Chalice of Renev

G000146922

This book is a work of fiction, all similarities to groups, organizations or individuals is purely coincidental and unintentional.

This book is a self-published piece of work and although it has been meticulously checked for mistakes, please be aware that some may remain.

Please note!
If you have not already read my previous book titled Eternal Struggle, I recommend reading that one first, as this book is set afterwards and contains spoilers.

Eternal Struggle can be found and bought online on Amazon.

Dear reader – thank you for taking the time to pick up my latest book. I have poured a lot of time and energy into it and I'm very grateful for your interest. I sincerely hope you enjoy reading my book as much as I enjoyed writing it. Thank you dearly, and if you enjoy this book, I only ask if you could mention it to any friends or family members who may also be interested in it. Please enjoy and once again, many thanks!

To my friend Lisa

Best wishes

Dorch wheel

X

Meadow kept slipping into a drowsy slumber as the trading cart she was riding in rumbled along the snowy, cobblestoned road. The gentle feeling of the carts wooden wheels turning and the creaking sound they created caused Meadow to rock back and forth, trapping her in a sleepy limbo. To top it off, the cart had a thick linen cover which sheltered her from the falling snow. Currently, Meadow was wrapped up in a warm woolly blanket like a new-born baby. She thanked her lucky stars she was able to hitch a ride from the generous travelling merchant, who just so happened to be heading her way. Graciously, the merchant had allowed Meadow to climb aboard his trade cart and ride alongside his goods. Which consisted of various wines, cheeses, alchemy supplies and ingredients, nothing too valuable really. However, Meadow couldn't fight the growls of her stomach any longer and helped herself to an apple or two along the way. She had the gold to afford them, but had to save every coin she possessed, for she needed it for something far more vital.

It was difficult to discern how much time had elapsed since she began her hitchhike, but it felt like an eternal voyage across the ocean at this point. "Hey, old timer! How much further do we have to travel? The boredom is starting to torture me!" declared Meadow, tightly clutching the snug blanket. The merchant, who was sitting at the front of the cart holding the reins, gave Meadow an icy glare as cold as the snowy mountain air itself. "Who're calling old timer!? We'll be there when we're there! Don't worry, I will shout ya when we arrive!" he barked in a weathered rusty tone.

Meadow gave a prolonged huff and rolled her eyes upon hearing his answer. "Fine, and thanks for letting me ride in your cart by the way, I think I would've turned into a block of ice by now if you hadn't been passing by" she replied. Happily, the old merchant tipped his leather hat to Meadow and rewarded her with a wrinkly, yet amicable smile. "Think nothing of it, can't understand why such a young girl like you is wandering this cold road alone though, don't you have any family, or are you a runaway?" he asked. The mere mention of family caused a shiver of sadness within Meadow and would likely reduce her to a teary shamble if she dwelled upon it too long. "No, I have no family anymore, just the pain of losing them" she uttered.

Thankfully, the old merchant decided not to pry too deeply, but also enquired just enough to seem caring and supportive. "Sorry for your loss young miss, I know how you feel; I lost my wife several winters back, we used to roam the roads together, travelling all over Resplendia with our wares" he uttered. A mournful sigh slithered from the old merchant as he watched the snow gracefully fall from the sky. "To this day even the smallest detail reminds me of her, but the memories we made together is what keeps her alive" he uttered. Meadow pondered his poignant words, her thoughts imprisoned in a state of reflective silence. "I'd love to forget what happened" she whispered a few seconds later. Rather than bunker beneath the woolly blanket, Meadow decided the mountain air would do her some good and gazed upon the stretching cobblestoned road in front of her. Enjoying the feeling of the faint snow as it gracefully fluttered from the sky. While the shaggy, golden furred galamare pulling the cart gave a soft neigh as it trotted along at a leisurely pace.

Meadow loved galamare; they were one of her favorite creatures, she adored the shimmering silver horns upon their heads. "Does she have a name?" she asked, nodding towards the beast. "Nope, no point since I'll be eating her once I arrive at the next city" the merchant answered in a serious tone. Instantly, Meadow's face turned ghastly white and she recoiled upon hearing the merchant's remark, "What? No, you can't!" she cried. Seeing her reaction, the old merchant burst into roaring laughter, "Ha, don't worry I only jest lass! Ya should've seen your face though!" he laughed. Wearily, Meadow hung her head and sighed before raising it again, giving the old merchant a miffed scowl, "Meanie!" she growled, turning her back to him.

Further and further the road behind Meadow trailed away. It had been roughly four years since she took her first step upon this journey, now home seemed like a million miles away. Not that it mattered anymore, the place she called home was long gone. Meadow watched the snow-covered cobblestones fade into the distance behind her and felt a moment of tranquil peace. Maybe it was because all was calm and the further from home she travelled, the easier it was to forget, but she knew the feeling wouldn't last.

Innocently, Meadow twirled her finger around a lock of her fiery, bright copper hair and emitted a jaded sigh. She stuck out her tongue and tried catching some of the falling snowflakes upon the tip. Before long, weariness soon got the better of her, "This is so, boring!" she declared. A soft smile followed by an amused chuckle left the old merchant's wrinkly lips. Yet, he also kept his eyes on the winding road of white in front of him, "Patience young one, always savor the journey!" he called. Admittedly, the view was rather serene to say the least. Mountains of icy rock towered towards the clouds, while entire forests of snow-covered pine trees enveloped the lush countryside. It culminated in a wonderland of white where Meadow could see for miles, the very air tasting like a bracing brew of elf blossom tea. "I guess so, maybe spending the rest of my life endlessly journeying like this wouldn't be such a bad idea" she whispered. A fleeting moment later, the wooden cart came to an abrupt halt when the merchant suddenly pulled back upon the reins. "Well, we're finally here! We've reached the Frostveil Mountains!" he declared.

Gleefully, Meadow hopped down from the cart and stretched the sleep from her arms and legs, "You're sure?" she asked. "Absolutely, see that long winding path that passes through the two mountains?" the merchant replied while pointing his finger. Meadow's eyes followed to where he pointed, "That's Frostveil Pass, keep following it and it'll lead you to the other side, eventually" explained the old merchant. Traversing the mountain pass looked like quite an ordeal, but Meadow was prepared. "Very well, thanks again for giving me a lift old timer!" she cheerfully replied. "Less of the old, and your welcome, but I still don't understand what you're looking for, you know no one lives in these mountains don't you?" asked the merchant.

Meadow caressed the shaggy, golden furred galamare pulling the cart and stroked its shimmering silver horns. "Someone lives here, someone important, and I shan't stop looking until I find him" answered Meadow with fiery resolve. "More likely you will freeze to death or get eaten by a pack of hungry wolves, but either way it's your life" replied the old merchant.

With a sudden crack of the reins, the merchant signaled the galamare to resume pulling his cart of wares along the snowy, cobblestoned road. "Either way you're on your own from here girl, I hope you know what you're doing" uttered the merchant, while giving Meadow a friendly wave goodbye. Meadow happily waved back as she watched him trail away, "Oh, by the way, I hope you don't mind, but I helped myself to a few of your apples!" she called. Upon hearing this, the old merchant began to wildly shake his fists around in the air. He comically shouted a string of inaudible curses while the galamare gradually pulled him and his cart away. "Okay, time to find me an alchemist!" declared Meadow as she turned her focus back to the snow-covered mountain pass and readied herself for the journey.

Once she had checked none of her supplies were missing, Meadow began the long, cold ascent into the snowy mountain pass and marched into the icy Frostveil Mountains alone. Despite being clad in layers of thick woolly garments, gloves, a scarf and a warm furry hat, the icy wind still chilled Meadow's bones. A howling blizzard had begun to stir soon after Meadow began trudging into the mountains, and it was engulfing her with all its wintery wrath now. Fluttering snowflakes had turned into pummeling hailstone and the further Meadow travelled, the deeper the snow became, until it was swallowing her knees. The screaming wind blew with the ferocity of a tormented banshee and caused Meadow to topple over and enjoy a face-full of snow more than a few times. Icy shivers crept along Meadow's spine, for she had been traversing the bellowing blizzard a little too long and the cold felt like it was freezing her soul.

Still, she trudged on, enduring the chilly bombardment of hailstones and sweeping snowstorms. "I must keep going; I will not give up, especially not because of some stupid storm!" Meadow grumbled. The fire in her heart bolstered her determination, like a blazing beacon of willpower that could repel the merciless, bitter cold. Meadow only wondered how long she could keep her fire burning. So far Meadow had been unable to find what she was looking forever, all she had discovered was freezing wind and deeper snow. "Come on, he must be here! The information I've gathered can't be wrong!" she yelled, huddling her head against the cruel storm.

Even warm clothes and a fiery determination was not enough to withstand this whirlwind of freezing white ice and Meadow's steps became increasingly clumsy. Her shivering began to intensify, her body soon to ceasing moving all together, "I can't go on!" she uttered in a cold whisper. Finally, after another bellowing blast of cold wind, Meadow toppled over like a falling tree and fell into the soft snow. Her entire body felt numb and as cold as death, movement of any kind became near impossible and she could feel the snowstorm gradually devouring her. Meadow was too cold to even crawl; instead, she curled herself into a ball and tried to find warmth, until she heard something in the depths of the blizzard. It sounded close and stood out, in fact, it sounded like a voice, "Hey, hey you!" she heard it call. Wearily, Meadow tilted her head upwards and gazed into the swirling blizzard to see the shape of a person emerge from within it. "Hold on! Do not let this blizzard sap the last lingering shards of life from you just yet!" called a man's voice.

Whoever this mysterious man was, he wore a woolly hat and a bandana over his face to protect him against the ravaging storm. "Here, drink this at once!" he declared, revealing a glass vial containing a mysterious blue liquid. Meadow was on the verge of passing out, hence she had little option but to open her mouth and swallow whatever mixture this man was giving her. "I thought my eyes were deceiving me for a moment, what's a young girl like you doing out here alone!?" the stranger cried above the snarling snowstorm. Strangely, the vial of curious mixture the man had given Meadow seemed to repel the onslaught of the cold, bitter wind, but she was still too weak to move.

Quickly, the stranger scooped Meadow up into his arms and stumbled through the snow as he carried her. "Endure the plight of this persistent, perilous squall a little longer girl! For my warm abode awaits nearby!" shouted the stranger. Soon, the frigid snowstorm swallowed Meadow and the man up and gradually, they vanished like a couple of wandering ghosts.

Panicked screams of frightened villagers filled the air, along with the burning scent of smoky ash and flames. Meadow hid beneath her bed like a helpless mouse as she watched Elijah obliterate her village and murder her loved ones with his demonic magic. It wasn't clear to Meadow what caused Elijah's outburst of hatred and rage, nor was it clear how he obtained his newfound demonic power. The only thing that was clear to Meadow was that Elijah was mercilessly hunting down and killing everyone in the village. His wrath was unforgiving; it was such a drastic change of behavior; Elijah and his sister Lucinda were always treated with respect and kindness by everyone in the village. Meadow was young, but she could not forget the harrowing events of that night. She covered her ears to try and shut out the chilling screams of the dead and dying, yet even that was to no avail. Still the sounds of suffering infiltrated her ears and she heard a familiar voice cry out, "Stop this Elijah, no more!" it screamed.

Beads of terrified sweat trickled along Meadow's face as she foolishly crawled from beneath her bed. She took a cautious peek out of the window to observe the slaughter taking place outside, "Mother!?" she worriedly whispered. On her knees, spitting blood and with a magical black spear piercing her chest was Meadow's mother. Fear engulfed her as she looked upon the hate filled visage of Elijah, he stood above her, his eyes glaring with boundless fury. Suddenly, Meadow's father arose from among the ashes like a noble phoenix. he raised his woodcutters' axe as he charged towards Elijah like an enraged minotaur, "Get away from her you monster!" he roared.

Elijah didn't even bother turning around to face Meadow's father. Instead he callously conjured a fistful of dark magic and cast his palm behind him, surrounding Meadow's father in a sudden surge of searing, black fire. Meadow stifled her gasp as she watched her father be consumed by the fearsome flames and be reduced to ash, yelling a final roar of agony before dying. Meadow's mother tried to pull the painful black spear of sorcery from her chest, but it wouldn't budge an inch. "Curse you Elijah, curse you to darkest pits of torment!" she hissed.

Elijah remained silent and cold, haughtily standing above her like an icy colossus, even though he was still a child, not more than a year older than Meadow. Finally, Elijah decided to end the pain of Meadow's mother, by summoning a magical sword of demonic sorcery in his hand. Elijah lopped off her head like he was chopping off the head of a fragile flower, leaving her lifeless corpse in the middle of the burning village. Meadow had to cover her mouth and muffle her gasp of hysterical terror, having no choice but to tearfully turn away from the window and wait for that harrowing night to finally be over. That was the last time Meadow ever saw Elijah again and she no idea where or what had become of him now. But his evil was forever seared into her skull, as was the scent of the smoke and the feel of the fire upon her skin. Shutting her eyes, covering her ears and huddling up in the corner was all Meadow could do. She felt like a powerless, lost puppy, whimpering at the horrible reality unfolding around her.

It was always at that point when Meadow would awaken; gasping for breath and drenched head-to-toe in sweat, this time was no different. She burst from her slumber and released a frightened gasp, while wiping the torrent of sweat from her forehead, "Mother!" she cried as she bolted up. Aside from the howling snowstorm outside, all else was silent in the rather elegant room she awoke in. "Gods how long must that nightmare keep haunting me?" she groaned. Wearily, Meadow flopped her head back and let it land upon the plush, scarlet bed she had been resting upon and blankly gazed at the ceiling, trying to collect her thoughts.

Fate had bestowed a cruel torment upon her, she had suffered such a traumatic ordeal at such a tender age and wished it were nothing more than a nightmare. Yet, the reality of it remained unchanged, the horror she witnessed was very real and was not content to vanish that night. Instead, the memory of it choose to haunt her dreams nearly every night since it happened and there was only one solution Meadow could think off to rid herself of such a bane. The bed Meadow awakened upon felt soft and cozy, a feeling she hadn't felt for a long time since starting her travels. She had awoken in a small, quaint bedroom, decorated with a sturdy oak dresser, a tall oak cupboard and various pretty paintings upon the walls.

As Meadow's senses began to focus, she started to perceive more soothing sounds, such as the crackling of burning firewood from the small stone fireplace in the corner. Achingly, Meadow climbed off the bed and stumbled forward, letting the thick warm blanket draped around her body gradually slip away, "Where am I?" she groggily whispered. "You're in master Clyde's house and it is, good, to see you awake" called a raspy voice from the doorway of the room. Meadow spun around to confront the voice and was greeted by the sight of a floating little imp, softly flapping its leathery wings. Two horns adorned its forehead, its skin was light purple like lavender, its eyes gleaming like a pair of burning rubies, its spiky tail coiled around the little pitchfork it wielded. Meadow erupted a piercing scream of fright upon seeing the fiendish little creature, resulting in her comically rolling and falling off the bed.

Her reaction and scream caused the imp to unleash an equally loud cry of fright and he swiftly retreated into the shadows of the corner. "What is the meaning of all this ruckus? Did you catch a glimpse of your reflection in the mirror again Styx?" called a voice from behind the bedroom door. A tall, slender man wearing a white cravat and dressed in a stylish, lapis-blue waistcoat with a smart ebony shirt that was rolled up at the sleeves stepped into the room. He had exquisite taste in clothing, but his hair was far from refined, it was of medium length and black as coal, yet bushy and wild like he had recently arisen from his bed.

Meadow found herself eased by his piercing yet peaceful blue eyes, eyes that seemed to harbor a mixture of inner turmoil and shimmering melancholy. In his arms he carried a polished silver tray with a steaming ceramic teapot, a ceramic floral teacup and a silver spoon resting upon it. Gently, he placed the tray on the dresser alongside the bed that Meadow had fallen off. "Ah, so your awake, took you long enough, you may look as sweet as a flower, but you sleep like a hibernating frost troll" remarked the man.

His comment caused Meadow to scowl and narrow her eyes at him. "How lovely, I hope you didn't rescue me simply to insult me?" she asked after picking herself up off the floor. "Oh, if you thought that was an insult you should hear yourself snore, it was like hearing the hungry rumbles of a giant's belly" answered mystery man. That was the last straw, Meadow angrily stomped towards the bushy, black haired man and shoved her finger into his face. "How dare you, do think that is any way to speak to a lady as lovely as I!?" she barked.

Calmly, the bushy haired man poured a cup of tea and held it out to Meadow. "How about we start with names first? Mine's Clyde, Clyde Alrime" he declared. Meadow's eyes twinkled with delight once he revealed his identity, "Ah! So, you're the alchemist!?" she declared. Amicably, Meadow accepted the cup of steamy tea from Clyde's hands and performed a curtsy, "My name is Meadow, Meadow Evershrewd!" she revealed.

Chalice of Renewal
Chapter 1
Welcome to the world of alchemy

An intoxicating aroma swirled over Meadow's senses as she inhaled the steam that floated from the cup of vibrant red tea, "This smell is wonderful, what kind of tea is it?" she asked. "Elm blossom tea, made with plomberry juice and hints of crimson fang, a kind of red thorny plant" replied Clyde. After exhaling a hearty gust of air from her mouth to cool her tea, Meadow took a timid sip from the cup and felt the delightful liquid revitalize her. "Tell me, how did you deduce that I was an alchemist?" asked Clyde as he watched her drink. "I didn't, not for certain" Meadow answered with a crafty smile.

Without a doubt, the tea Clyde had concocted for Meadow was the most delicious tea she had ever tasted, made all the sweeter with the miffed expression upon Clyde's face. "Don't look so irked just because I tricked you, I've been searching for you for the last four years" uttered Meadow after taking another sip. "Tracking you down and travelling here wasn't a walk in the park, let me tell ya!" she grumbled. Clyde couldn't resist raising an eyebrow, both in surprise and curiosity at the tenacity to which Meadow spoke of. "Really? And why pray tell have you gone to such lengths to find me? Bear in mind, I never wished to be found" he replied.

Meadow cupped both palms around the hot tea and rested her rear upon the plush bed behind her. "Your alchemy skill is legendary; you are the best and I need a memory erasing potion" she answered. The mention of such an exceptional and potent potion caused Clyde's eyebrows to shoot up further. "That is quite an exotic request, but what memory could be so dire to warrant such a potion?" he asked. Ripples formed in Meadow's tea as she stirred it with her spoon, and she gazed emptily at her reflection upon the blood red surface. "Four years ago, my village was attacked by a boy called Elijah, he slaughtered my family, my friends and burnt everything to the ground" she uttered.

Reciting the horrific tale took tremendous effort on Meadow's part, but she managed to persevere. "He possessed terrible demonic power and unleashed his wrath upon everyone, I think I was the only survivor" Meadow added softly. A cloud of silent darkness fluttered over the room, "I was only ten years old when it happened, I still hear the screams and feel the fire in my dreams" continued Meadow. "I survived by hiding, closing my eyes, and silently praying" she whispered. After telling her woeful tale, Meadow gulped down the last drops of her refreshing tea. "A scared little lamb tucked away in the shadowy corners of a burning village with naught but the noise of frightened screams to accompany you, your tale is indeed beyond woeful!" announced Clyde. His words were sympathetic, but his gestures and tone were dramatic, leaving Meadow puzzled as to how he truly felt.

Casually, Clyde rested both hands upon his hips and closed his eyes. "Now all becomes clear, I see why you sought me out and desire a memory erasing potion so badly!" he declared. Sternly, Clyde then thrust his finger into Meadow's face, causing her to jolt back. "However, your memories make you who you are! Often the most painful memories give us our greatest strength, you cannot undo what has been done!" he declared. Wearily, Meadow rolled her eyes and huffed, "I've heard this whole song and dance before and believe me I have given it much thought" she answered. "I don't care about strength; I just want to be at peace again! I want to forget!" she snapped.

Meadow's fiery demeanor caused little reaction within Clyde, other than a slightly irked frown. Meanwhile, Clyde's pet imp flew behind his shoulder and peeked over, "This girl isn't going to be a problem is she master?" he asked. Truthfully, Meadow completely forgot about the unique little creature, until she heard his hissing voice and saw him timidly poke out his head from behind Clyde. "Why do you have a pet imp? Are you mad?" she asked. Her apprehension and distrust were reasonably justified; imps had a reputation as being deceitful tricksters at best, or sadistic fiends at worst.

The fact that they all possessed demonic magic in some form was the cherry on top. "Styx is not my pet, he is my friend and I assure you he is harmless, unlike most of his kind there is no reason to be wary of him" answered Clyde. Calmly, Clyde stepped aside to reveal the imp called Styx, "Don't be afraid Styx, say hello" he instructed. Timidly, Styx gave a feeble wave to Meadow and introduced himself, "Greetings, a pleasure to meet you!" he nervously uttered. His humble demeanor reassured Meadow and she performed a graceful curtsy, "Tis a pleasure!" she answered. Once that necessity was completed, she shifted her focus back to business, "So, the potion?" she asked. This caused Clyde to rub his forehead and sigh. "Look, memory erasing potions are one of my rarest and most expensive potions, do you know how much they cost?" he asked.

Haughtily, Meadow revealed a bulging linen pouch that hung behind her hip upon the leather travel belt wrapped around her waist. She proceeded to empty the pouch of its contents, creating a shower of gold into her palm until it created a shimmering pile so large that some of the golden coins spilled onto the floor. "Will this be enough? I've been saving up!" she declared. Meticulously, Clyde took a few moments examining the pile of shiny coins in Meadows palm and squatted down to count the others that had fallen to the floor. "Nope, not even close" he answered aloofly.

His underwhelming reaction in the face of such an ample pile of gleaming gold caused an irritated scowl to appear on Meadow's face. "What? Oh, come on! That's more than a fair price for one potion!" she cried. "Believe me whelp, if I told you how much my memory erasing potions cost, you would age at least fifty years!" Clyde answered. Then he callously turned his back to Meadow leaving her frustrated and defeated. A huff leapt from Meadow's lips and she let her head powerlessly flop. "But, I really, really need it! I don't want to keep these accursed memories anymore; can't you show some compassion?" she wearily pleaded.

Clyde shook his head, "Sorry girl, but my compassion only extends as far as the gold in my pockets and you have nowhere near enough to fill them" he answered. At this point Meadow was on the verge of bubbling tears, evident by the sounds of her sniveling. Which unbeknownst to her, created a merciful glimmer of sympathy within Clyde's uncompromising heart. "However, I can see how much you desire my memory erasing potion, so I am willing to bestow it to you, under special terms" he said. Meadow's attention was ensnared once again and she raised her head high, her eyes shimmering with hope, "Yes, whatever it is I'll do it!" she cried.

Perhaps it was her tenacity that Clyde took a shine too, or maybe her spirt. Whatever it was; Clyde dramatically spun around to face Meadow again and pointed his finger directly in her face. "Meadow Evershrewd, I shall give you the memory erasing potion, on the condition that you work off the gold for it, by becoming my new apprentice in alchemy!" he announced. Silent awe swept over Meadow like a swift breeze, rendering her speechless and confused as to how she should react. Simultaneously, Styx freed a shocked gasp and began clapping with admiration, "Such an honor! My master has chosen his apprentice!" he declared. His continual clapping didn't aid the situation, it only served to bewilder Meadow further, "What? Is this a jest?" she asked. "I never jest girl, and correct me if I'm incorrect, but you said you were willing to do whatever it takes to get your little talons upon my memory erasing potion, did you not?" replied Clyde.

Frustration simmered within Meadow, but she mustered her patience and kept it concealed beneath a grumpy frown. "Fine, I accept your terms, but I don't even know the first thing about alchemy" she answered. An ecstatic smile spread over Clyde's lips, "Why, alchemy is art, it is life! It is the essence of combining the various wonderful and weird ingredients of the natural world!" he announced. "Then it's about distilling and mixing them into a magical potion, a marvelous medicine or a fiendish, potent poison!" declared Clyde with a playfully sinister tone at the end. It was clear to Meadow how passionate Clyde felt about alchemy, his merry tone and the brazen gestures he made while parading around the room were about as subtle as a drunken orc.

Lost in his own kingdom of euphoria, Clyde raised his hands to the sky and reveled in his moment. "Alchemy is the embodiment of change, it brims with mystery, bestows beauty and bubbles with creativity!" he lauded. "It creates and destroys life; it heals and hurts, its possibilities as infinite as the heavens! Why, the mere mention of alchemy makes me want to break into song!" Clyde added. Wearily, Meadow rubbed her face, "Please don't" she answered with increasing fatigue. Her tone caused Clyde to freeze in his tracks and scowl, "Your loss girl, I'll have you know that singing is just one of my many amazing talents!" he declared. "Yes, yes, I'm sure it is, so how long do I have to be your apprentice for? It's not going to take that long to work off the gold for that potion is it?" asked Meadow.

Clyde's passionate demeanor diminished at the sound of her apathetic tone and he sternly folded his arms. "Do you have someplace else to be girl? If so, I suggest you leave my home and brave the harrowing hail and screeching snowstorm from whence you came, is that the case?" He asked. Mournfully, Meadow averted her eyes from his inquisitive gaze and let her focus fall to the floor. "No, I have nowhere else to be, I have no home or anyone waiting for me" she uttered.

Clearly Meadow felt lost and alone and Clyde wondered if that's why he took her on as an apprentice. Or maybe it was because he felt lost and alone too? "Very well, then I think it is time to give you the grand tour" he replied. Clyde tried to console Meadow's melancholy by wrapping his arm around her shoulder, gently nudging her along with him as he walked. "Now come along, there is much to see and learn" he remarked.

Styx flapped his wings and flew close behind as he followed Meadow and Clyde through the rest of the house. "The room we were just in was the guest bedroom, that is where you shall be sleeping my dear" explained Clyde. Across the hall from the guest bedroom awaited the kitchen and what a kitchen it was. A long stretch of pristine oak worktops lined the kitchen wall. Immaculately clean and decorated with a giant bowl of fresh fruit and various colorful flowers, which acted as adornment. Along the wall, above the row of kitchen counters were several iron hooks, from which various, weathered cast iron pots, pans and wooden chopping boards hung. Resting in the center of the wall was a large oak shelf with a built-in knife holder, which held a plethora of various shimmering knives.

In the center of the room stood a beautiful dining table, also embellished with an array of fabulous flowers and shiny, silver candleholders. Built into the front wall of the kitchen stood a large, stone oven with a tall, slender chimney shaft which allowed the smoke to safely escape. In-between the narrow slit in its iron doors, Meadow could perceive the faintest flickers of fire as the mouth of the oven burned away. Carved into the left side of the kitchen wall was a magnificent white stone fireplace with a bundle of burning logs and a large iron cauldron.

Currently, the cauldron was filled with boiling water that calmly simmered away; no doubt it was used for making various soups and stews. Then of course was the gigantic, oak larder in the corner, the largest Meadow had ever seen and could surely fit enough food to feed a family of four for months. It was difficult to not be impressed at how efficient and immaculate the kitchen was. it possessed everything required to prepare and create every meal one could desire, "I take it you know how to cook then?" asked Meadow. Styx answered Meadow's question before Clyde could respond, seemingly wearing his master's pride. "Not only can my master cook, but he can concoct a hundred different blends of tea!" he bragged. Humbly, Clyde chuckled and treated the statement as a causal observation. "Ah yes, tea, the mistress that came and captured my love forever, after alchemy of course!" he remarked, before ushering Meadow onwards. "Next we have the foyer; it is the main hall of my home and also used as the portal room" explained Clyde.

The foyer was built of sturdy, elaborate oak and four thick wooden pillars decorated with lavish gold borders stood in opposite corners of the room, supporting the structure. "The portal room?" asked Meadow as her eyes surveyed the room, her attention being drawn to one interesting object in particular. The mysterious, unique object that drew Meadow's attention was the large stone structure that stood in the very center of the room. "Don't worry, you'll learn more about this room later" replied Clyde. It looked like a large stone pedestal of some kind, only it was quite low and circular in shape, like a giant stone coin. The texture of this intriguing stone structure seemed strikingly smooth and glossy too, like natural majestic marble. Strange engravings were inscribed into the circular stone structure; they encompassed all the way around and looked like runes of some kind, glowed with a faint blue aura and radiated a subtle, magical resonance.

Hastily, Meadow was steered towards the next room by Clyde, like he couldn't wait to show her what lay behind the next door. "However, the grandest room of all has yet to be revealed!" he declared, struggling to contain his excitement. An innocent glee filled his heart and his frolicking steps radiated joy, like that of a little boy receiving a pet griffon on his birthday, "Behold greatness!" Clyde proclaimed. With a twist of his wrists, he simultaneously turned the two wooden doorknobs upon the double oak doors in front of him and proceeded to throw them open. "Welcome to the world of alchemy!" he proudly declared.

A wave of wonder swept over Meadow as she witnessed the whimsical world that awaited on the other side. Her jaw practically dropped, "Wow, you really are passionate about alchemy!" gasped Meadow in awe. Upon parting the pair of double doors, Meadow emerged into a large, wacky workshop, devoted entirely to alchemy, "This is my laboratory, this is where the magic is made!" echoed Clyde's voice as he led Meadow around. Bubbling beakers containing various colorful liquids boiled away as they rested in iron racks over the flames of recently lit candles. Lined along the wall of the lab was a long stone worktop, strewn with mortars, pestles, alembics, flasks and potion vials of all shapes and sizes.

It looked cluttered and chaotic yet seemed to emanate a tidiness that only Clyde could comprehend. Hanging along the wall above the wooden worktops was a sturdy iron shelf, lined with thick glass jars, each one uniquely labelled and holding a variety of vibrant powders. As Meadow moved her gaze back to the cluttered wooden worktops, she noticed all manner of various measures, weights and scales scattered across it. An assortment of alchemy instruments was also spread across the wooden worktops. Tools such as calipers, tongs, potion racks and spatulas. Located on the other side of the room, opposite the wooden worktop, Clyde had been growing a gorgeous, flourishing garden, filled with flowers, mushrooms, beetles and bugs of every vibrant color conceivable. No doubt the fabulous array of fauna and flora Clyde had been cultivating were essential ingredients for his potion mixtures and Meadow was enthralled by the plethora of creatures on display.

Majestic butterflies and dancing dragonflies fluttered around the towers of fabulous flowers. While bewitching bugs such as colorful caterpillars and strange spiders crawled along the gardens soil surface. Meadow couldn't explain why, but she was instantly captivated by all the sights, sounds and smells of the alchemy laboratory, it was mind boggling and she hadn't the faintest clue where to begin.

Meanwhile, Clyde scrambled towards his lavish but cluttered oak desk, which was located right in the center of the room. He proceeded to promptly tidy away all the scattered scrolls, quills and sheets of parchment upon it. "You'll have to forgive the level of clutter; I've been engrossed with some rather fascinating experiments lately!" he declared. Undoubtedly, the most prominent feature in the alchemy lab was the colossal, fire spewing furnace looming on the far end of the room. It stretched towards the ceiling of the lab and possessed three thick, iron chimney pipes, all of which were puffing out hazy plumes of white smoke.

Placed inside the gaping maw of the fiery furnace was another large black cauldron this one the size of a barrel of rum. "Amazing, I bet you can create a lot of potions in that thing!" remarked Meadow in an impressed tone. "Ah, that cauldron is mostly for large orders of simple potion recipes, useful for when I have clients that need basic potions in bulk!" answered Clyde. His voice sounded scattered at the moment, mainly because he continued to diligently dash around the lab in an effort to clean it up. Alongside the giant roaring furnace, stood a huge oak cupboard with a glass covered door and what lay within captured Meadow's attention, "Amazing! So many potions!" she gasped. Inside the towering cupboard were rows and rows of various potion vials, each one containing a unique potion with an equally unique color. "Yes, this is my potion cupboard, inside is every potion I have ever made!" Clyde declared proudly.

Superb scarlet, terrific turquoise, enchanting emerald, splendid sky, passionate purple, beguiling blue, captivating crimson, glittering gold, wonderful white and ravishing rose. Every potion had its own heavenly hue of color, some even possessed a mixture of two or even three colors. For example, Meadow spotted a potion that had a mystifying azure blue color, mixed with a mysterious deep violet and traces of shimmering gold. The entire cupboard was a colossal cascade of captivating color and created a chasm of awe within Meadow. "They're all so unique and pretty, it's beautiful!" she uttered.

Every potion had a small label upon its vial too, likely to aid Clyde in identifying which potion was which merely by looking at its color and consistency. "Yes, beautiful indeed, but don't start getting any ideas about pilfering that memory erasing potion girl" he answered. Meadow's jaw suddenly dropped with shock, "Are you insisting I would stoop so low as to resort to common thievery!?" she cried. Clyde remained motionless, his glassy blue eyes blankly staring at her, his eyebrow quickly flicking up, "Indeed" he bluntly replied.

Secretly, Meadow cursed her luck and gave a grumpy scowl, but maintained her ruse of shock, "How dare you, I would never do something so dastardly!" she sternly replied. Still, Clyde's laboratory was a wonder and Meadow had seen every inch of it now, except for one final door that lay tucked away in the secluded corner. "What about that door? Which room does that lead to?" asked Meadow. A forlorn cloud of sadness swiftly loomed over Clyde's head as he silently gazed at the sturdy iron door, which was securely locked shut by a chunky iron lock over the keyhole. "Nothing, that room is forbidden and sacred to me, no one is allowed in" uttered Clyde in a soft tone as he swiftly turned away from the door. He and Meadow departed the elaborate laboratory and headed back to the kitchen, where Styx awaited them. "So, are you impressed by my master's laboratory?" he asked Meadow upon her arrival.

Meadow attempted to feign ignorance and casually flung her hair over one shoulder, while giving a shrug, "Yeah, it's pretty good I guess" she replied. However, her nonchalant attitude aggravated the little imp to no end. "Pretty good? You should be in awe! Your jaw should've dropped to the floor and your eyes should've been blinded with wonder!" cried Styx. "Now, now Styx, allow her to seclude her amazement, she may think her emotions are hidden behind stone walls, but to me, they are as clear as the rising sun" declared Clyde. Although Clyde's deduction skills were precise, Meadow didn't allow him the satisfaction of proof. Instead she quietly took a seat at the kitchen table, "Yeah, you keep thinking that old timer" she answered.

Her comment crushed Clyde with the ferocity of a plummeting meteor and made him gnash his teeth in riled frustration. "Old timer? Old timer!? Look at me girl! Do you see a single grey hair or wrinkle? Nay I say! Nay! For my age is only double yours! Give or take" he fired back. Impatience bubbled inside Meadow, like a geyser about ready to erupt. "Saying your only double my age still makes you sound old you know!" she answered. "Anyway, can we start now? I really want to work off the money for that potion" Meadow added.

Unfortunately, Clyde sneered at her request and stuck his nose into the air. "I admire your eagerness, but we must take small steps, you're still a naïve little girl from a nit-wit village, you've probably only just learned how to tie your own shoes, let alone how to make a potion" replied Clyde. It seemed Clyde was unaware of how insulting his remarks were, Meadow got the impression that he was very rusty with social interaction or he simply didn't care. His insolent comments still caused Meadow to scowl at him like a grumpy cave bear. "First, we need to know what we are making, which is why we shall await the arrival of my diligent delivery minion, known as Swiftwing!" declared Clyde. His declaration left Meadow more than a little baffled, but only a fleeting grain of time slipped by before a series of heavy knocks echoed upon the front door and ensnared everyone's attention. "Speak of the devil; he is on time as usual! Styx, journey to the front door and rescue our noble companion from the perilous ravages of ice and snow!" announced Clyde.

As Clyde's loyal little imp flapped his wings and lazily floated towards the front door, Meadow studied Clyde with perplexed curiosity, "Are you always so dramatic?" she asked. A frightful barrage of icy wind blasted Styx when he pulled upon the handle of the front door with all his might and yanked it open. "Welcome to our abode!" cried Styx while being blown backwards from the abrupt gusty gale. Meadow observed the new arrival as he entered and was admittedly surprised to see he wasn't human, "A harpy?" she noted.

Quickly, the stranger hurried into hallway, eager to escape the billowing snowstorm outside and promptly shut the front door behind him, "Greetings, who might you be?" he asked. Despite the stranger being clad from head to toe in warm, woolly garments, Meadow easily knew he was a harpy. The large pair of white wings upon his back and the curvy brown beak where his nose ought to be gave it away, "You first" replied Meadow. "Of course, where are my manners?" answered the stranger as he removed his fluffy blue scarf and the snow-covered goggles he wore upon his eyes.

Before the harpy had chance to speak further, Clyde sprung forth and interrupted him. "Ah, Swiftwing, my loyal lackey! Do you have the latest requests?" he asked. "How many times do we have to go over this Clyde? That's not my name, I'm not your lackey and yes I have them right here in my bag" wearily uttered the harpy. Once he had removed his thick leather gloves, the harpy proceeded to plunge his talons into the depths of the large delivery bag that slung across his shoulder, "Here" he said. A small stack of sealed envelopes was revealed from the harpy's huge delivery sack and he passed them to Clyde. "Excellent work Swiftwing, here is your well-earned payment!" declared Clyde as he passed a pouch of jingling coins to the harpy. With a jaded sigh, the harpy took the pouch of gold from Clyde, "Excuse me but, who are you? It's a little rare to see a harpy so far from Cloudvale" asked Meadow.

The harpy took a moment to shake the cold snow from his wings before answering. "My real name, which I wish Clyde would start using is Hector, and yes your right, harpies are quite rare to see on the surface of Resplendia" he replied. "I was born in the soaring sky city of Cloudvale, but I have always been fascinated with the surface below" added Hector. His stance then shifted to one of pride, "So I decided to become a courier in the hopes of seeing many sights and meeting many different races of people" Hector continued.

Travelling the land, never staying in one place and always seeing something or someone new, it was a dream Meadow could certainly resonate with. "Sounds like quite a noble ambition, I'm Meadow by the way, I've become Clyde's coerced apprentice" replied Meadow. Politely, she extended her palm to initiate a courteous handshake. Hector raised his arm and grasped Meadow's palm with his eagle-like talons and shook her hand, returning an amicable smile. "Clyde has an apprentice now? Interesting, he never considered himself the teaching type" he answered.

After perusing his mail, Clyde raised his gaze back to Hector and slammed his hands upon his hips. "You doubt my teaching proficiency Swiftwing? It matters not, for the world will tremble when I elevate this simple, country bumpkin girl into the archives of alchemical genius!" declared Clyde. Hector, Styx and Meadow remained motionless and gawked at Clyde silently, before Hector finally spoke. "Okay well, I still have many more deliveries to make" he uttered. "Okay Hector, it was nice meeting you, see you later and travel safe" replied Meadow. She kindly escorted him to the front door, only to be greeted by the same howling blizzard she had been caught in before. Hector placed his protective goggles over his eyes and wrapped his thick woolly scarf around his neck, before reluctantly leaving the warm embrace of Clyde's house. "I wish you would find a better place to live Clyde!" Hector cried as he marched into the chilly domain of blinding blizzards and shivering hailstorms.

Meadow mightily pushed the front door close against the onslaught of freezing wind and gasped a deep breath. "He's right, why couldn't you choose somewhere sunny?" she asked. Casually, Clyde strolled back into the kitchen with his letters in hand. "I like the isolation and that raging snowstorm outside ensures I rarely get visitors foolish enough to attempt traversing through it" he answered. All his attention was consumed by the small stack of letters he received. So much so that he nearly missed the doorway leading back into the kitchen and almost slammed face first into the wall.

Meadow watched him amusingly, "So, what's got you so engrossed?" she asked as she shadowed Clyde into the kitchen and slumped into one of the chairs. After a minute's silence Meadow was on the verge of asking again in a louder tone, until Clyde finally unearthed his face from the pile of letters. "Potion requests my dear, I must earn gold somehow" he remarked. "Lately, a lot of people have been requesting large orders of hair growth tonics and love elixirs, ugh! The vision of commoners and nobles alike is so limited!" Clyde added.

Carelessly, Meadow leaned backwards on her chair and rested her hands behind her head. "So, people send you requests to make potions, you make them, have Hector deliver them and then they give you the money?" asked Meadow. "Indeed investigator, how impressive that you managed to deduce all that on your own!" Clyde haughtily answered with profuse sarcasm. The signature vexed scowl Meadow was becoming known for appeared once again. "Are you sure your isolation from society was purely your choice? I'm beginning to think you were forced" she remarked. "Silence my minion, for we have bigger leviathan to fry than the mundane trivialities of society! For I have received not one, but two personal requests!" announced Clyde.

It sounded important, but Meadow was unaware how important, hence her reaction was devoid of all interest, "Oh, that's nice" she answered rather flatly. Peering over the peak of his letters, Clyde rolled his eyes and huffed, "I forget you are still my oblivious acolyte" he answered. "Sometimes I receive special requests, requests that I handle personally with my alchemy, usually to aid a village or town with a particular perplexing problem" he explained. That made a lot more sense to Meadow and as soon as her mind processed the words, it caused her to sit-up and lean forward with renewed interest. "Ah! So, you basically travel the land and help others with your alchemy?" she asked.

Clyde proudly folded his arms, raised his chin to the heavens and smiled, "I don't like to brag, but my alchemy has aided many in the past!" he declared. Unable to resist the alluring thought of travelling to new places and seeing new sights, Meadow tried to peek at the letters with special help requests. "So, you've got two? Where are we going first? What are we doing?" she asked. Before, she could glance upon the letters, Clyde hastily scooped them up. "Temper your curiosity my apprentice, I shall tell you in due time, all you need to know is that we are departing tomorrow, to a village called Oakpass! So, rest up!" he announced.

Chalice of Renewal
Chapter 2
To trick a trickster

Screams echoed all around Meadow, she couldn't block them out; they invaded her dreams and tormented her mind. All around her Meadow could hear her family, her friends, her entire village. All begging for mercy or uttering their last frightened cry, before Elijah conjured his dark magic and ruthlessly stole their life, as callously as snuffing out a candles flame. Panic and fire surrounded Meadow, while a fog of fear veiled the village, yet all Meadow could do was helplessly hide under her bed and pray that she was never found. Except this time, she was, this time she heard her bedroom door slam open and watched someone's feet slowly approach her bed.

Beads of terrified sweat dripped along Meadow's entire body, but she covered her mouth and remained as motionless as a marble statue, alas it was to no avail. The figures feet halted in front of Meadow's bed and everything went silent for a second. Until the glaring face of Elijah suddenly swooped under the bed and his demonic red eyes pierced right into Meadow. "Found you!" Elijah roared, before summoning the power of dark magic into his palm, fiercely gripping Meadow by the throat and pulling her from under the bed like a rag doll.

Elijah malevolently cackled as he watched her squirm and wriggle like a helpless worm and drained the life from Meadow until she was rendered little more than a lifeless skeleton. That's when Meadow finally gasped with fright as she burst awake from her horrific domain of dreams, her face flushed with fear and prickly sweat gushing down her body. "By the gods! Why does it always seem so real!?" she panted. Once she had collected her breath, Meadow shakily left her bed that Clyde had bestowed to her. Right now, Meadow couldn't focus, her mind was a muddled mess of melancholic memories and she had to take a momentary meander.

Her night-time walk led her to the kitchen, and to her surprise she walked in on Clyde, who was fully awake and sipping a cup of tea. "I see the mistress of sleep eludes you too, she can be a fickle maiden" Clyde uttered upon seeing her. "Just bad dreams, memories of a past I'd rather forget, so what's your excuse?" asked Meadow as she took a seat at the kitchen table. Clearly Clyde was deep in thought as he carelessly swirled around the teabag in his teacup with his spoon. "An alchemy dilemma, one born from the past, a dilemma that still causes me great strife to this very day" Clyde answered. Although Meadow secretly wished to inquire further, she fought off her curiosity. "You could always drink one of your memory erasing potions, I mean that's what I would do, forgetting might be the best option, for both of us, no more pain" she replied. For a few intense seconds, Clyde silently surveyed Meadow with a grouchy frown.

Clyde was no fool, "Your attempts to tug your talons upon the strings of my heart will do you little good, for I am a man of logic and you shan't get your potion any sooner!" he added. Fatigue filled Meadow as her face flopped upon the kitchen table and she released a weary sigh. "Oh, come on! Just let me erase my memories! Can't I work on a payment of one sip of potion a day or something?" she groaned. To Meadow's' dismay, Clyde remained firmly aloof to her plight and her pleas of desperation reaped no fruit. "I'm losing sleep over it; I'm nearly fifteen now and I'm getting wrinkles! Wrinkles!" cried Meadow.

Unfortunately, Clyde seemed utterly immune to her teary-eyed dilemma and finished drinking his tea before leaving the kitchen table. "Quell your distress girl, I am acquainted with the bane of wrinkles, but submitting to your trauma will ensure they remain!" he declared. Dramatically, Clyde slammed his teacup onto the kitchen table, bolted up and raised his fist to the sky, appearing to brim with strength. "Now return to your sanctuary of slumber, grasp the elusive strings of sleep and embrace them, as you would a fierce and noble unicorn of the celestial heavens!" Clyde decreed before leaving the kitchen. A baffled chuckle stumbled from Meadow's lips as she watched him walk out of the room and she couldn't help shaking her head. "I think only half of that made sense" she uttered.

It was difficult to discern whether it was morning or night, as the raging snowstorm howled beyond Meadow's bedroom window relentlessly. It was a never-ending tempest of frigid snow and she'd never seen anything like it before. Regardless, Meadow awoke when her body deemed it time and she rubbed what sleep she had managed to obtain from her drowsy eyes. "Morning, so you're awake at last? Good, my master requires your presence in the kitchen!" Styx loudly announced in a tone too jovial for Meadow to handle upon awakening. Although Meadow did as she was instructed, she trudged out of the guest bedroom and into the kitchen with about as much life as a shambling zombie fresh out of its grave.

Upon entering the kitchen, she spotted Clyde standing over the roaring firepit, scooping a large clay jug into the cauldron of bubbling water. "Ah, you're just in time for fresh tea!" he declared upon seeing Meadow behind him. Promptly, Clyde proceeded to pour the jug of boiled water into a pair of ceramic white teacups he had already placed out upon the kitchen table. Both teacups contained vibrant yellow flower petals that had been meticulously crushed, mixed alongside a slender green herb. "Today's tea is made from the sunflame flower and mixed with grimweed herbs, a perfect tea for eccentric minds who are suffering from an erratic night's sleep!" announced Clyde.

As soon as Clyde poured the jug of boiling water into Meadow's teacup, a hot plume of rising steam drifted over her senses, filling her with a subtle yet distinctly sweet aroma. "Mmmm, smells delicious!" she remarked. Clyde took his seat across from her and a pleasant, tranquil atmosphere passed over them as they sat in silence for a few moments, waiting patiently for their tea to cool. "Ah, it tastes as good at it smells and this is just what I need after the night I had!" uttered Meadow as she took a timid sip from her teacup.

Her approval pleased Clyde and he raised his teacup to her, before taking a sip himself. "I'm glad my apprentice, after all, I will need you at full focus today for what is to come" he replied. Meadow was intrigued, "And what's to come? I know we are going to Oakpass and the people there need help, but didn't they say what they need help with?" she asked. A refreshing gasp escaped Clyde's lips after he took a hearty swig of his tea, "The letter is somewhat vague" he replied. "A local prankster has been stealing the villager's belongings, peppering their houses with rotten eggs and tomatoes and painting the local livestock different colors" Clyde added. In truth, Meadow thought it was a rather petty case, not the kind an alchemist would investigate, "Sounds like a job for local guards or wandering mercenaries maybe" she uttered. "I agree, however, the local guards seem to keep falling prey to the pranksters snare traps and being flung upside down, thus they have been unsuccessful in identifying the culprit" replied Clyde.

The sweet taste of hot tea rejuvenated Meadow's spirit and rescued her drowsy senses from the clutches of sleep. "Whoever the culprit is, they sound skilled, it couldn't be one of the villagers could it?" she asked. "I suspect it is the work of a satyr, half-man half-goat creatures, they are tricksters by nature and enjoy pranking others, dense forests also happen to be their natural environment" replied Clyde.

Once Meadow and Clyde finally consumed the last drops of their nourishing tea, they decided it was time to prepare. "Well, I guess I should go to my room and pack for the journey, where exactly is Oakpass anyway?" asked Meadow. "I'm not sure my loyal little lackey, follow me and we shall check the map to be certain" answered Clyde as he marched out of the kitchen. Like a curious cat, Meadow tailed Clyde into the portal room and spotted Styx, his impish claws wrapped around a long velvet rope connected to a set of giant, stylish red curtains. "Alright Styx reveal it!" decreed Clyde.

At which point Styx gave a faithful salute and proceeded to pull the red velvet rope, which in turn parted the pair of plush scarlet curtains. Meadow noticed the curtains when she was being given the grand tour; she assumed they covered a large window like any other pair of curtains. Her amazement was justified when they instead revealed a gorgeous, gigantic framed map of the entire land of Resplendia. It was drawn with meticulous detail and upon exquisite parchment of the highest quality. Seeing the entire land of Resplendia beautifully illustrated upon such an imposing golden frame of perfect parchment made Meadow feel like a timid little ant. "So......this is Resplendia" she uttered with quiet awe. Clyde pulled the letter from Oakpass out of his pocket and rolled a library ladder from behind the curtains, the kind of ladder attached to a glossy wooden frame with wheels on the bottom.

Like a playful child, Clyde hopped onto the wheel ladder and rode it alongside the map with his body weight until it finally came to a halt. "Let me see, the letter states Oakpass is around thirty miles northwest of Greydawn, so its.........here!" declared Clyde, slamming his finger upon the spot once he found it. As soon as his finger touched the spot on the map, Meadow's jaw almost dropped to the floor. "That's over two-hundred miles from here! The journey will take forever!" cried Meadow. Her reaction was understandable, yet Clyde glanced back at her with an expression of weariness all the same. "My precious little apprentice, do you seriously not think I've already solved that particular little problem?" he replied. "Travelling comes in many forms my dear, traversing the terrain on foot is tedious and time-consuming, so remember what room you're standing in" Clyde added.

The cogs in Meadows head began to turn and she recollected the name. "The portal room, wait......you mean we're travelling by portal? How!?" she inquired. Clyde merely smirked at her blatant bewilderment, "Using the power of imp magic! Styx here is a prodigy at portal magic in particular" he answered. Meadow shifted her gaze towards Styx, who had fallen asleep. Yet, he also maintained flight by lazily flapping his purple wings and proceeded to casually pick his pointy ears with his long, impish tail. "Great, my confidence on this is simply astounding" replied Meadow with copious sarcasm.

In a gesture of support, Clyde placed his hand upon Meadow's shoulder. "Worry not my devoted disciple, over the years I have calculated there is only a seven percent chance of failure with the portals, Styx will get us there, right Styx?" he uttered. Clyde's voice roused Styx from his slumber, "I want to ride the unicorn!" Styx cried in dream speak upon awakening. Meadow however wanted to rewind the conversation a little, "Wait, hold on a second! Can we discuss that seven percent failure part some more!?" she exclaimed. "No time my apprentice, for time is of the essence and I have consumed enough explaining the basics to you!" Clyde decreed. Confidently, Clyde rested his hands upon his hips and suddenly laughed his lungs out like a delirious dictator. "Now Styx, Prepare the portal! Get us as close to Oakpass as possible, I shall venture to my lab and grab my harness!" ordered Clyde with hearty gusto. As soon as he finished announcing his orders like a merry pirate captain, Styx stood to attention and gave a salute, "Aye, aye master!" he declared.

Whilst Clyde nipped into his lab, Styx began the captivating process of creating the portal. A vibrant, pulsing aura of mysterious magical energy began to appear around his palms, shifting between hues of azure and violet. The mystical little imp focused his sorcery into the tiny pitchfork he wielded which seemed to act as a conduit for the magic. Carefully, Styx then proceeded to point it towards the large and ancient stone platform in the center of the room.

Meadow was bombarded with bewitchment as she watched the ancient runes carved into the stone circle radiate a mystical blue aura of flickering fire. What was perhaps even more incredible and bewildering than that, was the tremendously deep hum which followed soon after. A relentless booming hum that rippled the very air, echoing like it came from the depths of the earth.

After a minute or two the ritual was apparently completed, as the relentless rumbling finally ceased. The magical flames upon the runes surrounding the edges of the mysterious stone platform also faded. Everything went silent and Meadow allowed herself to relax and take a breath again. However, her heart nearly burst out of her chest when a sudden explosion of dark magic ruptured the air and momentarily rattled the room. "Eek!" screamed Meadow as she stumbled backwards from fright and fell onto her rump, her gaze becoming lost in a trance at the floating portal of swirling magic in front of her. It levitated over the center of the circular stone platform and never had Meadow seen something so beguilingly beautiful.

The whirling, mystical portal of magic radiated a luminous hue of ravishing red and alluring amethyst and looking into its swirling depths was like looking into a vortex of stars. Clyde soon returned with his elegantly designed harness, wrapped firmly around his body. Over a dozen glass vials were slotted into it, containing a vibrant variety of peculiar potions. "Well done Styx, good work as always, I guess there is little else to say, come my apprentice! It's time to step through the void of destiny!" he declared.

Naturally, Meadow was more than a little reluctant to step through the pulsating portal. However, Clyde placed a comforting hand upon her shoulder upon seeing the uncertainty in her face. "Fear not dear disciple, the only way one can overcome any frightful endeavor is to face it front on, march forth and accept what comes!" announced Clyde. Not an ounce of hesitation could be discerned in Clyde's steps as he kindly walked with Meadow into the portal. A sense of speechless awe overwhelmed Meadow as she allowed herself to be slowly devoured by the mysterious portal. For a few ephemeral moments of time it felt like she was wandering amongst the celestial realm of the heavens.

A cascade of color washed over Meadow, enveloping her in a palette of luminous light, but the entire spectacle was incredibly brief and abruptly faded. Clyde and Meadow suddenly emerged in a vast forest of towering trees and the sound of the humming vortex from whence they came disappeared. Vanishing from one place and appearing in another felt peculiar to say the least, and the vast variety of sounds of the forest engulfed Meadow immediately. "Incredible, it actually worked! Wait a moment though, how in the world are we supposed to get back!?" she cried. Dramatically, Clyde pointed his fist directly at Meadow to reveal a shimmering gold ring upon his finger, decorated with an alluring, azure jewel embedded within its center. "Worry not young Meadow, for I have this! A chatterstone!" he declared.

Curiosity cloaked Meadow as she watched Clyde move the ring to his mouth and speak into the stone. "Nice work Styx, we have arrived safely without being trapped in another dimension!" he said. "Thank you master, I am pleased to serve! Just let me know when you are ready to return!" echoed Styx's voice from within the ring. That's when it suddenly dawned on Meadow what purpose a chatterstone played, the purpose was within the name. "Ah, I see! So that's a chatterstone, it lets you communicate with your little imp! Pretty clever!" she remarked. Meadow had heard of chatterstones before, but they had become quite the rare oddity now. "Indeed, I can converse with Styx as long as he doesn't take his ring off" replied Clyde.

Once he had reclaimed his bearings, Clyde began scouring their surroundings to locate the village of Oakpass. "Now let us dawdle no longer my little lackey, tis time we aid the people of Oakpass in their plight!" he announced. "All well and good but where the heck is it? I expected to emerge right on the doorstep" answered Meadow as her eyes searched around. Thankfully, Oakpass wasn't too far from the spot they appeared, as Clyde soon located the little village nestled in the distant dense woods of the forest. "Aha! That must be it, come my trusty servant, the walk will do us good!" he proclaimed.

Without delay Clyde began marching into the mouth of the forest, "I still don't see why Styx couldn't just portal us right in front of the village" replied Meadow. "It creates too much attention if he portals me directly into a settlement, it is the magic of imps remember? Many are fearful of it" answered Clyde. The stroll through the winding wild woods was certainly serene. Meadow enjoyed the plethora of pleasant sounds echoing all around her as she ambled alongside Clyde, following the weary footpath worn into the earth. Whilst following the winding forest footpath, the sudden sound of rustling in the bushes nearby ensnared Clyde's attention. It caused him to briefly halt his advance and Meadow watched him with piqued curiosity, "What is it?" she asked. Like a vigilant stone statue, Clyde watched the cornucopia of dense bushes, waiting for another sudden rustle, which never came, "Nothing, tis nothing" he answered.

They resumed their traversal across the sprawling lush forest, Meadow allowing herself to become enchanted by the bracing fresh air and symphonic sounds of nature. Which is what likely caused her to overlook the tripwire in front of her feet. Meadow toppled over like a giant domino when the nefarious wire caught her leg. "What the heck!?" she managed to scream, as she fell face first towards a patch of murky mud. However, Clyde rescued Meadow from her clumsy fall when she felt a vigorous tug upon her arm. With a hearty tug he pulled her back, just in time before she received a mouthful of mud.

After Meadow had been rescued from the mucky maws of mud, Clyde squatted down and meticulously inspected the tripwire. "It would seem travelers are also fair game for our mischievous prankster" he uttered. Carefully, Clyde strode over the tripwire and held out his palm to lend Meadow a helping hand. "Wait till I get my hands on this trickster, I'll do more than prank them now!" Meadow growled.

Oakpass, after several more minutes of marching Clyde and Meadow arrived at the village's wooden palisade gate. It appeared defended by two blank grumpy guards, who wielded nothing more than shabby iron swords and worn wooden shields. Both grouchy guards eyeballed Clyde suspiciously, "Who're you!?" one of them lazily barked as Clyde approached. "I am Clyde Alrime, this is my apprentice Meadow Evershrewd, I am the alchemist whom your village requested for aid!" Clyde loudly declared. Dramatically drawing and flaunting the letter of aid from his waistcoat pocket. One of the guards suddenly snatched the letter from Clyde's hand and perused the writing upon it before handing it back and nodding his head. "Alright, go on in but don't cause us any trouble!" he barked. "Surprised you can even read" Clyde muttered under his breath as the letter was passed back to him.

Gradually the village gates were pushed open and made a long, weary groan. The first sight to greet Meadow and Clyde was the bombardment of tomatoes, eggs and flour upon the houses. Along with the cats, dogs, chickens and galamare all plastered in a colorful array of different dyes. Meadow and Clyde traded silent confused glances with each other after looking upon the village. Waiting to meet Clyde and Meadow was an elderly man wearing thick, circular brass spectacles and a beard so long and bushy it looked like he had a cloud stuck to his chin. "Ah, welcome!" he called out while waving. "My name is Albert, I'm what you might call the chief of Oakpass, you must be Clyde, the alchemist we requested" he added in a creaky tone.

As Clyde approached Albert, he extended his hand for a firm handshake. "Indeed, worry no longer sir, with me and my apprentice on the case, your woes will soon be a thing of the past!" he proclaimed. A wrinkly smile spread across Alberts lips and he gave an adorable chuckle, "Ha, good to see such passion in someone young, I thank you for your aid" he replied. "Hear that my little lackey? He called me young, guess you can retract your comment about calling me an old timer!" remarked Clyde. However, Meadow rolled her eyes and sighed, "Don't let it go to your head, this guy Albert looks so old he could make an ancient fossil seem youthful" she muttered.

After taking another glance around the village, Clyde turned his attention to Albert again. "So, tell me sir, do you have any suspects, anyone who may harbor a grudge towards your little settlement?" he asked. Dismay appeared in Alberts weathered eyes as he shook his head. "Not a clue, I've talked to everyone in the village including the children and not one of them knows, worse yet, every one of them have been a victim of these pranks" he replied. "Hmmm...it's possible someone in the village would prank themselves to appear innocent, but I believe this could be the work of a satyr" answered Clyde while rubbing his chin.

Clutched tightly in Alberts left hand was a short oak cane which aided him with walking. Clyde and Meadow followed behind Albert as he hobbled through the village, "Come, let me show you what we're dealing with" he said. "Oakpass largely depends on lumber and grain as our main sources of trade, we have the usual conveniences here too, a butcher, fletcher, baker, a general store and such" explained Albert. He halted his meandering upon reaching the sight of a frustrated villager who had been caught and strung up in a net rope trap. "Get me out of this thing!" shouted the ensnared villager. "This is the latest prank to befall us, happened not more than ten minutes ago and as you can see, we were in process of cutting him down" explained Albert.

Perplexity proceeded to infuse Albert's mind and he threw up his arms in frustration. "We can't deal with these tricks day in and day out any longer, it has made life in our village stressful!" he remarked. Thankfully, the unfortunate villager who had been ensnared in the net trap was cut down and released by a group of his friends nearby. "At the moment I'm afraid we don't have any gold to pay you for your services" said Albert. "But, if you manage to catch the culprit responsible for all this mischief and return our belongings, I would be more than happy to pay you" he added.

An itch quickly arose within the old chiefs long snowy beard, but Albert banished it with a good swift scratch. "Many of our valuable possessions and most of our gold has been stolen too you see, so I couldn't pay you right away even if I wanted to" he remarked. Clyde folded his arms and dwelled upon his thoughts. "Satyrs aren't malicious by nature, but they can be irksome, they enjoy being rascally and taking belongings from others" he uttered. Albert carried on leading Meadow and Clyde on his wander through the village, "Please do whatever it takes and all of Oakpass will be grateful to you, young man!" he croaked. Only to trigger another sneaky tripwire stretched between two trees as he passed between them. As soon as Albert triggered the tripwire, a wooden bucket of water tipped over from a lofty tree branch above and splashed all over him, soaking from him head to toe. "Please, we are desperate!" uttered Albert as he stood there, utterly drenched with a moody scowl upon his face. Meadow stifled a laugh on her face as she watched water drip from his head, while Clyde gave an adamant nod, "Leave it to us sir!" he declared.

Over the last couple of hours Clyde and Meadow had been searching for clues to the identity of the mischievous trickster, but impatience began to increase. "How the heck are we supposed to find this satyr? This forest is huge! How do you even know it's a satyr!?" she moaned. "You've uttered that same sentence several times now! Must you continue to make our already vexing ordeal even more so!?" declared Clyde. A stern glare flashed in Meadow's eyes as she stomped through the forest behind Clyde, only to be slapped in the face by a cluster of leaves from a nearby tree branch. "But how do you know which direction to go?" asked Meadow as she shoved the clump of leaves out of her face like a disgruntled ogre.

Before she received an answer, Clyde abruptly ceased his stride to inspect something intriguing embedded in the ground, "Because of these tracks" he replied. He and Meadow squatted down to examine the tracks further, although Meadow didn't fully know what to make of them. "They look like animal tracks but, they're in pairs……" she whispered. "A precise observation my delightful disciple, in pairs, in other words the animal that made these tracks was walking upright" replied Clyde.

Based on the size and shape of the tracks Clyde was easily able to conclude that they weren't paw prints nor were they padded. They were clearly hoof prints like that of a galamare, "Or a satyr" uttered Clyde. "Well, what are we waiting for? Let's follow the trail and catch this scoundrel!" growled Meadow as she began marching after the tracks which luckily led in a relatively straight line. Both kept a brisk but wary pace as they followed the trail of hoof marks deeper into the sprawling lush forest. Until they caught the ethereal sound of delicate musical notes echoing from up ahead. "Is that, music?" whispered Meadow as she cautiously inched through the obscuring bushes and closed in on the source of the sounds.

Although it took great effort, they both made sure not to rustle the flora and reveal their presence. "What could be making that music?" she uttered in a tone that was just barely audible. "Satyrs are curious creatures, music piques their interest, they adore listening and playing it, especially flute music which is what this music sounds like" whispered Clyde. They pursued the harmonious melody that gently drifted through the air, almost like the notes were luring them in with their enrapturing resonance until they finally saw it. After creeping through another clump of bushes they spotted the satyr.

Innocently, it sat with its back to them on a log, pressing its lips into a personalized wooden pan flute and blowing into it, "Looks like we finally found our quarry" whispered Clyde. Admittedly, the satyr didn't fill Meadow with trepidation in the slightest, it was much shorter than she expected, maybe the same height as an average child. "So that's a satyr? Are they dangerous?" Meadow whispered back. "No, not really, but they are a nuisance and can be very cunning and swift, we must strike quickly" whispered Clyde as he prepared to charge the satyr.

As soon as Meadow noticed him preparing to ambush the satyr, she immediately did the same, "Alright, let's do this!" she answered in an excited hush. Luck was on Clyde's side today and it pleased him greatly, the satyr was utterly unaware of his presence. Evident by the way it carried on naively playing its flute. "Now!" whispered Clyde as he bolted from the bushes and stormed towards the satyr who was no more than several feet away. Meadow leapt from the hiding spot and joined Clyde in his charge, only for them both to be suddenly ensnared in a hidden tripwire.

Before they knew it, Clyde and Meadow were scooped off their feet, flung into the air and dangled upside down by their heels in a dastardly snare trap. "What the heck!? What just happened!?" shouted Meadow as she flopped around like a fish on a line. "It was a trap! We should've looked before we leapt!" yelled Clyde as he squirmed around like a worm. Calmly, the satyr finished playing his song before arising from the wooden log which he sat upon, "Yes, you most certainly should have" it replied. "I knew you were following me all along, so I laid out some traps and played a song" said the satyr with a haughty chuckle as it turned to face them. Finally, Meadow received a good look at the satyr and the incredibly wild, sage green hair trailing down its back was the first thing she noticed. Two long, twisting horns stretched upwards from the front of its forehead and curled backwards. Thick layers of fur covered its arms and legs, possessing the same sage green hue as its hair. It clearly had the body, face and arms of a man. Yet possessed two legs like that of a goat and seemed to stand and walk upright with apparent ease like any ordinary human.

Despite her best efforts, Meadow failed to squirm free from her disconcerting dilemma, "Clyde, what are you waiting for? Use one of them fancy potions or something!" she shouted. "A good idea my dim-witted disciple, until you consider how am I supposed to drink one of my potions while upside down!?" Clyde fired back as he gently swayed back and forth. Both ended up colliding into each other from the natural swinging motion of the snares, which resulted in them butting heads. "Ow! What's your plan then? I haven't heard it yet, or could it be you don't have one!?" barked Meadow as she rubbed her head from the collision.

Their quarrelling caused the onlooking satyr to utter an amused chuckle. "Bicker no more, for I shall cut you loose and have you on the ground as you were before, but only if you can answer my riddles of which I have three, this is a fair deal do you not agree?" asked the satyr. Options were clearly in short supply, so Clyde decide to indulge the satyr's little game. "Very well if you really want to test our wits then so be it! Just know I shall laugh the moment your face crumbles under the pillar of defeat!" Clyde declared with certainty. An aura of confidence radiated from the satyr as he casually rested his rump upon the fallen tree log behind him once again. "I appear when the world is devoid of warmth and light, an orb of silver in the veil of night, what am I?" asked the satyr. Meadow pondered his puzzling riddle but struggled in her search to find an answer, while Clyde found it simple to solve, "Too easy, the answer is moon!" he replied. Receiving the correct answer so swiftly was something the satyr didn't expect and caused him to raise his eyebrow and sit up straight. "Well, well, so you do have a brain! But this is only the beginning of our game" he answered.

A cunning smirk appeared upon the satyr's face as he readied the next riddle. "I shine beautifully despite being old, battles are fought for me and honor is sold, what am I?" asked the satyr with a devious snigger. This one took Clyde a little while longer to ponder a shrewd answer, but he was certain he knew what it was. Meanwhile, Meadow was thinking so hard it looked like steam was about to erupt from her ears. "Ha, laughably easy, the answer is gold!" proclaimed Clyde with a hearty chortle.

Once again, the satyr was taken aback by how effortlessly Clyde solved his next riddle and this time it caused him to hop from his log and adopt a more serious expression. "Whatever, you think you're so clever, but one riddle still remains, and I guarantee it will be too much for your little brains!" he growled. Vertigo had begun to set in, making Clyde and Meadow feel lightheaded and dizzy. "Before I reveal my last riddle I must ask, what is your task? You must have a problem to solve, to follow me with such resolve" asked the satyr. "Our task is to put an end to the plethora of pranks that you've been plaguing the village of Oakpass with, and to return all the belongings you stole, now speak your last riddle!" Clyde answered with gusto.

Scowling vexation poured over the satyr as he glared at Clyde. "Very well, I am something only love can steal, without me life feels like an abyss and I can take an eternity to heal, what am I?" he replied. Again, Meadow hadn't the faintest idea what the satyr was talking about. As for Clyde, he contemplated the satyr's confusing conundrum, but felt confounded from having to consider the puzzle whilst upside down. Until at last an answer came to him, just as the satyr became smug with confidence. "Heart, the answer is heart!" Clyde abruptly spewed with glee. As soon as he declared his answer, the sight of the satyr's arrogant smirk fading from his face was all the proof Clyde needed to confirm he was correct. "Ha, I knew I'm right! I solved your riddles! I am a genius! Ha, ha, ha!" He laughed. The sight of him gloating made Meadow wearily sigh, "I think being upside down has made the blood rush to your head, if gets any bigger I'm worried it's going to explode" she uttered.

Meanwhile, the satyr continued to glare at them with clenched fists but managed to overcome the bitter taste of defeat that lingered within him. "Well done, cut you both down I will, but this game continues still, for if you wish to end my pranks catch me first to earn your thanks" decreed the riled satyr. A shiny gold necklace dangled around the satyr's neck, but Clyde and Meadow hadn't paid attention to it until the satyr suddenly raised it high up for all to see. "Pay attention fools, for I shall not repeat the rules" uttered the satyr. "I am not only a prankster, but an excellent thief and this shiny necklace belongs to the village chief!" he announced. Proudly, the satyr rubbed a speck of dirt from the gleaming gold and jeweled incrusted necklace he stole. "If you can remove it from my neck then I shall bother the people of Oakpass no more, of that you can be sure!" he proclaimed.

Back and forth Meadow and Clyde continued to swing, like a couple of dangling rag dolls whilst watching the satyr with an ample mixture of suspicion and frustration. "Only when this necklace around my neck is in your hand, shall I remove myself from this part of the land!" added the satyr. His delight quickly changed into nefarious glee. "But I'm giving you only a day, so I suggest you do not delay!" the satyr remarked, his fingers drumming together with villainy.

His jovial demeanor of being the mastermind in his little game made Meadow and Clyde scowl further. "Fine, we will play your game, you annoying little goat man! Now cut us down!" Meadow sternly barked. Although Meadow's harsh insults and demanding tone succeeded in their effort to rile up the satyr. The satyr was able to overlook it when he contemplated the giddy game of tag that was going to take place. "For solving my riddles, I shall set you free, but do not think catching me will be as easy!" proclaimed the satyr. Swiftly, he then scurried up the tree from which Clyde and Meadow hung and proceeded to untie them. As soon as their binding bonds were untied, Meadow and Clyde fell victims to the laws of gravity and felt their stomachs lurch as they suddenly plummeted to the earth. "Ow!" Meadow cried as she slammed into the mossy dirt.

While they were both still face in the ground, the satyr had already given himself a head start. "And now the game can begin, give chase if you wish to win!" he echoed, before scurrying into the depths of the forest. Angered by the satyr's juvenile trickery and irksome riddles and rhymes, Meadow furiously lifted herself from the mud and moss. "Alright, let's hunt down that annoying dung kisser!" she declared. "Soothe your fire my anxious lackey, we shan't catch that satyr merely by chasing, satyr are too fast thanks to those goat-like legs of theirs, it's time to call upon my alchemy" replied Clyde.

Once he had finished removing the remnants of rope coiled around his ankles, Clyde reached for one of the sealed potion vials upon his harness. "It is time for you to behold the power of alchemy my apprentice!" he proclaimed. His chosen potion was one that shimmered with a mesmerizing, silvery cerulean hue. "Okay, so what exactly will it do?" asked Meadow as she curiously gazed at the bottled vial of blue liquid.

Hastily, Clyde ingested the potion, "This captivating concoction is none other than a speed enhancing potion! I shall catch that impish prankster with sheer speed!" he proclaimed. A refreshing gasp erupted from Clyde's lips once he had consumed the vial of gleaming liquid and he proceeded to position himself in a running posture. "Now watch, and be amazed!" he declared, before rushing into the forest at remarkable speed. "Whoa!" cried Meadow as she watched Clyde whoosh into the woods faster than the fastest cerberii, the very leaves around him being flung into the air from the initial gust. Luckily, the satyr hadn't gotten too far, evident when Clyde began to hear the familiar sound of musical notes floating upon the current of the air. no doubt the satyr was pleasantly playing his little flute, confident in his victory.

That's when Clyde suddenly spotted the satyr sitting on a smooth circular rock up ahead. Casually blowing his lips into his wooden flute and creating a sonata of soothing music until the satyr also spotted Clyde. The satyr's serene little symphony was cut short and the sight of Clyde dashing towards him at great speed caused him to become spooked. A flustered panic swept over the satyr as he toppled off the rock and began scurrying into the forest as fast as his goat legs would allow him. "Yes, that's it! Run while you can little goat man!" Clyde uttered with a devilish smirk.

Thanks to his potion, Clyde was swiftly gaining on the satyr as he chased him through the winding labyrinth of trees, whizzing past bushes and shrubs like a whistling arrow. However, Clyde lost his momentum momentarily when he had to duck under a thick branch that nearly clobbered him in the face. Yet, the satyr was short enough that he could simply run right under it. "You merely delay the inevitable!" Clyde shouted as he locked eyes upon the satyr again and resumed the pursuit, the thrill of the chase bubbling within his beating heart. As fast as the satyr was, he couldn't match Clyde's speed now. Clyde was on a higher level and even zipping and zagging through the trees didn't help to evade him. Clyde had caught up with the satyr; he was no more than a few feet behind. Eagerly, he reached out his arms to grab the little prankster, until the satyr suddenly leapt into the air.

This puzzled Clyde, but only for a moment, as he felt the ground beneath him instantly sink away. "A pitfall trap!?" Clyde cried from the sudden plummet. To his dismay, the satyr had gained the upper hand once again. Clearly, he had been leading Clyde towards a well concealed pitfall trap, deceptively camouflaged amongst the forest foliage. There was little chance Clyde would've spotted it, even if he were walking. As he plunged into the hole's shadowy depths, Clyde was surprised how deep it was. Sadly, upon painfully colliding with the muddy earth, he realized it was too deep for him to escape it unaided.

To add insult to his wounded pride, the satyr haughtily stood above the devious pitfall trap he laid, gazed upon Clyde like he was a petty insect and arrogantly gloated. "Oh dear, if only you had kept your eyes on the path ahead, you may have caught me instead! But don't fret, our game hasn't ended just yet!" he taunted. Arrogantly, the satyr jingled the golden necklace swinging around his neck, "Out of that pit you must climb, to try again one more time!" he goaded. Before Clyde could utter a single word in response, the satyr swiftly took off into the forest again. Leaving Clyde frustrated and trapped at the bottom of a muddy hole, "Revel in your victory while you can!" he growled.

Meanwhile, Meadow was calmly inhaling the sweet scent of a crimson colored flower she picked while innocently humming, "Wonder what's taking him so long?" she uttered. Deep from within the forest, Meadow started hearing her name. It resonated through the winding woods and verdant vegetation, "Meadow! Meadow!" it echoed over and over. It sounded like Clyde, which caused Meadow to quickly hop to her feet and investigate, "Clyde? Clyde is that you!?" she called back.

As she tracked the echo of her voice through the maze of mossy trees and drew closer to its origin, it became certain that the voice belonged to Clyde. Until finally, she located him by almost stumbling into the gaping hole at her feet. Perplexity hooked Meadow, accompanied by a curious tilt of her head as she gazed into the deep pit burrowed into the earth, "What are you doing down there?" she asked. Clyde raised his head to meet her while a sullen cloud of defeat lingered over him. "Oh, I'm just waiting for my forest friends so we can have a tea party together! What do you think?" he grumbled. His profound sarcasm provoked Meadow, evident by the way she firmly planted her hands upon her hips. "I think that satyr gave you the slip and it looks like you need a hand escaping, so how about you try asking nicely?" replied Meadow.

After swallowing his pride and taking a hearty sip of humility, Clyde proceeded to ask nicely. "Fine, please would you be kind enough to assist me out of this hole Meadow?" he uttered. "Much better and yes, I would be glad to!" answered Meadow with a pleased grin spread across her face. At which point she dug her knees into the dirt and reached a hand into the deep hole for Clyde to grasp. After a substantial amount of huffing, wheezing and tugging, Meadow managed to hoist Clyde up just enough for him to reach out and grab the edges of the provoking pitfall trap.

The effort required was seemingly herculean, thankfully Clyde was able to climb out of the pit at that point, "You're much heavier than you look ya know!" Meadow panted. "I'll have you know my scrawny student; it is because of all my muscle mass, I'm stronger than I look!" Clyde pompously proclaimed. His bragging seemed baseless and only served to cause Meadow minor irritation, like a well-stuck splinter, "Right, of course, so what do we do now?" she asked. After climbing to his feet, Clyde rested his fingers upon his chin and contemplated what to do next. "If speed alone will not allow us to catch this satyr, then we need to approach without being seen, we need to be invisible!" he declared.

For the last few hours Clyde and Meadow had been tirelessly tracking their elusive quarry, following trails of broken branches, footprints and even the faintest rustling of bushes. "Can't we just give up and accept we lost track of it?" Meadow wearily sighed. "Never, I refuse to let that infuriating trickster stroll into the sunset with the last laugh! Besides, I accepted this request and I need to get paid" Answered Clyde. By this point a heavenly golden glow radiated over the entire forest, indicating the sun was at its peak. This also meant plenty of time remained to catch the satyr and snag his stolen necklace. However, with no sign of the satyr other than vague remnants of his presence to be found, Meadow began to feel waves of pessimism swirling around.

What delayed their hunt even further were all the tripwires the satyr scattered throughout the forest. Every so often Clyde would spot one and while overcoming them was a trivial task, keeping a vigilant eye open for them wasn't. After avoiding yet another tripwire, Meadow parted her lips and was on the verge of speaking, until Clyde shoved his hand over her mouth, "Shhhh! You hear that?" he asked. Meadow grumpily swatted away his hand from her mouth and listened intently, "Hear what?" she whispered, before suddenly hearing faint flute music. Beyond the blanket of lush bushes and trees, something caught Clyde's eye or rather someone. "At last, the prey is spotted!" he remarked in an excited hush when he finally laid eyes upon the infernal satyr once again. Quickly but quietly, Meadow scurried to his side and scrunched her eyes to study the scene ahead. Sure enough the satyr was there, naively performing that same cheerful melody upon his wooden flute. "Okay, so let's go over the plan again, we drink that invisibility potion of yours, sneak up to the satyr without the worry of being seen and we grab him!" whispered Meadow.

A cunning twinkle gleamed in the corner of Clyde's eye. "Precisely, this time it shall be our turn to dangle that satyr upside down and torture him with tedious riddles!" Clyde whispered back. Currently, the satyr sat upon a hill, remained motionless and rested its back against a towering oak tree. It was completely oblivious to Clyde and Meadow's presence and the fact that its attention was focused on playing its flute made the moment all the sweeter. "This is our best chance; we should not let it slip us by!" whispered Clyde.

From his harness of colorful potions, Clyde revealed a clear glass vial that contained a unique white liquid, almost translucent in form. "This is the invisibility potion, remember it only lasts a minute or two" he uttered. "So, we shall have to move swiftly but silently" replied Meadow as she watched Clyde uncork the glass vial. He raised it to his lips and took an ample swig, before passing the rest to Meadow. About half of the potion remained, but Clyde assured Meadow it would be more than enough, "Okay, here goes" whispered Meadow as she gulped it down. Surprisingly, it tasted rather sweet but had a distinct tingling that lingered upon her tongue. A mysterious sensation she couldn't quite describe and before she knew it, Clyde had vanished from all sight. "Wow, even your clothes have disappeared!" she uttered in an amazed hush. It was at this point she began noticing her hands and fingers became more transparent, until they completely faded away from all visibility. "Indeed, my old invisibility potion was rather embarrassing, I had to remove all my attire for it to work effectively, it was more than a little humiliating when it wore off" whispered Clyde.

Being invisible felt so empowering to Meadow, like she was an ethereal deity watching the world from the outside in. For an ephemeral moment it felt like she had vanished from all existence, along with the bad memories that haunted her. "Alright, time is of the essence my dear, I shall approach from the left and you shall approach from the right" whispered Clyde, shattering Meadow's whimsical moment of wonder. Nevertheless, Meadow followed his instructions and began to slowly approach the oblivious satyr from the right, taking meticulous care to avoid rustle when moving through the bushes.

If there was one quality Meadow could discern from the satyr, it was his ability to create music, for the melodic notes floating from his flute were heavenly to hear. "I wonder if all satyrs can play the flute so well" wondered Meadow as she warily encroached upon the creature. Until she suddenly stepped upon a fallen twig and snapped it underfoot and the distinct sound of splitting wood immediately followed. It caused the nearby satyr to instantly cease his flute playing and become alerted.

Meadow's gaze was so vigilantly fixated upon the satyr that she neglected to see where she was stepping. She thanked her lucky stars that her and Clyde were invisible as they were stood right in front of the satyr, no more than several feet away. Clyde and Meadow remained frozen on the spot with nervous beads of sweat dripping down their foreheads as they watched the satyr survey his surroundings. All the while, the time limit for their invisibility constantly counting down caused further anxiety. After it felt like a century had passed, the satyr finally rested his back against the rugged oak tree behind him and resumed playing his mesmeric melodies.

Gradually, Meadow and Clyde inched closer and closer, until they were finally within spitting distance of the seemingly unaware satyr. Once they had successfully reached him, Meadow remembered the plan and profound anticipation swelled in Meadow's heart as she prepared to pounce. She and Clyde decided to throw caution to the wind and quickly rushed the last several feet that remained between them and the satyr. With all haste Clyde and Meadow dashed towards the satyr, still completely invisible to the eye. This time Clyde was supremely confident in his plan to catch the cunning little trickster.

Both reached out their arms, ready to grab the satyr, until to their utter bewilderment, he quickly smiled and bolted straight ahead like he knew they were there all along. "What the heck!?" shouted Meadow as she watched him scurry past. To her dismay, another plan failed and to add insult to injury or rather injury to insult, Meadow and Clyde ended up painfully colliding into each other. "Ow, watch where you're going!" cried Meadow as her head slammed right into Clyde, causing her to topple backwards.

Clyde also staggered from the sudden impact and felt the wind be knocked out of his lungs, "How am I supposed to watch where I'm going when your invisible!?" he cried back. "Ow, okay you make a valid point! Just, let me recover a moment!" cried Meadow as she rubbed her throbbing skull. Meanwhile, the satyr who was nearby, listened to the bizarre scene with a perplexed expression. Until the invisibility potion abruptly wore off, "Ah I see, invisibility was how you tried to catch me!" he declared. "I expected more but it seems your both quite dense, don't you realize you cannot rely on only one sense?" spoke the haughty satyr, before dashing off into the woods again.

Twilight begun to appear over the horizon and although Clyde and Meadow were continuing their hunt for the satyr, the bitter taste of defeat still lingered within Meadow. "I still can't believe you didn't see such an obvious flaw in the plan, nothing is working!" She growled. Her tone irked Clyde and he angrily kicked away a stone near his foot. "Okay, I forgot that satyrs possess a keener sense of smell than humans and he picked up our scent!" he growled back. At this moment in time Meadow felt like she was on the verge of ripping her hair out, her infuriated scowl saying more than a thousand words could. "So, if we want to catch that satyr all we have do is think of a way to approach it silently, invisibly, really quickly and without giving away our scent, how hard can that be!?" she uttered sarcastically.

Clyde didn't possess a reply; he remained trapped in a state of speechless frustration and about the only way he could think to respond was with a weary sigh. At that moment, a nearby owl perched itself upon a thick branch above and echoed the air with its hooting. It felt eerie when combined with the fading amber light that had begun to infiltrate the forest. Meadow shuddered as she felt a brief chill creep over her skin, "Can't we just admit defeat and leave? This forest is starting to get a little dark and spooky" she uttered. However, her words caused Clyde to have a sudden surge of inspiration, evident by his expression when he turned around to face her. "Spooky? Hmmmm……interesting, you may have just bestowed me a brilliant idea my disciple!" Clyde cried eagerly.

Only the faintest glimmers of sunlight remained now. Yet, Clyde and Meadow strode through the murky forest with newfound confidence as they resumed their hunt for the sneaky satyr. "It's getting dark, soon we won't be able to see our hands in front of our faces" uttered Meadow. Shrugging off the ominous chill that slithered up her spine, a result of how eerie the forest had grown. However, her apprehension at the encroaching night only served to strengthen Clyde's faith in his plan. "Worry not, we're on the right trail, we are not far behind, that Satyr will not elude us a third time" answered Clyde.

Dusk had finally fallen upon the forest by the time Clyde and Meadow caught up with their quarry. They began to hear that same haunting melody being played from the satyr's flute, floating upon the eerie air. Clyde had become proficient at following the satyr's tracks now and keeping a vigilant eye open for any devious traps had become second nature. Still, finding the satyr took a little longer than Clyde desired. This time the satyr had chosen a mystical moonlit glade as his preferred stage of performance, his gaze currently fixated by the ashen moon in the starry sky. Clyde and Meadow watched the satyr innocently play his flute from a distance and waited until he ceased his melody, for that would be the time to strike.

From the shadows they patiently waited and watched, having no choice but to listen to the enchanting song that flowed from the satyr's flute. Until the music finally faded, and the satyr set his flute down beside him at last. "Now is our chance" whispered Clyde as he pulled another vial of potion from his harness, tugged out the cork that was wedged within its neck and handed it Meadow. This potion had a mysterious, mesmerizing blue hue, its liquid having a significantly thin consistency, almost delicate. "So, what does this do again?" Meadow asked. "This little mixture is none other than my ethereal potion, for a short time you will be completely intangible and utterly invulnerable to harm!" Clyde whispered with pride.

Slowly, Meadow raised the potion vial to her lips and began to imbibe the tasteless liquid. "Your footsteps will make no sound, you will have no scent and you will be able to phase though anything, and everything will phase right through you" explained Clyde. Once Meadow had consumed the potion, she eagerly awaited its effects and she didn't have to wait long. "What's going on? Is this supposed to happen?" she asked as she looked down at her body. Gradually her entire body became transparent, her flesh slowly faded away until she looked like an ethereal ghostly blue phantom. "It also has the added side-effect of making the drinker appear like a ghost" remarked Clyde as he looked upon Meadow's spectral visage. To test her temporary abilities, Clyde picked up a nearby stone and tossed it to Meadow for her to catch. As she held out her palms to receive it, the stone passed right through her and fell onto the ground as Clyde expected. "Okay, you know what you must do my apprentice, move quickly while the satyr is not playing his flute, for his flute is the very thing we must get our hands on" whispered Clyde.

So, the plan was set, and Meadow made sure to approach the satyr from an angle he couldn't see her from, taking advantage of his spellbound stargazing. Her footsteps made not a sound and Meadow felt like she was floating as she passed straight through the shrubs and bushes of the forest like they weren't even there. With silent speed Meadow approached the satyr from behind and once she was close enough, she leapt from the shadows to strike. "Ooooooooo!" she wailed while reaching her arms out to try and grab the satyr. She was determined to scare the satyr witless and she succeeded greatly. "A.... A ghost!?" cried the satyr as terror flooded his senses and he clumsily bolted into the woods.

The scare tactic was made more impressive by the fact that Meadow decided to phase half-way through a nearby tree so that only her upper body and face were visible. "Ooooooooo!" she moaned again as she watched the satyr flee in fear. It would've been impossible for the satyr to hear or smell Meadow approaching, hence it was an excellent plan Clyde cooked up, but it was only the first step. "Good show my simply amazing apprentice, I think that satyr will not sleep well for some time to come!" declared Clyde as he came running over.

Meadow, still in her spooky ethereal form burst into laughter, "I know! It was so funny; this whole plan was worth it for that part alone!" she cried with tears of joy. Clyde enjoyed watching Meadow revel in the prank they had just pulled upon the satyr. It felt so satisfying to turn the tables for a change, but now it was time for the next step. The beautiful, handcrafted pan-flute belonging to the satyr lay nearby and Clyde promptly scooped it up. "Just like I hoped, that satyr was so scared that he forgot to grab his flute, and now it is ours!" He declared, uttering a devious chuckle. Gradually, the ethereal potion that Meadow consumed began to wear off and her tangible flesh was restored, "You really think that flute will lure the satyr in?" she asked. "Yes, there is no better bait to capture a satyr, they are all deeply attached to the flutes they make, he will do anything to try and get it back" replied Clyde as he strolled away.

While Clyde went off to get everything prepared, Meadow remained behind. She stayed at the exact spot where she scared the satyr out of his senses; for she knew it wouldn't be long before the satyr returned. Return the satyr did, much sooner that Meadow was excepting, brave considering his ghostly encounter. "You? You're that girl! The apprentice of that man! Why are you here? What is your plan?" asked the satyr upon seeing Meadow. A delighted smirk spread across Meadow's face as she arrogantly crossed her arms. "The plan has already worked! That ghost you saw was me, we pranked you good!" she answered smugly.

Being pranked left the satyr speechless, his mouth literally becoming agape. "Oh, and we have your flute, it was just lying there so......finders' keepers!" Meadow remarked with evident bliss. "Where is it? Where is my flute!? It was not yours to loot! It was very dear to me you thief; you have caused me so much grief!" the satyr angrily shouted. His bout of furious frustration only fueled Meadow's delight further, "And now you know how it feels, how does that saying go? No honor amongst thieves!" she replied. A stern glare was the only answer the satyr had to give and Meadow wasn't finished toying with him yet. "Don't worry, if you want your flute back you just have to answer a simple riddle!" she declared.

A vexed scowl spread over the satyr's face, the empowerment of being in control clearly slipping away. "If you've lost something and know not where to look, return to where it all began, and you may find what was took" Meadow recited. Deeply, the satyr pondered Meadow's riddle, but it didn't take him long to deduce. "Ha, Easy! It is in the place where our game started! I shall retrieve my flute, and never again shall we be parted!" he cried, before darting into the forest. Meanwhile, Clyde had been preparing for the satyr's arrival and he knew he wouldn't have to wait long. "Soon everything will fall into place, he won't be able to resist a chance to get his flute back" Clyde uttered. He vaguely remembered where the satyr's game first started, Clyde couldn't remember the exact spot, but he knew it wasn't far away. Also, Clyde kept creating a clamorous cacophony with the flute he stole to ensure the satyr had no difficulty locating him. So far Clyde's plan worked exactly as he envisioned, the satyr overheard the discordant, wincing notes Clyde was played from the stolen flute and came running, eager to reclaim it.

Upon being confronted by the satyr again, Clyde ceased the dreadful din he was performing. "Such a nice flute I found, alas it seems I shall need more practice with it!" he decreed with a confident smirk. "I'm here to take back what you stole, if your plan was to enrage me then you succeeded in your goal!" growled the satyr. Surprisingly, Clyde tossed the flute onto the ground a few feet in front of him and shrugged, "I'm no thief, if you want it back you can have it" he uttered. Naturally this caused the satyr to be dubious and he warily surveyed the situation and noticed the poorly concealed pitfall trap Clyde had created in front of him.

A cunning smile spread across the satyr's lips upon spotting Clyde's pitiful attempt at trickery, "Nice try you thieves, but I see that bundle of grass and leaves!" declared the satyr. "Your trap is far too obvious, but I cannot deny it was a nice try!" announced the satyr as he ran towards his flute and easily leapt over Clyde's pitfall trap. It all worked out perfectly and Clyde watched with delight as the satyr leapt over the trap and eagerly dashed for his flute. Only for the satyr's joy to quickly crumble away and be replaced by the shattering tides of dismay.

The satyr felt a sudden, forceful yank upon his leg and before he knew it, he was abruptly scooped up and flung into the air, "No, a tripwire!?" He cried in utter panic. Like a fish on a line the satyr flopped around as he hung upside down, which caused the golden necklace to fall from his neck and drop to the ground. "Indeed, and one of yours to be exact, I knew you would be so fixated on reclaiming your flute that you wouldn't notice a second trap, especially one of yours!" replied Clyde. Effortlessly, Clyde then proceeded to pick up the shiny gold necklace from the muddy ground and jingled it around for the satyr to behold.

Within that same moment, Meadow came running through the bushes. She was out of breath but overjoyed when she saw the satyr dangling upside down from his own snare trap and the expression on his face looking like he just kissed a goblin. "Ha, so it worked! How does it feel now the boot is on the other foot goat-boy?" Meadow gleefully taunted. To further wound the satyr's pride, Meadow confidently marched onto the pile of bundled grass and leaves. Yet she failed to suddenly plummet beneath the ground, "And you actually fell for our fake pitfall trap!" she declared with a haughty laugh.

Seeing the fake pitfall trap was the final blow to the satyr's dignity and it left him utterly vanquished. "It looks like we are the winners of this game!" announced Clyde as he held up the gold necklace, its jewels shimmering under the increasing moonlight. "Very well, there's no point in remaining heated, you win, I am defeated" reluctantly uttered the satyr. The sweet taste of victory gracefully danced upon Clyde's tongue, causing him to cackle like a delirious mad scientist. "Ah, that precious moment when the enemy is conquered and admits defeat! Tis more beautiful than the sight of a hundred puppies in a field of roses!" Clyde declared. The sensation of triumph gripped Clyde and a hearty laugh of victory bellowed from his lungs, resonating through the forest.

Meanwhile, Meadow gawked at Clyde with a raised eyebrow, "I hate to interrupt your moment of wondrous whimsy, but what are we going to do with this little prankster?" she asked. Slowly, Clyde's ecstatic laughter subsided, finally fading to a weighty hum. "An astute question my adorable apprentice, we shall cut him down but keep him restrained, we need him to show us where he hid the villager's belongings" he answered. Clyde turned his attention to the dangling satyr, "Did you hear me? Show us where you hid the belongings you stole, then you shall receive your flute and your freedom!" He demanded.

A disgruntled grumble and a reluctant head nod were the best answer Clyde could receive from the satyr and true to his word, Clyde cut the satyr down. However, Clyde wasn't born yesterday and used the rope that snagged the satyr to bind his arms and kept him on a short leash. For Clyde knew full well that the satyr would likely flee at the best opportunity. Without delay, the satyr began leading Clyde and Meadow through the dark forest towards the stash of stolen belongings. "Remember goat boy, don't even think of trying to run for it, I've still got your flute and if you try to flee, I will smash it into splinters!" remarked Meadow in a stern tone.

After a fair amount of marching through the wild woods the satyr abruptly halted in his tracks. "This is the place, this is the spot, for my freedom and flute I trick you not" muttered the satyr. Upon cautiously studying the spot of ground where the satyr beckoned, Clyde could discern a giant letter X made entirely from small rocks, "And so X marks the spot!" he declared. It was time for Meadow to get her hands dirty, literally, "How come I have to do this? This is not a job for a young lady like me!" she grumbled as her nails clawed through the dirt. "Forgive any unpleasantness it causes you my sulky servant, but I must keep a close eye and an even closer grasp upon our little goat friend here!" answered Clyde. After a few minutes of mucky digging, a glimmer of gold shimmered from beneath the cold, earthy soil, "I think I've found it!" exclaimed Meadow.

Clyde inched towards the hole that Meadow had dug to take a curious peek, while keeping a tight hold upon the rope that bound the satyr. The more Meadow continued to scoop away the dirt, the more of the treasure trove she unearthed. Jewels, rings, bracelets, even a magnificent silver bladed and gold hilted sword, it had all been buried here. All those items alone would've fetched a hearty sum. But a thick leather sack containing something heavy is what captured Meadow's attention, "Look at this!" she remarked. Promptly, Meadow opened the heavy leather sack after she arduously pulled it from beneath the earth. An act that required both her hands and all her strength, "Goodness! That is a lot of gold!" she cried.

Meadow and Clyde were dazzled by the array of gold that greeted them upon gazing into the leather sack, "Yes, a lot of gold, too much in fact" uttered Clyde suspiciously. Contained in the sack was well over a thousand gold coins, which caused Clyde to remain firmly skeptical as he turned his attention back to the satyr. "I highly doubt a secluded hamlet like Oakpass possessed that amount of coin, I also doubt your that great a thief so tell me, where did you get all that gold?" he inquired.

At first the satyr eluded Clyde's inquisitive gaze, but when Meadow began to tap the wooden flute against her palm as a reminder, the satyr soon spilled his secrets. "Okay, a hooded stranger cloaked in black! He was the one who gave me the sack!" he answered. Confused glances were traded between Meadow and Clyde as they listened to the satyr speak further. "The man in black paid me to harass the village, all I had to do was prank and pillage" he uttered. This new piece of information was something Clyde was admittedly unprepared for.

Naturally, he couldn't help narrowing his eyes with dubious skepticism, "An intriguing fable you've woven there" he replied. Unable to contain his frustration the satyr started hopping up and down. "Tis no fable, I would prove it were I able! True I prank and deceive, but this time you must believe!" he cried. This time the satyr's anxious pleas and agitated hopping convinced Clyde, who decided to untie him. "Very well, for some reason I think your actually speaking the truth, Meadow, return his flute" said Clyde. Once the ropes binding the satyr were removed and he finally felt the wooden oak of his beloved flute again, he breathed a sigh of relief. "But you better not cause trouble again, cause if you do, we're gonna come after you, and we won't be nice!" barked Meadow after placing her hands firmly upon her hips.

It was remarkable how scary Meadow could be when needed, especially for someone so young and fair. "Yes, yes I understand! I have no more pranks planned!" The satyr nervously spluttered, quickly fleeing into the woods once and for all. It was a long trek back to the secluded little settlement of Oakpass and Clyde and Meadow were absolutely fatigued from the whole ordeal. "I need a bath and a five-course banquet right now" sighed Meadow as she clumsily shuffled behind. Although Clyde could relate to her misery, his mind was deeply fixated upon this mysterious hooded man that the satyr spoke of. "I wonder, why? What does this mean?" muttered Clyde as theories clouded his mind.

Carrying all the villagers treasured belongings made the journey more cumbersome, thankfully it was mostly all jewelry, the heaviest item being the large sack of gold coins. Unable to resist the shimmering allure of the coins, Clyde took another swift peek into the sack to gaze upon their golden glory. "Such an ostentatious display of wealth!" he whispered with gasped breath. For the time being, Clyde could not discern a logical reason for why the satyr was paid such a grand sum, just to play juvenile pranks and trickery upon the villagers. "Maybe a ridiculously rich noble who succumbed to boredom?" muttered Clyde as he pondered reasons. Whatever the reasons, the case was over and for now Clyde banished the topic from his mind upon seeing Oakpass come into view beyond the trees.

Dawn had begun to break by the time they arrived at Oakpass, the sight of the warm sun gently rising from beyond the woods felt radiant and seemed to ease Clyde and Meadow's fatigue. The two grouchy, blank-faced guards who defended the pitiful oak gates of the village immediately pushed them open upon seeing Clyde approaching and granted passage. Inside, the villagers were going about their mundane lives, but all of them abruptly ceased what they were doing upon noticing Clyde's arrival. "I guess they've been expecting us" Meadow remarked while jadedly shuffling her body onwards. "They've been waiting for us; they must be eager to hear our report" added Clyde as he shambled into the middle of the village like a resurrected corpse. Hastily, Albert the village chief came scurrying over like a wolf seeing a stack of meat. "Ah good you've returned, but you both look exhausted, please tell us you have good news" he said.

Meadow promptly placed the villager's belongings upon the ground and unveiled the bundle of cloth they were all wrapped in. "Here are all the missing items belonging to the villagers!" She declared. "And I believe this belongs to you good sir!" Clyde added as he removed the shimmering gold necklace he fought so hard to obtain from his neck and passed it to Albert. Delight struck Albert like a lightning bolt as his scrawny fingers reached out for the necklace. "Oh my, this necklace was a gift from my late wife before she passed, I feared I'd never see it again!" he replied, his wrinkled lips forming a creased smile. "Happy to be of service sir and you needn't worry about your prankster anymore; it turned out to be a satyr, but it's been taken care of" replied Clyde.

This news surprised and delighted Albert at the same time, "A satyr? Goodness, I imagine it wasn't easy to catch then! I never considered it could've been a satyr!" he remarked. After placing his beloved necklace safely around his neck again, Albert's face creased when he softly smiled. "Thank goodness that stranger in the black mask recommend your services to me!" he added.

His comment caused Clyde and Meadow to suspiciously glance at each other, "Excuse me sir, but how exactly did you find out about my services?" asked Clyde. "A hooded stranger dressed in black told me about you after he discovered the problems our village was facing, he told me to seek out Clyde Alrime" answered Albert. Again, Meadow and Clyde were left utterly baffled upon hearing this news; it couldn't just be a coincidence. "What did this stranger look like? Did you see his face?" asked Meadow. Sadly, Albert shook his head, "No, like I said he wore a black iron mask, normally I wouldn't have trusted such a man, but our village was desperate to be rid of our trickster" he replied.

None of it made sense, it had to be the same hooded stranger that paid the satyr to harass the village. "And after getting in contact with us, we show up to solve the problem this mysterious stranger caused, curious" muttered Clyde under his breath. A puzzled expression appeared within Alberts eyes, "Is something wrong?" he asked. As much as Clyde wanted to share his thoughts, he was far too tired to begin. Albert didn't seem to know anything more than he did anyway, "No, it's nothing" replied Clyde. Before finally leaving Oakpass, Clyde handed Albert the sack stuffed with gleaming gold coins. "Oh, we also found this sack of gold coins the satyr was stockpiling, I'm sure your village can make better use of it" said Clyde.

The sheer weight of the sack felt as heavy as a mountain to Albert and the look of utter surprise on his face as the sack was dumped into his hands was comical. "Gracious, are you certain? This is more gold than our village earns in a month!" gasped Albert as he let the heavy sack slam to the ground. Clyde gave him a final handshake before departing, "Worry not, my apprentice and I have already taken a small amount of gold from it as payment" he replied.

With the case concluded, Meadow and Clyde strolled along the bushy forest path they traversed upon first arriving. They waved goodbye, but were eager to depart Oakpass, for they were anxious to return to the snowy mountains and rest. "Why does it feel like we've been playing some childish game?" asked Meadow. "The stranger who paid that satyr to pester the villagers is the same person who told them about you; it's all been a complete run-around!" she groaned. Clyde couldn't think right now, his mind was clouded with confusion, but couldn't deny the truth within Meadow's words. It felt like they had been led on a pointless circle, like a couple of dogs chasing their tails. "We'll discuss it later, for now let's just return home" uttered Clyde as he closed his eyes and rubbed his throbbing temples.

After banishing the brief headache from his mind, Clyde raised his hand so that the ring upon his finger was near his mouth and proceeded to speak into the chatterstone. "Styx, can you hear me? We're done here, create a portal in same place you sent us" uttered Clyde. After a couple of seconds of silence, they heard Styx's voice abruptly echo from the ring. "Yes master, I hear you loud and clear, creating the portal now, make sure you're both stood back!" Styx answered in a raspy tone.

It took a minute or so, but after waiting patiently, the air was torn asunder by a sudden shockwave of magical energy. Just like that, the mystical portal of bewitching blue, ravishing red, glorious green and every other color conceivable appeared in front of Meadow. Gazing into the mysterious portal of magic was like gazing into the depths of the galaxy. At which point Clyde marched into its mystical void with Meadow in tow and they finally returned home.

Chalice of Renewal
Chapter 3
Spring Cleaning

Another howling blizzard battered itself against the snow-covered cottage, it seemed to work wonders in aiding Meadow with sleeping though. She couldn't remember the last time her realm of sleep was devoid of nightmares. It was either the sounds of the blustering snowstorm that helped her sleep or she was exhausted from chasing that satyr, either way she awoke with a well-rested stretch. Meadow rinsed her face with some fresh water in the bowl on her nightstand, brushed her hair and headed to the kitchen. "Good timing my sleepy servant, I have just finished preparing our morning tea!" declared Clyde as he watched Meadow shuffle into the room. Tea, the thought of drinking some right now sounded as delightful as drinking a vial of magical immortality elixir. "Thank you, Clyde, I would love some" replied Meadow as she slumped into one of the kitchen chairs.

After pouring some fresh boiled water into two teacups, Clyde joined her at the table and placed one of the cups of hot steaming liquid in front of Meadow. "So how did you sleep?" asked Clyde after taking a seat opposite her. "Surprisingly well, for once the cruel face of Elijah did not haunt my dreams" answered Meadow, taking a gentle blow upon her mug of swirling emerald colored tea. The aroma flowing from the tea was intoxicating and seemed to instill a sense of vigor, "Smells wonderful!" remarked Meadow.

Like an alluring maiden enveloped in a mysterious, musky scent, the tea lured Clyde deeper in with its sweet, dancing odor. "Today's tea is honeybrook herb and powdered petals from a demonbane lily, mixed with ripe plomberries, a perfect tea to enhance energy, immune system and purifying the body!" Clyde proclaimed. While waiting for her tea to cool, Meadow took a delicate sip. "So, what's on our agenda today? Are you going to start teaching me about alchemy?" she asked. "Rein in your wild galamare my dear disciple, did you already forget that I received a second letter requesting aid?" answered Clyde.

Blankly, Meadow tilted her head and shook the dust from her mind, "Oh yeah! I remember now, Hector gave you two letters, not one!" she declared. After taking a bountiful quaff of his tea, Clyde gave a refreshing gasp and nodded. "Correct little Meadow, although this next request has even more mystery surrounding it" he answered. His comment was as welcome as a tribe of goblins at a birthday party. "Ugh! Can't we take a day off or something? I'm still drained from dealing with that satyr" Meadow groaned. Unfortunately, her reluctance to commit in the face of adversity triggered Clyde's erratic behavior and he slammed both palms upon the table. "Never woman! We cannot rest so long as the helpless cries of the innocent continue to echo our way, for our duty is to dive headlong into the abyss and rescue them from their perilous plight!" Clyde proclaimed. Strangely, Clyde's passionate dedication to duty and aiding others only seemed to drain Meadow further. "Fine, where are we going?" she grumbled, powerlessly flopping her forehead upon the kitchen table. "This time we shall be visiting a town called Soulspring, I've been there before, but this is the first time they have requested my aid" answered Clyde.

Slowly, Meadow lifted her head from the table and enjoyed a delicious swig of her refreshing tea, "So, what is it they need help with?" she asked. "Some kind of poisonous green mist has enveloped the town and caused almost everyone to go mad, survivors managed to evacuate the town and thus have requested my aid" answered Clyde. Meadow already felt a sudden lurch of dread sway in her stomach. "A poisonous mist? What caused it? Better question, what the heck are we gonna do against it!?" she answered in a raised voice.

Calmly, Clyde leant back against his chair and took a thoughtful gulp from his silver teacup as he pondered the possibilities. His other arm remained outstretched across the table, drumming his fingers upon its surface. "What's fascinating about Soulspring is the water that runs through the town; it all comes from a mystical spring and grants health to those that imbibe it" Clyde remarked. Gears of logic continued to rotate inside Clyde's mind as he contemplated the potential cause of this new plight. "Apparently, the mystical spring from where all the healthy water stems, is watched constantly by a magical fairy, though I've never seen it myself" he added.

He and Meadow proceeded to sit in silence for several seconds longer, peacefully their drinking tea and pondering the implications. "So, you think this mystical spring is somehow connected to the poisonous green mist that's appeared?" asked Meadow as she consumed the last drops of her delightful tea. "Indeed, I do, but we won't know for certain until we see for ourselves, let us prepare my loyal little lackey!" replied Clyde after gulping what lovely liquid remained in his teacup. After such a splendid spot of tea, Clyde was thoroughly stimulated to save Soulspring from their perilous poison problem. Briskly marching out of the kitchen with renewed conviction.

Into the portal room did Clyde stride next, with Meadow trailing behind, "Styx, create a portal! Get us close to the town of Soulspring!" Clyde passionately declared. "Yes master, right away! Remember not to lose your chatterstone!" answered his loyal pet imp, before beginning the ritual of channeling his mysterious magic. Meadow pursued Clyde when he proceeded to enter his alchemy lab, "So what potions are you taking this time?" she asked. "I always take a mixture, we don't know what to expect, so it's best to try and prepare for any scenario my apprentice!" answered Clyde. Diligently, He loaded his potion harness up with as many potions as it could fit, but surprised Meadow when he handed her a harness of her own. "This one's yours, it's my old one from when I was still an apprentice, but it should fit you nicely!" he remarked.

Awe overcame Meadow for a couple of brief seconds as she gazed at the harness, rendering her unsure on how to react. "For me, really? My very own potion harness! Does this make me an alchemist then?" she gasped. Her reaction caused a nostalgic flame to flicker within Clyde's heart. "I guess so, but an alchemist in training none the less, now load up your harness with the same potions as me and I shall quickly explain what they all do" he replied. Once Meadow's harness was properly fitted, Clyde was kind enough to point out which potions she should take with her.

All of them were the same ones as his, but his explanation of what each of them did was so quick that Meadow barely had time to digest it. "Not that I'm complaining but, why did you decide to let me carry my own potions now? Was it simply the time?" asked Meadow. Clyde finished preparing the rest of his potions and made sure his harness was firmly attached, ensuring his vials didn't jingle around too much. "You will need your own my apprentice for I shall not lie, this could be a dangerous undertaking" he answered. A trembling shockwave suddenly rippled through the air, shattered the moment and shock the ground beneath their feet for a short second before subsiding. "Ah, Styx has no doubt completed the portal, let us be off!" declared Clyde.

In the portal room the swirling, humming doorway of strange sorcery awaited them, as did Styx with his little pitchfork proudly slung over his shoulder. "Portal complete master, you should arrive on the borders of Soulspring!" he hissed. "Excellent work Styx, tis best we do not appear too close, if this letter is to be believed that a poisonous mist has enveloped the town" replied Clyde. As he approached the mystical portal of magic, Meadow bravely joined his side, her fear of the stepping through the vibrant whirling vortex was not as intense as the first time. "Well then, off we go!" she cheerfully announced before leaping into its swirling depths. "She's adapting quickly!" remarked Clyde, an impressed grin on his face as he watched her dive in and he proceeded to stroll in after her.

Into the vibrant sea of cosmic colors, they plunged, through the portal's profound deepness. Until the resplendent array of hues faded, and they emerged into the dazzling warmth of sunlight. The glare hit their eyes as fiercely as a face full of burning torchlight at night. Still, it was nice to feel solid ground beneath their feet after floating through the portal. "Alright, now let's see where we are and where we need to be" uttered Clyde as he rubbed the light from his eyes. "Don't worry, I don't think it will be hard to miss" answered Meadow.

She looked to the horizon on her left, making Clyde turn his head and become overwhelmed with shock at what he saw. Soulspring was nowhere to be seen, it had indeed been utterly blanketed in a hazy, emerald mist that had devoured most of the entire island Soulspring rested upon. Clyde uttered a baffled gasp as he staggered a little closer, "Not just the island, but the entire lake too!" he cried. Soulspring was a town built upon an island in the middle of a lake, a lake with the most beautiful shimmering surface one could lay eyes upon, a lake that glistened like a valley of sapphires. Now however, its appearance was like that of a murky swamp, its crystal-clear waters replaced by a disgusting muddy green with plumes of foggy mist constantly rising from it. It was far worse than Clyde imagined, luckily, he spotted a small makeshift camp of survivors near the lake. "Come on, let's hope the people down there can give us more answers" said Clyde as he proceeded to meander towards the beach. "That poisonous mist has left everyone here homeless, we have to help them!" cried Meadow when her and Clyde looked upon the crowd of frustrated survivors.

All the survivors who were wise or lucky enough to flee, were now powerlessly watching their home be devoured by the miasma. Clyde halted his steps upon reaching the beach and approaching the shores of the icky green lake. "Only a handful of people are here, it would seem very few managed to evacuate before the mist spread" he remarked. "Clyde, I thought that was you! Thank goodness you're finally here!" a voice abruptly called from behind.

Upon turning around to meet the voice, Clyde was greeted by the sight of a young, cheerful fenix girl who threw herself at him and gave him a big hug. "Nera, Good to see you! You've grown up!" replied Clyde. Meadow watched the two of them tightly hug before exchanging delighted smiles. "You're a fenix? It's rare to see your kind beyond Scorchwind and especially living among humans" she remarked.

Fenix were a race of humanoid fox people, renowned for their agility and cunning, their shrewd wits and silver tongues also made them excellent traders and diplomats. Not to mention their swift reflexes and sharp claws made them proficient thieves and assassins. Their profound aptitude for learning coupled with their wisdom resulted in many of them becoming skilled wizards too. Meadow had heard of their race before; they were the newest race to join the civilized meeting table of Resplendia. Truthfully, Meadow had never seen a fenix before since they hailed from the far southern reaches of Resplendia. Somewhere in the vast, arid sea of sand in their home city of Scorchwind.

Nera held her furry hand out to Meadow for her to shake, "I believe this is the proper greeting for humans, a pleasure to meet you!" she said in a friendly demeanor. Meadow mirrored her amicable greeting and shook her hand. All the while being captivated by the fiery amber fur that covered her entire body. "Thank you, nice to meet you! I'm Meadow, Clyde's apprentice" she replied. Meadow heard that the fur of fenix came in a variety of elegant colors from snowy white, to rustic cinnamon, mysterious ebony and majestic honey.

With the greetings out of the way, Clyde returned to the matter at hand, "What happened here Nera? Tell me everything you know" he said. Melancholy swooped over Nera as she recollected what happened. "It was madness, the crystal-clear water that flowed from the fairy's spring suddenly turned green a few days ago" she answered. "When it did, a strange kind of poisonous mist started rising from it and covered the whole town!" Nera added with a slight hysteric cry. In order to control her emotions, Nera wrapped her long furry tail around her body and began gently stroking it. "Those that inhaled the mist, or the drank water went crazy and became violent, I was one of the few that managed to escape in time" she added solemnly. Her tale evoked nothing but swirling clouds of confusion with Clyde, causing him to rub his chin as he contemplated the catastrophe. "And the water that comes from the spring runs through the entire town, leading right into the surrounding lake, which is what poisoned that too" he remarked.

Nera abruptly took hold of Clyde's hands and clutched them gently with her paws, her gleaming golden eyes gazing hopefully at Clyde. "I'm so glad you got my letter Clyde, many of the survivors here have loved ones on the island, no one has been able to stop worrying!" she uttered. Clyde could clearly perceive the plight tormenting the people, he averted his gaze to the misty green lake and the towering haze of poisonous fog covering the island. "I promise I shall do everything in my power to banish this noxious miasma and bring the mystical waters of cerulean blue back to Soulspring!" Clyde decreed with fierce determination.

Despite uttering his promise, Clyde was uncertain as how to begin, evident by the silent tremble of doubt in his face. "I'm assuming you have a plan then?" asked Meadow as she looked on at the fog covered island. "I need to know what caused the water to become a river of poison, I need to get a sample and analyze it back at my lab, tis the only way to defend against it!" answered Clyde. With an air of caution in his steps, Clyde crossed the sandy surface of the beach, approached the sickly green lake and scooped a sample of the noxious liquid into an empty vial he pulled from his trusty harness. "Styx, I need a portal back at once" Clyde uttered into the chatterstone embedded within the golden ring upon his finger.

After patiently waiting a couple of minutes, a ripping shockwave shattered the air and a new magical portal suddenly burst into existence. "Portal created master!" echoed Styx's voice from the precious chatterstone. Meadow approached the swirling, vibrant void and was about to step in, until she felt Clyde's hand upon her shoulder. "No Meadow, you stay here, I can't have any distractions, I need complete focus" he ordered. Although she was slightly dismayed, Meadow reluctantly agreed with his reasoning for there was little she could do to help, "Okay, I understand" she answered. Clyde needed to be alone and fully analyze the water without thinking about anything else. "Thank you, hopefully I won't be long" he replied, before vanishing into the portal's endless depths.

Once the portal had disappeared and left no trace of its presence, the only sound remaining was the swishing waves of the vile green lake gently lapping against the beach. "He'll be back soon; Clyde is a genius! There's no one who knows more about alchemy than him, you're really lucky to be his apprentice" said Nera as she sat upon the soft sand. Night soon fell upon the lonely beach and Clyde still hadn't returned from his lab, "What's taking him so long?" whispered Meadow. "Relax, I have full faith in him, come sit by the fire and get warm" answered Nera as she poked the makeshift campfire she had constructed with an old wooden branch. The cozy allure of the glowing campfire lured Meadow in and she took a seat next to Nera and watched the dancing flames hypnotically. "So, how did you come to know Clyde?" she asked. "That's quite a long story, the short version is I left Scorchwind and the other fenix, I wanted to travel and see the world and it was during my travels I met Clyde who also had a journey of his own" replied Nera.

Wearily, she rested herself backwards upon her furry elbows and turned her gaze towards the starry night sky above, "It seems like so long ago now" she uttered. "I was almost dead when Clyde found me, I was suffering from a serious infection from a wound during my journey" Nera recited. Hypnotically, she watched a shooting star whizz past in the distance. "Using his alchemy Clyde was able to temporarily treat the wound just long enough to carry me here, to Soulspring" Nera concluded.

Her foxlike claws scratched through the sand, etching casual swirls into its surface. "It was Clyde who told me of the healing waters within Soulspring and their ability to cleanse the body of illness and disease" added Nera. "Clyde carried me all the way here on his back and the healing waters completely cured my infection, the people of Soulspring were also kind enough to allow me to live among them" she uttered. Nera's thoughtful scribbles in the sand gradually grinded to a halt and she chuckled poignantly, "If not for Clyde I would've died" she uttered. Her powerful tale resonated within Meadow's soul and further increased the respect she felt for Clyde. "Quite a fortuitous meeting you had, have you not returned to Scorchwind since?" she asked.

A dismayed sigh blew from Nera's lips as she shook her head reluctantly, "No, the fenix keep themselves very isolated" she replied. "The desert is harsh and unforgiving, so very few leave Scorchwind, as for me, I feel like my place is here and Soulspring has become precious to me" Nera added. That's when it dawned upon Meadow as to why Nera was so desperate for aid and why she wrote the letter to Clyde. "So, it makes sense why you want to save Soulspring so much, and like you said I'm sure we can rely on Clyde" replied Meadow. "We can, I know we can, he's done more than I can imagine for me, I just wish he could find a cure too" replied Nera.

Her last sentence ensnared Meadow's curiosity and she couldn't repel the temptation to inquire further, "A cure? What is Clyde searching a cure for? Is he sick?" she asked. Nera suddenly went meek and her eyes widened with regret, like she had just spilled the secrets to immortality. "It's why Clyde journeyed here all those years ago, he was searching for a cure, but even the healing waters of Soulspring couldn't help him and so he continues to search to this day" answered Nera. Her words were puzzling, relinquished no answers and only created more questions instead. "However, I cannot say more, if Clyde hasn't told you what he is searching for, then I can't either, all I shall say is he has his own inner demons" Nera uttered before falling silent.

Meanwhile, far across the land, in the snowy tundra of the Frostveil Mountains, Clyde was hard at work in his alchemy lab. "Confound it! I'm so close to creating a cure to this blasted poison!" he growled. After slamming his fist upon his workbench and rubbing the fatigue from his eyes, he swiftly resumed his work. "Any progress master?" asked Styx as he fluttered in while carrying a small silver tea tray. A steaming cup of tea lay upon the tray which Clyde eagerly took a sip from after Styx set the tray down nearby. "Almost, this poison is magical in nature, no doubt created by the fairy of the spring" replied Clyde. "Only the fairy who creates the healing water in Soulspring has the power to change it to something as vile as this, but why? Fairies are benevolent creatures by nature" he added while stroking his chin. A glimmer of concern gleamed within Styx's eyes as he watched his master diligently work. "Have you not learned anything else from this vile mixture master?" he asked.

Clyde leaned back and slouched against his chair as he continued to sip his tea, "Of course I have and vile is certainly the right word" he replied. "Anyone who consumes the water in this form or inhales the green mist it creates is driven berserk" Clyde explained. Impatience grew within Clyde, for he knew how desperately Soulspring required a cure. "Once turned berserk, their ferocity is like that of a feral animal and they will instinctively attack anyone who isn't like them" he concluded.

Styx could see the cogs turning within Clyde's mind, his focus utterly absorbed by the vial of potent poison. "The magical water of the spring is meant to bring clarity to the mind and cleanse the body, but now it's like the water does the exact opposite" Clyde remarked. It was at this point a revelation struck him, "Now it turns the mind wild and fills people with rage, but since the fairy altered the water, she must also be able to reverse the effects!" he exclaimed. Although Styx detested the idea of disrupting his master whenever he was so smitten with a new project, there was a lingering question he just had to voice. "Forgive me for asking master but, what about the girl? Why have you chosen her to be your apprentice? And is it such a wise idea considering the danger of your task?" he asked.

An irked sigh crawled from Clyde's lips as Styx's question briefly shattered his focus. "I came here hoping to escape distracting thoughts Styx, not to have them thrown at me" he replied. Humbly, Styx bowed his head, flapped his leathery wings and slowly fluttered out of the room, "Apologies master" he replied. "Truth is, I understand the loss Meadow has suffered and I know the allure of having your memories erased, but I'm hoping she will see that the past is also a place where our happiest moments lie" uttered Clyde before returning to work.

A warm tingle caressed Meadow's skin as she slept and caused her to be roused awake. The prancing flames of the campfire had long since perished and naught was left but a pile of smoldering ash. The pleasant tingle of warmth she felt came from the distant sunrise as its face had begun to peek from behind the towering mountains in the far horizon. "Its morning!" uttered Meadow in a surprised tone. Naturally a frustrated grimace fell upon Meadow's face when she tiredly crawled out of her bedroll and approached the edge of the beach to have a refreshing morning wash. Only to remember the water was magically poisoned, "I can't believe the morning light has already arrived!" she declared. "How much longer do we have to wait? I could've built my own ship and solved the problem myself by now!" Meadow grumbled with a parched throat.

Nera, who had been sleeping in her own bedroll nearby, awoke at the sound of Meadow's voice and passed her a leather-bound flask of water. "Place your trust in Clyde, I know he will be working as hard as he can" she replied. Just as Meadow was quenching the arid desert in her throat with the refreshing flask of water. A rippling shockwave of magical energy ruptured the peaceful morning air and a familiar mystical portal appeared nearby. From out of the portals abyssal depths strode Clyde, looking haggard and with large black bags under his eyes, "Greetings, I'm sorry it took so long!" he proclaimed. Meadow, Nera and what few survivors there were from the town of Soulspring all gazed upon Clyde expectantly, glints of hope twinkling in their eyes. "Clyde! Can you banish this miasma? Have you found a cure?" asked Nera. "Not so fast my furry friend, I'm afraid I have some good news and some bad news, and cleansing Soulspring of its poison problem will be no small feat!" Clyde replied.

After releasing a much-needed yawn, Clyde slowly approached the sandy beach, "You look exhausted, were you working all night?" asked Meadow. "Indeed I was, and I managed to create a cure, but there's only enough for one person" Clyde answered with evident weariness. An aura of dismay enveloped Nera and the other survivors, "Only one person can be cured?" Nera uttered, her voice frail and worried. "Worry not, for tis not all dire, there is only one person we need to cure; we must use this precious cure upon the fairy of the spring!" Clyde declared.

A wind of silence blew over everyone as they gawked at Clyde, completely unsure if he was being honest of having a jest, "Are you serious?" Meadow slowly uttered. "Clyde, even if we could safely approach the island, everyone in the town has gone mad, including the huge troll that guards the entrance to the fairy's cave!" proclaimed Nera. Despite hearing all the risks, Clyde drew two vials of liquid from his harness, quickly spun round to face Nera and dramatically held them up high. "Fear not, for I have also concocted these vaccines for us!" he announced. "These vaccines will protect anyone from the poisonous mist who hasn't already been affected, we will be immune to its effects, for a few hours" added Clyde as he held the two vials out.

Nera peered closely at the two shimmering vials of vaccine and the one and only true cure to the poison, her glassy reflection gazing back. "Why do we need to cure the fairy? Is she the source of all this?" she asked. "Yes, the fairy of the spring is the one who corrupted the water that flows through Soulspring, she is the only one who can cleanse the magical water" answered Clyde. Upon hearing the details of his crazy plan, it all became clear and sounded more like suicide with every passing second. "Okay, so all we have to do is reach an island veiled in poisonous mist, fight our way through a town of berserk villagers, overcome a raging troll guardian and cure a crazy magical fairy, all in the space of a few hours!?" cried Meadow. Although her reaction was rather hysterical, Clyde couldn't fault how accurate it was, "Yeah, that's about the size of it" he answered honestly.

A reliable wooden boat that the survivors used to escape the island lay upon the beach nearby. "That vessel there will be sufficient, come Meadow, there is not a moment to lose!" Clyde gallantly declared. Meadow couldn't yet decide if Clyde's tenacious passion was either inspiring or exhausting, but as his apprentice she followed him all the same. "And here I thought we were just going to sit around making potions all day!" she groaned. Nera marched behind them with a determined stomp in her steps, "Wait, I want to come with you!" she barked. "And I want a magical floating castle made of solid gold" Clyde swiftly fired back as he diligently prepared the boat to sail.

His ridiculing reply caused a vexed frown to flare within Nera's shiny amber eyes. "I'm serious Clyde! Soulspring is my home and I don't want the whole speech about its too dangerous for me, blah, blah, blah!" she answered firmly. "Last time I checked Clyde it's been several years since you've visited Soulspring, you'll need a guide to the fairy's spring, especially if you're on a time limit!" Nera fiercely added. Her logic gave Clyde a moment of thoughtful pause, evident by the way he suddenly spun his head towards her. That's, actually a very good point! Curse your astute logic and get in!" Clyde growled.

Nera happily hopped into the boat with a grin and with a hearty heave of the oar Clyde cast them away from shore, "Okay, drink up!" he ordered. One of the tough glass vials containing the vaccine against the perilous mist was instantly thrust into Meadow's face. "Okay, but I really hope your right about this" answered Meadow as she nabbed the vial out of Clyde's hand. Meanwhile, Clyde popped the cork top off the second vial he was holding for himself. "Meadow share half of yours with Nera" he uttered, before promptly gulping the potion down his throat. "Nera is roughly the same age, weight and height as you and children don't require as high a dosage to achieve the desired effects, there should be enough for both of you" he added, wiping his lips upon his sleeve.

After taking an ample swig, Meadow passed the remaining vial of vaccine to Nera, "Fine, but you really don't want to refer to me as a child again!" Meadow grumpily fired back. At first Meadow couldn't taste any flavor to the vial of vaccine. Until the taste abruptly kicked in and her tongue was assaulted with an onslaught of bitterness, "Eugh! By the gods that tastes disgusting!" she cried. Nera had the same reaction upon quaffing the remaining vial of liquid and the bitterness hit her like an icy gale, "I heartily agree!" she declared while sticking out her tongue.

Clyde however, seemed utterly impervious to the vaccine's repulsive aftertaste. "Endure it young ones, I did not have the luxury of making it palatable, but for the next several hours we should be completely immune to the effects of the mist!" he proclaimed. Meadow hypnotically gazed at her reflection cast upon the vile green lake as the sturdy wooden boat gently crossed its poisoned waters, "I wonder why the fairy would do such a thing" she uttered. "That's the mystery we need to solve, after all, the fairy's magic is what created the healing waters of Soulspring" answered Clyde.

Closer and closer they sailed towards the misty miasma, but impatience began swirl inside Meadow, her attention fixating upon Nera's long bushy tail. Gently, she ran her fingers along Nera's fiery fur, unable to repel the tantalizing curiosity of how it felt. Nera raised one of her paws and playfully slapped Meadow upon the hand, "Hey, hands off the tail!" she sternly cried. "Sorry, it's just I've never met a fenix before, I've read a little about your race in books, but I'm still fascinated, you're like a fox, yet walk and talk like a human" Meadow uttered. Her comment reaped an amused chuckle from Nera who briefly flashed her fangs with her wide grin. "It's okay, I was fascinated when I met humans for the first time, better adapt quickly though, there are far stranger creatures than me in this world" she replied.

Although most of the island of Soulspring was shrouded in mist, a small lonely dock gradually came into view. "Alright, we can tie the boat up here" Clyde cautiously whispered as he slowly rowed alongside the dock. All three of them quickly disembarked their vessel and Clyde securely tied it to one of the sturdy wooden mooring posts. "You're our guide Nera, lead the way, but remain vigilant" uttered Clyde. "Okay, follow me" ordered Nera as she began traversing the hazy green mist, which was thankfully not as thick as it appeared when seen from afar. "Stay alert now, any of the villagers we encounter will be infected and hostile towards us" Clyde whispered as he carefully crept behind.

To their good fortune the dock and the twisting rocky path that lead towards Soulspring were devoid of any villagers. Hence, it wasn't long before they reached the grand white marble archway to the town. It acted as the entrance into Soulspring; its elaborate iron lattice gates left flung open and beyond the gates with no guards, Nera could discern the familiar majestic courtyard further ahead. Clyde, Meadow and Nera all took cover and squatted behind the lofty marble pillars of the archway and peered upon the scene ahead. "Looks pretty quiet, I can't see anyone just yet" whispered Meadow. "True, but this accursed mist certainly is making it a little harder to see" Nera whispered as her eyes searched every inch of the courtyard for any traces of activity. For several seconds they waited, expecting something to happen or someone to appear, trepidation was their leash and it kept them tethered. Finally, Clyde advanced forward and roused them to action. "Okay, we cannot wait forever, it looks empty but stay vigilant and remain quiet" he whispered as he warily inched his way further into the misty town.

Like a trio of rats, all three of them scurried into the shadows, hugging the walls. Seeking concealment behind the safety of whatever cover was large enough to obscure them from view. Soulspring seemed silent and peaceful at first glance, but signs of violence and madness could be found all over. Shattered windows, broken pots, smashed crates, barricaded doors and piles of smoking ashes from long dead fires. Despite the surrounding anarchy, Meadow could perceive the beauty within the town even with the hazy mist covering most of it.

A towering, magnificent marble fountain sculpted in the image of a graceful fairy stood in the center of the majestic courtyard Meadow was currently creeping across. It was clear the people of Soulspring adored the benevolent fairy that bestowed the bountiful healing water the town was renowned for. Which made the fairy's apparent betrayal even more baffling. An eerie shudder traversed Meadow's spine as she looked upon the marble fountain of the fairy, which constantly spewed a stream of sickly green water from its mouth.

There was no doubt the water flowing from her mouth was supposed to be a crystal-clear blue color instead. "So, the water from the mystical spring runs through the entire town?" asked Meadow in a careful whisper. A sudden noise from somewhere ahead caused Meadow and the others to hastily scamper into a nearby alcove and patiently wait for things to settle, albeit with a firm feeling of tension. After waiting several precious moments, all three of them relaxed upon meeting with nothing but more silence. "Yes, the magical healing water runs through the entire town with the help of aqueducts built into the island" answered Nera. "That marble fountain is just one of many, built across different parts of the town; the water flows directly into the lake surrounding the island" Nera added as she took lead again.

Meadow succumbed to a fleeting state of fascination upon hearing Nera's explanation. So much so that she neglected to see the nearby clay vase next to her that she unfortunately knocked over while sneaking behind. Time slowed down in that moment and dread surged through Meadow as she had enough time to watch it topple, but not enough time to try and stop it. A frightful shatter echoed across the courtyard as the vase collided with the ground and smashed into dozens of pieces. Sadly, this provoked the worst outcome and the noise of the shattered vase captured the attention of a nearby horde of berserk, infected villagers.

Within the next heartbeat, a swarm of volatile villagers burst through the front doors of the many buildings surrounding the courtyard like a pack of savage cerberii. "Hide, now!" ordered Clyde in a hushed gasp. Beads of tense sweat trickled along Meadow's forehead as she ducked into a nearby alcove built into the side of some stone steps, which were also partially blocked by a stack of wooden crates.

Clyde and Nera darted to the left and took shelter in a nearby doorway opposite Meadow that managed to barely fit them both with a bit of a squeeze. They remained still as statues and as silent as a crypt in the dead of night. However, their hiding spots were far from effective and Clyde knew it would only be a matter of time before they were caught. It was far too risky to remain where they were; they had to make a move and quick. "Invisibility potion!" Clyde whispered to Meadow as he pulled one of his small glass vials from his harness. Meadow nodded, carefully watched which potion Clyde held in his hand to make sure she consumed the right one and firmly tugged the oak cork off the top. "Down the hatch" she whispered as she gulped the vial of glittery grey liquid down her throat.

Before taking a sip himself, Clyde passed a second vial of the invisibility potion to Nera, who gladly imbibed it without question. Hastily, Clyde drew another vial of invisibility potion from his lifesaving harness, thanking his own prudence for bringing two batches instead of one. However, their anxiety began to intensify when they started to hear the frenzied stomps of the villagers draw closer and closer. "Their coming this way!" whispered Meadow in a panicked hush.

Ominous snarls accompanied the berserk villagers as they approached her hiding place. Their feet finally came into view as they patrolled the courtyard and Meadow knew she would been spotted any second now. Fright filled her soul, she slammed her eyes shut and waited to be caught, while Clyde and Nera continued to nervously hug the wall. A few seconds passed and nothing happened, causing Meadow to slowly creep her eyes open, only to see one of the savage drooling villagers glaring right at her.

Meadow had to clamp her hands over her mouth to stifle a horrified scream, but she soon realized the villager was glaring through her, not at her. Slowly, she moved her hands away from her mouth only to see that they weren't visible anymore. Meadow released a silent gasp of relief; the invisibility potion had worked and just in time. Two maybe three minutes was all the time they had though, and the nearby group of villagers blocked their path. Clyde had the clever idea of picking up a nearby rock while they weren't looking in his direction and hurled it through the air. It took a couple of seconds, but Clyde soon heard the impact as it collided against something far off, causing the mob of mad villagers to mindlessly chase it. "Meadow, where are you?" whispered Clyde once the horde had left their earshot and were out of harm's way.

A nearby piece of red cloth that lay upon a crate opposite Clyde began to eerily float into the air on its own, "I'm here!" whispered Meadow as she waved the red cloth around. "Okay, there are more villagers ahead, let's move quickly and quietly, I know you can't see me but head towards the large sandy building at the end of the courtyard" whispered Clyde. Meadow poked her head out and peered towards the building he mentioned and spotted it right away, "Okay, it looks pretty far but okay!" she answered in a trembled tone.

Like a group of silent ghosts Clyde, Meadow and Nera all began creeping across the untidy courtyard. Taking special care not to bump into anything or anyone, a task that was admittedly harder than it looked. Many of the mad villagers were still skulking around and avoiding them became quite the challenge. Meadow would have to stop and abruptly change direction whenever one of them decided to suddenly move into her path. This happened a few times and every time it did Meadow would be engulfed in a sudden surge of panic and frustration.

Having to remain completely still, steady her breathing and suppress any noise made it even more difficult. It felt so tense to be so close to the villagers, yet unable to be seen. Fright leapt into Meadow's heart again when she inched forward some more, only to be confronted by the fierce face of another feral villager that had bumbled into her path. What was perhaps most disturbing was how this malevolent mist had affected the villagers. It had rendered them drooling, snarling husks of their former selves, their eyes bulging with hatred and madness. Now more animal than man, their indiscernible menacing growls were unnerving to hear, and the sight of their hands tightly gripped around steel axes, daggers and swords unsettling to behold.

With upmost caution Meadow meandered around the hostile villager in her path, avoiding him like he was the grim reaper. She continued to quickly scurry across the courtyard, aware of the time limit of the potion, without a doubt not much time remained. It had certainly taken two minutes to traverse the courtyard, thankfully Meadow had almost reached the rendezvous point. Urgency began to build within Meadow, but as she approached the wooden front door of the sandy stone building, it suddenly swung open by itself, like a ghost had just walked through, "Clyde!" Meadow whispered.

Hastily, Meadow scampered for the door of the building, eager to duck out of sight, but her scamper turned into a frantic bolt when she noticed her invisibility wearing off. Gradually, Meadow came back into view for all to see and while she was still in the open, causing a swift gale of panic to billow over her. Fortunately, she was able to recklessly scurry into the open doorway while only risking a couple short seconds of exposure. At which point she hastily shut the door behind her and breathed a deep sigh of relief.

Invisibility had worn out its welcome and unfortunately Clyde and Meadow had none left to drink, all they could do was hope they didn't need it again. "Is this a blacksmith?" asked Meadow as she surveyed her surroundings and the expertly crafted shimmering steel swords, shields and suits of armor scattered around the room. Nera reacted to her question with a proud nod. "Indeed, it is, the only blacksmith in Soulspring, but the quality of the arms and armor made here were the finest around for miles" she replied. "We shouldn't linger here too long; reveal a new path for us to pursue my furry friend!" declared Clyde after taking a glimpse out of the nearby window to ensure they were safe.

His comment aroused an amused chuckle from Nera, who pointed one of her furry fingers towards a door nestled in the back of the store. "That door will lead us to the alleyways, they're built like a maze, but I know them well, the alleyways should be pretty quick unless we find trouble" Nera replied. By Clyde's estimation, roughly two hours remained before the vaccine they imbibed wore off and the poisonous mist turned them into drooling mindless husks of madness. "Good enough, we still have sufficient time" Clyde responded.

Upon departing the temporary protection of the abandoned blacksmith, Clyde drew another vial of potion from his harness and passed it to Nera. "You take lead again Nera, this should help, it's a life detection potion" explained Clyde. As Clyde dangled the vial of viscous violet liquid in front of Nera, she gazed at it curiously, "What does it do?" she asked. "For a brief time, you shall be granted the power to perceive the life essence of everyone wherever you look, regardless of where they are hidden!" Clyde remarked with a haughty tone.

Nera could certainly see how essential such a skill could be, so she swiftly swiped the vial of strange liquid and swallowed it down. "Nice! It tastes quite tingly, but it should come in handy" she answered. To ensure it worked, Clyde promptly hid behind a nearby crate, "Alright, what do you see Nera? Can you see me?" he asked. "Incredible, I can see your life essence, it glows so brightly!" Answered Nera in an amazed gasp. Clyde then left his little hiding place, smug at Nera's fascination. "Lead on Nera, navigating these twisting alleyways should be a breeze with your new sight" replied Clyde.

Being able to perceive the life energy of others around her regardless of where they were hidden proved to be quite the boon. Nera lead Clyde and Meadow through the winding misty alleyways, halting whenever she spotted danger. "Two more villagers around the corner but they have their backs to us, if we move quickly, we should be alright" whispered Nera as she cautiously crept further. With silence and stealth, the three of them swiftly swooped past the oblivious infected villagers and into the secluded safety of the alleyway opposite. Until Nera's new vision caught the sight of a few more luminous life signs gradually approaching from around the next corner in front of them. "Three more coming from around the corner!" she whispered with urgency.

Without delay, Clyde, Meadow and Nera hastily scattered out of sight and patiently waited for the danger to pass. Soon, three drooling, growling villagers came menacingly stomping around the corner just like Nera foretold. Thankfully, they were none the wiser and trudged right by. A fragile sigh of relief escaped Nera as she left the confines of the doorway she had been silently hiding in, "Okay, shall we continue?" she asked.

Her relief was brief, as her head slammed right into the chest of a fourth villager that abruptly stumbled around the corner, his fierce glaring eyes piercing right through her. A stifled scream suddenly erupted within Nera's throat, combined with a tremendous surge of terror. Luckily, Clyde bolted from his refuge behind a thick oak barrel and smashed the corrupted villager over the head with a nearby clay pot he nabbed. It shattered into several fragments upon impact and made a distinct smashing sound, alerting the other villagers nearby, "I don't understand, why couldn't I see his energy!?" cried Nera. "The potion must've worn off just at that moment!" declared Clyde as he gripped Nera by the wrist and pulled her along as he began to run, prompting Meadow to do the same.

Nera was still in a state of surprised shock; thus, Clyde had to take lead and urgently chose the left path when he was suddenly confronted with an intersection. Behind him, he could hear bestial snarls and frenzied footsteps upon the cobbled alleyways. An enraged swarm of afflicted villagers mercilessly pursued them and there was little time to ponder which path was the correct one. Alas, Clyde soon discovered he chose poorly when he, Meadow and Nera all turned the corner to meet with nothing more than a dead end.

Dismay descend upon them like a flock of ominous crows and Meadow approached the solid stone wall that barricaded their path and powerlessly slammed her fist against It. "Great, we're trapped!" she uttered with fluster. "I have to say, being hunted down by a mob of crazed infected villagers was not how I imagined I would go out in life!" Cried Nera with increasing hysteria. Meanwhile, Clyde maintained his composure and swiftly drew one of the potion vials from his harness. "Now, now, let's not lose our heads just yet" he replied in a calm demeanor.

Nera spotted the crowd of snarling villagers come stomping around the corner, axes and daggers tightly clutched in their hands. "We won't have to lose our heads, I think they're gonna do it for us!" she cried. Urgently, Clyde held up the potion so Meadow could see it clearly. "Meadow, Ethereal potion, now!" he barked, before hastily yanking the cork off and gulping it down like it was pumpkin juice. Meadow nodded her head and reached for the potion that had a mysterious, azure hue and proceeded to pop the cork off the top. She proceeded to promptly guzzle down the delicate, slithery liquid before passing half of it to Nera, "Down the hatch, and quickly!" she exclaimed.

There was no time for Nera to ask what this potion did, as the frenzied villagers encroached closer and closer with every sinister footstep. Instead she threw her curiosity to the wind and quaffed the vial of mysterious liquid. Suddenly, Meadow's heart leapt into her throat as one of the savage villagers raised his arm and violently hurled the axe he was holding through the air, directly at Meadow's head.

The deadly gleaming blade of the axe struck Meadow right between the eyes but proceeded to phase right through her and strike the stone wall behind. To her great fortune the ethereal potion kicked in at the last second. Just like that time when they hunted the satyr in the forest near Oakpass, Meadow had become ghostly, her flesh replaced with that of a phantom. It wasn't just her of course, Nera and Clyde had also become spectral. "Ah, excellent! The potions effect activated at just the right time, come you two, we may now move on!" Clyde announced without worry. Calmly, he then strolled towards the dead end that lay at the end of the alleyway and proceeded to effortlessly pass through the study stone wall like it wasn't even there.

Nera watched with wonder as he vanished beyond the wall. While Meadow's worrisome state quickly withered away when the horde of heinous villagers swung their weapons at her only to hit nothing but air. Their beastly snarls intensified as they surrounded Meadow and violently lashed at her, becoming increasingly frustrated with every missed attack. "Well Nera, shall we?" said Meadow with haughty delight. A brief chuckle leapt from Nera's lips as she watched Meadow smoothly glide straight through the villagers as though they were rendered nothing more than noisy air. "Right behind you!" answered Nera as she pursued Meadow towards the wall.

Both girls used their intangible ghostly bodies to shadow Clyde straight through the wall. Absconding the wicked clutches of the corrupted villagers and emerging in a rather opulent residence on the other side. "About time you decided to join me, lucky the potion didn't wear off as you came through or you would've been stuck inside the wall" said Clyde who waited patiently. Lavish curtains draped the giant glass windows of the house they had infiltrated, and ornate silverware spread across a vibrant red tablecloth covering a long, oak banquet table nearby. "I know this place; this is the mayors house!" declared Nera.

The sickly green mist that had arisen from the corrupted spring water had also invaded the mayors house, defiling the very air around them. "The cave leading to the fairy of the spring isn't too far from here" said Nera. Before quickly leaving the residence, something strange caught Clyde's eye. "Wait a moment, all the plants here are withered and dying" he pointed out. "I don't think watering the plants are on anyone's list of priorities right now" Meadow sarcastically answered, oblivious to whatever point Clyde was making.

Upon inspecting one of the wilted plants more meticulously, a dreaded thought occurred to Clyde, causing him to shudder. "Now that I think about it, we've not seen any healthy plants or flowers since we entered Soulspring" he said. "It hasn't been that long since the mist spread, these plants shouldn't had died at this rate, there must be only one explanation" Clyde added with unease in his voice. Meadow and Nera exchanged worried glances and waited for him to cease the suspense. "This noxious mist isn't just corrupting all life, its slowly killing it all too!" Clyde gasped. His gloomy observation sent a chilling shiver along Nera's fur and caused her eyes to widen in panic. "Oh no, the villagers! We have to hurry!" she cried. Time was not their ally, meaning haste was of the upmost importance, Clyde took lead and left the mayor's residence through front door with urgency in his stride. "Come my compatriots, we have not a second to waste!" he announced.

Upon leaving the mayors majestic manor, the three of them were suddenly confronted with the sight of a looming mountain nearby. "There it is, the mountain where our spring water comes from!" Exclaimed Nera. "The mountain is formed upon the island itself, the entrance to the fairies cave is built into the side of it, we just have to cross the bridge up ahead" she added, recklessly running onwards.

Fearing the worst, Clyde chased after Nera through the thin veil of malevolent mist, "Wait Nera, don't just hurtle into the unknown!" he called. Meadow rolled her eyes in frustration and proceeded to hurry after them, "This is not what I expected when I became an apprentice!" she groaned. Soon after, a long, white stone bridge that stretched over a babbling stream of putrid green water came into view. However, their tracks were instantly halted when they began hearing deep, menacing growling resonating from further beyond.

Tremors of heavy, booming footsteps trembled the earth and from out of the murky haze emerged a looming, hulking beast with eyes as fierce as burning rubies. Shaggy, chestnut colored fur covered the imposing beast's thick muscular body and its deep monstrous snarl rippled the air, "I think we've found the troll!" declared Meadow. Frantically, Clyde reached for a potion latched securely in his harness, "Meadow! use steel-skin potion now!" he shouted. Meadow obeyed the orders of her master and grasped hold of a vial of steel-skin potion and consumed it without hesitation.

Meanwhile, the fearsome guardian troll began storming towards Meadow, intent on crushing her like a bug. "Nera, drink!" cried Meadow as she passed what remained in her vial to Nera. Fascination swept over Meadow as she watched the flesh upon her bones change form and turn silver like shimmering steel. "What's happening!?" she cried, gazing upon her new steely fingers. Soon her wonder quickly shifted to pain, as the mighty troll swung his huge fist and punched Meadow right in the face.

Meadow was promptly sent flying backwards through the air and crashed straight into Clyde behind her. "Oof!" groaned Clyde as Meadow slammed into his chest and knocked him over, resulting in the two of them crumpled upon each other in a messy pile. "Ouch, that really hurt, you big bully!" Meadow shouted to the troll, quickly picking herself up from the hard-stone ground and rubbing her sore cheeks of steel. "Trust me, if not for my steel-skin potion you wouldn't have a face to rub right now!" replied Clyde as he gathered his bearings and pulled himself up. His skin had also becoming like shimmering steel at this point and a roar of anger burst from the troll. It was quickly silenced however, when Nera charged at the slobbering beast and used her foxlike reflexes to leap onto the trolls back and quickly scaled to the top of its head.

Rage erupted from the troll as Nera rode upon its head like she was trying to tame a wild wolf and it wasn't just Nera's skin and fur that had become solid steel now. The potion also affected Nera's sharp fox claws, changing them into miniature steel daggers, which she used to try and scar the bellowing beast's eyesight. Although Nera was victorious in partially blinding the beast in one eye with a couple of deadly swipes of her claws, the troll proved too powerful. It thrashed and flailed its hulking arms around wildly, until it managed to seize hold of Nera with its might grasp. Spit splattered Nera's face as the terrifying troll opened its jaws and roared, then used its formidable strength to slam her face first into the ground.

Meadow urgently dashed at the monster, determined to try save Nera from her dire predicament. Until the tyrannical troll tossed Nera towards Meadow like he was throwing a pillowcase. For the second time, Meadow skidded across the ground as Nera whizzed through the air, her head slamming into Meadow's face. Both girls lay face up in a confused daze for a second, while the troll took a running jump and leapt into the air, determined to crush into dust under its enormous weight. Seeing the snarling behemoth plummeting through the air towards them roused Meadow and Nera out of their confused daze. Frantically they rolled themselves out of the impact area and were felt fortunate that the steel-skin potion still protected them from harm.

Clouds of billowing dust scattered as the huge, hairy feet of the troll slammed into the earth, causing a colossal crack to appear and creating a shuddering tremor to ripple through the ground. "We need to overpower this brute, Meadow! Drink a vial of enhanced-strength potion!" shouted Clyde as he reached for one of his vials of precious potion. After popping the cork, Clyde swiftly swallowed his own vial of strength potion and felt the invigorating power it bestowed flow through his veins. Using his newfound strength and a fist made of reinforced steel, Clyde simply charged right up to the beast and leapt right into its body. Since the troll stood over ten feet tall, hitting its face was a little out of reach, yet Clyde succeeded in landing a powerful blow to its body. A blow powerful enough to cause the troll to stagger backwards and fall onto its stinky, hairy rump.

A howl of pain and fury bellowed from the troll as its hind was forcefully slammed to the ground, while Meadow had just finished drinking her strength potion. "Alright, now it's my turn!" Meadow shouted, rapidly charging the toppled monster and ploughing her fist square into its face with as much might as she could muster. Meadow rattled the troll's yellowish teeth when her empowered punch connected, causing the creature to topple backwards and fall flat onto the ground face up. "Wow, did I just do that!?" Meadow declared, her voice filled with fiery gusto, her eyes agape as she gawked upon her steel fleshed fist. Yet it was too soon to celebrate, for the enraged troll painfully arose and started to relentlessly slam its heavy fists onto the ground in a hateful tantrum.

Approaching the beast in such a berserk state would've proven dangerous and risky, therefore, Meadow and the others wisely hung back and watched what it did next. Furiously, the enraged troll grabbed a nearby bench made of solid white marble, lifted it up high and hatefully launched it at Meadow. It proved a futile concern though, as Meadow used the effects of the enhanced strength potion still coursing through her body and caught the flying marble bench as it flew at her. With her newfound strength, catching the bench felt as easy as catching an apple from a falling tree and she handled it with ease.

A delighted grin spread over Meadow as she marveled at her strength, "Hey, dung breath! Have a seat!" she shouted, throwing the marble bench right back at the beast. With tremendous speed, the solid marble bench whizzed across the air, back towards the troll, crumbling in half upon painfully smashing into the creature's dense skull. For a few moments, the troll clumsily staggered around, like it had guzzled down a dozen barrels of rum. Finally, after a deep and weary roar, the troll collapsed face first onto the ground like a freshly chopped tree. Its bulky body caused a brief quake as it hit the ground and this time it stayed down. "Looks like we finally gave it a time out!" declared Nera with a sigh of relief. "Yes, and not a moment too soon!" replied Clyde as he watched the shiny steel covering their skin slowly vanish, returning their flesh back to its delicate state.

With the troll's fiery wrath doused, the three of them were free to cross the bridge leading to the cave of Soulspring's fairy unobstructed. "Fatigue may be devouring you like a leviathan devours a ship of its sailors but alas, onwards we must charge my courageous comrades!" declared Clyde as he heartily headed for the bridge. Meadow rolled her eyes and shook her head in disbelief, "He certainly has a way with words" she sighed. Meanwhile, Nera pressed her hand against her rib as it ached from an abrupt burst of laughter, "Clyde, he hasn't changed one bit!" she chuckled. Across the white stone bridge, they travelled, navigating the eerie green mist and watching their step for fear of falling into the rushing river of revolting green water beneath. The gaping entrance to the fairy's cave emerged closer into view, an aura of dread surrounding its dim doorway. "Alright, I have no idea what to expect here since a demented fairy is not something I have ever encountered" uttered Clyde.

A feeling of foreboding flaunted within Meadow and Nera and fear filled their footsteps as they followed Clyde into the fog of gloominess. Dying, oil-wrapped torches dotted the walls of the cave indicating that they hadn't been changed in a while. Yet, it also indicated it was safe for people to wander this cave before all this madness had transpired. Strangely, the further into the cave they delved, the brighter it became, until they perceived an eerie, otherworldly green glow shimmering upon the rocky walls in a clearing up ahead.

As they approached the clearing, it became evident that the glow was coming from the mystical spring of magical water located in the center. "This is the spring, but the water isn't supposed to be green!" gasped Nera. "Just as I suspected, it was the fairy's magic that tainted the spring, but where is the fairy?" he asked. Soon, Clyde received his answer, for a chilling screech burst their ears from behind them and as they spun around, they were all suddenly confronted by the fairy.

Meadow's image of the fairy was completely awry, she imagined a cute, tiny creature no larger than a mouse, unable to do more than spray magical golden dust around. Instead, she was confronted with a tall, slender creature with shadowy, violet colored skin, armed with razor sharp nails upon each of her fingertips and large, ethereal, blood-red wings. The fairy attacked Meadow from behind with a shrieking swoop from the ceiling, knocking her down and glaring into her soul with ruthless red eyes. One of the fairy's hands was gripped tightly upon Meadow's neck and Meadow began to feel weak, her skin gradually becoming pale and her body cold as ice, "What's happening!?" cried Nera. "The fairy is using her magic to drain the life energy from her body!" yelled Clyde, swiftly running at the demented fairy and ramming into her, using all his strength to help Meadow escape.

Both Clyde and the mad fairy went tumbling across the ground, while Meadow gave a delightful gasp as she felt her lifeforce filling her soul once again. "Quickly, we have to pin her down!" shouted Nera. Seeing no better chance than now, Nera seized the opportunity and charged at the fairy, attempting to subdue her while she was floored. "Nera wait!" cried Clyde as he staggered to his feet. Except, it was too late, even while she was down the frenzied fairy proved she was not defenseless.

The fairy quickly conjured bizarre magic from her palm, spraying a mysterious purple mist into the air. Unfortunately, Nera ran headlong into the small hazy cloud, breathed it in and quickly collapsed in an awkward heap like a lifeless doll. "My.... body.... I.... can't.... move!" uttered Nera in a stiff voice. "Great, the fairy's magic has paralyzed her!" growled Clyde as he pulled the glass vial containing the cure to the corrupting fog from his harness and rolled it towards Meadow. "I'm going to grab the fairy and when I do, you need to pour that cure down her throat, do you understand my apprentice?" he asked, gazing hopefully back at Meadow. Swiftly, Meadow scooped up the vial and nodded, "Leave it to me!" she answered with firm devotion.

At the same time, Clyde reached for another potion fastened securely to his trusty harness, removed it, yanked the cork stopper from the top and hastily imbibed the entire brew. Meadow caught a brief glimpse of the potion before Clyde drank it, it was a vile black color, almost oily in hue. Now the fairy's frightful glare was fully fixated upon Clyde. However, once Clyde consumed the mysterious mixture, he reared his head back, before belching a blanket of blinding black smoke from his mouth. A piercing screech erupted from the fairy, echoing the walls of the dimly lit cave as the cloud of choking smoke briefly blinded and confused her.

Using this ephemeral window of opportunity, Clyde hastily slipped behind the bewildered fairy and seized her, "Now Meadow! Use the cure!" he shouted. Gradually, the haze of shadowy smoke that Clyde puffed from his mouth vanished and Meadow perceived him once again, furiously wrestling with the writhing fairy. Fairies may have magical abilities, but luckily for Clyde their strength wasn't much greater than an average human adult. Even so, the fairy put up quite a struggle, thrashing like a wave in a stormy sea.

Maintaining his hold upon the flailing fairy was proving more arduous with each passing second, thus Meadow had to act fast. She approached the frantic fairy with haste yet waited until she was close before popping the cork off the vial of potion she held at the ready. It wasn't difficult to entice the fairy to open her mouth since she kept shrieking relentlessly like a howling gale, the vexing part was for Clyde to keep her still. Frustration grew within Meadow, but a distant memory flashed through mind of a time she was ill and had to take medicine she didn't like, so she did the same thing her mother did. "Shut up and take your medicine!" shouted Meadow, ramming the vial into the fairy's face and forcing the precious remedy down her throat.

A little of the cure spilled, but Meadow managed to make the fairy swallow most of it. Gradually, the fairy's hysterical thrashing began to subside, her shrill screeching changing to wailing gurgles. Suddenly, the corrupted fairy started to suffer from shuddering convulsions and Clyde quickly released his grasp upon her as she collapsed to the cold floor of the cave. The gargling fairy started rolling upon the ground like a puppy in a puddle of mud, except with evident agony. "Did it work?" asked Meadow as she watched the madness unfold. After taking several steps back to keep his distance, Clyde waited patiently. "Yes, whatever it was that corrupted her is trying to oppose the cure I concocted, but knows it is losing" he answered. Heaving gasps resonated from the fairy until a disgusting torrent of repulsive ebony liquid violently spewed from her mouth. "It's over" uttered Clyde once the volley of vile vomit had ceased and what happened next was a truly majestic transformation.

Meadow gazed upon the fairy as her violet skin changed to a healthy, golden copper, her flowing hair changed from shadowy black to radiant blonde and her fierce crimson eyes changed to calming turquoise. The imposing, ethereal blood red wings upon her back also altered in hue, shifting to a captivating azure blue color. "Thank you, I owe you a great debt for cleansing that malevolent scourge from my body!" uttered the fairy with a jaded gasp, wiping her mouth clean with her arm. Wearily, the fairy staggered to her feet while Meadow and Clyde gawked upon her renewed beauty, "It was truly no trouble at all" Clyde answered in a cheery tone.

At last the numbness in Nera's bones began to fade, the fairy's paralysis hex finally wore off and she was able to move once more, "Ugh, that was unpleasant!" she declared. Seeing the fairy returned to her natural state again caused a ripple of rapture to shiver in her heart and she gleefully sprang towards her the second she was up. "It worked, your healthy again! Does this mean you can cure Soulspring too!?" she hopefully asked. "Yes, young one, I can cleanse the tainted spring here in my cave using my magic, for it was I that corrupted it to begin with" answered the fairy, caringly resting her hand upon Nera's shoulder.

Fatigue lingered in the fairy's steps as she approached the sickly green water within the large mystical spring and she feebly knelt beside it, plunging her hand straight in. Using her magic, the fairy slowly dispelled the curse she had inflicted upon the water, finally purging it of all impurities and changing it back to a beautiful, crystal clear blue. "With the water in the spring purified, it won't be long until all the water in Soulspring and the lake becomes pure again, for my magical spring is the source of it all" explained the fairy. A breeze of delight swept over Clyde and the others upon hearing these words, "Thank the stars, the veil of noxious mist should also vanish in time" added Clyde. "But I don't understand, why did you taint Soulspring's water? What caused you to become that monster we fought?" asked Meadow.

Without a doubt those were the questions everyone desired answers to most. Although it proved a struggle for the fairy to recollect what happened, she slowly began to assemble to pieces, "Follow me" she answered softly. Another chamber lay deeper within the cave, beyond the enchanting spring and the fairy led them inside, "This is my chamber where I rest" she explained. Burning candles inside shimmering gold holders lit this new chamber and lavish banners draped the cave walls. Opulent rugs of soft fur spread across the floor while plush pillows adorned a snug bed and ornate jars containing a wide variety of flowers decorated the room. "The people of Soulspring are very grateful to me and this is how they show their generosity, I guess being a magical fairy can have its perks" wearily joked the fairy.

Achingly, she sat upon her soft bed, clearly still drained by the whole ordeal. "I remember, I was trying to sleep when it happened, I remember seeing a mysterious figure sneak into my chamber" she explained. "I couldn't see the strangers face, they were clothed in a black robe and wore a black iron mask, they must've assumed I was asleep as they were very secretive about entering" the fairy added. A mixture of surprise and trepidation fluttered inside Clyde's stomach as soon as the fairy mentioned the black masked man, "What happened? What did he do?" he asked.

A brief, unpleasant tinge flashed through the fairy's mind as she reminisced the events, forcing her to woefully rub her temples. "I remember the stranger kneeling and placing a small glass bottle on the ground in front of my chamber entrance, then he left without a sound" uttered the fairy. The haze veiling the fairy's thoughts steadily vanished with each passing second. "It was a potion of some kind, I remember waking up the next morning and drinking it, I assumed it was just another generous offering" she uttered. A frightful jolt trembled along the fairy's skin, along with a shimmer of sorrow in her soulful eyes. "That's when I changed, soon after I drank the potion, I felt a darkness that was not there before, I felt hatred and madness, but struggled to remain in control!" gasped the fairy.

Questions continued to mount, and the mystery of the masked figure grew more sinister with every mentioning. "What kind of potion does that? Who could make something like that? And who is this masked stranger? Why would he do such a thing?" asked Nera. "It was no potion, but rather a poison, one meant to appear as a nourishing apple to a fair maiden, yet tainted within its core, as for the masked stranger, his or her identity and motives remain an enigma" replied Clyde.

Weariness revealed its unpleasant face once again when the fairy hunched over and held her palm against her eyes. "Thank you for all you have done, but I feel I must rest a while" she uttered weakly. "Of course, we shall take our leave, Soulspring and its people should return to normal soon, me and my apprentice were glad to be of service" answered Clyde after taking a humble bow. Nera was kind enough to escort them out of the cave and back across the stone bridge. "Words alone cannot express my gratitude Clyde, I knew Soulspring could depend on you, a grand reward is more than fair" she remarked.

However, Clyde remained modest to the very end, "Ah, worry not about such trivialities, you're a friend Nera, aiding you and bringing a smile to your face is reward enough" he replied. Suddenly, Nera wrapped her furry arms around Clyde and tightly hugged him, unable to repel the swirls of joy swelling within her. "Thank you so much Clyde, for everything!" she declared. Clyde cherished her adoring embrace and hugged her back, "Anytime my foxy friend!" he answered, gently patting her on the back, before breaking away after a couple of seconds. Now it was time for Clyde to depart Soulspring and return to his cozy abode nestled among the chilly Frostveil Mountains. "Styx? We're coming home, kindly create us a portal, only this time create it within the town of Soulspring itself" Clyde uttered into the chatterstone embedded into his ring.

A few seconds of silence passed until they heard Styx's raspy voice, "Right you are master, I shall create it at once!" he echoed. Before the portal was created, Nera decided Meadow was worthy of a thankful hug as well. "It was a pleasure meeting you Meadow, thank you for your aid, I know you shall make a fine alchemist one day!" she declared. "Oh, well you know, I'm just glad I could help!" replied Meadow somewhat awkwardly. The idea of her becoming an alchemist wasn't something she was prepared for, and yet she was now the official apprentice of an alchemist. It was only then, when Nera said it aloud did Meadow truly grasp the reality of her position. "It was nice meeting you too Nera, you're a good friend" uttered Meadow, hugging her tightly.

A thundering boom suddenly ruptured the air, causing Meadow's hair to flail around wildly. The explosion originated from behind her, a mysterious humming sound joining it soon after. Meadow and Nera broke their hug, the magical portal had been created, its swirling mouth of luminous colors beckoning Clyde. "Ah, looks like Styx created the portal not too far away from us, come my apprentice, tis time we returned home!" Clyde passionately proclaimed. "Home? Never thought I'd find another place to call home again" Meadow replied in a thoughtful tone as she approached the whirling portal of sorcery.

Her and Clyde decided to take a final look back at Nera and waved goodbye. Then they faced the rumbling portal with its captivating array of luminous color and plunged into its dazzling depths. Into the endless vortex of radiant energy, they dived, the doorway of the portal vanishing from all existence behind them, leaving Nera alone. "Goodbye Clyde, I hope you find what you're looking for, I hope you find a cure, she needs it and you need her" Nera Whispered.

Chalice of Renewal
Chapter 4
An eye for an eye

two weeks had passed since Soulspring and currently, Meadow was meticulously pouring a vial of turquoise liquid into a small glass beaker containing an unusual amber liquid. "Now remember, you have to pour a little at a time and mix too" instructed Clyde. A timid flame burned brightly upon a small wax candle beneath the beaker, causing the pumpkin colored liquid inside to gently bubble away. "Did you remember to add three spoonsful of powered mermaid-tear flower?" asked Clyde. "Yes, three spoonsful of powered mermaid-tear, and I grinded up the sunflame flower petals then added them to beaker before pouring, just like you told me" answered Meadow.

Although it was a rather simple potion Meadow was concocting, Clyde watched with unshakeable fascination. It seemed the art of alchemy bewitched him regardless of its complexity. Meadow shared his captivation in the process of alchemy, for her focus and obsession with perfecting the mixture relentlessly enthralled her. As Meadow continued to carefully pour more of the turquoise liquid into the beaker of amber liquid, she pondered what new majestic color it would create. "Add and mix, add and mix, add and mix" she kept chanting to herself, taking the nuggets of knowledge Clyde had bestowed so far to heart.

A wave of wonder cascaded over Meadow when she noticed the mixture slowly change into a bewitching, twilight blue. It was a shade she hadn't expected to see, but one that captured her attention with its lustrous sheen. One that evoked a sense of magical mystique, made all the greater by the subtle sparkles scattered across its surface. There was little doubt that the array of sparkling dots within the mixture was a result of the powered pixie wing, another vital ingredient. "Okay, now we just leave it to boil for several hours, well done my dexterous disciple!" Clyde decreed. Supportively, Clyde then gave Meadow a playful pat upon her back. "You have just created your first water-breathing potion, now you shall be able to swim among the creatures of the sea without the constant concern of air!" Clyde proclaimed.

With a restless huff, Meadow removed the leather lab gloves and the circular black goggles she wore. "As fascinating as this is, can you tell me how much more I have to work to earn that memory erasing potion?" she asked. Slowly, Clyde removed the black goggles he wore and kept tapping his finger against his lips, gazing at the ceiling deep in thought. "I'd say, based on the amount of times you keep asking me, your still not even a fraction of the way there" he answered. Hearing his response caused Meadow to comically flop her face onto the wooden workstation in defeat, "Then please, just end my life now!" she groaned.

Calmly, Clyde leaned closer to the simmering mixture Meadow had just concocted and observed it closely, his attention beguiled by its bubbling beauty. "Is it truly so important to have your memories erased?" he asked. A stern scowl veiled Meadow as she spun her head. "You already know how important this is to me, Elijah still haunts my dreams, I can rarely get a good night sleep without the image of him murdering my parents!" she growled. Clyde turned to face Meadow and stuffed his hands into his pockets, "You know, I can make a potion to help with sleep" he answered in a dry, witty tone. His attempt at humor failed to amuse Meadow, evident when she crossed her arms and glanced away from him, "You just don't understand" she replied.

Her thoughts wandered for a moment, "Elijah grew up in the same village as me, he was always very quiet and kept to himself, but seemed like he had a good heart" Meadow uttered. "Do you know what it's like to lose someone you love? Especially to someone whom you trusted?" she asked with a somber tone. Something akin to sympathy or empathy twinkled within Clyde's shimmering eyes for a moment as he silently contemplated Meadow's words. Normally, Clyde would've banished the silence with a witty comment or frivolous banter. So, Meadow found his shroud of thoughtful silence somewhat peculiar, "It's getting late, we should turn in" Clyde eventually uttered.

Later that night, a freezing gale was howling away outside the window of the cozy cottage as usual and Meadow's sleep was restless, as usual. She rolled and writhed like a rat caught in a trap, her mind imprisoned within a realm of horrific nightmares. "No, stop! Don't hurt them! Have to run!" she muttered. Elijah roamed her dreams once again, like the grim reaper of sleep, forcing Meadow to the feel the searing flames, hear the chilling screams and witness the chaotic bloodshed all over again. Meadow trembled beneath her bed like a helpless lamb, covering her mouth with her hands and watched the window in front of her. Watching shadows scurry by it and the hazy orange hue of the rising flames reflected in the glass.

Except this time in the nightmare, Elijah suddenly pounced out from the side and glared in through the window. He was cloaked in shadow with burning red eyes that spotted Meadow beneath her bed and pierced right through her. Such a frightful nightmare forced Meadow awake, her terrified screams rivalling that of the shrieking blizzard beyond. But her pulse began to calm once she realized it was another nightmare. Breathless and drenched with sweat, Meadow fell back against the soft embrace of her pillow and rubbed her face wearily. Meanwhile, Clyde who was wide-awake in the other room, lay on his bed, grumpily staring at the ceiling, "I have to do something about this" he groaned.

Five more nights of disrupted sleep passed, and Meadow awoke to another frosty morning. She cherished the feeling of fresh warm water splash against her rosy cheeks as she washed her face and changed into fresh attire. However, her heart abruptly leapt into her throat and she gave a frightful squeak upon opening her bedroom door, for the devilish face of Clyde's pet imp was the first to greet her. The serenity of her morning was promptly shattered, "Styx, for crying out loud!" she yelped while recoiling backwards. "Good morning Miss Meadow, master Clyde has requested you join him in the kitchen for tea, he has something he wishes to discuss with you" uttered Styx in that same slithery voice.

Meadow rubbed the sleep from her eyes, her face still reeling from surprise. "Sure, just let me pick my heart up off the floor! Were you just lingering around my bedroom door waiting for me to open it?" she asked. "I did exactly as my master instructed, apparently he has made a rather intriguing discovery that you will likely want to hear" answered Styx as he hovered along the hall, flapping his little leathery wings. A fresh, steaming pot of tea lay on the center of the kitchen table when Meadow followed Styx into the kitchen, "Young Meadow is awake and present master!" announced Styx. "Thank you, Styx, you have fulfilled your duty admirably!" replied Clyde as he poured himself a fresh cup of tea. Meadow sternly stomped towards the kitchen table, her face contorted with crankiness, "Fulfilled his duty admirably? What, you mean scaring me half to death!?" she grumbled.

A beaming smirk spread across Clyde's lips as he raised the cup of tea to his face and inhaled its invigorating aroma, completely ignoring Meadows words. "Ah, the tea smells wonderful today!" he declared. Powerlessly, Meadow shook her head and rolled her eyes with futility, before grabbing the pot of hot tea and pouring herself a cup. "So, what's so important that you had to have your little minion scare me awake?" she asked in a flustery huff. "Your nightmares, you have been losing sleep because of them and consequently so have I, however, I think I have found a solution to remedy this vexing plight once and for all!" he dramatically announced.

Delight instantly began bubbling within Meadow, her eyes gleaming with hope, "You saw the light at last! Thank you so much Clyde!" she declared. "I'm not giving you the memory erasing potion" Clyde quickly answered, instantly crushing the cheery twinkle in Meadow's eyes and causing her blissful grin to vanish. However, before she had chance to utter a single word, Clyde raised his index finger to interrupt her. "What I am giving you, is the knowledge that you won't ever have to concern yourself with this Elijah character again" he said. An aura of intrigued silence enveloped Meadow, Clyde triumphed in ensnaring her ear. "For the last five days me and Styx have been gathering reports across Resplendia, to find out what became of this Elijah" he added.

Clyde decided to take a moment to grab the sweltering tea pot and top up his teacup before continuing. "I'm hazy on the details, but I think you may find some clarity if we travel to a town called Greydawn" he added while pouring. "I've heard of Greydawn, it's supposed to be rather unremarkable, aside from the towering grey stone walls surrounding it" answered Meadow. Casually, Clyde leaned back in his chair, crossing one leg over the other and clamping his warm teacup in both hands. "As mediocre as Greydawn may be, it will be our destination for today" he replied. A whirlwind of wonderful flavor swirled within Meadow's mouth when she took a much ampler quaff of the marvelous tea Clyde had concocted. "This may be the most delightful tea yet, what's in this one?" she asked. "Today's mixture of benevolent brew consists of elderking root and chasmberry, both are the main ingredients to create a tea that is both beneficial to the immune system and aids in keeping skin looking younger!" remarked Clyde.

In a gesture of gratitude, Meadow raised her teacup and bowed her head, "To good health and looking healthy then" she proposed. "So, you've never been to Greydawn? Or perhaps know anything about it?" asked Meadow in-between sips from her teacup. However, Clyde shook his head, "Never had a reason to go there, I know it's more racially tolerant than many other settlements, accepting visitors such as orcs, skarl, centaur and pretty much any other race" he replied. It pleased Meadow to hear a settlement employ such a diverse stance, it proved that racial disputes were becoming less and less common. "Nice, it's about time all other races were accepted in Resplendia" she answered.

Clyde tipped his head in agreement, yet a sense of dismay still lingered over him. "I agree, sadly there are still many parts of Resplendia which harbor animosity to any race beyond their own" he replied. "Humans were the first to discover and settle in Resplendia over three thousand years ago, the elves followed a short time after and both races managed to live in relatively harmony with each other" Clyde continued. Once again Meadow reached for her teacup and inhaled the swirling plume of steam ascending from it. "Right, the racial divides started afterwards, when the harpies, skarl and fenix appeared" she replied.

Discussing the history of Resplendia over tea made Meadow reflect upon all she had learned through her studies on the topic. "From what I learned, the harpies appeared in Resplendia and the skarl came after, both races living as nomads, wanderers without homes" she uttered. Her historical knowledge impressed Clyde, evident by his raised eyebrow and tilted head, "I'm glad to see history isn't completely lost upon our youth just yet" he replied. Meadow cracked a smile and chuckled, "The fenix appeared in Resplendia next, settling down at the city of Scorchwind in the Burning Plains" she added. The invigorating aroma drifting from the tea banished the lingering sleep from Meadow's mind and rejuvenated her senses. "Wasn't it around two-hundred years later when the orcs and the goblins appeared in Resplendia?" she asked. "It certainly was and that's when the Green Banner War started, a bloody stain upon the archives of Resplendia's history, when orcs and goblins formed an alliance and tried to conquer all of Resplendia for themselves" uttered Clyde.

Once his teacup was devoid of delicious tea again, Clyde reached for the handle upon the pot. "Despite the fact that was over two-hundred years ago now, animosity towards the orcs still exists to this day" he said. Alas, upon attempting to pour out the tea he soon discovered the pot to be as empty as a sirens heart. "Oh dear, looks like morning tea is over my dear disciple, I guess we should get going" he declared. Quickly, Meadow slurped down the last droplets of her tea and unleashed a refreshed gasp. "By the way, if we are talking about which is the oldest race in Resplendia, then surely it would actually be the centaurs wouldn't it?" she asked. "Centaur and satyr and technically yes, they were here long before humans, of course they don't build cities and empires like humans do" answered Clyde as he headed towards the portal room.

Clyde's devilish imp helper Styx was already situated in the portal room. Floating lazily in mid-air using his eerie little wings and with his sharp magical pitchfork at the ready, "Where to this time master?" he hissed. Cheerfully, Clyde hopped upon the rolling ladder and wheeled it along the gigantic, elaborately illustrated map of Resplendia fixed to the wall and came to an abrupt halt in the middle.

He pressed his finger upon the exquisite parchment, pointing at one spot. "This is the spot where Greydawn lies and so our target is revealed! Please prepare your portal at once Styx! The time to sail into the horizon of adventure has risen once more!" he decreed. "Great, you've gone nuts again, are you sure there wasn't something else in that tea?" Meadow jest as she reclined her head back and gazed closer at their destination. Clyde retaliated with a haughty laugh, "Mock me if you will my defiant disciple, but the very essence of my soul informs me that the key to banishing your nightmares lies in Greydawn!" he replied with glee. It seemed Clyde was more excited about this venture than Meadow was, but he did have his own reasons for doing this too. "Once your nightmares have been quelled, I shall no longer have to hear them, I too shall have a peaceful night's sleep!" cried Clyde with maniacal laughter.

Dramatically, Clyde pointed his finger directly at Styx, "Styx, begin the portal process, we can't get this done soon enough!" he declared. "Aye, aye Captain Clyde!" answered Styx, obediently standing to attention and responding with a playfully salute. Vigor seemed to be bursting more than usual within Clyde today, as he leapt from the ladder and placed his hand upon Meadow's shoulder. "To the laboratory my little lackey, we must equip ourselves!" he proclaimed. Meadow followed behind his trail of hasty frolicking and joined him in the alchemy laboratory. "Are you expecting trouble?" she asked as she watched him gear up his harness with a variety of potions, including the one that granted enhanced strength. "Always be prepared my dear, that is the code of any alchemist worth his weight" replied Clyde, eagerly outfitting himself with a potion for every consequence he could conceive.

Meadow flicked her fiery hair backwards for a moment and grabbed her harness. "I suppose it never hurts" she replied as she began equipping her harness with the same potions Clyde had picked. Until Meadow noticed that she was short by one, "Hey I'm missing a potion!" she remarked. Quickly, Clyde examined her harness and deduced which potion was missing, "Invisibility potion, I've got the last batch, we'll have to make some more when we get back" he replied.

Suddenly, a thundering boom echoed from the portal room, shattering the peaceful air. "Sounds like the portal is ready, hopefully we shouldn't need our potions anyway" uttered Meadow as she departed the lab. Inside the portal room, Styx had conjured another portal upon the circular stone pedestal with glowing runes. "Portal ready master, travel safe and bring back souvenirs!" Styx playfully rasped. "Very well, it is time to voyage into the horizon of mystery and adventure once again! Time to traverse this mystical realm of sorcery and" Clyde declared before being interrupted by Meadow. "Ugh, can we just go!?" she groaned after rolling her eyes and proceeding to march impatiently towards the portal. A grumpy scowl spread across Clyde's face as he followed her, "I'll have you know, that just cost you an extra week of working for me my disruptive disciple" he replied.

Into the swirling portal of magic, they stepped without further delay and were instantly washed away by the waves of sorcery once again. A few fleeting moments later, they emerged upon the other side, casually ambling from out of the portals mystical mouth like they were enjoying a summer stroll. "It seems Styx brought us very close this time" remarked Clyde as he glanced at the many flabbergasted onlookers working in the nearby fields and upon the main road. After taking a quick survey of her surroundings, Meadow chuckled upon seeing the astonished faces of the nearby commoners. "Yeah, it's like they've never seen two strangers suddenly appear from out of a mysterious magical portal before" she replied with sarcasm. "Never mind, the trivial wonders of the common folk aren't our concern today, let us proceed young Meadow!" declared Clyde.

With gusto in his stride, Clyde sauntered towards the looming grey walls of Greydawn and their imposing oak gates which currently wide open, sadly he didn't make it very far. Two guards clad in chainmail wielding shiny steel spears and large wooden shields crossed their weapons as Clyde approached, hindering his advance. "Not a step further stranger, we saw that magic you stepped out of, who are ye?" asked one. "Do not concern yourself my troll-breathed friend, my apprentice and I are alchemists, we are here to do some shopping and we simply travel by means which your common minds would be unable to fathom" Clyde earnestly replied.

Both guards remained steadfast and vigilant, retaliating to Clyde's words with stern glares, while Meadow slapped her palm against her forehead in frustration. However, the two guards traded amused glances with each other and burst out laughing. "Very well, welcome to Greydawn strangers and enjoy your stay!" said one of them while chuckling. They proceeded to raise their steel spears, blocking Clyde's path no longer. "Many thanks and good day to you noble guardsmen, continue to perform your duties valiantly" uttered Clyde as he strolled by.

Various vendors peddling a variety of items lay beyond the hulking gates inside the town, accompanied by bustling patrons and the droning of pleasant chatter. Jovial curiosity entangled Clyde when he passed a couple of stalls, one selling a selection of spices while another peddled an assortment of colorful herbs. "The prices here are seducing to say the least, I must investigate further!" declared Clyde as he skipped towards the stalls with glee. Meadow placed one hand upon her hip and began tapping one of her feet impatiently, while also observing Clyde with suspicious narrowed eyes.

Curiosity entangled Clyde tighter as he strolled further ahead and noticed a large, crowded market packed with a plethora of stalls and stands draped in majestic banners and colorful cloth. Naturally, Clyde flung himself at the marketplace, a deluge of childish innocence flooding over him. "Such a fabulous array of stores, I must peruse their goods at once!" he proclaimed. Once again Meadow watched him with suspicious scrutiny, both arms firmly folded, "So, the shopping was the reason you were so eager to come here!?" she called. "Don't be absurd, I'm merely looking, I promise we shall attend to your needs in a minute!" Clyde called back as he poked his nose through the hordes of chattering shoppers.

Two hours later, a rather satisfied expression smeared Clyde's face as he carried the bulging sack of shopping he had swung over his shoulder. "Come along my apprentice, let us not dawdle!" he uttered. Meadow, who also carried a small leather sack brimming with recently bought goods suddenly fired a scornful glare his way, "Merely looking!" she grumbled sarcastically. After a little exploring around the town, Clyde finally found what he had been searching for. "Ah, there it is, this is what I brought you here to see!" he declared as he rushed on ahead. Meadow quickly chased after him, huffing slightly from the weight of the sack slung across her back, "Okay, just wait up!" she cried. Further ahead lay a large open square, decorated by a towering statue of majestic marble, "Here it is!" declared Clyde as he gestured his arm towards it. Strangely, the statue was of a young girl with horns adoring her head and a spiky demonic tail entwined around her legs. A golden nameplate was also embedded upon the pedestal of the statue, "Elma Rosewish?" Meadow whispered.

Although the statue was admittedly magnificent to behold, Meadow failed to see why it was necessary for her to witness it, "You brought me here to see a statue?" she uttered. Wearily, Clyde hung his head and sighed, "This is not just any statue my apprentice, rumor has it this is a statue of the girl who destroyed Elijah!" he announced. His words quickly seized Meadow with shock, causing her to become speechless and gasp with disbelief. "I just wish the statue provided more information about her; it seems to be vague on details" remarked Clyde as he inspected the sculpture. "Actually, that's not true, Elma never killed Elijah, she actually banished him to another realm" uttered a firm voice from behind.

With a swift spin, Meadow and Clyde turned to greet the mysterious voice and were confronted by a handsome young guard with sea-blue eyes, snowy skin and long golden hair. "I couldn't help but overhear you, my name is Angelo, I'm captain of the guard here" he said. "A pleasure to meet you Captain Nosy, do you know anything more of this girl Elma, me and my apprentice are intrigued in learning more" replied Clyde, holding out his hand for Angelo to shake.

However, Angelo kept Clyde's hand waiting, marching right past him and taking a sincere, profound gaze upon Elma's statue. "I can tell you more than almost anyone, I was the one who kept hunting her down" he answered softly. "Elma was half-demon herself you see, she had the terrible power of dark magic at her fingertips, just like Elijah, but unlike Elijah, she was pure and kind, never wanting to use her demonic sorcery hurt or kill anyone" Angelo continued. Mournfully, Angelo stretched out his arm and powerlessly leaned against Elma's statue, as though an invisible fog had just drained him of his energy. "I hunted her like she was some evil monster to be exterminated, simply because it was my duty" he uttered.

With great care, Meadow approached his side and softly placed her hand upon his shoulder. "Would you mind telling me what happened? What became of Elma and Elijah?" she asked in a gentle voice. Such a tale may have left a bitter taste lingering inside Angelo, evident by the way he began rubbing his temples, "Why do you care?" he asked. Meadow's soulful gaze pierced deeper into Angelo's abyssal blue eyes and she firmly clenched Angelo's hand, "Please" she uttered. Finally, Angelo yielded his steely heart to her, "Elijah used his dark magic to conjure a portal to realm of Diablos, one of the gods of our world, the god of demons and darkness" he replied. "Elijah believed making darkness and demons common would change everyone's judgmental, archaic views, in his own twisted way he sought to make a more open-minded world" Angelo added.

After taking a moment to recompose himself, Angelo straightened his uniform and rested his palm upon the hilt of his steel sword. "Elma stopped Elijah by hurling him into the dark portal he created, sadly, Elma died soon after from a wound Elijah had caused, a wound originally meant for me" he uttered in a somber tone. Peering closer at the golden nameplate upon the pedestal of Elma's statue, Clyde recited a few more words engraved upon it. "Elma Rosewish, savior of Resplendia? Your telling me she saved all Resplendia? Why isn't that greater news!?" he remarked.

A graceful white dove swooped down and rested upon the base of Elma's pedestal at that very moment and Angelo smiled upon seeing its purity. "History is written by the victors, or in this case the survivors, only a handful of people witnessed Elma's noble act" Angelo replied. "I was there alongside Elma and her friends in the final battle against Elijah, hence why I spread her tale to as many willing ears as I can" he added. An aura of wonder swathed Clyde as he gawked upon Elma's statute with profound astonishment. "Apologies for all the questions my good man, my apprentice Meadow is a victim of Elijah's cruelty and we came here so she could find closure, also the shopping is good" said Clyde. A shimmering gleam of remorse appeared within Angelo's eyes as he turned his attention towards Meadow. "My sympathies young miss, many suffered at the hands of Elijah, including me, he destroyed much of what I cherished" he uttered solemnly.

To further illustrate his empathy of how Meadow felt, Angelo knelt in front of her and gently held her hand. "I promise you; Elijah can no longer hurt you or anyone else, he was banished and trapped forever inside that dark realm" he whispered. His voice brought solace to Meadow and the knowledge that Elijah had been stopped and exiled to another realm entirely beamed a ray of hope upon her heart. "Thank you, I needed to hear that" she answered. "So, you witnessed all this with your own eyes? How exactly did a captain of the guard in Greydawn become tangled up in such a tale?" asked Clyde inquisitively.

Stoic silence was the only answer Clyde received as Angelo arose from his knee and briefly adjusted the silver clasp upon his belt, deciding to speak only when he was ready. "It's a long story and I don't have time to tell it, Greydawn is facing a dire problem at the moment" he replied. "Really? Well color me intrigued! My assistant and I might be able to help you in that regard, we offer our alchemy services to aid anyone in need, for a price of course!" declared Clyde.

Doubt clouded Angelo like fog on a mountain as he inspected Clyde from head to toe, "And what is the price of being bestowed your services?" he asked. "That, good sir depends entirely upon the perils that plight you and your settlement, but since you were able ease my disciples' weary heart, I'm sure I can arrange a deduction in my rates" Clyde answered shrewdly. Impatience clearly grew within Angelo; he didn't strike Meadow as the kind of man who had time for smooth talkers. "Fine, I shall accept any aid I can get, just know this is a dangerous task, not one for foolish gold chasers" Angelo replied firmly. "Nor is it a task meant for alchemists with their vials and herbs, more a task fit for warriors armed with sword and shield" he added with a degree of ridicule in his voice.

Proudly, Clyde placed his hands upon his hips and stood tall. "You should not underestimate the power of alchemy my foolish friend, for anything is possible using the miraculous mixtures we make!" he declared. Angelo remained unconvinced and let out a haughty sneer, likely believing a sharp blade was the best solution to a problem. "Trade caravans on route to Greydawn have been attacked lately, we don't know who or what is doing it, but I'm fairly certain it wasn't bandits" replied Angelo, swiftly dismissing Clyde's boasting.

With a slight nod of his head, Angelo gestured Clyde and Meadow to follow him. "No bodies have been found, no survivors remained, even the galamare that pulled the caravans were hauled away" he explained as he strolled. "No fired arrows were seen around the area, all bodies were picked up and carried away and all the valuable cargo remained intact, the attackers only stole food" uttered Angelo as they departed Elma's grand statue. Clyde's gaze wandered as he walked, his finger bent and pressed against his lip as he remained deep in thought. "It would take something of great strength to carry away the corpse of a galamare" he replied.

They took the scenic route and strolled through a grandiose garden of verdant green, brimming with vibrant flowers of all varieties. "The attacks happened along the western road, which is covered in a dense forest" explained Angelo. "That would explain why the culprit's identity remains a mystery, must be difficult for your guards in the watchtowers to see" replied Clyde as he followed closely behind.

Playfully, Meadow sauntered along the walls of the stone planters that surrounded the ravishing flowers, keeping her arms held out to try and maintain her balance as she moved. "The last attack came just a couple of days ago, making it the third caravan of goods we have lost along the western road, I'll escort you to the crime scene since it remains mostly untouched" said Angelo. Meadow skipped ahead of them and frolicked through the gorgeous gardens like a playful pixie, stopping to sniff the flourishing flowers at every chance she got. "My apprentice may seem quite carefree, but I assure you she takes her duties seriously, she can be scary when she needs to" remarked Clyde. Angelo chuckled as he watched Meadow prance past the planters of tulips and roses, "Sounds like Elma" he uttered softly.

They departed Greydawn through the western gate and it took roughly an hour to reach the spot. Angelo escorted them along the sun-soaked road and into the deep sprawling forest that lay beyond the comforting sights of the city watchtowers. After strolling around a curvy bend of road, the sight of two guards, several ripped linen sacks and a few smashed crates came into view. "Here we are, this is what remains of the crime scene" declared Angelo. Both guards instantly sprung to attention and quickly saluted Angelo when they saw him approach, "Captain Angelo, sir!" cried one of them. "At ease, these two are alchemists, I've brought them to aid with the investigation and examine the crime scene" explained Angelo as he marched closer.

Right away Clyde discerned that there wasn't much to investigate, at least not on the surface, "So, how untouched is this crime scene?" he asked. "Very, this attack happened a day ago, but Captain Angelo ensured guards were always stationed here and it's been watched vigilantly" answered one of the guards. Meticulously, Clyde studied the scene, trying to visualize what transpired. "So, no bodies, no survivors, no witnesses, the galamare pulling the caravan was taken too, only food was stolen, but why take the bodies yet leave evidence of an attack?" he pondered. A bloodstained longsword lay strewn upon the ground nearby, "Looks like someone put up a fight and managed to draw blood, but not much" uttered Clyde.

Expensive jewels, rings, ornaments and amulets were spilling from out of the leather sacks. "Even the stupidest bandits would've seen the gain from looting such lavish items, this was not a crime of profit" Clyde remarked. "There's some more blood over here but it looks dry!" declared Meadow who was diligently examining the woods surrounding the crime scene. Clyde swiftly jogged to her side while carefully navigating the spot, "The humidity would've no doubt hastened the drying process" he replied. "Still, there is enough blood here to examine, perhaps the culprit's blood? Maybe a cut caused from the sword I saw earlier" Clyde theorized as he continued his inspection.

Meadow squatted down and fixed her gaze closer upon the scattered droplets of dried blood that covered the grassy ground and a nearby tree. "I'm no expert but, this blood seems different" she remarked. "Your intuition serves you well my disciple, this blood is far too thick and much too dark to be human blood, this is a blood of a monster, which would explain why only food was stolen" answered Clyde. Deeper within the sylvan forest, Meadow's focus was snatched by the sight of strange tracks, "Here, I think these tracks might lead somewhere!" she declared as she keenly chased the trail. "Looking at the foliage it would seem that something heavy was dragged through here, likely the galamare" noted Clyde as he vigilantly inspected the trail of crushed shrubs and weeds.

A set of imposing footprints that travelled alongside the trail also gave Clyde a moment of pause, along with a frightful shudder. "Look at these footprints, whatever created them is large, exceptionally large!" he gasped. Calmly, Angelo strolled over to join the investigation and curiously peered upon the tracks. "Perhaps a troll? Or maybe an ogre?" he speculated with his hand rested warily upon the hilt of his sword. "Trolls don't stray far from their caves and ogres lack the intelligence to locate a main road and attack traders as they travel by" answered Clyde, rubbing his chin.

Without a single droplet of fear on his face, Angelo started stomping through the woods and boldly following the tracks, "In that case we follow the trail and see for ourselves!" he declared. Angelo's march was steadfast and brisk, so much so that Clyde had to hastily give chase or risk losing sight of him. "I'm surprised to see a guard captain taking such direct action in this matter, you do realize my apprentice and I can more than handle whatever creature awaits!" boast Clyde as he jogged alongside.

Unable to swallow such a remark, Angelo's stern gaze flickered towards Clyde, before firmly resting upon the forest again. "Innocent people have been killed, I refuse to sit back and do nothing, I am the captain of Greydawn, but that title rings hollow if I do not have the power to defend it!" he growled. "Well said, but you might need help so count us in!" cried Meadow as she ducked under a drooping branch of tangled bushes and scurried after them. Thankfully, the midday sun still hovered in the air, acting as their stalwart protector against the arrival of night. "I confess, the manner of creature that committed this crime still eludes me" admitted Clyde. "We know for certain its a beast with great strength, it's pretty intelligent and has quite the gluttonous appetite too!" remarked Meadow as she cavorted between the gaps in the trees.

A nearby skittering sound and the snapping of a wooden branch caused Angelo to abruptly freeze in his steps and tighten his grasp upon the hilt of his blade. "Stay alert, there's no telling where this monster could be hiding!" he whispered in a firm hush. Gradually, Angelo relaxed his hand, releasing the rigid grip his polished steel gauntlet had upon the hilt of his shimmering longsword after encountering nothing but the pleasant chirps of birds. "All seems calm, let us continue the hunt, just don't drop your guard, forests are excellent locations for ambushes and can conceal even the largest of foes" uttered Angelo as he resumed his march.

Clyde heeded his wise words and warily wandered through the wild woods while maintaining a balanced distance apart, "Worry not, my minion and I have seen our fair share of peril, right Meadow?" he asked. However, when Clyde swung his head to glance back at Meadow, he noticed her body language had become mellow, her focus drifted, and a subtle smile stretched her lips, "You seem happier" he noted. Meadow's movements were whimsical, almost aimless as she strolled along, devouring the radiant slits of sunlight slinking between the gaps of trees. "I keep thinking about what Angelo said, about the fate that has befallen Elijah, coming here was an excellent idea, I think it has given me a little more peace, so thank you Clyde" she replied sincerely.

Caution was apparently flung to the wind, for only Angelo seemed to be paying attention to the monster's tracks, evident as he watched Clyde and Meadow casually banter between each other. "Well, that was our purpose in coming here, hopefully it shall cleanse your mind of nightmares and grant me a peaceful night's sleep, I've started noticing the bags under my eyes" Clyde answered. A playful harmony resonated between them and Meadow gave Clyde a teasing shove, "Don't worry, I'm sure you've got a potion for that" she jest. Meanwhile, Angelo silently watched them with arms folded and a raised eyebrow and waited for them to finish their chatter. "Hate to interrupt your pleasant conversation, but maybe we could focus on the ferociously strong monster we're supposed to be hunting, you know the one that's attacked three caravans and killed several people?" He remarked.

Angelo's sarcasm was so thick it felt like wading through a viscous swamp, "Apologies, I assure you we will…." Began Clyde, before abruptly halting his speech and curiously sniffing the air. "Do you smell that? I smell something delicious cooking nearby!" he spluttered while inhaling the wonderful new aroma. Like a tempting adder, the aroma crept over Angelo and Meadow too, seducing them with its heavenly scent. "Guess we should follow our noses for now, who knows, maybe we can find someone who can tell us what happened" remarked Angelo.

Without a shred of hesitation, the three of them pursued the divine odor, tracking it to its source, their noses acting as the guides through the lush, labyrinthine forest. The deeper they travelled the more potent the aroma became, until they finally ceased their hike upon hearing the crackling of nearby firewood. Angelo took lead, navigating around a towering mossy rock, peering curiously around the corner, swatting away a lengthy strip of ivy that dangled in front of his face. A huge blazing campfire lay ahead with the roasted carcass of a galamare resting upon a crude makeshift spit above the snapping flames. Burst leather sacks brimming with food also surrounded the roaring campfire, "I think we've found the culprits campfire" uttered Angelo as he studied the scene. Unfortunately, before anyone could utter a single word further, the sudden sound of fierce rustling from amongst the trees above caused everyone to avert their gaze upwards and lay their eyes upon the fearsome monster looming over them.

Deep, ominous snarls ruptured from the monster's maw as it rested upon the towering pillar of rock. It gazed down at Clyde and the others like a hulking gargoyle with its one and only bulging veiny eye, "A cyclops, of course!" gasped Clyde. With a mighty roar the muscular mountain of monster leapt from the tip of the tall rock formation and slammed its giant feet into the earth, causing a titanic tremble to cascade across the ground. Clouds of dirt and dust scattered into the air like a swarm of moths as the beast landed and it took a few seconds for the rumbling echo to subside. Fear froze Clyde and Meadow as they gazed upon the giant cyclops, its growling visage rendering them speechless and unable to act. "Don't just gawk! Scatter!" boomed Angelo's voice.

Thankfully, his stern shouting snapped Clyde and Meadow back to their senses and they swiftly spilt-up. Scurrying like rats, just in time to avoid the slamming fist of the hulking cyclops before them. Another brief quake followed as the monster's fist smashed into the earth, causing a swarm of leaves from the trees above to shake loose. Angelo took advantage of this opportunity, astonishing Clyde and Meadow with the way he instinctively approached the monster and gracefully dashed along its thick arm, effortlessly maintaining excellent balance. However, the beast began to quickly rouse again, and Angelo deduced he wouldn't have time to deliver a killing blow. instead he raised his shimmering sword and plunged the blade into the cyclops's shoulder.

A growl of agony erupted from the cyclops, causing it to wildly flail its colossal arm in retaliation. Luckily, Angelo elegantly hopped from the beasts back, his radiant golden hair flowing as he flew. Once Angelo had safely landed upon the ground behind the cyclops, he raised his sword and recovered his posture, maintaining a disciplined stance while vigilantly watching the creature thrash around.

After a couple of seconds, the cyclops held its glaring eye upon Angelo and took a furious running stomp towards him, leaping high into the air, determined to crush Angelo like a pitiful insect. It was a tactic Angelo was honestly unprepared for, fortunately his life was saved at the last second. Something with terrific speed suddenly whooshed to his side and shoved him out of harm's way. As the cyclops's gigantic feet smashed into the ground causing another tremendous shudder, Angelo looked upon his speedy savior with bewilderment, "Where did you get such speed!?" he gasped. A smug grin spread over Clyde's face as he dangled an empty potion vial in the air, "Enhanced speed potion my friend, always handy in a pinch!" he remarked.

Meadow had also guzzled down her vial of speed potion and within the blink of an eye scooped up a small rock and tossed it at the cyclops with great speed. "Hey, ugly!" she taunted. A tiny cut appeared upon the back of the cyclops's head as the rock collided, enraging the brute further and causing its attention to now fall upon Meadow. Like a hungry hound chasing a meat cart, the cyclops charged towards Meadow and with the ferocity of a roaring tsunami, it raised its gargantuan fists and attempted to pummel her into oblivion.

Thanks to the speed potion Meadow took however, she was able to easily whizz out of the monster's path leaving nothing more than a swirl of dust behind. Cockiness swathed Meadow as she watched the cyclops's massive fist clumsily smash into the oak tree where Meadow was standing, splitting the timber asunder and causing it to topple over. Alas, to Meadow's dismay, the tree was quickly falling straight towards her. "Eek!" she cried as she used her enhanced speed to swiftly dash from beneath the ominous shadow of the toppling tree.

It was too close for comfort, the giant oak slammed into the earth mere inches behind her. The impact caused a rumbling tremor to resonate through the entire forest and resulted in Meadow losing her balance and painfully skidding across the ground. Before Meadow had time to gather her bearings and recompose herself, the cyclops had already begun menacingly stomping towards her, eager to grind her bones into seasoning. Fear devoured Meadow as the snarling monster bent down and reached its huge hand towards her, on the verge of scooping her up within its crushing grip. Once again Clyde rushed to the rescue with the aid of the speed potion he consumed, froze in front of the cyclops and flung a handful of dirt he had gathered directly into the beasts bulging eye.

A Roar of confusion erupted from the cyclops as it staggered backwards, violently swinging its muscular arms around with all the grace of a drunk goblin. Within this brief window of opportunity, Clyde assisted Meadow back onto her feet. "Do not become too calm my apprentice, be aware of your surroundings" he uttered as he pulled her from the dirt. After using its arm to wipe the scattered dirt from its large protruding eye, the cyclops gradually recovered its vision. Only to see Angelo valiantly charging forth with his sword unsheathed and the shimmering shield he carried upon his back now raised. Retreat was an absurd concept to the cyclops, instead it retaliated by charging right back at Angelo. Furiously, the beast swung its enormous fist in an upward arc as he approached, no doubt wanting to knock Angelo into the heavens. With elegance and timing Angelo dodged the creature's formidable blow and used his momentum to roll beneath the cyclops's legs, delivering a swift slash of his sword upon the beast's ankle as he passed. Searing rage then filled the cyclops, causing it to recklessly turn around and swing its gigantic arm towards Angelo.

This time Angelo failed to evade the blow and the monsters formidable fist slammed against his steel shield. It resulted in a booming din which echoed through the tranquil forest and caused Angelo to be propelled backwards. Angelo grimaced from the impact and was rendered powerless as he flew across the air with great speed towards Clyde who happened to be stood in the path of his trajectory. Sadly, Clyde failed to react in time and felt the wind get knocked from his chest as Angelo slammed into him headfirst.

Both men skidded across the dirt and grass, tumbling into a messy roll and ending up in dazed heap. "Get off me alchemist!" growled Angelo as he woozily staggered to his feet. "Hey, I cushioned your impact, your welcome!" shouted Clyde, batting the dirt off his outfit and uttering a weary sigh. Meanwhile, Meadow had gathered a dozen small rocks and decided to assault the cyclops from the right, "Hey eyesore, over here!" she yelled. Meadow quickly succeeded in ensnaring the brute's attention, "How about a rock storm!?" she declared, bombarding the cyclops in a speedy salvo of stone.

Since Meadow was still under the effect of the speed potion, her hailstorm of rocks was like a shower of tiny meteorites. Sadly, her rock supply quickly depleted, and she knew the speed potion had to be ending soon. Scrapes and cuts covered the cyclops's arms since it had the intelligence to raise them and guard itself against Meadow's rocky onslaught and it wasn't too worse for wear. Furiously, the cyclops unleashed a trembling roar, wrapped its hulking arms around a nearby boulder and mustered all its strength to rip it from the earth. "Okay, you win, your rock is bigger!" uttered Meadow as she nervously watched the colossal brute raise the giant boulder above its head, clearly planning to lob it at Meadow and turn her into paste. By this point the speed potion had undoubtedly wore off, so Meadow hastily drew a new vial of potion from her harness, ripped off the cork and gulped it down as fast as she could. At the same time, the towering cyclops hurled the humongous boulder towards Meadow with all its might. The huge hunk of stone whizzed through the air and collided into Meadow, smashing into her face, cracking asunder, crumbling apart and creating a fearsome boom upon impact.

Frantically, Clyde rushed to her location as he watched the scene unfold, clearly concerned about her wellbeing, "Meadow!" he cried. Angelo daringly dashed straight towards the cyclops with fire in his heart and fearlessly flung his sword towards the beast, managing to strike it right in the ribs. A deep, bellowing growl of anger rumbled from the creature as it recoiled in pain. Worse still, Angelo was now unarmed and knew he needed to recover his blade as quickly as possible. Hence, he used the toppled tree from earlier as a steppingstone and courageously leapt towards the cyclops. Yet, he aimed his leap for his sword which remained embedded in the belly of the beast. Using his momentum, Angelo managed to grasp the hilt of his sword as he gracefully swung at it and use his body weight to rip the blade clean from the creature's flesh.

While this was unfolding, Clyde checked upon Meadow who was thankfully unscathed from the giant boulder that smashed into her. A dense layer of steel now covered her skin, "Ah, Steel-skin potion eh?" remarked Clyde. Meadow winked and playfully stuck out her steel tongue, "We must end this my apprentice, time to use the strength potion!" declared Clyde.

The cyclops retaliated against Angelo with a dirty backhand strike. Luckily, Angelo was able to defend against the attack with his shield, but the blow still rattled his bones and flung him backwards again. Angelo painfully gasped as his back slammed against a tree behind him. He also failed to keep a tight grasp upon his shield, which the hulking cyclops suddenly scooped up. Promptly, Angelo shook away the daze that clouded his vision, only to see the dreaded cyclops hurl his own shield right back at him like it was a discus. Resulting in Angelo having to frantically skitter out of the way to avoid getting his head lopped off.

The sturdy steel edge of Angelo's shield slammed into the tree where his head was, stabbing deeply into the oak or Angelo's face if he had acted a second later. Meanwhile, Clyde and Meadow had consumed their strength potions, bestowing them tremendous physical might, "Ready my dear?" asked Clyde. Currently, Clyde was using his newfound strength to grab Meadow by the arms and effortlessly swing her around in a circle, "Ready!" yelled Meadow. Using all his enhanced strength, Clyde timed his throw, released his grip upon Meadow's arms and flung her through the air, towards the cyclops's snarling face. "Woo-hoo!" Meadow delightfully cried as she rapidly whizzed through the air, catching the colossal cyclops by complete surprise and walloped it right in the face with a formidable fist made of steel.

Combined with the strength potion she had taken, Meadow managed to deliver quite the powerful blow, enough to render the mighty cyclops utterly stunned. Meadow tumbled across the ground, rolling a fair distance, but remained unharmed thanks to her steel skin. At the same time, Clyde seized advantage of this opportunity, striking while the iron was hot. Meadow's punch had caused the lofty tyrant to totter, its legs wobbled like jelly, with a little more effort the beast would topple like a crumbling pillar in a strong breeze.

Possessing the power of the effects of the strength potion, Clyde hastily scooped up a large piece of rubble leftover from the shattered boulder. He lifted the rock, which was as large as his own head and effortlessly launched it towards the staggering cyclops like he was throwing a common beach pebble. His aim was precise, the hurtling hunk of rock smashed into dozens of smaller pieces upon colliding into the cyclops's ugly head, creating a burst of cloudy rubble on impact.

A weary growl erupted from the one-eyed brute as it finally toppled onto its rump, utterly dazed by the attack, but it still attempted to arise and put up a fight. "I'm glad I made one of these!" declared Angelo, heroically dashing towards the collapsed creature and pulling a strange vial from his waist belt. He promptly tossed the vial at the nearby spire of rock jutting from the earth and it shattered upon impact, exploding in a dazzling burst of celestial white light. It temporarily blinded the creature along with Clyde and Meadow too, "A flash bomb!?" yelled Clyde as he covered his eyes. Strangely, Angelo remained unaffected by the burst of light, "Sorry, but I believe in an eye for an eye!" he snarled at the toppled monster. Once he was close enough, Angelo then mercilessly thrust his blade, stabbing it right into the large, dazed eye of the cyclops.

It was over, a final grunt of defeat murmured from the mighty cyclops as it took its last breath, while Angelo gracefully drew his blade from the creature's eye as it lifelessly collapsed. Once their vision had returned, Clyde and Meadow rushed to Angelo's side, watching in wonder at the sight of their vanquished foe. The forest became tranquil once more with sound of chirping birds and the soft summer breeze fluttering through the air, "It is done" Angelo gently uttered.

Just like that, Angelo slowly placed his sword back in its sheath and gradually walked away. "That vial of exploding light, how were you immune to its effects?" asked Clyde as he watched Angelo wander further. "May the dawns light guide our hand as we purge the monsters that defile this land, this is our oath and we are bound by the light, as we destroy the demons that prowl in the night" chanted Angelo upon collecting his shield. Upon uttering these words, Clyde gasped with surprise, "That's the oath of light! I see, so you weren't always a guard captain!" he remarked.

A sly smile spread across Angelo's lips as he glanced back at Clyde. "Thank you both for your aid in this matter, the western road will be much safer for any travelers now!" Angelo declared with a humble bow. Hastily, Meadow returned a thankful bow of her own. "And thank you for telling me what became of Elijah, I imagine I shall sleep much better knowing he cannot harm anyone again" she replied. "If the two of you accompany me back to Greydawn I shall see you are both suitably compensated for your efforts" Angelo answered with hearty gratitude. Yet, Clyde raised his hand to reject his offer and shook his head. "That shall not be necessary good sir, we were happy to be of service and the solace you have brought my apprentice is reward enough!" he remarked.

Angelo cracked a smile of admiration, seemingly inspired by Clyde's act of gallantry, "Well then, all the best to both of you, wherever life leads you" he replied. Playfully, Angelo rubbed Meadow's hair and raised her chin, so her gaze met his. "Never forget girl, there is always a light in the darkness somewhere and once you find it, you'll never lose sight of it" he uttered. As the soothing sunlight graced Meadow's skin, a tender smile appeared upon her lips as she watched Angelo take his leave and gradually fade into the forest. "Well then, I guess our work here is done" she whispered happily.

Chalice of Renewal
Chapter 5
Fire and ice

Like a griffon stalking its prey, Meadow watched and waited until the moment to swoop down and pounce was ripe, "Alight, slowly!" she whispered with intense breath. Warily, she shadowed her quarry while also keeping her presence concealed, until the moment to strike began to materialize. "Now!" cried Meadow as she lunged forward with her glass jar in hand, swiftly scooping the elegant blue beetle inside and held it upright to prevent it escaping. "Okay, I got one! What potion is it for again?" asked Meadow as she waltzed out of the colorful botanical garden Clyde had created inside his large alchemy lab. "Take care when transporting it my dear, that beetle is a vital ingredient for making ice resistance potion" Clyde answered, his face buried in another concoction he was creating.

Before bringing the beautiful blue beetle over to Clyde, Meadow made sure to shut the study wooden door to the garden behind her. "Are you sure one is going to be enough?" she asked as she carefully set the jar upon the worktop next to him. "Yes, one should be enough for one quick batch, did you shut the garden door behind you? I don't wish to repeat what happened a few days ago, took us forever to find all the spiders!" Clyde answered.

It had been two weeks since the cyclops incident and although the occasional nightmare still plagued Meadow's mind, they were much rarer now and her sleep had improved quite a bit. In that time Clyde had also spent almost every waking moment teaching her the fundamentals of alchemy, which she was picking up quite well. "Yes, I remembered to shut the door this time" answered Meadow as she watched Clyde work. However, he abruptly ceased the mixing he was currently doing with his mortar and pestle and gestured Meadow to take over. "Okay, you keep on grinding the ingredients away, including the beetle, tip it into the mortar and crush it into the mixture but don't be too rough with it" instructed Clyde.

Meadow's face turned ghastly white as she took hold of the pestle with one hand and tipped the jar containing the beetle upside down with her other. "I hate this part, I'm not a fan of bugs but still, it's a living thing!" she whined. "It is part of the intricate process of alchemy my apprentice, regardless of how cruel it may seem, alchemy is the art of transformation and creation, often it entails changing the properties of a living organism into something else entirely" replied Clyde. A revolting crunching sound made Meadow's tongue twist as she quickly crushed the blue beetle beneath the stone pestle. "You've given me this speech before, in turn we consume the creature for our benefit, ensuring it fulfils a greater cause" she uttered with revulsion. "Well remembered my disciple, there may be hope for you yet!" Clyde declared while diligently pouring a vial of oil extracted from anemone flowers into a glass flask of simmering water. "You know, I think that might be the part that disgusts me the most, the fact that we drink concoctions that sometimes contain crushed up bugs" replied Meadow as she gently grinded away.

Thankfully, it didn't take very long for the beetle to become mixed in with the powdered catoblepas tooth that Clyde had already pulverized with his pestle. "Okay, that looks good!" Clyde cheerfully remarked as he peered over Meadow's shoulder. "So, why do we need ice resistance potions?" asked Meadow as she followed the next step. Gradually she poured in the mixture of crushed beetle and powdered catoblepas tooth into the bubbling flask of anemone oil and water. As the glass flask hung in its iron holder above the flickering candle, Clyde tenderly swirled the mixture with a long wooden spoon. "I shall explain soon my dear, but I assure you it will be vital" he answered.

All that was left to do was wait patiently, Meadow knew the mixture would need a few hours to boil before it would be complete, "So what should we start making next?" she asked. Before Meadow gave Clyde a chance to reply, her attention was snatched away by the lonely iron door located in the corner of the lab, "Hey that door!" she remarked. "You never told me what's behind it, you told me it was forbidden" uttered Meadow as she leapt from the wooden stool she sat upon and curiously inspected the iron door.

Meadow's proximity to the door alarmed Clyde, causing him to dash in front of her and block her advance, "Indeed I did, and it shall remain that way!" Clyde exclaimed. "Oh, come on, there's no need to be so defensive, I can't even get in there anyway since you've locked it tight, just tell me what's inside!" Meadow demanded with tenacious curiosity. Despite Meadow's relentless snooping, Clyde remained evasive and began ushering her out of the lab. "There is nothing in there that concerns you my prying pupil, now come! It is time for tea!" he firmly announced.

Impatiently, Clyde pushed Meadow out of the lab, continuing to ignore her barrage of questions. "Wait, I want to see what skeletons are in your closest, you're not doing anything creepy are you? I bet you've got a helpless princess locked up in there and your using her as a poor test subject for your experiments!" declared Meadow. A steaming pot of fresh tea awaited them in the kitchen, brewed recently by Styx. "Greetings Master Clyde and Miss Meadow, your morning tea is now ready!" hissed Styx, bowing upon seeing them both tussle in. "Thank you, Styx, that will be all for now!" Answered Clyde in a frustrated tone while firmly steering Meadow towards the large kitchen table and promptly shoving her into one of the wooden chairs.

After serving the pot of tea upon a polished silver tray, Styx obediently bowed his horny head, flapped his little leathery wings and fluttered out of the kitchen. "As you wish master, as always it's nice to see you two getting along" he replied in a sarcastic tone. Delight gleamed within Meadow's eyes as she reached for the handle upon the teapot, "Ah, morning tea! Can't beat it!" she merrily announced. Wearily, Clyde took a seat opposite her and vented a jaded gasp, "Truly, taking on an apprentice is no simple task, especially one as annoying as you!" he groaned.

After gently pouring herself a cup of steamy hot tea, Meadow raised her cup in the air towards Clyde. "Cheers to me, for being the best apprentice you could ask for!" she declared, a beaming grin of mischief spreading over her cheeks. "Lower your cup at once my maddening minion, for I reject your deceitful toast!" Clyde sternly replied after reaching for the teapot and tipping the hot, odorous liquid into his teacup. A bitter frown fell upon Meadow and she playfully stuck her tongue out at Clyde, "So which tea is this?" she asked, heartily inhaling the ravishing aroma that drifted from her cup.

A distinct spicy hint tingled the tip of Meadow's tongue as she took a humble sip. "Styx concocted this one, I asked him to make one with grinded dragontail mushroom and crimson fang thorns, a tea perfect for resisting frigid weather and common colds" replied Clyde. "Sounds nice, so what's on our agenda today?" she inquired. Unsurprisingly, a howling blizzard was bellowing outside as usual. "The clue is in the tea my dear, we must not let warmth elude us, for today we must traverse the snowy tundra surrounding the Frostveil Mountains" answered Clyde. An icy chill shuddered over Meadow's shoulders as she turned her gaze towards the kitchen window and looked upon the shrieking storm of white outside, "We're going outside? In that? What for?" she asked.

Clyde raised his steaming cup of tea to his lips for a moment and took a tame sip of his spicy brew. "Remember a couple of weeks ago when I said our stock of invisibility potions were depleted? Well, out there lies one of the ingredients required to create more" he explained. "Really? I don't remember that; do we really have no invisibility potions left?" replied Meadow as she wrapped her palms around her cup of boiling tea and felt the serene warmth caress her skin. Meanwhile, Clyde let his forehead fall into his palm, "You know, for someone who desires a memory erasing potion, your memory seems quite capable of erasing itself!" he uttered with sighed breath.

An irked frown appeared upon Meadow's face in retaliation to his comment. "To put it simple and short, we need a special ice crystal to create invisibility potions and they exist a short walk away in a snowy cave outside" Clyde explained. "And I assume that's why we need ice resistance potions? To endure the frigid winds beyond?" replied Meadow after taking an ample quaff of her tea now that it had cooled.

Surprisingly, Clyde shook his head and chuckled. "Alas no, we just need to wrap up to weather the glacial gales that relentlessly bombard these plains, no we need the ice resistance potions in case we encounter a fogfur" he answered. With a tilt of her head, Meadow gazed at Clyde quizzically, "And what in the world is fogfur?" she inquired. "Something I surely hope we do not encounter; they are giant beasts with razor sharp claws and fangs that run with great speed on all fours" answered Clyde. Using words to explain the ferocity of a fogfur proved a difficult task for Clyde, "To paint a clearer picture, imagine a giant woolly snow tiger crocodile hybrid if that's possible" he added.

If such a creature existed, then Meadow shuddered with dread upon receiving the image in her head. "I'm not surprised you've never heard of one, they are very elusive creatures, very few have laid eyes upon them and lived to tell the tale" uttered Clyde. "They have a most unique defensive ability, able to quickly shed their woolly fur at will and create a blinding field of mist, hence the reason why few have ever seen one" he remarked. Meadow was unable to decide whether she should be fascinated or frightened by them, "So ice resistance potions will give us the advantage against these creatures?" she asked in a trembled tone. "Only against their frost breath, another nasty little trait these monsters possess, one blast of their misty breath will freeze you solid, I'm being sincere when I say fogfurs are one of the deadliest monsters in all Resplendia" replied Clyde.

Hearing this, Meadow flung her arms in the air and collapsed against her chair, "Okay, that's it! I officially declare you insane!" she announced. Admittedly her reaction was justified, but Clyde simply chuckled it away. "Now, now, do not create fear and worry where none yet exists, we may not even encounter such a creature" he answered calmly. Although his positivity was admirable, it didn't spark much morale within Meadow, "Can't you just buy your ice crystals like a normal person?" she sighed. Meadow knew it wouldn't be that simple and she was proven right when Clyde shook his head. "Sorry to burst your hopeful little bubble, but merchants rarely sell them, they melt if contained for too long and if they are sold, they're always extremely expensive" he replied.

Oddly, Clyde chortled to himself and Meadow fired a prying gaze his way, curious at what could be so amusing. "Forgive me, I'm merely laughing at the irony of our situation" he uttered. "Normally, I keep an invisibility potion to one side, that way I can use it to sneak into the cave and collect the ice crystals I need without worry, that's how I keep making a constant supply of them" Clyde added. Meadow consumed the final drops of her tingly tea and made her delight obvious with a refreshing gasp. "If you always have one for an emergency then why have you run out? What's changed this time?" she asked. "You, I failed to include you in my deductions, it was you who consumed the last invisibility potion" answered Clyde taking an ample quaff from his cup and devouring his tea. Morning tea was finished, but it would take a few more hours before the ice resistance potions would be ready. "Right, let us head back into the lab my dear, there are still a few other potions we shall require, should fate curse us with the encounter of a fogfur" uttered Clyde.

For the last few hours, Meadow and Clyde had been diligently devising a few different potions, thankfully, they didn't take as long to create as the ice resistance one. "Did you remember to add three dashes of grinded wyvern claw?" asked Clyde as Meadow meticulously chopped the spicy nightfire nuts in front of her into tiny pieces with a knife.

Once she had chopped the vibrant orange nuts into small fragments, Meadow proceeded to carefully tip them into a nearby glass boiling flask. "Yes, I remembered, and I also made sure to distil the poison out of the scorpion tail" she replied. "Very good, the life detection potions are coming along nicely, I've nearly finished extracting the oil from the shadow-weave lilies, the raven beaks and rainbow moths have already been grinded and mixed" uttered Clyde. Once he had extracted the last drops of oil from the mysterious purple flowers by using an intricately designed filtration apparatus, Clyde took a step back and removed his goggles, "Now we wait again!" he declared.

Clouds of colorful smoke ascended from the pair of large flasks of simmering liquid as they boiled away above the burning candle holders. One flask created a vibrant plume of orange, while the other produced a hazy mist of violet. Meadow couldn't resist being enslaved by the captivating colors, the tranquil sound of liquid gently bubbling and the mysterious odors floating through the air. "I have to admit, I see now why you have such profound passion for alchemy, the intricate process and the beauty of what it creates, its bewitching to say the least!" gasped Meadow in delight. Proudly, Clyde folded his arms and gazed upon his creations with admiration, "Indeed, I'm glad to see the world of alchemy has begun to enthrall you as it did me" he replied. "Have you never really seen alchemy at work before?" Clyde asked while removing his leather gloves and allowing himself to rest his rear upon the chair at his desk. Gleefully, Meadow took a carefree stroll around Clyde's alchemy lab, inspecting the many other tools, devices and ingredients with deep fascination.

A whirlwind of wonder swept up Meadow and she felt powerless to resist it as she innocently waltzed around Clyde's lab. "I've never seen alchemy like yours, the village I grew up in had an alchemist by the name of Lucinda, but she only made tonics and remedies for various injuries and illnesses" uttered Meadow. Her fingers glided over the various alchemy tools and apparatus that were laid out on the workbench, feeling the sensation of their textures upon her tips. "Sadly, Lucinda was executed by the village when they discovered her basement, she was using ingredients that were forbidden by Resplendia's laws" added Meadow.

As she recalled the tragic tale, it suddenly dawned on Clyde that she hadn't shared many details of her village. "I still don't understand why she had to die, she used her alchemy to help people, but my village had always been stuck in archaic ways of thinking" Meadow uttered. It was impossible for Clyde to contain the simmering frustration he felt, hence he had to unleash it in the form of a heavy huff. "Let me guess, they were afraid such ingredients would taint their souls or some such nonsense? There are far too many outdated laws in Resplendia that many believe they must follow!" he puffed.

The foolishness of archaic minds never ceased to irk Clyde. "There's still a law that states it's illegal to feed a unicorn plomberries during a full moon and you'll be cursed with a fine of five-hundred gold for crying out loud!" huffed Clyde. Once again, Meadow glanced the secret door in the corner, the one leading to a secret room that Clyde kept tightly locked. "Well, when Lucinda was executed by the village, I think it caused Elijah to snap, after all, Lucinda was his sister" she answered.

Curiosity kept luring Meadow in with each passing second she gazed at the mysterious iron door, wondering what secrets Clyde was concealing. A frightful chill crawled along her neck when she considered if the secrets he hid were dark. "Let me guess, ravens' eye? Imps tongue? Goblins ear? Such ingredients seem ominous, but they are hardly perilous, only ingredients such as human flesh is truly forbidden" replied Clyde. Finally, Meadow managed to tear her attention away from the mysterious door and back to Clyde. "I know, my mind has never been as archaic as the people in my village, I personally saw no problem with it, Lucinda was making potions that helped people" she answered. Recalling that tragic day summoned a forlorn fog over Meadow, "Sadly, the people of my village didn't see it that way" she uttered. "They took the law into their own hands and killed Lucinda, believing that ingesting such ominous ingredients was as great a sin as cavorting with demons or something" Meadow added. Her words were swiftly joined by an irked eyeroll, "Such is the mentally of mediocre minds, they will always fear what they don't understand" answered Clyde. A sad chuckle suddenly crept out of Meadow, "I think that's what Elijah thought too" she whispered.

After waiting for around an hour, Clyde finally concluded that all the potions were ready. "Right, that should do it! Tis time for us to prepare my apprentice!" he declared while springing from his chair. Four empty vials of strengthened glass hung upon a wooden wall rack nearby. Clyde proceeded to carefully pour the flasks of freshly made potion into each of them, "Two for each of us my dear" he uttered. Meadow strapped on her alchemy harness and swiped the swirling vials of newly concocted potion from Clyde's outstretched hand, "So what do these ones do again?" she asked. "That one is life detection potion, it will allow you to see the residual life energy of any living thing even if it cannot be seen by the naked eye" replied Clyde as he pointed to the potion with a mysterious violet hue. The other vial of potion was like looking at a jar of lava, it glowed with a vibrant fiery hue of gold, "That one is called fire-breath potion, it shall be vital should we encounter a fogfur" remarked Clyde. Clyde and Meadow loaded up their harnesses with a variety of other potions, preparation was essential, "Alright, time to find us some ice crystals!" Meadow cheerfully declared.

Departing into that frozen tempest naturally required warm clothing, thankfully Clyde had more than enough to spare. "I admire your spirit my loyal lackey, but hold your britches for a moment longer, we must ensure we have all we need before traversing the bellowing blizzard beyond!" answered Clyde. "Here you are, I think this should fit well enough, but you'll need some gloves too!" he declared. A thick woolly coat was flung at Meadow, along with a fluffy warm hat, a long soft scarf and a pair of large cotton gloves.

Soon Meadow looked like a glorified clothes rack from all the garb buried upon her, but she quickly burst from her fluffy tomb. "You do realize I travelled here by myself? I already have warm clothing remember?" she uttered. Clyde remained silent and blank for a moment before answering her, "Oh, well why didn't you say so?" he casually replied. An arrow of frustration pierced Meadow mixed with a dose of fatigue and she had to muster an army of patience, lest her fiery nature result in her quarrelling with him. "Well? Let us proceed my daydreaming disciple, those ice crystals shan't gather themselves!" announced Clyde. Reluctantly, Meadow allowed her head to powerlessly droop as a symbol of surrender, "Ugh! I'm almost hoping I do get eaten by a fogfur" she sighed.

Layers of thick, furry attire enveloped Clyde and Meadow, causing them to feel a sweltering flush. Neither of them minded though, for they knew it wouldn't last as they approached the front doors of the house. "I assume no portals today master?" asked Styx who awaited in the portal room, in that same raspy voice, which continued to sound deceitful and malevolent. Imps were mostly devious and mischievous by nature, which is why it still felt so jarring to Meadow, to encounter one that was loyal and helpful. "Not today my winged friend, today is a day of respite and relaxation for you, and a day of freezing toil for us" answered Clyde as he adjusted the cozy handknitted scarf coiled around his neck. Playfully, Styx twirled his miniature magical trident and flashed his rows of sharp gleaming fangs into a smug grin. "As you wish master, I'm certainly not going to dispute your decision, maybe I'll have a cup of tea, do some reading and have a hot bath" he bragged. A frown as bitter as the icy gale outside appeared upon Meadow, "Well, won't that be lovely!?" she grumbled.

Words alone could not banish the toothy smugness Styx felt today, "Indeed it shall Miss Meadow, I'm looking forward to a day indulgence!" he boasted. "You've more than earned it Styx, keep in mind Meadow that when Styx creates one of those portals, it places a considerable strain on him both physically and mentally" added Clyde. Learning such a fact caused a lingering swathe of sympathy to shroud Meadow. "Truly? I had no idea, should we be traveling by portal then? I feel a little guilty now" she uttered. "Feel no guilt Miss Meadow, I create the portals for a good cause, tis tiring but the fatigue is easily remedied with a nice nap afterwards" answered Styx.

In all honesty, Meadow hadn't considered the intricacies of the mysterious portal magic that Styx wielded until now. She deduced by this point that the large circular pedestal made of mysterious marble acted as a sort of stage for Styx's portals. The magical runes inscribed upon the pedestal seemed to react and glow whenever a magical portal was being created, further evidence that it was a vital tool for the portals. Maybe the magical marble pedestal kept them stable, Meadow would only be guessing though, but she also noticed Styx channeled his magic using his trident.

In fact, as far as Meadow knew, all imps used their tridents to create the magical hexes they loved to afflict others with so much. Their tridents seemed like conductors and for Styx, the pedestal was the stage. "I don't understand though, is it not possible for Styx to just portal us to this ice cave? It might be tiring but at least it's a lot less dangerous" said Meadow. Her suggestion was promptly crushed by the way Clyde shook his head and refused to indulge the idea further. "Much too vague, his portals are based on geography and need an accurate destination to focus on, hence the huge map on the wall, I can't tell Styx to portal us to the nearest ice cave" he replied with slight satire.

There was little point delaying it any longer, Clyde stretched his arms and threw open the front doors of his house, confronting the blinding storm of white awaiting on the other side. "Stick close to me my apprentice! Hopefully, we shan't be long!" Clyde cried over the howling wind as it swiftly intruded the warm walls of the house. Speckles of snow began to gradually accumulate across the floor, which caused Clyde to urge Meadow out of the doors quicker. "Well, this looks delightful!" declared Meadow as she left the warm embrace of Clyde's house and felt her feet suddenly sink beneath the chilly sea of deep snow. Hesitantly, Clyde joined Meadow and felt his legs disappear into the depths of the snow when he began the voyage into the frosty whirls of wind. Meanwhile, the cozy walls of the candlelit house and the thought of creating new alchemy concoctions over constant cups of tea kept beckoning Clyde back.

Such cozy thoughts were banished however, when Styx slammed shut the front doors behind them, a task which proved difficult against the bellowing gale. "Well, let us depart my dear! Let us plunge into the heart of this storm and prove it futile against our impervious determination!" Clyde cheerfully chirped. Sadly, his attempt to bolster morale quickly vanished as soon as their feeble trudging began. Traversing the deep snow was like trying to wade through a murky swamp, made even more laborious by the relentless blasts of wind. Soon, they became like two tiny dots upon a fresh white canvas. The icy tundra of the Frostveil mountains swallowed Clyde and Meadow like a tidal wave crashing upon a wounded ship at sea.

Thankfully, the layers of thick clothing they wore kept the temperature tolerable. What irked Meadow most was the pace at which they travelled; it was maddening to say the least. More than a few times Meadow had taken a tumble, falling flat on her face and having to endure a mouthful of freezing snow. The screaming squalls of icy wind only served to confuse her senses further. At one point, Clyde lent her a helping hand from yet another fall, only to lose his own footing and topple over with her. This resulted in them rolling through the snow like a couple of infants still learning how to walk. It would've been hilarious for anyone who watched, Meadow just thanked her lucky stars that they were the only two crazy enough to be travelling out here.

After picking herself up from the eighth or ninth fall, Meadow used her scarf to wipe away the bitter snow stinging her rosy cheeks, "How much farther!?" she shouted over the shrieking tempest. "Remain stalwart my little lackey, I think I perceive our cave ripe for plundering over yonder! We must not falter now, not when we are so close to grasping the hilt of destiny!" yelled Clyde with gusto. His manner of speech was eccentric and quirky at the best of times, here it was yet another thorn in the side. "Do you ever take a day off!?" shouted Meadow as she trudged past him to see where he was pointing.

Beyond the blustering blizzard and frigid field of snow in front of them, Meadow was barely able to see the opening of an icy cave up ahead. "At least it will give us some shelter!" she yelled. Shelter from this howling tempest of ice sounded like a delight, so naturally Clyde and Meadow ploughed through the snow and hastily headed towards the lonely cave. Within its cold, rocky walls they were able to find some modicum of warmth, more so than outside. "Ah, behold! We have arrived at our journey's end my disciple!" echoed Clyde.

Unlike Clyde, Meadow was more than a little wary of speaking above a whisper, "Quiet! Didn't you say that fogfurs like to dwell within caves like these?" she asked in a low hush. This time Clyde had no choice but to bow to her wisdom, "Indeed I did, and your words echo truth, silence shall be our greatest ally" Clyde answered in a whisper. Softly they proceeded deeper into the cave's icy innards and it was rather spacious for a cave, which didn't bode well since it increased the likelihood of a fogfur lurking somewhere inside. The deeper they delved, the more ice started to appear, until it literally began to cover the walls and ceiling like a giant shimmering mirror.

Meadow found it utterly beautiful to tell the truth, removed her thick gloves and allowed her fingertips to glide and grace across the caves captivating, glacial surface which felt smooth and icy to the touch. Every footstep they took created a crunch upon the thin layer of snow that covered the ground. Luckily, there were no signs of any creature dwelling within the cave just yet, "Ah, up head!" uttered Clyde with hushed glee. Meadow had to quicken her steps to catch up with Clyde and avoid falling behind, "Perhaps a less rash approach?" she replied as she pursued him. Yet, what awaited further ahead was a truly magnificent sight to behold.

Shimmering clusters of beautiful ice crystals lined the ground, walls and ceiling of the cave, radiantly sparkling like a cavern of stars. Meadow emerged into the large clearing and gazed upon the array of twinkling crystals all around her with wonder. Being surrounded by such a secluded chamber of majestic, sapphire colored crystals was enough to even banish the chilly veil of air. "Amazing, guess it was worth coming here after all!" gasped Meadow. Clyde joined in and admired the marvelous scene around them, "Yes, it really is something!" he uttered. The lustrous beauty of the crystals was so beguiling that Clyde and Meadow briefly forgot their whole purpose for seeking out the cave. "Keep watch for anything ominous my apprentice" asked Clyde who revealed a small hammer and chisel from the large leather satchel strapped over him. Eagerly, he then pounced upon a nearby cluster of crystals with his hammer and chisel and got to work.

The captivating cluster of blue crystals radiantly reflected their gleam within Meadow's iris as they laid upon it. "I take it these are the crystals you need?" she asked, her voice bouncing between the reflective walls of the icy cavern and echoing deeper within. Clyde stuffed a large chunk of ice crystal into the satchel slung over his shoulder and proceeded to diligently chip away at the next one. "Yes, these crystals are one of the essential ingredients I need to concoct my precious potions of invisibility" he answered. So far everything was going smoothly, and Clyde's satchel started to look quite bulky, "Here, start filling your bag up" he uttered after gently tossing a chunk of crystal at Meadow. Meadow caught the shimmering piece of ice in her hand, caressed its mesmerizing cool surface and stuffed it into the empty satchel she carried.

As Clyde continued chipping away at the root of crystal clumps, Meadow kept her eyes sharp and vigilant, "Are we done now? We have enough, don't we?" she asked. "Patience my hasty helper, we should plunder as many precious crystals as possible, after all, we should not leave the jaws of victory without taking every tooth!" Clyde declared eccentrically. His quirky demeanor caused Meadow to grimace as she turned her attention away from him, but the chipping of his hammer and chisel began to irritate her.

Chip, chip, chip, the noise kept echoing along the icy cavern walls incessantly until Meadow had to rub her temples to keep a headache at bay. To shut the noise of relentless chipping out of her skull, Meadow's gaze wandered to the sparkling array of crystals embedded within the cave walls and ceiling once again. Truly, it was a delight to behold, one that lulled her defenses like a trio of singing sirens upon a lonely rock at sea. Hence, why Meadow didn't notice the ominous growling until it was too late. "Stop, stop!" she gasped while listening intently and watching the corridor leading to the cave entrance with wary, worried eyes. Clyde immediately ceased his chipping and listened closely, but he didn't have to listen long for the creature responsible for the dreaded growling soon stomped into view and flaunted its fangs.

Never had Meadow seen such a creature, it slowly crawled into the cave on all four of its furry white paws while wagging its thick, scaly tail. Copper colored scales covered the underside of its body, while the top half of its entire body was coated in dense shaggy fur as white as snow, "I'm guessing that's a fogfur!" gasped Meadow with apprehensive breath. Slowly, Clyde placed his hammer and chisel down and carefully rose to his feet, proceeding to gradually back away. "It must have come home to rest, gently start backing away!" he whispered intensely.

Fogfurs were much larger than Meadow expected and the one in front of them was huge, easily stretching over the height of fifteen feet. However, the white furred beast appeared even more imposing when it leaned back and stood upon its two hindlegs. Once it joined Clyde and Meadow in the large clearing of the cave, it glared at them with its snarling reptilian head. It was just as Clyde had described, like a giant furry tiger mated with an alligator and this was the result, "What now!?" uttered Meadow as she gazed upon the daunting beast. Using the razor-sharp claws upon one of its forelegs, the fogfur carelessly scratched its large scaly belly and rumbled the cave with a deep menacing growl. "Now my dear, we run!" cried Clyde as he desperately dashed deeper into the cave without another moment's hesitation. Meadow suddenly snapped free from the frozen fortress of fear that gripped her and frantically followed Clyde before the fogfur had chance to chase.

It gave them a lead of about three seconds, then they heard the frightful roar behind them and witnessed the sight of the fearsome fogfur suddenly pursuing them. Meadow uttered a spiteful curse under her breath, if only the creature hadn't entered the cave from the entrance, she and Clyde could've sneaked out. Alas, the fogfurs bulky body blocked the entrance from whence they came and delving deeper into the cave was now the only option. Meadow cursed their situation further when she realized the tunnels of the cave continued to be large enough for the fogfur to follow, "Keep running, don't look back!" yelled Clyde.

Mercilessly, the fogfur hunted them, its savage snapping jaws lined with sharp deadly fangs were eager to taste blood. It ran on all fours and was frighteningly fast for its size, the only stroke of fortune Meadow could find was the fact that the cave tunnels had many twists and turns. That was the only reason the fogfur hadn't already caught up with them and wasn't picking their bones clean. "Ahead, I think I see another way out!" declared Clyde. Meadow prayed Clyde was right, as she avoided the fogfur by following him around another tight, twisting corner of the cave, resulting in the fogfur slamming face first into the wall as it tried to savagely maul her.

A growl of anger bellowed from the fogfur as it shook its head from the impact and regained its fierce gaze upon Meadow and Clyde once more. It was a long dash, but an exit from this icy nightmare lay ahead, Clyde was correct, now all they had to do was survive long enough to reach it. Behind them, the fogfur grew ever closer, Meadow was certain she was going to be its lunch any moment now and dismay struck when she felt her feet slip from under her. The pathway leading to the cave exit was coated in a layer of slippery ice and all downhill too, effectively turning the tunnel into a chilly slide. Clyde was also powerless to maintain any trace of balance and clumsily toppled over the moment his feet touched the ice. "Whoa no!" were the words he chose to shout as he plummeted down the icy tunnel.

Both Meadow and Clyde slammed into each other as they slid along the ice at whizzing speed, problem was, the fogfur followed them. It too was rendered helpless when its paws touched the stretching layer of frost, losing its balance and feebly gliding along the slide of ice behind Meadow and Clyde at formidable speed. Being chased down a hill of ice by a giant fogfur at an alarming pace wasn't something Meadow ever imagined would happen to her. "This is crazy!" screamed Meadow as her momentum gradually kept increasing. Despite the imminent danger the fogfur posed, it was rather amusing when Meadow glanced back. She saw the large, furry creature flat on its belly, spinning in a circle behind her, with all four of its paws stretched out.

Eventually, the slippery ice slide came to an end and a face-full of snow greeted Meadow. For her, Clyde and the fogfur swiftly slid from out of the cave's cold tunnels and into the chilly mountain air again. It certainly wasn't a graceful halt, Meadow tumbled over and rolled clumsily into the field of deep snow, tasting the bitter frost upon her lips, before the momentum she had gathered finally ceased. Clyde landed nearby, his face buried beneath a blanket of frosty snow and it took a few seconds before he stirred again. "Well, that was fun!" groaned Clyde as the snow crumbled off his body when he pulled himself up. Meadow remained spread out like a dazed snow angel, watching the plumes of white frosty air that appeared from every breathless gasp. Yet, the sudden sound of deep roaring from behind, roused her and Clyde to action much sooner, "Next time please buy your ice crystals!" shouted Meadow.

From beneath the depths of the snow the fogfur arose, shaking the thick layer of snow from its body and stood upon its hindlegs, becoming a snarling tower of fluffy ferocity. A shivering aura of dread veiled the area as the fogfur glared at Meadow and Clyde and as they gazed back at the looming beast, time within this glacial domain froze. Besides the screeching bursts of freezing wind, all else became silent, it wasn't until the fogfur went back on all fours and began to menacingly prowl closer that Clyde shattered the silence. "Meadow, steel-skin potion now!" Clyde shouted as he reached for one of his vials of magical liquid strapped tightly within his harness.

Urgently, Meadow fumbled for the steel-skin potion in her harness but watching the fogfur ferociously charging towards her didn't aid her concentration. Luckily, she managed to pop the top off the vial and guzzle down the liquid in time. Shimmering steel started to coat Clyde and Meadow's skin, filling them with a sense of safety as the stampeding fogfur fiercely leapt through the howling blizzard and pounced upon Clyde. Globs of slimy drool dripped upon Clyde's face as the fogfurs snarling jaws loomed over him. Suddenly, the fogfur lunged forward and clamped its savage gnashing fangs upon Clyde's arm.

If it hadn't had been for the steel-skin potion, Clyde would've already been torn to shreds like a scarecrow in a hurricane. Clyde raised his arm to protect himself out of instinct and the fearsome fogfur grimaced as its fangs felt the taste of cold steel. Regardless, the fogfur remained latched onto his arm and started viciously gnawing on him, while Meadow hastily rushed through the deep snow to help. However, approaching the creature proved difficult, as Meadow received a brutal smack to the face from its thick thrashing tail which whipped around wildly.

Once again, the steel-skin potion verified its effectiveness as Meadow flew across the snowy field from the blow. Her body spun out of control as she sailed through the air, slamming face first into the snow. Clyde regained some control over the beast, but he knew the steel-skin potion wouldn't last much longer and had to act fast. "Unhand me foul creature!" yelled Clyde as he clenched his steely palm into a fist and began frantically punching the fogfur on the nose. After several smacks, the fogfur relented, released its deadly grip and performed an abrupt, leaping backflip to create distance from Clyde, landing on all four paws again.

This time the fogfur was much more wary as it watched Clyde regroup with Meadow who was pushing herself up from the snow. Generously, Clyde gave her a quick helping hand when he came stomping over, "It's fast for its size!" declared Meadow. "Yes, and wild too, we mustn't rush in against such reckless ferocity" uttered Clyde as he vigilantly watched the fogfur which was currently shaking its body and shedding its fur. The creature's unique ability soon became evident as strands of white fur floated into the air and evaporated into clouds of hazy mist. "It's creating a field of fog, drink your life-detection potion!" yelled Clyde over the screeching gale.

Soon a dense field of cloudy fog blanketed the area, but Meadow and Clyde grabbed the correct potions and gulped them down while they could still see their hands in front of their faces. Unfortunately, the steel-skin potion wore off, meaning their flesh had no protection against the beast's lethal fangs and claws. "Remain focused Meadow, concentrate and tell me if you see it, for the fogfur can see through its own mist clearly" uttered Clyde as he pressed his back against Meadow's.

Vigilance was now vital; Clyde and Meadow remained firmly back to back and watched the whirling field of fog that had shrouded them. Somewhere, deep in the depths of the chilly mist, Meadow could swear she heard fogfur snarling menacingly, or it could've been the sound of the roaring blizzard around them, it was hard to tell. Until, something suddenly caught Meadow's eye, a glowing hue within the fog, like a lighthouse during a stormy night. "I see something, something glowing, its coming right at me!" cried Meadow. "That's the fogfur!" shouted Clyde as he spun around and glimpsed upon the creatures glowing life energy, a feat made possible thanks to the life-detection potion.

In the next frantic breath, Clyde dived at Meadow and the two of them slammed face first into the soft snow and were successful in evading the fogfur as it pounced at them from the refuge of the mist. A fearsome roar erupted from the beast's lungs as it galloped back into its fortress of fog. "Keep your eyes open, that glow is the beast's life essence, it's the only way to see it in this blinding mist!" declared Clyde. Only a second after he uttered these words, Clyde spotted the same luminous glow of life in the distance and it was heading straight towards him at fierce speed. "Duck!" shouted Clyde as he grabbed Meadow's shoulders and pulled her down along with him, just in time to avoid the charging fogfur which stormed right over their heads.

Once again it retreated into the refuge of the mist after another failed pounce, but that didn't discourage the fearsome fogfur from trying a third time. "Quick, roll to the side!" yelled Meadow as she spotted the radiant glow of energy hurtling towards her again with great speed. Clyde obeyed her order and hastily rolled to the right, while Meadow performed a frantic roll to the left, evading the fogfurs savage claws as it pounced and dashed in-between them at the last second.

Finally, the fogfurs mist faded and despite the howling storm of snow relentlessly bombarding them, Clyde and Meadow could see much more clearly now. Amazingly, the fogfur had already started to grow back most of the fur it had shed to create the fog, further proving how unique this fearsome creature was. Alas, it suddenly stood tall upon its hind legs, raised its head to the sky and took a deep gulp of frosty mountain air, "Ice breath! It's using its ice breath!" shouted Clyde. Meadow knew what to do even before Clyde told her, and he watched with admiration as Meadow reached for one of the ice resistance potions they brewed.

Quickly, Meadow removed the vial of hardened glass from her harness. She yanked the cork out of the neck which made a distinct popping sound and she proceeded to guzzle it down like fresh plomberry juice. Clyde had already done the same thing and it was fortunate that the potion took effect almost immediately. Meadow could already feel a weird chill flowing through her body, a chill that felt cold but not icy. Particles of frost began to fall from Meadow and Clyde's skin, like they were sweating snowflakes and a thin veil of swirling mist surrounded their bodies. This all transpired within a couple of seconds, lucky since the fogfur opened its gaping jaw of gleaming fangs and unleashed a hissing blast of freezing misty breath that blew over Clyde and Meadow.

Even with the power of the ice resistance potion in her system, Meadow still shuddered as she felt the fogfurs frigid breath envelop her. "Be thankful your only shuddering, the icy breath of a fogfur would've normally turned you into an iceberg by now!" yelled Clyde. Meadow barely heard his shouting over the hissing blast of mist coming from the fogfurs maw and the bombarding blizzard as well, "Ugh! I still feel freezing!" she hollered back.

Despite having tremendous resistance to the cold, the icy mist still stung their eyes like the frosty bite of winter, forcing Meadow and Clyde to raise their arms and shield themselves. After several seconds, the current of frigid mist subsided and the fogfur had to rest its lungs, causing Clyde to spring into action. "Now Meadow, drink that vial of black potion we made!" he shouted. For the moment, the fogfurs icy breath ability had rendered it breathless and tired, but Meadow knew it would be mere seconds before it attacked again, "This one!?" she cried as she reached for the vial. She didn't even wait for Clyde to answer, instead Meadow ripped the cork from the neck of the glass vial and hastily ingested the admittedly icky looking black liquid.

As soon as she ingested the horrid liquid and it touched her tongue, Meadow immediately spat it out again for it was the most revolting thing she had ever tasted. Luckily, spitting it out was the point as Meadow unleashed a vile stream of black gloopy liquid from her mouth. It was like she was suddenly vomiting oil and it splattered all over the fogfur. Some of the sticky black liquid landed in the fogfurs eyes as well, causing it to stumble around, shake its head and paw at its face in a confused panic. "Ugh! What was the point in that again?" asked Meadow with disgust still lingering upon her tongue. "It's immensely flammable" answered Clyde as he gulped down his vial of glowing fire-breath potion and proceeded to spew a searing blast of flames from his throat a couple of seconds later.

Fire engulfed the fogfur and the sticky black liquid that remained stuck within its snowy fur was set ablaze, causing the frosty beast to become a howling inferno. It roared with tremendous agony and chaos ensued as the fogfur wildly lashed its tail, swiped its claws and lunged its body across the snow in a frightened attempt to extinguish the flames. It was to no avail, the sticky, shadowy liquid from the black potion remained stuck and the flames from the fire-breath potion continued to spread like wildfire.

Clyde and Meadow stayed far away from the fogfur as it violently thrashed around. In its confused and frightened state, it also failed to notice the edge of the snowy cliff it had rolled itself towards, until it toppled right over the side. A final echoing howl was the last Clyde and Meadow heard from the burning beast as it plunged over the snowy cliff and into the icy seawater and jagged rocks below.

A sigh of weary relief finally drifted from Meadow's lips, along with the repulsive aftertaste of that black oily potion she drank. "Okay, I think that's enough excitement for one day!" she groaned. At the same time, Clyde reached for a vial of clear liquid attached to his waist belt, popped the cork off and swiftly guzzled it down, "Which potion is that?" asked Meadow. "It's called water!" gasped Clyde as he swallowed the entire vial and proceeded to stick his tongue out so he could catch droplets of snow upon the tip. "Fire-breath potion, it leaves a pretty spicy kick!" he declared once the lingering taste of flames upon his tongue had finally diminished. Once again, they were alone with the wailing tempest, but the day's events caused Meadow to utter a weary gasp, sit down and flop backwards onto the soft bed of snow, "Ughhhh!" she groaned.

Chalice of Renewal
Chapter 6
Elf problems

It had been a few days since the battle in the blizzard against the beast with ice breath and things had been relatively placid. Currently, Meadow was hunched over a bubbling flask of azure colored liquid in the alchemy lab and reached for a small glass jar containing a sickly green liquid. "So how much troll urine do I need to add again?" she asked. "Add around three tablespoons" answered Clyde who currently had his head buried in his desk in the middle of the room. A repulsive stench drifted from the jar of troll urine as soon as Meadow twisted the lid off. "Ew! I don't even want to know how you get this stuff! Do you actually drink it?" she asked with a grimace. "Heavens no girl, it isn't meant for potions! Believe it or not, troll urine is a vital ingredient for concocting lotions for younger looking skin, I have clients who request it and no, you really don't want to know how I get it" answered Clyde.

Troll urine for younger looking skin, the irony of putting something so vile on your skin to make it look younger and healthier made Meadow chuckle. "These clients of yours, I'm assuming they don't know?" she asked. Clyde raised his head and a sly grin spread across his face. "Oh, if they knew, I certainly wouldn't get delivery requests sent to me anymore, the judgment of the uneducated is rivalled only by their ignorance" he replied.

After scooping a wooden spoon into the glass jar of troll urine, Meadow tipped three spoonsful into the boiling flask of blue liquid. Then she promptly screwed the lid back on the jar, sealing away the noxious odor. "So, what's grabbed your attention so intently? You've barely even left your desk all morning" asked Meadow as she came wandering over to Clyde like a curious cat. Upon seeing her approach, Clyde quickly leaned his body upon the pile of tattered parchment spread messily across his desk, attempting to conceal his work, "Nothing, nothing!" he declared.

Yet, Meadow managed to catch a glimpse of something when she leaned over his shoulder and took a closer gaze, "The Chalice of Renewal? What's that?" she asked. "Nothing that concerns you, it's just very important work and quite frankly I've been falling behind with it, what with all the irksome distractions I've been having!" Clyde answered in a flustered tone. A familiar miffed scowl appeared upon Meadow's face, accompanied by crossed arms. "Irksome distractions? I really hope you're not including me in that!" she growled. A series of heavy abrupt knocks at the front door saved Clyde from hammering another nail into his coffin.

Styx kindly fluttered into the room to answer the door, "I shall get it master" he hissed. A screeching gust of frosty wind rushed through the halls of the house the moment Styx pulled the front door ajar, revealing the visitor on the other side. "Ah greetings Hector, welcome to our humble abode!" Styx declared, before being flung back by the icy gale. Hector the harpy stumbled in from the blustering blizzard outside and summoned all his strength to push the door shut behind him, which was quite the tiring task against the onslaught of wind.

Fortunately, Meadow jogged over to assist him, slamming the door shut and silencing the howling tempest again. "Ah, thanks Meadow! Delightful to see you again!" Hector breathlessly gasped. "Nice to see you too Hector, what brings you here?" asked Meadow as she watched him remove his fluffy blue scarf, snow sprinkled goggles and bask in the warmth of the house. After shaking the mountain of snow from his body and feathery white wings, Hector opened the gigantic delivery sack that hung around his shoulder, reached his talons into its depths and began rummaging around. "Yes Swiftwing, enlighten us as to why you have traversed across these frozen peaks and plains of snow to grace my palace of potions with your feathery presence at once!" declared Clyde. Naturally, Clyde's manner of dramatic speech caused Hector to wearily slouch, "How many times do I have to tell you Clyde? My name is not Swiftwing" he sighed.

From the leathery depths of his delivery bag, Hector revealed two letters addressed to Clyde and held them out for him to take, "Two new letters requesting your aid, I have to say I'm surprised how many you've been getting lately" noted Hector. Clyde felt jaded as he swiped the letters from Hectors outstretched talons. "See, my apprentice? Distractions abound!" Clyde proclaimed, marching into the kitchen with a slight huff. His dramatic demeanor caused Meadow to produce an elusive smile, "Well since you're here Hector, would you care to wet your beak with a cup of tea?" she asked. "I wish I could Meadow, but I'm afraid I still have far too many deliveries to make" answered Hector as he coiled his warm fluffy scarf around his neck. Just as Hector was about to brave the blustering squall of freezing wind again, he turned his head towards Meadow. "By the way, how's it going so far? Being his apprentice?" he asked.

At first this question froze Meadow like the breath of a fogfur as she was unsure how to answer. "Well.... I guess it's going okay, I'm learning a lot, I feel fascinated by alchemy and its rather fun, although Clyde can be a little quirky sometimes" she replied. Something resembling a smile appeared upon Hectors beak and he gently patted one of his eagle-like talons against Meadow's shoulder. "That's just part of his charm, as much as I can't believe it, Clyde is a genius of alchemy despite being an oddball" uttered Hector in a hush. "Meadow, my steadfast servant! Assemble in the kitchen at once! There is a grave matter that calls our alchemy to action!" Clyde called from the kitchen.

Cheery chuckles drifted from Meadow and Hector as they looked at each other and playfully shrugged, "Well I should get going, a harpy's work is never done!" declared Hector. "Farewell and fly well Swiftwing, may your spirit remain gallant against the frosty ravages of the aloof mountains beyond!" Clyde suddenly announced upon popping his head out of the kitchen. The only response Hector could muster was rolling his eyes and shaking his head, "Take care out there Hector" said Meadow as she helped him with the front door. As usual, the house was instantly engulfed in a shrieking bombardment of icy air and snow, "Until next time!" Hector cried as he gave a wave, flapped his white wings and flew away.

Today the merciless gale sweeping through the frosty mountains seemed more potent than usual and it took a hefty amount of shoving from Meadow and Styx to shut the front door again. Once it was finally closed however, Meadow shook off a thin layer of snow that had gathered upon her hair and proceeded into the kitchen with a chilly shudder. "So, where are we going this time?" she called. Clyde was already sitting at the table holding a cup of freshly poured tea and lazily leaned against the back of his wooden chair while contemplating the letter. "It would seem the elves of Crestwood desire my aid" he replied. Crestwood was the capital city of the elves, but Meadow only heard of it through rumored mutterings and whispers, she'd never laid eyes on it before. "I've always wanted to see Crestwood! It's supposed to have houses built right into the trees!" Meadow proclaimed while pouring herself a cup of tea from the steaming pot in the center of the table.

Clyde took a timid sip of his hot tea and gave a humble nod, "Indeed, Crestwood is a city built by the elves hundreds of years ago when they first arrived in Resplendia" he answered. "Crestwood is the largest forest in Resplendia and rather than separating themselves from nature, the elves live comfortably amongst it" Clyde added. As the plume of delicate swirling steam from Meadow's teacup floated up, Meadow hypnotically gazed down at it, "What's todays tea?" she asked. "This morning's tea is made using a combination of sea thorn, elf blossom and wisewind herb, everything to calm one's senses and keep one as focused as a freshly fired arrow!" answered Clyde.

Taking a gentle sip, Meadow discovered this tea had a distinct sharp taste to it. Like a sudden burst of sunlight had erupted within her mouth and faded within the next fleeting second, "Mmmm......tastes so unique!" she remarked. "So, we're going to Crestwood to help the elves, what is it they need aid with?" asked Meadow as she repositioned herself behind Clyde to acquire a better glance at the letter. It was easy for Meadow to perceive the gloomy clouds of troubled thoughts already brewing within Clyde's mind. "It seems a capamandra has been plaguing the elves and has killed several of them already" he answered.

Although Meadow was reluctant to ask, she knew it was better to find out, "Great, what the heck is a capamandra?" she inquired while caressing the warm teacup in her hands. Clyde wet his whistle with a swift swig of tea while ruminating upon the words within the letter. "Basically, a giant, carnivorous plant-like monster that captures prey with its cunning vines and devours them with it is sharp fangs" answered Clyde. A familiar aura of chilly dread enveloped Meadow like an eerie mist as she pictured the monster in her mind, "Sounds pleasant!" she uttered in a perturbed tone. "Indeed, capamandra are known for ensnaring and devouring prey as large as adult orcs and they have a nasty poison too, but what's really strange is Crestwood isn't their natural habitat" added Clyde.

After shaking off her cloak of shuddering fright, Meadow leaned forward and inspected the letter closer, "Then why or how did it get there?" she asked. "I have no idea, but it can't remain there" Clyde answered after placing the letter back upon the kitchen table and taking a hearty quaff of tea. Dealing with a poisonous plant monster sounded like a perilous endeavor, but Meadow immediately thought of an easy solution. "Why not just use fire? It is a plant, right? Fire seems like the most effective method" she said.

Upon uttering these words Clyde's face shifted to a shade of chalky white, his expression contorted and completely aghast. "Good heavens no! No, no, no! Fire is forbidden in Crestwood!" he proclaimed. "Crestwood is home to the centaurs and treants too, its not just elves that reside within that sprawling forest and they have formed a binding pact that forbids using fire other than for cooking and warmth" Clyde added. So much for that idea, Meadow had a sinking feeling it would've been too easy to just burn the monster out. "So, how is your alchemy going to get you out of this one?" she asked with slight ridicule. Clyde quickly spun his head and gave Meadow a haughty glare, arising from the kitchen table and pompously parading out of the room. "For your information I already have a plan!" he proclaimed.

After consuming the last little bit of tea in her cup, Meadow gave a refreshing gasp and pursued Clyde, "Guess it's time to prepare again" she uttered. By this point Meadow already knew the drill, she shadowed behind Clyde as he marched towards the alchemy lab. "Styx, we're going to Crestwood so prepare us a portal!" he ordered as he passed through the lobby. "As you wish master!" answered Styx with a humble bow and a dab of hearty gusto, flaunting his unwavering loyalty.

Captivation consumed Meadow the moment she entered the alchemy lab again, it was a feeling that happened every time now. Like she had been whisked away like a leaf on the wind to a world of wonder. Witnessing the whimsical world of alchemy provoked a deep-rooted passion with Meadow that until now had always lain dormant. Seeing the colorful ingredients, the quirky tools and the various intricacies of the art awakened her passion even more. Each time she entered the alchemy lab it had a new odor, some were delightful, others were dreadful. This time the lab had a distinct sweet but fiery aroma to it like burning strawberries. "So, what card is the legendary alchemist Clyde hiding up his sleeve this time?" asked Meadow as she waltzed down the few wooden steps leading into the lab, her fingers gliding across the brass banister.

As usual, Clyde outfitted his alchemy harness, filling every single pocket, pouch and holster with whichever potions he believed would be vital to the new task he received. "We can't use fire, but I have something almost as effective!" he declared. Meadow approached him and observed his harness, visually noting which potions he was taking from his plentiful stock and mirrored his loadout. For now, she lacked the experience or wisdom to customize her harness. But steel-skin and enhanced-strength potion were two she had become remarkably familiar with. For an adventuring alchemist they were like bread and butter and this new assignment they were about to embark upon was no exception. "Behold, my universal plant killer!" Clyde declared after using a personal key to unlock the magically enchanted cabinet in the corner of the lab which contained every potion Clyde had ever made.

The entire cabinet was a fabulous cascade of colorful vials. Clyde had his own stock of regular potions of course, but the cabinet was like a collector's display case. In his hand Clyde held a vial of sickly, snot green liquid that had a somewhat sticky form. Meadow's gaze ignored it, instead her eyes fixated on the translucent vial of memory erasing potion in the cabinet. So close yet so far, Clyde told her once that the cabinet itself is enchanted with powerful magic which rendered it indestructible and impervious to tampering. Not to mention the lock was crafted by a master locksmith, meaning it was near impossible to pick. Whether there was any truth to these statements was not for Meadow to know, but Clyde had always been a man of his word, he had always delivered on every declaration he declared. Using the key was seemingly the only way to open the cabinet, not that Meadow would ever stoop to common thievery to obtain what she wanted, she enjoyed entertaining the thought though.

Meadow's enthralled gaze upon the memory erasing potion was quickly shattered like a falling mirror by an abrupt eruption of force that ferociously resonated through the air. It caused a slight tremor but no doubt it was the sound of Styx's magic signaling that the portal was ready for use. Clyde still dangled the vial of emerald colored potion in front of Meadow's face, gently swaying it from side to side waiting her to react. "Hello? Are you still home in there? What has embedded its talons into your attention and ensnared it so?" asked Clyde quizzically.

Hastily, Meadow shuddered away her transient daydream of stealing the memory erasing potion and masqueraded an aura of normality. "Oh, nothing, nothing, just didn't get enough sleep I think, so what does this plant killer of yours do?" she asked. Clyde's narrowed; dubious expression immediately made Meadow regret asking such a foolish question. "Well, in case the name doesn't give it away, it kills plants" answered Clyde with tremendous sarcasm. Maybe meadow earned that little dose of sarcasm, but she still scowled at Clyde anyway, "Yes, I gathered that part, but I'm sure there's more to it" she uttered. Clyde securely slotted the poison in his harness and nodded, "It shall kill the monster in seconds, I have dealt capamandra before, hence why I created such a vile poison, problem is it must be ingested" he explained.

Swishing tides of trepidation crashed upon Meadow when she contemplated Clyde's plan. "So, we have to pour that poison down the creatures throat? We have to get close to a dangerous plant monster that eats people?" she asked. "Precisely my astute minion, once the perilous plant has consumed my potent poison, it shall wither and melt away faster than a snowman in the Burning Plains!" Clyde dramatically decreed.

Just like that, Clyde swiftly closed the cabinet containing his entire collection of concoctions, ensured it was locked securely and marched out of the room with a brisk pace. Meadow hadn't even a chance to utter a single word further, thankfully the prospect of witnessing exotic new places such as Crestwood rallied her motivation. She departed the alchemy lab and followed the deep humming sound of magical energy. It resonated from the mystical portal Styx had created upon the large, circular pedestal made of marble in the middle of the room. "Portal ready for your departure master, please ensure you have all your belongings and no eating or drinking during the journey!" declared Styx in a playful tone.

Once again Clyde stood at the very mouth of the floating portal and gazed into its infinite mystical swirling depths. Like he was a pioneer beholding a brand-new horizon of vast potential, "Very good Styx, into the unknown we go again" he uttered. Meadow understood the mood he was setting, she admired his dedication to the dramatic, which is why she hated running it, "Except it's not the unknown, we know where we're going" she answered. A grumpy scowl smeared Clyde's face as he twisted his head to Meadow and was on the verge of speaking. Yet, Clyde held his silence, likely knowing arguing with Meadow was fruitless and entered the glowing portal instead, "Travel safe!" hissed Styx. Meadow returned Styx's words with a kind bow and approached the levitating magical doorway of myriad swirling colors. "I'll bring you back something nice this time!" echoed her voice as she plunged into the vast vortex. Although she had travelled by portal more than a few times now, the view within the mysterious dimension still mesmerized Meadow to her core.

The best way she could describe it was like floating through a tunnel of cascading colors and shooting stars. At a speed that wasn't so slow that it became tedious and not so fast that everything blurred together, becoming nauseating. No, the speed at which her and Clyde traversed this majestic realm of vibrant color and shimmering light was perfect. Meadow wished it lasted a little longer as it was always over after a few seconds. All good things come to an end, and so did this as Meadow spotted the luminous rays of radiant light at the end of the dimension quickly approach, which always indicated the end of the journey. Resplendent light embraced Meadow, yet it was neither harsh nor blinding and was over faster than she could blink. Sure enough, she emerged out the other side of the portal in a new location with Clyde waiting to greet her.

Naturally, the magical portal vanished into thin air leaving no trace that it ever existed and this time it had whisked Meadow and Clyde to a gigantic, sprawling forest. It was like a labyrinth of trees and they stretched towards the sky, higher than the towers of most castles, "Hopefully Styx hasn't dropped us too far from Crestwood" uttered Clyde. "Yes, one would hope" replied Meadow as she surveyed her surroundings and listened to the plethora of pleasant chirps echoing through the air. That was until her heart froze with fright and she unleashed an alarmed gasp when a sharp arrow flew right in front of her face at whizzing speed and pierced into a thick tree beside her.

The sudden arrow surprised Clyde too and he quickly whirled his head towards its origin point to witness a group of elven hunters standing atop a stony ledge looking down upon them. "That was merely a warning shot!" barked the one leading them. There were five of them altogether, but the one leading them was the only one not pointing his bow. Instead, he haughtily stood with one hand upon his hip, examining Clyde and Meadow like they were insects. The other four elves kept their bows vigilantly pointed at Meadow and Clyde with arrows at the ready. "I demand you explain this rude interaction at once! My name is Clyde Alrime and I'm the alchemist Crestwood requested for aid!" barked Clyde. Upon hearing Clyde explain himself, the leader of the elven hunting party relaxed his glare and gestured to the other elves to lower their bows. "So, you're the alchemist?" uttered the elven leader.

With a gentle leap, the elven leader hopped down from his lofty vantage point upon the rock and landed firmly onto the forest floor to meet Clyde on his level. "I heard we were seeking aid from an outsider, but I'll be honest, I'm doubtful an alchemist could be of any use to us, you're a liability at best" declared the elven leader in a haughty tone. His attitude infuriated Meadow and she couldn't repel her tongue any longer. "Excuse me? First you shoot at us and then you mock our offer to aid you? Didn't your mother teach you the proper way to welcome guests!?" she snapped.

Meadow was already finding it taxing to stomach these elves, she disliked their arrogant stance. How they stood with perfect posture and their noses turned up, the fact that all the elves were over six feet tall made it worse. All the rumors Meadow had heard about the elves were becoming true, they all had pristine snowy skin, slender builds and cheekbones that were sharper than a pair of assassin's daggers. For the moment, only their arrogance matched their beauty as they continued to study Clyde and Meadow with unflinching expressions of blank superiority.

Their eyes were the next unique feature that Meadow noticed, their eyes were sharp, focused and contained colors that were practically impossible for any human to possess. The leader of the elven hunting party was a perfect example, for his eyes gleamed with a radiant hue of solid gold which matched his flowing honey colored hair. "I refuse to apologize for being cautious girl, this is our territory and we shall fire our arrows at whatever we want and insult whatever we like" uttered the elven leader. Meadow grew ever more impatient with the elves pompous attitude, luckily traveling with Clyde had made her slightly more tolerant. "My name is Silvas, I'm one of Crestwood's master hunters, we were hunting nearby when we heard a sudden boom, we came to investigate and spotted the two of you" Silvas explained with cocky flick of his hair. There was little doubt it was the portal they heard as it materialized into existence. "And that gave you cause to fire an arrow at us?" asked Clyde, an irked tone still lingering in his voice.

Silvas shouldered his bow and casually placed one hand upon his hip, "We thought you may have been connected to that stranger in that black mask" he answered. Hearing this caused Clyde and Meadow's eyebrows to suddenly shoot up in surprise. "Stranger in the black mask?" replied Meadow, trading a wary glance with Clyde. "Yes, I don't know who this black masked stranger is, but he must've brought the capamandra here, the attacks started soon after he appeared, but he was also the one who recommend your help to us" answered Silvas.

Once again Clyde and Meadow wished to scratch their heads in confusion, for they didn't know which was the bigger mystery. The identity of this masked stranger or why he was causing problems only to provide Clyde as the solution. Regardless, Clyde shrugged it off and treated it as normal for the sake of looking professional. "Very well, me and my apprentice shall dispatch the capamandra that hinders your hunting with all haste!" he declared. "But I shall need to meet with your leader Fivilon Relus, for it was he who wrote the letter and requested my aid did he not?" added Clyde. Silvas regarded Clyde with guarded suspicion, but soon gave an affirmative nod. "High elf Relus is our current leader yes, and if you must meet with him follow us, we shall guide you to Crestwood" he answered.

Styx managed to create a portal close to Crestwood as the trek through the dense forest was short but sweet. Vibrant flowers spread like wildfire across the forest while marvelous mushrooms of myriad colors adorned the hulking trees. "This place is so beautiful, like something out of a dream!" uttered Meadow with delight. Further ahead was an imposing wooden gate of astoundingly elegant design. Intricate swirling patterns were carved into the wood and the gate was no doubt crafted using some of the surrounding trees. Connected to the gate was an equally imposing wall made of exquisitely crafted oak that stretched and circled all around Crestwood. Two elven guards protected the gates with sharp spears and unflinching vigilance but stood aside once they saw Silvas approach. "Welcome back master Silvas!" one of them declared as they slowly pushed the gate doors open.

A sudden cyclone of amazement swept up Meadow once her eyes saw what lay upon the other side of the great wooden gates, "Amazing!" she gasped. "Welcome to Alfr Hemos which means Elf Haven in our tongue, of course you know it as Crestwood" uttered Silvas as he marched passed the guards and through the gate with his hunting party in tow. Meadow hadn't the faintest clue what to be astonished by first. Whether it was the colossal wooden water wheel near the center, constantly spinning beneath a rushing waterfall that led into a sparkling giant river. Or the towering trees which were dotted with wooden walkways and huts carved into them. Faint flickers of candlelight shimmered from inside some of the huts and Meadow could see many elves in the distance casually going about their day.

Rope swings and ziplines stretched across the city from one tree to another. Whenever Meadow looked up, she was fascinated to see elves use them to quickly traverse between the trees like graceful chimps. Perhaps the most magnificent sight to behold, was the towering oak statue of an elf, crafted with the pose of him holding a long wooden staff in one hand and his other arm stretched out with a wooden eagle perched upon it. "Who is that a statue of?" asked Meadow as she peered upon it while following Silvas's hunting party. Silvas took a quick glance at the statue and smiled admirably. "High elf Myrus Elgard, he was the first high elf to come to Resplendia and settle my people here" he answered.

Nature had become a vital part of elven life here in Crestwood and they lived among it seamlessly, utilized it for all it was worth, and no part of nature was squandered. This became particularly evident to Meadow as she passed through the marketplace and strolled by the wooden stalls where elven merchants peddled their wares. Various mushrooms were on sale by one merchant, flowers for all occasions by another. Some merchants sold the freshest fruit and veg Meadow had ever seen, while another sold delicious freshly caught fish.

Suddenly, Clyde stopped in his tracks for a moment and his attention was ensnared by a nearby elven merchant selling exquisitely crafted wooden trinkets. "Hold a moment, I wish to make a purchase!" declared Clyde. "This isn't the time, Lord Relus is waiting human!" Silvas impatiently growled, ceasing his focused march. Clyde revealed a handful of glimmering coins and offered them to the elegant, female elf merchant who smiled happily. "Oh, hush up Silvas! There's never a bad time to sell to a customer!" she answered. Silvas folded his arms and began tapping his foot irritably, releasing a low, muted groan, but the elven merchant grateful accepted Clyde's coin and passed him something in return.

Once their exchange had concluded, Clyde gave a humble bow to the beautiful elven merchant with flowing chestnut hair who also bowed in return. Clyde turned to Meadow and held out his purchase to her, "Here you are my apprentice, something to remember the journey by, it's said to make those with a troubled past feel lighter and luckier" he uttered. A delightful flutter flowed inside Meadow's heart as she gazed at the wooden pendant dangling from the end of his finger. "Clyde, this is lovely! Thank you!" she managed to finally utter. The pendant was made of repeatedly polished oak giving it a mirror sheen and intricate elven symbols were carved into it and swirled together, forming an elegant pattern.

Meadow promptly raised the pendant over her head and allowed the soft, dark red dyed rope entwined through the pendant to fall upon her shoulders. The pendant comfortably dangled around her neck, "That was so thoughtful Clyde, I love it!" Meadow declared after giving him a tight hug. Meanwhile, Silvas sternly glared at them both, "Are you finished? Can we meet High-elf Relus now? Or did you come to Crestwood just for the shopping!?" he growled. With a weary sigh Clyde nodded, "Yes, yes, please lead on, I guess we shouldn't keep the haughty highness waiting" he answered.

Silvas scowled, turned his back and escorted them towards a large wooden lift, elegantly crafted and engraved with a plethora of elven symbols. "This lift takes us to the top of the great oak, the largest tree in Crestwood, High-elf Relus awaits there" uttered Silvas as he stepped onto the platform. Clyde and Meadow joined him, while Silvas nodded his head and gestured for his posse of fellow hunters to cease following and disband. "I have to ask, you been to Crestwood before?" Silvas inquired while activating the lift. Intricate wooden cogs constructed around a fascinating pulley system is what made the lift move, triggered when Silvas pulled the large wooden lever towards himself. "I have actually, but it was over a year ago at least" answered Clyde. "And what dire circumstance warranted your aid?" asked Silvas as he ascended upon the lift, gazing upon the city of his people as its splendor laid bare. Clyde folded his arms and watched the city pull away beneath his feet, "I never met your leader last time, I merely came for ingredients" he replied.

Whilst they chatted, Meadow watched the forest city of Crestwood fall further apart from beneath her feet as she leaned over the wooden lift. The knowledge that places such as this existed was enough reason to rejoice, for Meadow yearned to witness the exotic variety of life and how it lived. The city was crafted into nature itself and it was simultaneous sonata of serenity and bustle. A deep sense of peace lulled Meadow into a hypnotic daydream as she watched elves in the distance swing and zipline across the lush city of trees and wood. However, her captivation was abruptly broken by a sudden jolt, which came from the elegantly crafted oak lift upon reaching its destination. "We have now arrived at the peak of the great oak, the home of High-elf Relus, so pay him respect!" Silvas sternly barked.

Silvas took lead and accompanied Clyde and Meadow further on. Crossing the circular wooden platform built into the side of the gigantic great oak tree and towards a gaping hallway literally carved into the great oak itself. As Meadow followed behind Silvas, her eyes enlarged in disbelief, for she couldn't believe she was entering the colossal innards of a giant tree, "Impressive tree house!" she gasped. For now, Silvas ignored the subtle sarcasm in her tone and led them deep into the heart of the tree, along its oaken halls which were brightly lit by hanging torches.

Elven guards clad in light leather armor and armed with sharp spears and oaken shields lined the walls of the grand hallway. Watching and guarding with unyielding vigilance and loyalty. "High-elf Relus, the human alchemist known as Clyde Alrime and his apprentice request an audience with you!" Silvas declared. Dropping to one knee and bowing his head to an opulently crafted oak throne further ahead in the hall. Sitting upon the majestic throne of oak was High-elf Fivilon Relus who silently watched them approach, his demeanor lofty and dignified.

Despite being an outsider, Clyde still had to submit to etiquette and bowed his head upon drawing closer, glancing at Meadow and gesturing for her to do the same. Of course, Meadow rolled her eyes first and tediously sighed, reluctantly bowing her head too. "High-elf Relus, I am Clyde Alrime and I'm here to respond to your request for aid!" announced Clyde. His words emptily echoed through the soundless halls of the great oak, for High-elf Relus continued to silently inspect them, his stern lofty gaze piercing the very air. "You came highly recommended to me alchemist, the stranger in the black mask was very insistent that I hire you for this job" High-elf Relus eventually uttered.

On one hand, Clyde appreciated the increased business he was receiving thanks to the running mouth of this masked stranger. On the other hand, the mystery of this stranger and his motives frustrated Clyde, especially when Clyde remembered the masked stranger was the culprit. "I assure you Lord Relus, my apprentice and I are worth every piece of gold, we shall purge any plight your suffering from, dutifully and diligently!" boast Clyde. Slowly, Relus arose from his exquisitely carved throne of oak and strolled down the few steps leading up to it. "Thank you, for this dilemma is serious; a dozen of our finest elven hunters have already been killed!" he uttered gravely.

Clearly elven leaders made it a point of how noble and dignified they were. Meadow noted this by the long silk robe Relus wore, dyed an elegant forest green color and decorated with intricate swirls of gold along the chest and sleeves. Jewelry adorned Relus in almost every place where Meadow could see his pale snowy skin. Thick gold bangles embedded with sparkling gemstones dangled around both his wrists. Each of his fingers wore a gleaming gold ring lined with silver engravings. A delicately crafted amulet of oak similar to Meadow's also draped his neck, but his possessed a gleaming purple gemstone in the center. To further flaunt his exalted position, Relus wore a polished oak crown atop his head, a crown lined with faint golden trimmings, a crown crafted with considerable care.

The gleaming array of gold and glittering gemstones swathing Relus's body matched his golden hair that had a shine rivalling the sun. Meadow noted how long his hair was, for it nearly touched the floor and appeared like a waterfall of gold. Despite being so long, it still appeared elegantly trimmed and didn't cover a single part of his pristine youthful skin of purest white. His appearance was immaculate and elegant beyond words, made even more striking by his eyes. It seemed unfathomable to imagine any jewel or gemstone more beautiful than the elven eyes of Lord Relus, for his eyes shone a radiant golden-green and were as imposing as they were alluring.

Elegance, grace, beauty, formality, the elves held all these traits in high regard. Yet, combined them with being at one with nature while also maintaining a disciplined warrior code, Meadow couldn't decide whether to admire them or be envious of them. "The capamandra creature that has encroached upon the forest seems to heal very quickly, so I'm reluctant to send any more of my hunters after it" explained High-elf Relus. Clyde already knew sending more hunters after the capamandra would be an unwise decision. Since it wasn't native to Crestwood it wasn't a surprise that the elves weren't trained in how to hunt and slay it. "The few scouts that have survived tell me the capamandra blends into the forest and uses its vines to pull its prey in without warning" added High-elf Relus. It was clear the situation irked Relus by the way he released an elusive frustrated snort. "The creature has been a step ahead of my best hunters, it knows when to retreat and how to ambush, making us the prey now!" he grumbled.

As dangerous as the capamandra was, Clyde found his thoughts dwelling upon the man in the black mask, what was his game? This was the third time now and it began to bother Clyde greatly, for he felt like little more than a puppet on a string. It came as an obvious conclusion that the man in the black mask was the true mastermind behind these events and should be prioritized. "One more thing High-elf Relus, this man in the black mask, did he reveal anything else about himself? Perhaps his name or where he might be heading?" asked Clyde. Sadly, Relus shook his head, "No, I'm afraid not, he simply snuck into my quarters and warned me of the capamandra creature" he answered. "After warning me of the capamandra, the masked stranger told me to hire you and then left without a word, but only a day after his appearance, the attacks happened" Relus added.

Wearily, Relus rubbed his eyes, "Naturally, I was suspicious of the stranger" he uttered. "But since I've lost many good brothers and sisters to this creature, I'm more than happy to throw you two at the problem instead" Relus coldly added. Being used as fodder for the capamandra wasn't something Clyde and Meadow found particularly enjoyable. What kept Clyde biting his tongue was the idea that they were well-paid fodder. "Well, you may now lay your concerns to sleep, for me and my dedicated apprentice are on the case and we shan't rest until you can serve this capamandra in a salad bowl!" declared Clyde with gusto.

High elf Relus raised one of his eyebrows in slight admiration and gave a very minor bow of his head. "Very well, then you may now take your leave, I wish you well in your hunt" he answered. However, just as Relus was turning his back, chief hunter Silvas abruptly added his own voice, "Lord Relus, with your permission I wish to aid them in the hunt!" he exclaimed. For a small fragment of time, High-elf Relus lay his lofty gaze upon Silvas, before giving a slight shrug. "Permission granted" he uttered before turning away and resting his refined rear upon his oak throne again. Then, Clyde, Meadow and Silvas promptly took their leave and departed the wooden hall carved into the side of the towering great oak tree and eagerly began their quest to hunt the capamandra.

Into the depths of Crestwood's lush, sprawling forest they ventured, and the elven gates of the forest city had long vanished into the untamed wilderness behind them. At this point, it had been a couple of hours since they left the city's wooden walls. "Such a majestic domain of life, it thrives everywhere you look, it must be wonderful to live so free and naturally!" uttered Meadow, evidently enraptured by the torrent of nature's sights and sounds. Yet, Silvas suddenly sneered at her sentence as he cautiously prowled through the forest, searching for signs of the capamandras presence. "It's not as alluring as you may think girl, a cruel food chain exists within these woods and if you're not careful nature will test if your predator or prey" he answered. "Or the hunter or the hunted? I only ask because I'm not sure which we are at this very moment" added Clyde as he studied the ground, keeping a keen eye open for potential signs.

After picking up a broken tree branch and studying it for the presence of anything dangerous, Clyde carelessly flung it aside, "At this moment in time I feel like we're the latter" he uttered. His comments irked Silvas enough that he ceased his prowling for a moment and turned to scowl at Clyde. "I'm one of the best hunters in Crestwood, I know this forest like the back of my hand, and I know where the creature was last seen, so believe me when I saw we are the hunters!" he growled. Clyde could've retaliated with the notion that the elves weren't accustomed to hunting a monster as exotic as a capamandra but froze his words when something in the bushes caught his eye.

One of the trees had something smeared upon it, something wet, sticky and slimy, so naturally Clyde eagerly examined it, "Hold that thought!" he answered as he dashed past Silvas. Whatever this mysterious green liquid was, it held enough importance to cause Clyde to kneel by it and study it further, "What is it human? Speak quickly!" demanded Silvas. "Saliva, capamandra saliva, its been here and based on the wetness and consistency, it was here fairly recently" replied Clyde as he took a quick glance around. Another sign quickly revealed itself to him, "Looks like we might have a new idea as to where to go" he uttered, nodding his head towards something.

Silvas turned his gaze to where Clyde gestured and quickly spotted an elven arrow, one that had been fired and found itself firmly lodged into a tree. "Cleary someone fired at something, lets follow the direction it points!" declared Silvas as he swiftly stomped past the tree with the embedded arrow and deeper into the words. "Hey, wait for us!" called Meadow as her and Clyde briskly chased after him, only to freeze in their tracks a minute later by the grimmest sign of all. All three of them stumbled upon several skeletal remains, scattered bones covered in dirt and blood. All surrounded by bows, swords and arrows, crafted with the distinct elegant style of the elves. As Silvas mournfully looked upon the skeletal carcasses of his elven brothers and sisters, he shut his eyes, hung his head and uttered something in his native elvish language. Meadow interpreted it as a prayer for the fallen. "Is this why you were so keen to aid us in our plight? To serve a hearty dish of vengeance upon the carnivorous creature that claimed these hunters' lives?" asked Clyde.

After uttering his elven chant of peace for the dead, Silvas opened his eyes again and released a deep sigh. "I knew every single one of the elves I hunted with, these are my people, I met their families and ate with them at their tables" he replied. Sorrow then shifted to anger, "Besides, I refuse to be upstaged by humans, it is our blood that has been spilled, it is our prey to hunt and that masked stranger is next! I know he had something to do with it!" growled Silvas. Alas, his anger must've alerted the attention of the creature, as Meadow felt something coil firmly around her ankle, giving her just enough time to see it was a green vine, before she was abruptly dragged away into the forest.

Her screams of surprise and terror made Clyde and Silvas spin. "Meadow!" cried Clyde as he watched her powerlessly claw at the dirt and branches as she was forcibly pulled into the dense foliage. "Now human, the prey is here!" shouted Silvas as he swiftly drew his bow and dashed into the woods after Meadow with all haste. Fear filled Clyde's steps as he frantically chased after Meadow, while guilt clouded his mind, "Hold on Meadow! I'm coming!" he yelled. The thick green vine wrapped around Meadow's ankle dragged her through the rough vegetation and filthy mud. Until she was lifted into the air upside down and finally got a close look at the capamandra.

The long vine tightly wrapped around her leg was one of several slithering, flailing vines. All were connected to what Meadow could only describe as a hulking body of shaggy moss. Vibrant flowers and fungus grew upon its mossy physique, as did an array of spiky, poison tipped thorns. Without a doubt the capamandra was ominous to behold and made more menacing when it opened its jaws and emitted a shrill, piercing screech. Stranger still, was the fact that the creature could part its jaws to such a gaping extent, it was like looking into a deep, black cave, one lined with a myriad of razor-sharp teeth.

Despite her struggling, Meadow could not wrest herself free from the squeezing grasp of the monster's vine. It remained tangled around her leg, and the capamandra seemed hungry as it pulled her closer to its slobbering maw. "No, no, no! Is this how it ends? Becoming plant food for a pile of moss!" screamed Meadow as she swung from side to side, dangling above the carnivorous creature. She may've met her demise too, if not for Silvas suddenly bursting through the nearby bushes, aiming his bow and hastily firing a sharp arrow. An arrow that whizzed through the air at great speed and struck the capamandra's vine. A shrill shriek of pain erupted from the capamandra and caused it to release its constricting grip upon Meadow, dumping her to the ground like a sack of potatoes.

Without delay, Meadow frantically scurried away and Silvas dragged her onto her feet by offering her a helping hand. "We need to make it digest my plant killer poison!" declared Clyde when he joined a second later. Again, Silvas took aim with his bow and unleashed another sharp arrow at the writhing muscular mass of vines and moss. "Keep your petty vial of liquid bottled human, enough elven arrows will bring this creature down!" shouted Silvas. "If only it were that simple, you pointy eared buffoon! The capamandra heals too quickly to be slayed by something as primitive as arrows!" Clyde yelled back as he watched Silvas swiftly fire arrow after arrow.

After shooting the fifth or sixth arrow, the capamandra retaliated and viciously lashed one of its many vines at Silvas, painfully pummeling him in the chest and knocking the wind from his lungs. As Clyde watched Silvas helplessly roll across the dirt, he tried to devise a way to safely approach the capamandra and pour the plant killer down its gnashing maw. Clyde's first solution was to simply run right at it as fast as he could and managed to duck under one of the creatures whipping vines as it swung towards him. His attempt was valiant, but the capamandra brutally struck him across the face with a second lashing vine and Clyde was sent hurling through the air. A groaning gasp of agony leapt from Clyde's lips, his vison became dazed by the blow and his back slammed against a nearby tree, "Okay, I think I need a different approach!" he wearily sighed.

Things quickly shifted from bad to worse when Clyde heard a thundering, grumpy moan echo behind him, "Uh Clyde? That tree is moving!" shouted Meadow. Dread conquered Clyde's senses for a moment as he glanced upwards at the looming tree behind him, "So much noise! Who disturbs my sleep!?" bellowed the tree. "Oh no, it's a treant!" shouted Clyde, quickly scurrying away like a frightened mouse, just in time to avoid getting stomped under the treants mighty oak foot.

Meadow remained speechless as she gazed with awe at the towering treant, watching it slowly rouse itself to life. Its thick long branches becoming arms and two hollow holes in its face becoming stern, glowing eyes. It was truly terrifying to think that such a creature was hiding in plain sight so close to them. Meadow would've found it incredible, if its anger was directed at someone else right now. "Great, nothing is crankier than a treant that has been disturbed from its sleep!" declared Silvas as he watched the sentient tower of lumbering oak furiously stamp towards them with ominous intent.

Even the capamandra was intelligent enough to avoid becoming entangled within this perilous conflict. Hence it seized this opportunity to slither away into the depths of the forest, "The capamandra, it's escaped!" shouted Silvas. "Focus on the here and now!" barked Clyde as he dived towards Meadow and slammed into her, rolling them both out of the treants path when it raised its two, hulking oak fists above them and slammed into the earth. Although Clyde and Meadow safely avoided the attack, the treants huge wooden fists caused a brief tremor to ripple across the ground when they smashed into the forest floor.

Dirt scattered into the air from the impact and the roaring treant came charging at Meadow and Clyde before they had chance to recover. It quickly scooped them both up within its tight oak grasp, "Do not disturb my sleep again!" boomed the treant as it tightly held them both within its two clutching fists. The grip in which the treant held Clyde and Meadow was far too tight to escape despite how much they struggled and Silvas knew he had to act, so he aimed his bow and readied an arrow. However, the treant must've been feeling merciful today, as it decided to fling Meadow and Clyde through the air instead of crushing their bones.

Helplessly, Meadow and Clyde sailed through the air like a couple of unwanted toys and slammed right into Silvas. This caused all three of them to tumble backwards and clumsily fall down a steep grassy hill. Unable to control their momentum, Clyde, Meadow and Silvas continued to roll down the sides of the hill, their faces getting scratched by dense clumps of bushes and becoming caked in dirt. Thankfully, the hill finally came to an end and when it did, all them of them painfully collapsed into a crumpled heap upon one another like a pile of dirty garments, "Ugh, so that went well!" groaned Meadow.

Angrily, Silvas shoved aside Clyde who remained sprawled on top of him and tried to stand up, yet he froze upon hearing a series of strange noises coming from all around them. "Oh, this must be a jest!" declared Silvas, once he studied his surroundings and noticed several strange, large mushrooms circling them. Some of the mushroom caps were deep purple with blue spots, while some were rosy red with purple spots, Regardless, Silvas knew what kind of mushrooms they were. "What? What is it?" uttered Meadow once she recovered her bearings, only to see the mushrooms all had stern, scowling eyes. Unfortunately, they had rolled right into a nest of fungoid, strange monsters that possessed the appearance of oversized mushrooms. All the fungoid creatures stuck their long purplish tongues out in disgust as they circled around Clyde, Meadow and Silvas. "Hope you're ready for some shut eye!" declared Silvas as the nest of fungoid belched a hazy purple mist into the air, which Clyde and the others inhaled, causing them to be promptly knocked into a deep, intoxicating slumber.

During her deep, drowsy rest, Meadow dreamt of a domain most familiar to her, a realm soaked in flames and echoing with chilling screams, she dreamt of home. Or at least that's how home last appeared to her, with Elijah unleashing his demonic fury upon the village, hunting the people like frightened lambs. Sadly, Elijah was a monster created by the village itself and Meadow could still hear her parents' voices calling to her, echoing within the darkness, but it always ended the same way. Elijah's burning flames of anguish would devour her, his demonic anger leaving a trail of sadness and hatred upon the souls of all it touched. Only when Meadow's life was snuffed out like the flame upon a candle, did she finally wake, and this time was no different.

The mysterious, intoxicating mist that the fungoids belched from their mouths finally wore off and Meadow bolted awake with a surprised gasp and a flutter in her heart. Wearily, Meadow rubbed the icky clusters of sleep from her eyes before noticing her rump rested upon Silvas's chest, "How long were we out for?" she groaned. Silvas, who was spread out like a starfish upon the forest floor, began to twist and squirm from what appeared to be a long, wonderful slumber. Meadow was more than a little envious that she often couldn't find the same level of serenity in her sleep.

Suddenly, Meadow's ears caught the incessant sound of an ogres rumbling stomach from behind her, but when she turned around, she was delighted to see it was only Clyde snoring. Like Silvas, Clyde was also messily sprawled out and oblivious to world, until he began to gradually awaken. "Ugh! What happened? What time is it?" he groaned in a drowsy daze. "Its early morning, we must've slept for a dozen hours at least" uttered Meadow as she climbed off Silvas and shook the stiffness from her arms and legs. A miffed expression overcame Clyde once he noticed Silvas's foot resting comfortably upon his head. "We must not delay any longer then!" he declared, shoving Slivas's leg aside and crawling to his feet. Silvas was the last to fully awaken, and he did so with a relaxed stretch and a refreshed yawn. "Wakey, wakey princess! Don't mean to rush you, but we have lost vital time hunting that capamandra!" grumbled Clyde.

Slowly, Silvas rubbed the fatigue from his elven eyes, "Hold your tongue human! It is you who disturbed that treant and landed us in that fungoid nest!" he growled. "This is what happens when you send a human to do an elf's job, trusting you was a mistake!" Silvas added in a bitter tone. Frustration flailed inside Clyde from the absurdity of his comment, "Are your saying this was all my fault? You're the one who refused to listen to my plan!" snapped Clyde. "You mean your plan to make the monster swallow that vial of poison you've concocted!?" Silvas fired back. A scoff of arrogance followed, "Such a plan is doomed to fail if you cannot even approach the creature! A few more of my arrows and it would've been slain!" Silvas shouted.

Seeing Clyde and Silvas butt heads like two territorial taurian was enough to make Meadow rip her hair out. "Can't we please just use fire to deal with the creature!?" she cried. That proved to be a mistake, for her statement was greeted with nothing but harsh glares from Clyde and Silvas, "No!" they both shouted at the same time. "That treant, the one that flung you aside like a rotten apple, this forest is filled with many more, fire is only allowed within the walls of my people, breaking that pact means going to war with the treants!" cried Silvas.

The tone of his voice and piercing scowl in his eyes made it crystal clear to Meadow how seriously the races of Crestwood treated the topic of fire. "Okay, okay! Fire is forbidden!" she nervously uttered. "It isn't just the treants, the forest of Crestwood is home to the centaurs too, the pact of forbidden fire is shared between all of them and breaking it means going to war with them as well" added Clyde. Gradually the tension and frustration subsided, "All we must do is pin the capamandra down, but its many vines keep attackers at bay" Clyde uttered. His mind became lost in thought as he mentally devised a new strategy, "If we can control its vines, keep them occupied, we can leave the creature open to attack" uttered Clyde.

His plan sounded logical enough to make the pointy elven ears of Silvas prick up, "And how do you propose we accomplish such a task?" he asked. "I have two unique potions that should do the trick, but it shall take all three of us working together in order to defeat that writhing mess of moss and vines" answered Clyde. Confidence brimmed from Clyde as he deviously analyzed his little scheme. "Before I can outsmart that perilous plant with my superior intellect, we must first track its trail again!" he announced. A crafty grin smeared Clyde's face, no doubt caused by the awe he regularly faced from his own genius. "It won't be long until victory is mine to claim you walking pile of shrubbery!" uttered Clyde with a cunning laugh. His quirky bursts of buoyant madness had become both jarring and admirable to Meadow by this point, "Are all humans this eccentric?" asked Silvas as he watched Clyde. A humiliated sigh drifted from Meadows lips when she remembered she was Clyde's apprentice, "No, just him" she answered.

For a while the trail of the capamandra grew colder than a hug from an undead maiden. The creature was proving to be elusive and despite the natural beauty of the forest, Meadow grew impatient, "Still no signs!" she groaned. "Keep your wits about you girl, this forest is perilous to the unguarded, honestly, you wouldn't last a day without us!" answered Silvas in a stern tone. Meadow vented her impatience by swiftly kicking a small rock by her feet. "Yes, yes, I'm aware of how perilous it is, the trees are alive! The mushrooms are alive! Is there anything in this forest that isn't alive!?" she growled.

Before a dispute could erupt between the two of them, Clyde quickly spun around and pressed his finger against his lips as a gesture for them to hush. "Quiet, I think I heard something!" he uttered in a frantic whisper. Silvas immediately took shelter behind one of the thick trees and vigilantly peered from behind it. "Where? Which direction?" he asked in a low hush, while Meadow blankly froze on the spot. Suddenly, the forest became eerily silent as the three of them stretched their hearing, trying to catch the smallest echo of anything ominous. Except there was nothing, not a single sound, "It could've been a bird or something" uttered Meadow. "No, it's the capamandra, it's here!" answered Clyde with a nervous gasp as he knelt to inspect a pool of gooey green saliva splashed upon a jutting rock nearby. The saliva was identical in color and consistency to the type he had seen previously and before Clyde could utter a word further, he was alarmed by an abrupt rustling sound from behind.

There was just enough time for Clyde to jolt up, spin around, stumble backwards and see the four strands of long vines swiftly burst from beyond the bushes and pounce upon him, entangling his arms and legs. "Clyde!" cried Meadow as she watched his ensnared body helplessly slam to the floor and be dragged away through the shrubbery like a freshly caught animal carcass. Sharp twigs and pointy pebbles scratched and clawed at Clyde as the capamandras vines forcibly pulled him through the forest. "Clyde, hold on! We're coming!" shouted Meadow as her and Silvas charged through the dense foliage. "We meet again!" roared Silvas with fury in his voice upon rushing through the blanket of leaves and twigs to rest his glare upon the screeching capamandra once more.

Meadow watched the flailing creature raise Clyde into the air like a fish ready to devour a dangling worm, "We have to rescue Clyde!" she cried. Luckily, Silvas was already on the task and drew a sharp arrow from his leather quiver, aimed it with his trusty bow and let it fly with remarkable accuracy. A shrill screech wailed from the capamandra as the arrow struck its vine, releasing its grip upon one of Clyde's arms. "Here, this is the plant killer poison!" shouted Clyde. With one of his arms now free, Clyde reached for the poison resting within his harness and tossed it towards Silvas, "Stick to the plan!" added Clyde as he squirmed and struggled.

The precious vial of poisonous plant killer sailed through the air towards Silvas's outstretched palm. Despair soon struck however, when the capamandra lashed one of its vines and knocked it out of reach before he could catch it. As the vial of potent poison rolled across the forest, Meadow breathed a sigh of relief when she noticed it remained undamaged. It was lucky Clyde's potion vials were made of a specially hardened glass. "Grab the vial!" barked Silvas as he aimed his bow and continued to fire a swift and ruthless assault of arrows, all while ducking and dodging the capamandras other four whipping vines.

Although Silvas's arrows proved futile in doing anything other than distracting the creature, distracting it was more than enough, "Meadow, I don't have infinite arrows!" he shouted. "Alright, I'm getting it now!" Meadow cried back as she quickly dived in-between the thrashing vines when she spotted an opportunity and swiftly scooped up the vial of plant poison. "Good job girl!" Silvas shouted upon seeing Meadow snag the vial. Alas, this moment of relief caused Silvas to be diverted and he failed to dodge one of the monsters lashing vines.

It felt like being struck by the tail of a dragon and a gasp of pain leapt from Silvas's lungs as the capamandras vine whipped him across the face. It sent him rolling across the dirt and despair soon struck again, for as soon as Meadow laid her hands upon the vial, the capamandra used its other four vines to swiftly entangle her, "Silvas, the vial!" she shouted. Meadow knew there wasn't much time, so she threw the vial of poison towards Silvas before the capamandras vines had time to tighten up. All eight of the capamandras vines were now preoccupied with keeping Clyde and Meadow tangled and contained, one vine for each of their limbs. But that was okay, for it was all a part of Clyde's plan. "Now Silvas, use your arrows! Give me and Meadow an arm free!" shouted Clyde as he resisted against the capamandras gripping vines with all his might.

Haughtily, Silvas chuckled as he scooped the vial of plant poison up off the ground. "It's a good thing I saved two!" he yelled back, vigilantly aiming his bow and shooting his last two arrows, one for Clyde and one for Meadow. His aim was perfect, the arrows stabbed into the vines that constricted Meadow and Clyde, giving them each an arm free again. "Now Meadow, use stone-form potion!" yelled Clyde at the top of his lungs. A shrieking wail spewed from the capamandras maw the moment the arrows struck its vines. At the same time, Meadow used her free hand and reached for the potion Clyde had told her to consume. She recognized it right away, and the vial containing it had an unusual dusty grey texture to it, "Bottoms up!" she declared. Imbibing the peculiar potion proved tricky with the way the capamandra was flailing them around, its enraged screeching piercing the air of the peaceful forest.

Despite such difficulty, Meadow and Clyde managed to quickly pop the corks off their potions and swiftly guzzle them down without delay. The stone-form potion took effect and it did exactly what Clyde said it would, Meadow watched with awe as her entire body quickly turned into solid stone. The same thing happened to Clyde, he became a living statue of stone, which in turn made their bodies highly resistant to damage and immensely heavy. A thundering tremor briefly rumbled the earth as Clyde and Meadow's stony bodies slammed into the ground. They became far too heavy for the capamandras vines to keep them dangling in the air.

Before the capamandra could release its long coiling vines around them, Clyde and Meadow each grabbed all four vines and held them tightly. "Now don't let go my apprentice, keep a tight grip upon its vines!" shouted Clyde. Thanks to the stone-form potion Clyde and Meadow had become living statues and were able to bind the capamandras vines with their immense weight. It was time to put the next part of the plan into action and Clyde stomped his way to the left. Meanwhile Meadow plodded her way to the right, and both kept a tight clutch upon the capamandras bunch of squirming vines. It couldn't escape this time, Meadow and Clyde acted as anchors to stop the creature from slithering away and by creating distance between each other, they left the monster wide open.

Their colossal weight made it impossible for the writhing pile of living moss to pull its vines away, it was now defenseless and immobile. "Hurry Silvas! the potions we took won't last for long!" shouted Clyde as he held onto the bunch of squirming vines, using his newfound stony strength and weight to keep the creature trapped. With its vines all securely constricted by Meadow and Clyde, nothing could stop Silvas as he charged straight towards the mossy monster with the vial of plant killer poison in hand. As soon as Silvas reached the gnashing, screeching jaws of the carnivorous capamandra, he popped he oak cork off the vial of plant poison. "For my fallen brothers!" he growled before pouring the sickly green liquid into its malevolent maw.

Yet, the creature had one last trick to play and suddenly propelled the sharp poisonous thorns covering its body outwards. It was a last resort defense against attackers that came too close, one Silvas was unprepared for as he stumbled backwards and collapsed when a few of the toxic thorns stabbed his neck. "Silvas!" Cried Meadow as she watched him fall unconscious. At the same time, the capamandra began violently writhing and shrieking sharply, its symphony of frightful wailing becoming increasingly loud, but it didn't have to suffer such agony for long.

After several seconds, the deadly creature ceased its fierce twisting. Its shrill screeching soon falling silent like the whispers of the dead, its mossy, emerald green body gradually changing to a dull, ashen grey. All the life from its body withered away like a dying weed. The poison had fulfilled its duty and the capamandra soon became little more than a clump of decayed sludge. Yet, seeing Silvas lying there utterly lifeless caused a rumbling storm of dread to stir within Meadow's stomach. "Oh no, is he?" asked Meadow as she came running to his side, unable to finish the sentence. "No, not without me, without me he would surely be as dead as a necromancers dinner party, luckily I'm so well prepared!" boast Clyde as he confidently strutted over.

From within his trusty alchemy harness he pulled one of his glass vials, this one contained a mixture that was gloopy and lavender in hue. "I'm familiar with the capamandras particular strain of poison, so I made sure to concoct some good old antidote just in case, it will banish that vile venom as sure as the sun banishes shadow!" he declared. Hastily, Meadow snatched the antidote from Clyde's hand faster than he could blink, "Then there's no time to waste you crackpot!" she replied in a stern huff. That familiar popping sound echoed next to Meadow's ear as she yanked the cork stopper from the neck of the vial and carefully poured the precious remedy down Silvas's throat. Once the vial had been emptied, Meadow took a step back and stood alongside Clyde. "You sure you've brought the right one? It's not going to turn him into a goat or inflate him to the size of a cottage and make him explode?" she asked nervously. An insulted scowl abruptly spread upon Clyde's face. "You dare question my skill and intellect my doubtful disciple? Has all our time together still not made you aware that you're in the presence of genius!?" he proclaimed.

Meadow felt jaded and allowed her face to fall into her palm, "The only thing I've become aware of is how much of an oddball you are" she groaned. Tremors of trepidation still rippled within her soul upon seeing no visual reaction coming from Silvas's body, however, Clyde remained positive and smug. In the end he had good reason to be, as Silvas began to suddenly rouse from his lifeless slumber. "Ugh, I feel like I've consumed an entire barrel of orc ale!" he moaned as he slowly dragged himself up. Clyde aided his ascension by offering a hand. "Tis fortunate you're in the presence of such talented alchemists then, for that poison in your blood would've made your sleep eternal if not for my antidote!" He proclaimed.

A flicker of humility flashed within Silvas's eyes as he accepted Clyde's hand of support. "I see, so it was your alchemy that saved me, I guess I owe you my thanks" Silvas reluctantly replied. Once he was back on his feet, Silvas turned to face the withered pile of rotting weeds that the capamandra had become. "So, it is done, my people no longer need to fear being prey again!" he uttered with relief. "It's still a great loss that some of your people lost their lives to it" replied Meadow as she mournfully placed her hand upon Silvas's back.

Strangely, Silvas chuckled, "Save your tears human, I know my brothers and sisters will live on in spirit and become one with the forest, they will rest, now that they have been avenged" he uttered. The sun had begun to sink beneath the horizon by the time Clyde, Meadow and Silvas completed the trek back to Crestwood. Along the way, Clyde's mind remained fixated upon the mystery of the black masked figure, who was he? Was he the one that brought the capamandra here? For what reason? And if so, why lure Clyde in to fix it? There were far too many questions and not a single fragment of an answer. "It doesn't make sense; this masked figure has caused trouble three times now" muttered Clyde.

Meadow overhead him and related to his confused frustration, "And each time he's caused trouble, he's recommended us to clear up the mess!" she growled. "Whoever he is, he's playing some kind of pointless game and getting people killed!" Meadow added. Delight washed over Silvas when the sight of Crestwood's main gate suddenly came into view. "We shall keep a keen eye open for this masked stranger should he appear again, but for now, Crestwood owes you a debt of gratitude!" decreed Silvas. Two different elven guards were defending the gates this time, but they immediately lowered their wooden shields and sharp spears and stood aside upon seeing Silvas approach.

Once again, the splendor of Crestwood was laid bare and Meadow watched the scenic forest city with fascination as the wooden lift carried her high into the treetops. Her, Clyde and Silvas enjoyed the calming backdrop as they ascended higher and higher towards the peak of the great oak to meet with High-elf Fivilon Relus again. Gently, Meadow caressed the charming oak pendant Clyde had purchased her from the elven market. She gazed at the quant houses carved into the colossal trees and the giant spinning waterwheel near the center. Resisting the sight of such profound tranquility and beauty was futile and Meadow watched the elves living as one among nature, swinging and sailing across the air on their sturdy rope swings and ziplines.

Eventually the expertly crafted wooden lift came to an abrupt halt, indicating that they had reached the very peak of the tremendous great oak tree. "Come, High-elf Relus will no doubt be eager to hear our report" uttered Silvas. Clyde and Meadow obediently stepped off the wooden lift and followed behind Silvas as he paced with pride across the oak platform and into the giant hall carved into the side of the tree. High-elf Relus was already sitting upon his lofty oak throne, draped in a fresh silk robe and sipping what looked like wine from a goblet made entirely of wood. "Chief hunter Silvas, your back! Please give your report" he ordered upon seeing them return. Loyally, Silvas bowed his head and knelt before High-elf Relus and recited the tale of what transpired between him and the capamandra in the wild and winding forest.

Relus stayed silent as Silvas spun the story, his aloof gaze remained unflinching, his slender elven fingers coiled around his goblet as he raised it to his rose red lips and took a sip. "And so, you see lord Relus, I owe these humans my life, if not them I would've been another victim of the capamandra" explained Silvas as he concluded his report. Silence followed for several moments, until High-elf Relus took the time to arise from his throne. Dominantly, he strut towards them, goblet still dangling between his fingers, "I see" he uttered.

His demeanor remained as haughty as ever, but Meadow could tell there was something different this time. "Then it seems we were wise to employ the services of two such skilled alchemists" Relus added. "I admit I had my doubts but, it seems the two of you have performed your duty admirably and deserve a reward" Relus continued, raising one hand and snapping his fingers. Instantly, a nearby elven guard came hurrying over, clutching a bulging sack filled with what appeared to be the shape of gold coins. "I trust this will adequately compensate you for your service?" asked Relus after taking another sip from his goblet. Clyde politely bowed his head and claimed the sack crammed with glimmering gold coins from the nearby elven guard. "This will be more than adequate lord Relus, it was a pleasure to be of assistance" he replied.

Seeing Clyde so formal and humble was a little jarring, but Meadow remembered that he was a professional alchemist. It was important to maintain healthy relations with potential clients, especially ones that paid as well as the elves did. "Seeing your city for the first time was a joy Mister Relus, it is truly beautiful!" Meadow anxiously uttered, swiftly bowing to escape eye contact. She had never been proficient at knowing how to act around important people. Referring to High-elf Relus as Mister Relus left Clyde and Silvas utterly speechless.

However, something akin to a little smile spread upon Lord Relus's lips as he gazed upon her. "Thank you, you are welcome here anytime" he answered, before walking back to his throne. After overcoming the surprise that Meadow got away with what she said, Silvas held out his arm and offered his hand for Clyde to shake. "Words alone cannot show my gratitude Clyde" he uttered. Happily, Clyde gripped Silva's open palm and gave it a firm shake, "It was nothing my friend, I'm just glad I was able to aid your potent plant problem!" he replied in a hearty tone. "Yeah, not bad for a human!" Silvas declared in a jovial jest, giving Clyde a playful slap on the side of his shoulder.

Seeing the two of them shake hands and exchange pleasant banter was a delight for Meadow to witness, especially considering they were both a different race. "Let us hope I don't have to swoop in and rescue you again anytime soon!" replied Clyde as he turned to leave and walked away. "Until next time Silvy!" Meadow happily declared as she waved goodbye and chased after Clyde, leaving Silvas to fold his arms and watch them depart, his lips spreading into a content grin.

Chalice of Renewal
Chapter 7
A web of misfortune

Delicately, Meadow tipped the glass vial containing powdered minotaur horn into the bubbling flask of boiling water. She remembered she only needed to pour in about half, for any more than that would cause the mixture to become too potent. She had already thrown a handful of elf-blossom and crimson fang petals into the mix, along with extracted chasmberry juice. Now it was simply a matter of stirring until it changed to the correct shade. A most unique odor crept into Meadow's senses when she hovered her nose over the mixture. An aroma laden with sweetness, but with a distinct, fierce kick of spice. It was a scent difficult to discern, one that reeked of mystery and when the mixture began to alter its color, it only served to mesmerize Meadow further.

She was utterly enthralled by the way the mixture gradually changed its consistency and hue. Becoming viscous and possessing a color that was just as challenging to describe as its scent. It was a vibrant and bold color, yet deceptively elegant, a color infused with a baffling blend of deep scarlet, rich violet and garish magenta, culminating in a truly captivating concoction. It had been three days since the capamandra incident at Crestwood and Clyde concluded that a few days of rest were in order. Although, while he had spent the last three days taking it easy, he made sure to give Meadow plenty of homework.

Hence, the reason why Meadow was currently hunched over the flask of bubbling brew, watching it like a perched gargoyle. She didn't mind though; by this point the world of alchemy had deeply embedded its captivating claws within her. Clyde hadn't woken yet, but as Meadow watched the flask of mysterious mixture upon its iron holder above the candles flickering flame, she heard a weary yawn echo behind her. Turning her head, she noticed Clyde standing at the doorway entrance to the lab, his hair looking like a bird's nest. His eyes were still drowsy with sleep, "Morning dear Meadow" he managed to slur out. "Morning!" Meadow cheerfully answered, returning her gaze to the bubbling brew, her attention utterly consumed by it.

Clumsily, Clyde walked down the wooden steps leading into the lab, his brain still adrift in a sleepy trance, "How goes the mixture?" he asked. A gust of swelling pride whooshed over Meadow and she took few steps back to admire her creation further. "I'd say very well, I've completed all the alchemy formulas you gave me, but I think this might be my best work yet!" she answered. Clyde meandered over to Meadow's most recent homework, inspected it meticulously and found himself to be extremely impressed.

The consistency, color and even aroma of the mixture was practically perfect, so much so that Clyde even gave a supportive nod and smile. "It seems exceptional in every way and I can always tell a good mixture from a bad one, well done my apprentice" he replied. For a few moments longer, Clyde and Meadow watched and listened intently to the glass flask of uniquely colored liquid as it gently bubbled and boiled away. Despite his status as a master of alchemy, it seemed Clyde could still be a victim of its allure. "By the way, didn't we receive a second letter from Hector? One that requested our services?" asked Meadow, breaking the enthralled trance. Casually, Clyde leaned away from the mixture of melodic bubbling liquid and folded his arms. "Indeed, though I've yet to rip the envelope asunder and peruse the delicious details lying within" he answered.

It astounded Meadow how Clyde could make the idea of opening a letter sound so dramatic, "Well, perhaps we might want to get ripping and perusing?" she suggested. "Tame those wild taurian stampeding within you my precious pupil, lest they drag you headlong into peril, I will peruse the contents of the letter in due time, for I'm sure the fate of entire land does not rest upon its shoulders" he answered. Time was Clyde's ally, anyone who requested his help never expected it right away, for they were unaware of Styx and his ability to portal Clyde across the land. This meant that Clyde could easily deal with whatever ordeal he was tasked with at his own leisure. If he ever had a client that whined about his tardiness, Clyde could always blame it on travel time.

However, his apathy on this matter caused a jaded sigh to flutter from Meadow. "Ugh, so typical, so you're just going to play the I'll get around to it later card? Why are you boys all the same?" she groaned. Naturally, her choice of words provoked a frown laced with ire from Clyde. "Being prepared is half the battle my hasty helper, and I shan't dive into danger until I'm sure you and I are at our best, you cannot always depend on me, understand?" he replied. Meadow raised a surprised eyebrow at his response since it sounded somewhat sincere and sane. "Did your master often rope you into danger too then? I've noticed you never mention your past, what were you like as an apprentice?" she inquired.

Asking such questions caused Clyde to become speechless and blank, but a brief flicker of sorrow shimmered in his eyes. "I never had a master, everything I learned, I learned on my own" Clyde answered solemnly. As Meadow watched Clyde amble out of the alchemy lab, she felt a lump of regret fall into the pit of her stomach, "Now if you'll excuse me, I have a letter to tend to" he added. Meadow could tell she had broached a delicate topic, one that Clyde clearly wished to keep buried, "Didn't have a master? That was a poor lie" Meadow whispered to herself.

Spirits were soon lifted by a pot of fresh steaming tea in the kitchen once Meadow had fulfilled a couple of lingering duties in the alchemy lab. "Mmmm, smells good! Which tea is it today?" she asked upon walking in. "Today it is a blend of honeycomb, crushed silver-queen petals and cherrybutter herbs, a tea that is both delicious and a boon to one's health" answered Clyde. He had already begun pouring himself a cup and once it was sufficiently filled, Clyde took a delicate sip from the steamy mug, his eyes darting across the second letter he had just opened. "Who requests our aid this time?" asked Meadow, pouring herself a hot cup of tea and embracing the heavenly aroma that swirled from within and tingled her senses.

Clyde took a seat at the large oak table in the kitchen and gently placed the letter down. "Looks like we're going to Deepshade, the home of the skarl, apparently a strange monster is lurking beneath their streets and abducting people" he answered. Meadow had heard only a little of the skarl, she heard they were a race of humanoid rat people. They also frequently indulged in thievery and assassination work, for their rat-like bodies made them highly swift and agile. "Deepshade, if I remember my history correctly, wasn't that a human city that fell to the orcs during the Green Banner War?" uttered Meadow as she sipped her steaming cup of sublime tea.

Clyde retaliated with an impressed nod, "Correct my apprentice, it was a human city which the orcs sacked during the Green Banner War many years ago" he answered. "Near the wars end, the skarl attacked and took it from the orcs and made it their home ever since" he added. Today the tea was remarkably sweet, and Meadow felt a soothing warm tingle in her cheeks as she imbibed it. "Today, Deepshade remains a decrepit husk of its former glory, the skarl have always been nomads looking for a home" uttered Clyde. Meadow leaned back against her chair and gently swished her tea around, "I hear it's become a wretched hive of scum and villainy" she remarked. "True, many thieves and rogues roam the city streets, keeping their daggers sharpened and their eyes peeled for an opportunity to make some gold" answered Clyde. His description of the of the city painted a rather unpleasant image, but it didn't end there. "And yes, the city is dirty, ruined, suffers from overpopulation and muggings are common if one wanders down the wrong alley" he added.

Deepshade didn't sound very inviting, but Meadow knew it wouldn't keep Clyde away, his tenacity to solve a problem was admirable to say the least. "But fear not, many skarl are honest traders' merchants and workers just trying to earn a living, proving Deepshade isn't entirely terrible" added Clyde. After taking another quenching gulp of rejuvenating tea, Meadow smacked her lips together. "So, what's this strange monster that's been abducting people?" she asked. "The letter isn't quite clear as it seems no one has managed to glimpse the creature and lived to tell the tale, but I'm sure we'll receive a clearer description when we arrive, I have my own theories though" answered Clyde.

Once again, his eyes shrewdly perused the letter, searching for the slightest hint to answer the mystery of what the next adversary would be. "It scuttles through the shadows of the sewers with swift speed, blends into the darkness and strikes with deadly intent, leaving nothing but the frightened screams of our people behind" Clyde recited as he held the letter near his face. Hearing such an ominous description caused an icy shudder to trickle along Meadow's neck. "Doesn't sound very pleasant and I have to say, the idea of plunging into the depths of a dark nasty sewer to hunt some icky monster doesn't rest well with me!" she declared.

After swigging the last droplets of his tea, Clyde thumped his teacup down and arose from the kitchen table. "Nor I, but that is the job and we must prevail my perturbed pupil, so let us venture forth and display our valor against the tyranny of fear!" Clyde boldly announced. His dramatic announcement caught the pointy purple ears of Styx who fluttered in with his little flapping wings. "Have you decided on a destination master?" he hissed. "I have indeed my most marvelous minion! Today we journey to the ruined rathole known as Deepshade!" Clyde declared as he waltzed out of the room. Styx pursued him with avid passion, "It has been quite a while since you last visited there master, I shall begin creating the portal at once!" he replied in a slithery tone.

Within the wonderful walls of the whimsical alchemy lab, Clyde was diligently preparing his alchemy harness, packing it with as many premade potions as possible. Of course, it could only hold so many, so he had to choose wisely like always. Meadow soon wandered in and watched Clyde, who already had half his alchemy harness stuffed with colorful concoctions. "So, what have you packed?" asked Meadow as she glanced upon the vibrant vials covering his body. This time however, Clyde refused to allow her to see which potions he had picked. "Actually, I believe the time has come for you to pick your own potions my pupil, tailor your harness wisely and ask yourself what you shall need" answered Clyde.

Upon being presented with such a choice, Meadow became like a timid rabbit in front of the gleaming fangs of a vicious cerberii. "What shall I need? I do not know, why are you letting me choose now?" she asked. "Because, my little lackey, if you are to follow my footsteps you need to also think on your own two feet, who knows when I may not be there to protect you?" Clyde answered sincerely. Normally, Meadow would just mimic whatever selection of potions Clyde had picked. Having to prudently pick her own potions for a change proved dauting to say the least, "Okay, I shall choose the first one for you" uttered Clyde.

He proceeded to causally toss a vial of potion towards Meadow which she quickly caught in her hand. "It's a potion that should prove quite useful, one I've been trying to perfect for a while, but now it is ready" explained Clyde. Meadow's attention was utterly hypnotized as she gazed upon the glass vial she held within her palm. The liquid was icy blue in color and thin plumes of tiny white mist swirled inside of it. However, before Clyde had a chance to tell her what the potion did, a thundering eruption rippled through the air, causing a deep roaring resonance. Meadow knew that noise well enough to know what it meant. "Sounds like Styx has prepared our portal, do not dawdle my dear, pick your concoctions and join me at the pedestal!" declared Clyde, briskly marching out of the alchemy lab.

Meadow held back a bitter curse towards Clyde, for she despised being in situations where she had to make crucial decisions while under pressure. "Okay, think! What will I need?" she whispered while gazing upon the vibrant array of potions. Since she would be heading into sewers, Meadow decided she may need some shadow-vision potion. Seeing in the dark would no doubt be vital, so she took two vials in case it didn't last long enough.

Enhanced-strength potion was always essential, so Meadow decided to take two vials of that as well. Along with a vial of sticky-sludge potion, fire-breath potion, smokescreen potion and invisibility potion. Only problem was, Meadow and Clyde were still in the dark on what kind of monster lurked beneath the depths of Deepshade, making preparation even more difficult. Her harness still had room for several more potions, so she decided to take a vial of sleepy-gas potion, ethereal potion, two vials of enhanced-speed potion and an extra vial of fire-breath potion.

By this point Meadow's harness had become quite crammed, she couldn't take every potion with her of course, but was confident enough with what she had picked. Perhaps her greatest concern was not what potions she had picked, but if she was taking enough of them with her, she even considered removing a couple and doubling up on others. Thankfully, she resisted the temptation of reviewing her selection of potions, the thought that Clyde would undoubtedly cover anything she was lacking aided in soothing her trepidation. With her harness now adequately outfitted, Meadow decided not to waste another second. She briskly departed the alchemy lab and hurried towards the portal room where Clyde and Styx awaited her.

As usual, Meadow was greeted to the sound of humming magical energy. It originated from the swirling portal of colors upon the circular marble stone pedestal and resonated the entire room. "Well, you join us at last my dallying disciple, if you took any longer preparing, I feared I'd have to leave you behind" uttered Clyde while subtly inspecting Meadow's harness. A bolt of vexation struck Meadow and she sullenly flicked a dangling strand of fiery hair over her shoulder. "Go ahead, I'm pretty sure I wouldn't miss the chance to go crawling through a nasty dark sewer" she replied.

Clyde quickly retaliated to Meadow's comment with another one of his blatant insults. "Be that as it may, I would rather have you by my side, your talent for carrying extra potions makes you a glorified mule" he impudently uttered. The sheer insolence and audacity behind his comment caused Meadow to smite him with a fearsome glare. Luckily, Styx interrupted their bickering before it could snowball, "I trust the two of you are done now?" he hissed. Slowly, Clyde began striding towards the luminous assortment of whirling colors contained within the floating mystical portal. "Yes, yes, we are ready Styx, into the vibrant void we march!" he valiantly declared. Into the magical doorway of cascading color Clyde entered, vanishing from sight as he stepped through, with Meadow following close behind. "Be a good little imp!" she teased to Styx, before playfully leaping into the portal.

Floating at great speed through a mysterious dimension drenched in every color imaginable had still not become tedious. Meadow expected it to, but any other method of travelling seemed mundane and dull to her now. To be able to travel using these mystical portals was truly a luxury and made her feel like she was really flying upon a current of color. Soon, the ride ended as usual, with both Meadow and Clyde emerging from the vibrant realm and back into the real world, except this time it was quite a blatant contrast. Icy raindrops splashed upon Meadow's skin the moment she appeared from within the portal.

A sudden gust of chilly wind swept through her dress, causing her to shiver, "Well, this looks bleak!" she uttered. She was no doubt referring to the ruined city of stone that stood upon the lonely hill across the horizon, which reminded her of a neglected rose that was slowly withering away. In all fairness, the dark gloomy clouds and relentless salvo of rain weren't aiding the city's appearance either. "So, that crumbling ruin is where the skarl live?" asked Meadow as she began following Clyde towards it. "Yes, the city of Deepshade a city fraught with sneaky thieves, devious scoundrels and merciless cutthroats, so keep your wits about you" answered Clyde.

A rough grassy ledge, slippery from rainwater awaited, but Clyde showed his chivalry and offered Meadow a hand and assisted her down. "What I don't understand is, if Deepshade was originally a human settlement, then why aren't humans trying to take it back?" asked Meadow as she took Clyde's hand. Carefully, Clyde assisted Meadow along the slippery grass hill, ensuring she didn't take a tumble. "Humans have tried to negotiate ownership of the city, but since it was captured by the orcs during the war, the skarl have argued that it was up for grabs" replied Clyde. As Deepshade drew ever closer, more of its ancient wounds became visible.

Rotting siege ladders still clung to parts of the walls, as did the claws of large siege hooks and giant iron spears, no doubt fired from mighty ballista. "The skarl were tired of wandering and Deepshade became the perfect opportunity to claim a city of their own, they also claim the city is their reward for helping in the war" uttered Clyde. Clearly the city of Deepshade had weathered quite a storm of war in days long gone. The murky clouds and dreary rain seeming like an echo of a somber past, "So, why not try and restore it?" asked Meadow. "The skarl aren't exactly proficient craftsmen, building is not often in their repertoire of skills, thievery and assassination is" answered Clyde, his voice trailing quieter as they approached.

A weary wooden drawbridge overlooking a filthy moat was the only visible way to enter the city, so Clyde and Meadow approached the crumbing stone gateway in front of it. Over a dozen skarl covered the stone gateway like leaves covering a tree, they were obviously stationed as guards, but it was jarring for Meadow to witness. All of them were sprawled across different sections of the stone gateway, sitting, squatting or lying upon it like a pack of watchful hawks upon a wall. All of them were armed with daggers, spears or bows and clad in lightweight scraps of cloth, leather and scruffy shawls. Most of the rat-like skarl appeared unfriendly and suspicious, with many of them possessing bite marks and blade scars upon their bodies.

Suddenly, one of them leapt from the top of the gateway and barred the path onwards once Clyde and Meadow grew closer, "Hold strangers and state your business!" he demanded. Slowly, Clyde revealed the letter of aid from his pocket while protecting it against the ravages of rain. "My name is Clyde, and this is my apprentice Meadow, we are alchemists responding to a request for help!" he called. This caused the suspicious skarl guard to take a more relaxed stance and he casually approached Clyde. Meadow watched the furry humanoid rat stroke his long whiskers as he peered closely at the letter which Clyde held in his hand. "Very well, your both free to enter" replied the skarl in a somewhat sly tone, keeping an uncomfortable glare upon them. Respectfully, Clyde gave a humble nod of gratitude and strolled past the skarl guardsman, Meadow only wished she could mask her unease as well as Clyde did. A tingly shudder traversed Meadow's shoulders as she glanced upwards to the swarm of vigilant skarl sprawled along the stone gateway. All of them watched her with their beady rat eyes as she passed through the gateway beneath them.

Crossing the battered oak drawbridge was the only visible way to enter Deepshade. But it wearily creaked and groaned the moment Clyde and Meadow placed their feet upon it, causing them to ponder how safe it was. Especially since it was held by such rusty iron chains and hovered above a deep gaping moat that looked about as clean as an ogre's outhouse. "I certainly wouldn't desire a dip in there!" uttered Meadow as she nervously peered over the side. Despite the fear of the drawbridge breaking and plummeting them into a moat of filth, Clyde and Meadow made it across without incident.

Scattered along the crumbling high walls of Deepshade were more skarl, all lazily watching the horizon. Meanwhile, Clyde and Meadow began to hear bustling chatter upon the other side of the city's main gate. "Welcome to Deepshade, enjoy your stay!" uttered a nearby skarl gate guard with a tone that sounded satirical. Nevertheless, the skarl guard lay his furry paws upon a rusty iron crank embedded in the wall next to him and began rotating the eroded mechanism. The scratched iron gate obstructing the entrance began to make a splitting screeching sound as it gradually rose and revealed the city of Deepshade.

Meadow struggled to find the right words to describe what she witnessed once her eyes rested upon the inside of the city. It was utterly decrepit, yet teeming with life and activity, "Okay, so where do we begin?" she asked in a daunted tone. Chaotic, was probably the best way Meadow could describe it. For as decayed and crumbling as the city was, skarl covered its many nooks and crannies. Their long furry tails and beady eyes could be seen in every single ruined watchtower and upon every rickety rooftop. It was a bustling hive of anarchy with skarl adorning every part of the city. A crowed market square awaited Clyde and Meadow as soon as they emerged, and they were swiftly assaulted by a horde of greedy skarl merchants.

It felt overwhelming to say the least and Meadow could hear the avarice in their voices as the swarm of skarl merchants chanted cries of bargains. They shoved the shiny trinkets they peddled into Meadow's face, likely because any race that wasn't a skarl were a gullible sightseer ripe for a good swindling. "Hey, you two!" cried a voice over the noise of coin hungry merchants. It was difficult to discern from which direction the voice came, but the person responsible soon revealed himself when he dashed in to save Clyde and Meadow from their unfortunate predicament. "Give our guests some space! Go on, get out of here!" he barked.

Gradually the crowd of skarl merchants reluctantly dispersed and returned to their little street stalls upon getting swatted and shoved away. Clyde and Meadow owed their rescue to a young skarl boy with admittedly exquisite white fur, albeit dotted with specks of dirt. "Sorry about that, skarl merchants are like griffons upon a herd of galamare when they see new faces" uttered the boy. Amicably, the young skarl boy held out his fluffy white paw, offering a handshake. "My name is Rittz, I'm one of the best tunnelers in Deepshade, are you two the alchemists we were expecting?" he asked. Respectfully, Clyde reached out his hand and shook the boy's paw. "Indeed, we are and thank you kindly for your timely rescue from those greedy ravens, but we need more information about the perils that plight your city" he answered.

This caused Rittz to coil his long scaly tail around his body and anxiously fidget with the end. "In truth we don't know what is down in the sewers, we've sent three groups of mercenaries to investigate and none of them have returned" he nervously replied. Meadow found his apprehension unusual, the disappearance of a dozen sell-swords shouldn't cause such unease, "Why do you care? There must be more to it" she inquired. Her insight forced Rittz to sigh and disclose the truth that had been causing him turmoil, "A few days ago our packmaster went to investigate too, but he also vanished" he uttered. "The packmaster is our leader, he settles disputes in the city, organizes the trade line, ensures the merchants aren't being greedy, the packmaster is also my father" Rittz added solemnly.

Evidently Rittz was concerned by the wellbeing of his father, his shaky voice and nervous twitching were clear indicators. "I see, well worry not fur-face! Me and my admirable apprentice shall delve into those slimy sewers and rescue your father....... for a price" Clyde declared. Such a statement sounded a little harsh to Meadow, but kindness didn't buy fresh alchemy ingredients or food supplies. Rittz didn't seem to mind though, "Of course, but let us discuss price after you've fulfilled the job" he shrewdly answered.

After a flick of his long white whiskers, Rittz gestured Clyde to follow him. "My only request is I join you, being one of the best tunnelers means I know the sewers like the tip of my tail and you'll both be lost in five minutes without me" he uttered. While following Rittz through the bustling bazaar filled with covetous skarl merchants, Meadow had to duck and dodge her way past the crowded sea of hustling customers. Cries of fresh goods and great bargains resonated the air. Not to mention Meadow couldn't walk five feet without a skarl trader pushing some trinket or bauble near her face in a greedy attempt to flog it off.

The incessant noise of bartering between merchants and customers coupled with the relentless rush of activity was causing Meadow to succumb to a headache. "Ugh, can we go somewhere quieter!?" she yelled. Thankfully, her prayers were answered when they reached the end of the chaotic marketplace and emerged into the main city streets. "Stick with me and don't go into any dark alleyways" uttered Rittz. Immediately after saying this, Meadow took a quick glance down a nearby murky alleyway they happened to be passing. Her gaze was quickly met with the beady glares of a few sinister looking skarl who were casually learning against the wall. An eerie shiver crawled over her and she hastened her steps, eager to escape their sight. "Why do the skarl care so much about a monster in the sewers anyway? It can't hurt you down there can it?" she asked. "We skarl are immune to nearly all diseases and poisons, so we use the sewers as a means to travel across the city quickly, also many of our thieves and those with a bounty on their head use it as a sanctuary" answered Rittz.

His reply struck a chord of confusion in Meadow and rendered her speechless, while Clyde chuckled upon seeing her naïve reaction. "Wait, so you openly provide refuge for criminals and thieves?" asked Meadow once she had recovered from the blow of surprise. Rittz quickly shuffled to the side in order to avoid the path of a couple of nasty looking skarl rouges, clad in black leather armor and armed to their fangs with daggers, arrows, longswords and scimitars. "Yes, everyone here is free to live as they please, we have few laws and most crimes are ignored if you can get away with it" Rittz answered.

It sounded like chaos, where the crafty thrived and everyone always looked out for themselves unless there were coin in it for them. A true city of scoundrels and scumbags, where all that seemed to matter was money and survival. "My father the packmaster, he is the only one who commanded any shred of respect and authority around here, most don't care that he is missing, but I know Deepshade will fall into anarchy without him" uttered Rittz. Just as he said this, Meadow and Clyde witnessed a nearby brawl erupt between a group of skarl, it was unclear how the fight started but both furry thugs began clawing at each other fiercely.

Several skarl spectators watched intently and began goading them on with excited cheers, some even started throwing down coin to make bets. "Well, even more anarchy than usual" added Rittz while observing. Rittz led Clyde and Meadow onwards, taking them past a rowdy ruined tavern filled to them brim with drunken skarl patrons yelling songs of befuddled revelry. All of them clumsily swinging their tankards of ale and mead back and forth. It looked like a den of pure drunken disorder, with skarl constantly falling over their tails, arm-wrestling each other and regularly engaging in sloppy fistfights over the slightest quarrel.

A shriek of agony erupted from one of the skarl patrons when a dagger painfully plunged right into his paw. It seemed like him and another skarl had been playing a game, trying to stab the dagger into the table as fast as possible without the blade touching his paw. Obviously, their game had gone awry and it broke into another violent drunken scuffle between the two rats. Spectators around them simply laughed, cheered and clanged their tankards of beer together. A deluge of joy spilled over Meadow when they finally travelled past the dilapidated tavern of turmoil and it trailed into the distance behind them. "How much further?" she asked impatiently.

Before Meadow could receive an answer, she and Clyde were suddenly ambushed by a giggling group of skarl children. "Not much further, we're close to the sewer entrance now!" Rittz answered back in a raised tone. He had to raise his voice above the innocent laughter coming from the flock of skarl children who were playfully prancing around Clyde and Meadow, ogling the many vibrant potions strapped to their bodies. "Hey there, nice to meet you all! Do you like our pretty potions?" asked Meadow in a cheerful tone, stroking a couple of the children upon their furry noses. Clyde on the other hand, he detested the idea of being surrounded by a bunch of bratty rat children and firmly brushed them away. "Stand aside rat boy! I have a duty to perform and there is no time for games!" he declared in an irked voice. "Oh, come on Clyde, they're really cute!" Meadow jovially replied, a cheerful smile spreading across her face as her hand tenderly caressed the children's fuzzy ears and wispy whiskers.

Yet, Rittz was wise to their scheme and marched over, shaking his head at Meadow's gullibility. "I'd be more vigilant if I were you, skarl children tend to have sticky fingers" he uttered while pointing his paw. Immediately, Meadow gave her head a swift twist and caught one of the skarl children behind her attempting to dip his paw into her satchel and pinch whatever he could find. Their ruse was shattered, and Meadow glared at the little ring of furry robbers with both hands planted firmly upon her hips. "I see, so you're just a pack of pilfering pickpockets! Well next ask nicely before trying to take something!" she barked. Her furious demeanor caused all of them to scurry away in fright and Clyde couldn't resist holding his sides as he released an irresistible chuckle. "The ferocity of my apprentice is truly terrifying to behold!" he laughed.

Casually, Rittz shrugged his shoulders and allowed himself to chuckle too, "Come on, its just down this alleyway" he uttered as he led them onwards. "By the way, how did you come to learn of Clyde's services?" asked Meadow as she shadowed Rittz down the narrow crumbling walls of the secluded alleyway. Her heart became aflutter as she awaited his answered, "A mysterious man in a black mask told me of your skills" replied Rittz. "He instructed me to seek out Clyde Alrime, a talented alchemist who would surely solve your problem" he added.

Frustration engulfed Meadow like roaring waves crashing upon rock, for his answer was the one she didn't wish to hear, causing her eyes to slam shut and her fists to tightly clench. Clyde rested firmly in the realm of confusion, his mind feeling like it was lost in a swirling veil of mist, but he didn't say anything or react visually. Yet, his silence spoke the loudest, at least to Meadow it did, she knew Clyde was merely masquerading the turmoil stirring inside him. They followed the rat-like Rittz, but felt like they were the rats instead, caught up in a mysterious game again.

A miserable square shaped sewer grate awaited them at the end of the grimy, crumbling alleyway. Rittz proceeded to approach it, clamp his paws around the rusty iron bars and lift the grate lid upwards, "Here we are!" he declared. Disgust besieged Meadow as she peered into the shadowy hole only to be assailed by a putrid stench that smelled worse than a necromancer's bedroom. "Ugh, should've brought a potion that blocks smell!" spluttered Meadow in a choking heave and recoiling backwards. The foul funk continued to linger in her nose long after she had moved away. "Tis fortunate I planned ahead and arrived sufficiently equipped then isn't it my forgetful little minion?" replied Clyde in a haughty tone, revealing two vials of luminous blue liquid.

After promptly yanking the cork stopper from the neck of one of the vials and gulping it down, Clyde handed the second vial to Meadow. "Behold, a potion that nullifies your sense of smell!" he revealed. Despite this being delightful news for Meadow, she still harbored a tinge of spite towards herself for overlooking something as obvious as the stench they would encounter within the sewers. It served as harsh suspicion to Meadow that she still wasn't ready to prepare her own alchemy harness and blemished her confidence.

The stench wafting from the grate of the sewers was vile and Meadow couldn't wait to purge it from her nostrils, "How long does this potion last?" she asked. "It's a very simple formula so it should be pretty potent, it ought to last a few hours at least" answered Clyde. Meadow tugged the cork stopper from the glass vial and guzzled the potion down in one and just like that, her sense of smell was gone. All traces of the disgusting sewer odor were nullified, but Meadow soon wished Clyde had given her a warning about the taste. For her throat was immersed in a taste so repulsive that she would've welcome a tankard of goblin pee to wash it down. "Ugh, a shame it doesn't nullify taste too!" spluttered Meadow as she reeled in disgust at the revolting flavor that now rested upon her tongue.

A state of amused befuddlement loomed over Rittz as he watched their droll banter play out. "I cannot believe I'm trusting the life of my father to these two!" he uttered, before descending the iron ladder leading into the dark sewers. Clyde waltzed his way past Meadow, giving her a somewhat ridiculing pat on the back as he passed by. "Come on my loveable lackey, time for us to plunge into this den of darkness and filth!" he declared. Reluctantly, Meadow followed Clyde into the murky sewer tunnels, her tongue still dangling out of her mouth from the dreadful taste of the potion. "Ugh! Honestly, this is no place for an elegant young lady like me!" she grumbled as she mounted the dirty ladder.

Darkness quickly devoured Meadow and Clyde as they plummeted beneath the crumbling and chaotic city walls and streets. Their only source of light coming from the narrow sewer grate they had just descended from. Suddenly, Rittz gave a sharp squeak of pain and swiftly leapt to one side, his outburst causing Meadow's heart to feel like it was ready to burst. "What? What is it!?" she gasped in a surprised jolt. Rittz caressed his long scaly tail, trying to gently rub out the pain of having Meadow's foot trampled upon it, "My tail, watch where your stepping!" he cried. "You must be heavier than you look" Rittz casually added while stroking his tail, his comment causing an angry scowl to smear Meadow's face. But she managed to muster her might and let it slide, having her hands upon her hips said enough. "Okay, enough comedy children, let us find your father, but stay vigilant, this is a perilous undertaking!" declared Clyde.

Rittz responded with a concurring nod, refusing himself to be deluded by how risky their venture may be. "Hopefully, no one else will be down here, word has spread about how dangerous the sewers have become and most refuse to gamble their lives" he replied. "Navigating this labyrinth of shadows shall be difficult, so its time to drink up Meadow, I hope you brought some shadow-vision potion" uttered Clyde as he reached for one of his potions. This time he grabbed a potion that possessed an enchanting shade of deep violet and quaffed the entire mixture once he had popped off the cork. "This one should also last a few hours, correct?" asked Meadow as she mirrored him and drew one of her own shadow-vision potions from her harness.

After Meadow had twisted off the cork stopper and swallowed every drop of the bewitching purple potion, Clyde gave her a reassuring nod. "Yes, these potions should last for a few hours, hopefully that should be enough time, otherwise we shall have to navigate this filthy maze in the dark" replied Clyde. After consuming the vials of shadow-vision potion, Meadow was astounded when she watched the darkness around her be instantly banished. Not to mention the visual effect it had upon their eyes was an admittedly splendid sight to behold. Clyde's eyes now possessed a radiant glow and appeared like two luminous golden gems among the sea of shadows, "Your eyes, they are glowing!" cried Meadow. "As are yours, their majestic gleam is visible even within this dreary domain of darkness!" Clyde proudly declared. As the fog of gloom flooding the sewers vanished, Meadow's sight became as clear as a crystal ball. "Remarkable, I never imagined it would work so well! It's like having candlelight for eyes!" she gasped.

Possessing the ability to see in the dark and being utterly immune to any smell were undoubtedly tremendous boons have if they were to traverse a filthy dark sewer. "Follow me, I shall show you the place where my father and his scouting party were seen last" uttered Rittz, his voice echoing along the filthy stone tunnels of the sewer. Clyde and Meadow pursued Rittz as he took lead but kept a comfortable distance as the tunnels were cramped and tactically perilous if they were attacked. "I guess having access to these tunnels really does come in handy for travelling around the city, and for those who wish to hide, I suppose disease isn't a concern either" uttered Meadow in a low hush.

Rittz kept his fluffy ears alert for any suspicious noises and maintained a wary stance as he vigilantly prowled onwards. "Correct, and using these sewers were how my people snatched Deepshade from the orcs many years ago, we swarmed them from below while most of them slept, or so the stories say" he whispered back. It was fortunate for Clyde and Meadow that Rittz had offered his aid, for without his guidance they would've surely been lost in this dreary labyrinth of muck.

Meadow had already lost count of how many twists and turns they taken within these taxing tunnels; she also worshipped the power of alchemy right now. Granting her eyes the ability to glow like a pair of blazing fireballs and pierce the veil of shadows with such luminous light was one blessing of alchemy that Meadow didn't take lightly. Without such an advantage and without her sense of smell nullified, Meadow could only shudder with dread at the image of how much more hellish wandering this maze of murkiness would be. Overhead, Meadow could still hear the muffled noise of chatter, shouting and laughter.

Life above the surface proceeded as normal, the entire city was utterly unaware of her presence right beneath them. Being immune to almost every single disease and illness and having access to these sewers painted a much clearer picture for Meadow as to why they were a haven for all manner of devious crooks and criminals. "Okay, we turn here" uttered Rittz as he cautiously crept around another slimy corner leading left, his furry white paw swiping away a thick clump of cobwebs in his path. Clyde warily tailed him, his attention becoming curiously captured by the torn remains of the cobweb as it passed him by, "Hmmmm……" he mumbled.

Upon turning the next corner and advancing along another section of mucky tunnel, Meadow and Clyde had to regularly raise their hands to swat away a persistent barrage of cobwebs. It didn't take long for Clyde to notice the deeper they delved into the sewers, the more cobwebs appeared, and they grew in both size and strength, something Meadow and Rittz failed to identify. Eventually, Rittz led them to a large open section of the sewers formed in a cross shape and three new directions now lay at their feet. "This is as far as I can guide us, my father and his scouts were last seen here" uttered Rittz.

Calmly, Clyde inspected their surroundings for any clues, his focus once again ensnared by a nearby cluster of cobwebs which he proceeded to glide his finger across. "These webs are far too large, I have a feeling if we follow the webs, we shall find the nest and the source of the problem" uttered Clyde as he studied the silvery vein of strikingly strong cobweb. Suddenly, Meadow's face lost all color, becoming pale like a fresh fallen layer of snow, "Find the nest? You can't possibly mean!" replied Meadow with a fearful tremble in her voice. Her words were abruptly cut short by the sound of mysterious scurrying nearby. It was brief and difficult to detect which direction it came from. Until a large slimy glob of disgusting saliva dropped from the ceiling and splattered upon Clyde's boot, forcing him to gaze upwards and be met with sheer terror.

Crawling upon the ceiling above Clyde was exactly what he suspected. A giant hissing spider, glaring at him with its copious collection of eyes, its sinister fangs poised to strike as it pounced upon him. Luckily, Clyde was quick to react and desperately rolled out of harm's way at the last second. "As I thought!" he declared while Meadow's eyes swelled with fright upon seeing the eight-legged horror. Its size matched its repulsive terror, for it rivalled an adult taurian in both height and length, its body a vibrant orange with lime green markings swirling upon each of its slender long legs. Fear assailed Meadow and Rittz, seizing their senses and rendering them too terrified to even gasp. "Stay back, I've got this!" barked Clyde as he reached for one of his potions. Alas, the spiders sudden ambush had rattled Clyde's focus which resulted in him making a fatal mistake. He didn't check his flank for the possibility of a second spider.

Clyde learned this the hard way as a second identical spider crawled into the room from one of the nearby sewer tunnels and fired a thick thread of sticky webbing towards him. This time Clyde was unable to react and gave a gasp of panic as he was swiftly wrapped up to his neck within the spiders tremendously tough webbing. Only to be hastily dragged away like a brush being swept across a filthy floor. Even Clyde surrendered to fright, his cries of terror echoing along the grimy stone sewers walls as he was hauled away. Meanwhile, Meadow had just enough time to watch him helplessly struggle against the cocoon of confining webbing before he disappeared.

As for the first spider they encountered, it had already set its creepy eyes upon Rittz. It unleashed a viscous strand of webbing upon him while he was still in a state of staggered fright. "No, no! Get this off me!" he cried, using his rat-like claws to frantically slash and tear his way to freedom, but it was to no avail. Like Clyde, Rittz was also quickly rendered defenseless, vulnerable and at the unforgiving mercy of the giant hairy horror. Meadow suddenly snapped into action and reached for one of her precious potions, sadly she soon realized she was too late. Rittz was forcibly dragged away by the spider as it swiftly scurried into the filthy innards of the sewer. His desperate cries for aid chased him into the tunnels, echoing with fear, leaving Meadow veiled in silence and utterly alone.

This was a dilemma Meadow never hoped or expected to find herself in. She was unable to contact Styx since Clyde still wore the ring containing the chatterstone and a cloud of uneasy turmoil quickly fell upon her. To make matters worse, the guiding light bestowed upon her eyes faded like ashes on the wind and the ominous sea of shadows swiftly ambushed her once again. It came as a great surprise to Meadow; she couldn't believe they had already been wandering these revolting tunnels for three hours already.

Fortunately, Meadow brought a second vial of shadow-vision potion and eagerly twisted the cork stopper from the neck of the glass vial and raised it to her lips. the radiant glow within the vial aided in identifying which potion was the correct one in this realm of darkness. A few seconds after she gulped the luminous liquid contained within the vial, the shadows began to vanish, and her eyes radiated that delightful golden glow again. It felt wonderful to be able to see with such enhanced vision and banishing the gloomy domain of darkness around her calmed Meadow's flustered soul. Sadly, it also meant she only had three hours left to find Clyde and Rittz. "Okay, Okay, I just need to remain calm and figure this out, where would those spiders have taken them?" uttered Meadow in a stressed tone while taking some deep breaths.

Taking a couple of minutes to gather her thoughts and soothe her rattled nerves was a far wiser strategy than frantically running away in a panic and becoming more lost. "The nest, Clyde's last words! He said we need to follow the webs to find their nest! That must be where they've been taken!" gasped Meadow. Nervously, Meadow took her first steps into the seemingly abyssal tunnel she saw the spiders drag Clyde and Rittz into. But her heart began beating louder than a roaring wyvern as she navigated her way through the sticky veil of cobwebs.

Cobwebs draped the tunnel and the deeper Meadow travelled the stronger they became. Meadow deduced that the toughest webs might be the newest and upon reaching a junction, she quickly learned something else. Only one of the tunnels possessed cobwebs, "Maybe that's so the spiders know their way back, perhaps they're afraid of getting lost down here too" whispered Meadow. Reluctantly, she pursued the trail of sticky webs, drawing ever closer to their source, but she froze her steps upon hearing horrible hissing nearby. Beads of terrified sweat trickled down Meadow's neck like raindrops, but despite the potential peril, she hesitantly peered her head around the grimy tunnel corner. Pure fright greeted her, for as soon as Meadow peeked around the corner, she was instantly welcomed by the dreaded visage of a giant screeching spider. Its fearsome hissing and repulsive face caused Meadow to squeak with terror and stagger backwards, almost tumbling straight over.

Without delay, the enormous arachnid seized Meadow's moment of fluster and unleashed a thick stream of sticky webbing and began swiftly wrapping her up. Frantically, Meadow fumbled for one of her potions the moment the webbing reached her knees, ripped the cork off the top and quickly quaffed the entire vial like an orc in a drinking contest. By the time the spiders coating of constricting webbing had reached her shoulders, the potion had kicked in and Meadow's entire body suddenly turned ghostly. She consumed the ethereal-potion and her body was now spectral like that of an azure phantom. Thus, allowing her to easily slip through the webbing, dash right through the dreaded spider blocking her path and escape.

However, just because she was intangible didn't mean she was invisible. The frightful eight-legged abomination ruthlessly chased after Meadow, violently swinging its slender front legs to strike her. Naturally, its attacks phased right through Meadow's ghostly form leaving her utterly unscathed.

It may as well be swiping the air, but the spiders speed was daunting to say the least and Meadow knew she had to create some distance. Hastily she darted down another section of sewer tunnel on her right, which caused the repulsive creature to scurry straight past her, giving Meadow a few seconds to gain some distance. Behind her, Meadow could hear echoes of the monsters ghastly scurrying legs and hideous hissing, it was on her trail, hunting her like prey. Despair awaited Meadow around the next corner as she confronted a dead-end and her ethereal potion suddenly wore off. Her ghostly body changed back to one of flesh and bone and she could her the vicious terror chasing close behind her.

Soon, the horrific creature came scurrying around the corner upon its eight slender legs, spotted Meadow and promptly charged towards her with fiendish intent. Fortunately, Meadow had already wrenched the cork stopper from the neck of her next vial of potion and guzzled it down. This one was a vial of sticky-sludge potion, which had a bright gooey green color with a texture that was remarkably dense. Upon drinking it, Meadow swiftly spurted a long stream of vibrant green goo out of her mouth. The repulsive spider was splashed with the sticky green sludge and quickly immobilized as the treacly goo rendered it near impossible to move.

Although the taste was as bitter as a witch's scowl, Meadow shook it off and swiftly reached for her next potion. This time she grabbed a vial containing a liquid that glowed with a burning orange color. It was fire-breath potion, and as soon as Meadow ingested the vial of fiery liquid, she unleashed a scorching plume of flames from her mouth. Unable to move an inch from all the sticky green goo, the giant spider was powerless as Meadow's blast of searing hot fire engulfed the beast. causing it to utter a piercing collection of painful shrieks as it burned to smoking ash.

It was difficult to deduce how much time had passed within these dank dreary sewer tunnels. But Meadow didn't want to waste a single fragment of time as she searched for Clyde and Rittz. She could still feel the fiery sensation of the fire-breath potion frolicking upon her tongue. Meadow simply prayed she wouldn't have to consume one again, for her nerves were still rattled from that last horrific encounter.

With great speed Meadow dashed along the winding sewers tunnels, making sure to follow the cobwebs the whole way, "Come on Clyde, where are you!?" she muttered. Meadow had consumed one of her enhanced-speed potions, granting her the ability to run faster than a centaur chasing a herd of delicious deer. It was a wise decision on her part, for she had no way of knowing when her next vial of shadow-vision potion would wear off. However, it felt like the tunnels would never end and Meadow felt increasingly flustered as she whizzed through them. "I don't like this; I don't like this! Never thought I would be the rescuer for a change!" she jabbered with dread. Her lack of focus cost her dearly, for as Meadow whooshed along another cobweb covered sewer tunnel, a long line of thick webbing shot out from around a corner and acted as a tripwire.

Meadow's attention was so preoccupied that by the time she saw the line of sticky webbing in front of her feet she was powerless to leap over it. "Darn it!" she cried as her legs were swept out from under her. Because of her speed and momentum, Meadow flew across the air and travelled some distance after tripping over the sneaky wire of sticky webbing. Soon she crashed and rolled across the mucky ground with a painful thud. It took a few seconds for Meadow to collect her bearings and recover her dazed senses, unfortunately a few seconds was all the time the giant spider behind her required.

As soon as Meadow dragged herself up and turned around, the beastly terror was already in her face and menacingly hissed at her, before spewing a large trail of sticky webbing. It laid the tripwire and caused Meadow's tumble, now it attempted to ensnare her in a constricting veil of web and drag her back to its lair. Unfortunately, Meadow had no more ethereal potions left, so she had to think fast. This time she swiftly reached for a vial of enhanced-strength potion and swigged it all down just as the spiders sticky webbing reached her chest. It was lucky she acted so fast, as by the time the potion kicked in, the hideous creature had managed to wrap Meadow up to her neck in its horrid webbing and was ready to haul her away.

Thankfully, with the enhanced-strength potion coursing along her veins Meadow gained the strength of a minotaur and easily ripped her way to freedom. Tearing the spiders webbing apart and making it looks as effortless as plucking weeds out of a garden. "Now, you've made me mad!" growled Meadow as she bravely overcame the fear of facing such a vile creature, grabbing the spider by its long front legs when it tried to swing at her. Using her immense strength, Meadow raised the hissing arachnid off the ground by its front legs and flung it aside like a rotten apple. As its giant, bright orange body slammed against the wall, Meadow quickly used this opportunity to swallow her vial of swirling, violet colored sleepy-gas potion and belched out a dense hazy cloud of purple mist. Before the mighty spider could recover from getting lobbed and slammed, the fog of mysterious gas enshrouded it, causing it to become lax and docile, finally falling into a deep slumber.

Clyde told Meadow that he concocted the idea of sleepy-gas potion from the living mushrooms creatures known as fungoid. With the giant spider now asleep, it was ripe for vanquishing with ease. Killing a creature while it was defenseless, even one as loathsome as this overgrown arachnid was something Meadow wasn't thrilled about, but she accepted it as part of her duty as Clyde's apprentice. They were here to eradicate the pests plaguing the people of Deepshade. If Meadow didn't destroy it while she had the chance, it would run rampant and continue to abduct and feed upon the citizens.

With that thought in mind, Meadow casually reached for her last fire-breath potion, slowly twisted the oak cork from the neck of the vial and imbibed the spicy luminous liquid. A second after she had consumed the vial of vibrant mixture, Meadow unleashed another scorching stream of fiery flames from her mouth and watched the sleeping spider be engulfed in a blazing inferno. Naturally, this woke the spider from its slumber and its frightened shrieks echoed along the stone walls of the sewer. But, as vile as the creature was, Meadow couldn't help feeling a stab of remorse for its suffering. Not wishing to look upon the creatures flaming corpse any longer, Meadow turned her back to it and boldly resumed her search for Clyde and Rittz.

The thrashing tornado of terror in her heart began to quell now that both beastly spiders had been vanquished and gave her the courage to call out. "Clyde! Clyde! Can you hear me!? Tell me where you are!" Meadow hollered into the echoing depths of the labyrinthine sewer tunnels. As she travelled along another stretch of tunnel, Meadow started to feel like she was on the right path, as more layers of sticky spider web tried to hinder her advance. Their strength was remarkable, and Meadow had to swat her way through the tatty tunnel of webbing with more vigor than she predicted. "Clyde! Clyde! If you can hear me, let me know where you are!" she called. Her voice resonated along the filthy tunnel, drifting deeper into the miserable maze of muck, but Meadow froze her steps when she heard a voice call back to her. "Meadow, It's Clyde! I'm down here!" it cried.

Without a doubt that was the sound of Clyde and Meadow immediately quickened her pace, delight pouring over her as she pursued the echoing trail of his voice. It sounded near, but Meadow kept encouraging Clyde to call out to her. "I think I'm close! Keep calling to me!" she cried while tearing the clusters of cobwebs in her path asunder. "I'm here but embrace a dose of caution! Those wretched spiders could be anywhere!" shouted Clyde, his voice echoing from around the nearest sharp corner. After hearing his voice, Meadow heard Rittz abruptly call out a moment after, "Do hurry, I do not relish the thought of being a snack for these vile pests!" he shouted.

Upon tracking his voice to its source and turning the corner, Meadow emerged into a large clearing and finally found Clyde and Rittz at last. "Well, well, better late than never I suppose!" remarked Rittz. "Apologies for the delay, I became tangled up with some less than amicable creepy-crawlies, I guess they saw me as the appetizer!" replied Meadow as she hurried into the web strewn room. Clearly this was where the spiders made their nest, with the rotting skulls and bones of their victims still littering the ground. Various weapons and armor now caked in web and dirt belonging to unfortunate victims also lay scattered across the floor.

As for Clyde and Rittz, they remained encased in webbing and stuck to the wall in the corner like fresh meat stored on a shelf to be saved for later. Their heads were the only exposed part of their bodies, likely to avoid any chance of suffocation. "Don't worry, I did it Clyde! I used my potions and I managed to vanquish those nasty critters for good!" Meadow proudly declared while snatching a nearby steel dagger from the skeletal fingers of a victims remains. Using the daggers steel blade, Meadow began cutting into the binding cocoon of webbing that bound Clyde, for he surely couldn't wait to feel freedom once more. "Really? You slew all three of those spiders?" asked Clyde.

His question caused Meadow to abruptly cease her cutting and she raised her head, confusion shimmering in her gaze, "Three?" she answered. Suddenly, a sticky thread of webbing wrapped around Meadows ankles and forcefully flung her off her feet. Before she even realized what was happening, Meadow's entire world was literally flipped upside down. She was quickly rendered dangling and helpless, "Another one!?" she cried in panic. An ominous hissing sound echoed from above and Meadow soon came face to face with the culprit.

It was indeed a third giant spider, possessing a bright, bulbous orange body and long slender legs adorned with swirling green patterns like the others. It had been hiding or perhaps sleeping in a large alcove above the room. But now it had captured Meadow in its web and rendered her a swaying sausage ripe for eating. Luckily, Meadow still grasped the steel dagger she found earlier in her hand and swiftly lunged her body forwards. Frantically, she started cutting through the web wrapped around her ankles. Her desire to be free intensified as the spiders sharp drooling fangs neared her face, "Come on!" Meadow screamed as she feverishly cut into the webbing.

For a spilt second the repulsive spider retracted its body, before suddenly pouncing off the wall and lunging at Meadow, eager to sink its fangs into her neck and devour her. Just at it pounced however, Meadow felt the steel dagger slice through the line of webbing tangled around her ankles, causing gravity to immediately take hold and plummet her to the ground. She landed with a rough thud, but quickly shook off the impact and scrambled to her feet, only to see the vicious giant spider now scurrying towards her. Unfortunately, there wasn't enough time to consume a potion just yet. Instead Meadow dived for a worn, cobweb covered shield scattered amongst the skeletal remains, snatched it up and raised it just in time to block one of the spider's powerful strikes.

It lashed at her with its two long front legs and struck the steel shield with tremendous force, so much so that Meadow staggered and stumbled backwards from the attack. Naturally, the vile creature didn't stop there, it maintained its relentless assault and kept stabbing and swinging at Meadow with its front legs. Thankfully, Meadow managed to keep clumsily blocking its strikes with her shield. After being pressed against the wall with nowhere else to scurry to, Meadow ducked as the spider lunged its hideous hissing face straight at her.

Smoothly, she evaded the creature's sinister fangs and rolled beneath its hairy underbelly unscathed and emerged behind the beast. Meadow wasted no time in reaching for one of the precious potions strapped to her harness, deciding it best to drink one while the spiders back was turned. This time she picked the smokescreen potion, a potion possessing a peculiar ebony shade, but with a liquid consistency that was both thin yet hazy and after popping the cork off, she swigged it down. By the time the monstrous spider had recovered its sense of direction and flashed its slimy fangs at Meadow, Meadow had already unleashed the effects of the smokescreen potion.

A giant cloud of black smoke suddenly spewed from Meadow's mouth and enveloped the horrid arachnid. Confusion ensued as the billowing haze of smoke obscured its sight and allowed Meadow a fleeting moment of precious respite. "How I wish I brought one more fire-breath potion, what can I do!?" cried Meadow. At least this ephemeral window of opportunity allowed her to scurry away from the dreadful creature and plan her next stratagem. "You needn't resort to fire to vanquish every foe, consume that new potion I concocted!" declared Clyde who watched Meadow from his webbed shell.

Glancing down at her harness, Meadow remembered the potion Clyde was referring to. It was the one which had an icy blue shade with swirls of faint white mist filling the pocket of air in the vial. Despite not knowing its effects, Meadow trusted Clyde's judgement, swiftly yanked out the cork, raised the vial to her lips and quaffed the entire mixture in one. A trembling shiver swept over Meadow's body as she drank the cold potion, it tasted light but incredibly chilly, like she had just consumed a bowl of fresh fallen snowflakes. Meanwhile, the cloud of eclipsing smoke faded, and the repulsive sight of the spider came back into view. It wasted little time fiercely scurrying towards Meadow, who was now backed into an infuriating corner. Yet, as the sinister spider mercilessly advanced upon her, Meadow unleashed the full effect of the alluring icy blue potion upon the beast and sprayed a blinding blizzard of frosty white air from her mouth. It lasted for several seconds and as the frigid white mist swept over the giant spider, it was rendered immobile until gradually freezing entirely.

Soon Meadow had changed the creepy-crawly into little more a shimmering, sparkly ice sculpture, albeit a rather repulsive one. "I see, frost-breath potion!" gasped Meadow, with white plumes of frost still drifting upon her breath. "Indeed, a marvelous miracle of alchemy if I do say so myself, but do not dally my dear, for that unsightly insect shan't remain frozen forever!" answered Clyde. At this point Meadow felt she had endured these hideous creatures enough for one day and refused the spider a second longer to potentially thaw out, "Then I guess it's time to break the ice!" she declared. Not a single fragment of hesitation entered Meadow as raised the steel shield she found and suddenly hurled it at the frozen monster, shattering it into numerous shards of ice.

Seeing the insidious spider shattered into a myriad of frozen fragments brought much-needed tranquility to Meadow's thundering heart. "Breathe easy my apprentice, it's over now! To overcome such an ordeal unaided speaks volumes about your courage and willpower" uttered Clyde. "Even so, tis not an experience I wish to repeat anytime soon!" answered Meadow as she approached Clyde and began cutting him free using the dirty dagger she found earlier. Her hands still trembled, from the peril of the situation and the terror that came with it. but something else existed within Meadow now, a firmness, a resolve that burned brighter than ever. Perhaps it had always been there and merely waited for a trial by fire to be awakened. The memories of Elijah had always haunted her dreams and infused her heart with fear, but Meadow proved that her fear could be conquered.

After a rigorous amount of cutting, Meadow concluded that one grimy dagger wouldn't be enough to cut through the sticky shell of webbing that bound Clyde. "It's not going to work, but what other option is there?" she muttered. "Don't give up now, I believe in you Meadow! Also, I really need to pee, so put all your strength into it and hurry!" demanded Rittz who grew increasingly fidgety.

His words proved helpful caused Meadow to have a sudden epiphany, "Put all my strength into it? hold on a second!" answered Meadow as she reached for her last vial of enhanced strength potion. "Don't worry, you'll both be free in no time!" declared Meadow as she uncorked the vial of liquid and pressed the neck of the bottle to her lips, baffled at the fact that she didn't think of this sooner. Like always, upon drinking the container of magical mixture, Meadow didn't have to wait long to feel its effects. Immediately, she felt the strength of a stone golem coursing through her veins and now, the cocoon of webbing was no match for Meadow's might.

Vigorously, Meadow proceeded tear it asunder with ease just as lightning tears the sky, ripping Clyde to freedom with her bare hands. Being able to move all his appendages again was a luxury Clyde never imagined he would miss and cherished his liberty once more. "Ah, how truly delightful it feels to stretch, I was growing ever so stiff in that constricting cocoon!" he gasped. Not wanting to delay and risk losing the potions effect, Meadow swiftly tended to Rittz, employing her temporary colossal strength upon the coat of spider web that contained him. Ripping it apart like she was plucking the feathers from a plump goose, until Rittz was also able to join Clyde in his admiration for freedom. "Ah free at last, I must say I prefer to be constricted by choice!" he crudely joked.

Luckily, his uncouth jest flew right over Meadow's head, "And now we can resume our search for your father, he's got to be down here!" answered Meadow with hearty optimism. Optimism that Rittz didn't share sadly, for he raised his furry paw to silence her potent jubilation and released a dreary sigh. "There is no need to continue the search, I found him already" he replied, mournfully approaching a pile of skeletal remains in the murky corner. "Skarl eyes see through the shadows and I spotted my fathers ring before you found us" uttered Rittz as he knelt beside the bones of his father and wrested the silver jeweled ring from his skeletal finger.

The ring was majestic and evoked sentimental value within Rittz, and he proceeded to slide it upon his own finger. Then used a few moments of reflective silence to kneel by his father's skeleton and honor his memory, regardless of how painful it was to behold. "Oh no, I'm so sorry for your loss" whispered Meadow once Rittz had finished kneeling by his father's side, although she was quite surprised by how well Rittz was handling it. Yet, a teary glimmer twinkled within the deepest corner of Rittz's eye, a glimmer Rittz hurried in wiping away with his paw. No doubt a twisting storm of anguish and turmoil churned within Rittz's heart right now, but visibly he remained unshattered. "Apologies aren't necessary, my father was foolish to place himself in harm's way!" he grumbled. "Your father was the packmaster, he was brave and noble, placing the needs of the people before his own, there is nothing foolish about that" Meadow replied sincerely.

Unfortunately, Rittz swiftly rejected her sincerity with a quick scoff, "Exactly, he valued the lives of others before his own, but what can he value now?" he asked. "Looking out for yourself has always been the code of the skarl and this only proves why!" Rittz added bitterly. Silently, Rittz strolled away, suppressing his frustration beneath a mask of coldness, "Come, the job is done!" he called. Departing these filthy dark tunnels was a thought that Meadow deeply cherished, especially since her shadow-vison potion had worn off some time ago. This meant that her and Clyde had to rely on Rittz to guide them back.

Skarl eyes pierce even the shadows, a statement that held weight right now. For without Rittz's natural ability to perceive beyond the veil of darkness around them, Clyde and Meadow would be as two shipwrecked survivors drifting aimlessly amidst a lonely sea. Stumbling through the gloomy tunnels was far from fun, but Rittz took lead and proved why he was one of the best tunnellers in Deepshade. Not once did his steps cease and not once did he lose his sense of direction. "We are not far now, I used to love playing in these tunnels when I were but a young rattling, after today though, I'm not sure these tunnels will fill me with the same joyful nostalgia again" echoed Rittz's voice.

Meadow grimaced at his words as she followed behind them, Rittz would no longer think of these tunnels as the place him and his friends played together. Instead it had become the place where his father was captured by giant hideous spiders and most likely eaten alive. It made an already bleak atmosphere even bleaker, seemingly squeezing any last drop of hope dry. Thankfully and ironically, a ray of light appeared, during their darkest moment.

Small, slithers of light crept through the ceiling, enough that even Clyde and Meadow could see them. "Here we are at last, I'm eager to leave these tunnels, something I thought I'd never say!" declared Rittz. He released his furry paw which was joined to Meadow and Meadow released her other hand that was joined to Clyde's, for all three of them had remained linked in order to remain inseparable. Now there was no need, for a burst of radiant sunlight washed over Rittz's furry face as he climbed the iron rings built into the wall and lifted the sewer grate above. Fresh, rejuvenating air greeted each of them as they climbed out of the foul shadows and emerged into the glorious light of day. "Ah, I truly never knew how much I cherished the purity of fresh air in my lungs, nor the resplendent light of the sun until both were snatched away from me!" gasped Clyde.

Sadly, the loss of Rittz's father left a bitter taste in their mouths, ensuring their victory was a hollow one at best. Something Meadow and Clyde were unaccustomed to, "So Rittz, what will you do now?" asked Meadow. A solemn cloud loomed over Rittz as he gazed at his father's ring upon his finger. "I guess I am now the new packmaster, the closest thing the skarl have to a leader, yet I doubt I can lead them even half as well as my father did" he answered. In a gesture of support, Meadow placed her hand upon his shoulder, "But surely your people do need leading? Deepshade needs organizing, they need someone who commands their respect" she uttered. Despite her effort, Meadow only served to make Rittz sneer, "Have you learned nothing during your time here? Deepshade is a city of thieves, scoundrels and villains, it is pure anarchy!" He grumbled. "No one could command order or respect here, least of all me!" Rittz frustratedly added.

Against her better judgement, Meadow tried to console Rittz a little more, "Your father could, could he not?" she asked in a heartfelt tone. "I'm not my father, but I will bear his title of packmaster, I shall bear it with both reluctance and disdain!" grumbled Rittz, the loss of his father clearly cutting him deeper than what he wished to show. Rittz then led Meadow and Clyde through the ravaged, rat filled streets of Deepshade. Past disorderly crowds consisting of skarl who were either brawling over a heated dispute or utterly drunk out of their minds, or both.

Once they reached the bustling bazaar, navigated the chaotic crowds of perusing patrons and made their way through the maze of market stalls, Rittz ceased escorting them. He travelled with them right up to the main gate which they entered and offered them a final nugget of gratitude. "Well, although we weren't able to rescue my father, I still believe your effort was valiant and worthy of merit, I thank you greatly Clyde" said Rittz. Unable to hear such praise, Clyde raised his hand to stop Rittz uttering a single word further, unable to accept any kind of glory this time. "Your thanks is appreciated, but also inaccurate, it was my disciple Meadow who saved your fur today and mine too if I had any! It is her that should be basking in your gratitude" he replied.

It was impossible for Rittz to refute such a claim and he corrected his blunder by offering Meadow a sincere bow. "Indeed, it is you whom we give our deepest thanks to Meadow!" he uttered. Meadow humbly recoiled herself into a shy shell, a slight blush blooming in her cheeks, for being the heroine was not something she ever envisioned. "Oh, well I was merely happy to be of assistance!" Meadow awkwardly blurted out. Suddenly, the potion they took several hours ago that nullified their sense of smell wore off. This caused their noses to be quickly assailed by the revolting stench they had accumulated on their clothes from within the filthy sewer tunnels. "Ugh! The smell nullifying potion has ended!" cried Clyde with disgust. "I gathered that genius! I think a much-needed bath is required when I return, a beautiful young lady like me can't go around smelling like this!" Meadow declared with a grimace.

Rittz couldn't refrain from chuckling at them both, "Plunging into those dark tunnels was no easy task, especially for anyone who isn't a skarl, your efforts will be rewarded with coin, I only ask you wait here while I retrieve it" he said. Although a sack stuffed with gleaming gold coins would be a welcome sight to behold, today Clyde felt like he couldn't even accept the scraps off a goblins dinnerplate. "Any payment you wish you give for our services must go to Meadow, it is her that should accept the reward and decide how best to spend it" answered Clyde. Rittz nodded his furry head in agreement and twirled his long whiskers, his attention falling upon Meadow. "Your master speaks truthfully and virtuously; your reward is rightfully earned Meadow" he added. Adamantly, Meadow shook her head at the notion of payment. "Keep the gold, use the money to aid Deepshade and its people, you've already lost your father today, you needn't sacrifice anything more" she answered.

Such a display of kindness stirred mixed feelings deep within Rittz. He had always believed in survival of the fittest and placing one's needs above the needs of others, this had always been the code of the skarl. Rittz's father, the previous packmaster was the exception, he tried to change this mindset and perceive the bigger picture. His father wanted to create a greater sense of harmony for his people, rather than them being perceived as thieves and selfish rogues all the time. "Your father may be gone Rittz, but he still lives on in you, carry on his title to the best of your ability, I'm sure that's what he would've wanted for you one day" uttered Meadow with sincerity. Rittz met Meadow's earnest gaze and nodded, "Your right, I shall do my best! For Deepshade, for my people and for the memory of my father!" he declared.

After finally waving goodbye to Rittz and bidding him a fond farewell, Clyde and Meadow decided it was time to depart Deepshade, the city of sin and home of the rat-like skarl. Clyde and Meadow traversed the groaning wooden drawbridge and passed under the crumbling stone gateway again. It hadn't changed, dozens of skarl were still lazily strewn across it like cats in a tree. Most of the skarl watched Clyde and Meadow with vigilant suspicion, while a few others were casually playing with their daggers, using them to clean their nails and such.

Clyde waited until they had passed under the dilapidated gateway and escaped the watchful gaze of any skarl before preparing to speak into his chatterstone. "I wish to commend you again my apprentice on a job well done, you displayed bravery and cunning to overcome your ordeals, Ah! You remind me so much of myself!" Clyde decaled. His egotism resulted in Meadow wearily rolling her eyes, baffled at how he could be so arrogant. "Oh thanks, I'm so glad I'm becoming like the great and valiant Clyde Alrime, the one who screamed like a little girl when he was being dragged away by a spider!" she replied.

Her comment served to smear the haughty grin from Clyde's face and replace it with a grumpy twisted scowl. "Styx, be so kind as to create a portal in the same place again" grumbled Clyde, refusing to acknowledge Meadow's jest. "Yes master, I shall begin conjuring another portal at once, but I hope you're not too dirty from your ordeal, I just cleaned the floors!" echoed Styx's raspy voice. Now the only thing left to do was wait for Styx to create the magical portal and ferry them home. Clyde had some serious words of wisdom to share with Meadow first. "All jesting aside, I would advise you to shield your emotions and not invest them in our clients, not all investments yield fruit my apprentice, Rittz must follow his own path and we came to do a job, nothing more" uttered Clyde.

Until the portal was created, Meadow silently pondered his words, she reflected upon them since they weren't the words of an erratic mad scientist for once. Clyde's words led Meadow to conclude that she may have stepped over the line a little with Rittz, even if it did create a seemingly good outcome. Life suddenly seemed very much like alchemy in a sense, for every action there was an equal reaction, some words and actions seeming like potions and some seeming like poisons. Such a moment of deep, reflective thought brought an equal slither of fascination and fear to Meadow, "I see, so we must choose our choices wisely" she uttered. However, half of her words were abruptly drowned out when the mystical portal suddenly exploded into view, rupturing the air with a thundering boom.

Clyde began walking towards the floating doorway of vibrant magical energy, but Meadow had one last question on her mind. "Clyde, do you think he was behind this? That mysterious masked figure?" she asked. "Maybe, I honestly don't know, but I enjoy the thought of finding out who he is" answered Clyde as he gradually vanished into the depths of the swirling vortex of colors.

Chalice of Renewal
Chapter 8
An imp-possible ordeal

Since meeting Clyde, Meadow had learned to cherish moments of tranquility, moments of respite, moments like the one right now. Meadow had added the correct quantity of ingredients, after grinding them down and distilling all their impurities to ensure her next concoction would be a beneficial one. All that was left was for Meadow to sit back, relax and observe the pair of bubbling glass beakers as they boiled above the fluttering flames of the candles beneath them. "I remembered to add a pinch of powered najala claw" she uttered. Her words went unanswered by Clyde, whom had his nose buried deeply within the piles of parchment upon his desk.

Two weeks had passed since their terrifying tribulation in the twisting sewer tunnels of Deepshade, and since then, Clyde had barely pulled himself away from his desk. Clearly whatever Clyde was researching was of great importance to him, but he still made sure to give Meadow a new task each time she fulfilled an older one. Ensuring Meadow kept learning the intricate art of alchemy was a duty Clyde never abandoned, his role as her teacher was one he took sincerely, it simply confounded him how quickly she was advancing.

Outside the cozy walls of the house another snowy blizzard was howling away, yet it seemed serene when Meadow watched it from the luxury of the window. Listening to the muffled whistling of the snowstorm and the gentle bubbling of alchemy flasks sounded like music to Meadow's ears. Perhaps Clyde chose wisely when he selected this spot to make his home, the solitude and regular squalls of blustering snow made it so peaceful. "I also remembered to extract two spoonsful of oil from sunflame petals" uttered Meadow. Once again, her words went unheard, for Clyde's mind may as well been in a different realm right now. His attention remaining ensnared by the notes upon his desk, his hand relentlessly scrawling with ink and quill.

Meadow causally dangled her feet over her chair and playfully kicked them back and forth, watching the bubbling flasks of liquid with unyielding captivation. Alchemy persisted in fascinating Meadow, and her passion for the elaborate art hadn't dulled in the slightest. In fact, it was quite the opposite, her passion for alchemy burned brighter than the roaring flames of a dragon's breath. Evident by the way her she rested her elbows upon the alchemy workstation to move her face closer to the beakers of vibrant brew.

Her eyes gleamed as they peered closely at the beakers of liquid, one of which had become a gooey emerald green, while the other had changed to a luminous pumpkin orange. The fact that Meadow worked so meticulously and poured all her passion into something so creative gave her a sense of pride and accomplishment, making alchemy feel even more rewarding. However, curiosity persisted in pestering Meadow the more she glanced at Clyde and his quill feverishly scrawling away, so Meadow decide to investigate in her own way.

She hopped down from her chair and left the two bubbling beakers of potion unattended for a moment and quietly crept towards Clyde. Her presence went completely unnoticed, Meadow could've been a herd of stampeding centaur and Clyde would've still failed to notice her considering how close his face was to his desk. Meadow took shelter behind Clyde's desk cherishing the suspense and relishing the moment until she could no longer resist the urge to spring up like a jack-in-a-box. After counting to three in her head, Meadow commenced her sly scheme and suddenly burst from behind Clyde's desk like a cobra pouncing upon its prey, "Boo!" she yelled upon leaping from her hiding spot. "Aghhhh!" screamed Clyde as he jumped out of his skin and bolted backwards in his chair, toppling right over and sending a bunch of parchment paper scattering like fresh blown leaves.

Meadow achieved a greater outcome than she could've hoped and held her aching sides as she staggered around in utterly relentless laughter. "By the gods that was funny! Oh Clyde, if only you could've seen your face!" she chuckled. Clyde's furious scowl only added to the amusement. "That was neither cute nor funny my maddening little minion and you're lucky I didn't mistake you for a deadly assassin and swiftly detained you!" he growled. Tears of amused laughter relentlessly rolled down Meadows cheeks. "Oh Really? A shooting star could've smashed through the roof and you would've failed to notice me based on how distracted you were!" she replied while wiping her tears away.

Clyde simply pulled himself up off the floor in a fluster in and began grumpily scooping up the sheets of scattered parchment paper. "What has captured your attention so greatly anyway?" asked Meadow as she slowly tilted her head and gazed upon a sheet of upside-down parchment paper that had landed near her foot. Instantly Meadow recognized a name, "The Chalice of Renewal, I remember seeing that name before, that's what has you so distracted isn't it?" she asked. Although Clyde desired to lie and squirm his way out of her question, he could tell Meadow would pierce right through any ruse at this moment. "Okay, yes! Yes! I confess, the Chalice of Renewal is why my focus has been so enamored of late" he reluctantly answered. The hooks of curiosity sunk deeply into Meadow and she dared to inquire further, "So, what is the Chalice of Renewal exactly? Why is it so important?" she asked.

Instead of receiving a straight answer, Clyde decided to oppose Meadow instead, "Must you ask more questions my mouthy minion?" uttered Clyde in a weary sigh. Sadly, his elusive nature backfired and only served to urge Meadow to inquire further. "Must you always evade them?" she answered in a fiery tone, slamming her hands upon her hips. Her persistence was both admirable and vexing and resulted in Clyde's fatigued surrender. "Fine, the Chalice of Renewal is a legendary goblet said to change any liquid into any other the holder desires, be it water, wine or whatever else" answered Clyde.

Grouchily, Clyde bent over and scooped up several pages of scattered notes off the floor. "Aside from that, it is said that liquid poured from the chalice can revert anything back to its healthiest form, cure any disease or illness, restore lost hair or sight, essentially a complete renewal" he added. Such a fantastical legend sounded miraculous to say the least, but Meadow clung onto a healthy dose of disbelief. "You don't really believe a silly fairy-tale like that do you? It's probably just another ancient children's story" she remarked. Her lack of faith disturbed Clyde, so much so that he made his passion for the legend of the chalice abundantly clear. "After all you have seen you still doubt the wonders of this world, you deign to fall to blissful ignorance at the magical miracles of this land!?" he proclaimed. Clyde's obsession with this fabled Chalice of Renewal soared like a burning phoenix the moment it was challenged, ambushing Meadow and causing her to recoil. "Okay, okay! No need to unleash the wrath of the gods upon me! It clearly means a lot to you" she uttered.

After taking a moment to pause, Clyde's ardent flames began to soothe, and he offered Meadow and apologetic bow. "Forgive my minor outburst of passionate mania, the chalice does mean a lot to me, I've spent years searching for it" he replied. As incredible as the Chalice of Renewal sounded, Meadow wondered if such a legend was truly worth chasing with such unyielding devotion. "It almost sounds personal, why do you seek it so much?" she asked. "Cease your questions for you shall divulge no more answers from me my disciple!" Clyde sternly replied. After reorganizing his pile of notes, Clyde diligently resumed his focus upon them. "My lips upon this topic are sealed tighter than the doors of a princesses bedchamber and as your master I urge to return to your own studies instead of meddling in mine!" Clyde declared.

Clearly, he wished to speak no more upon the matter, but his eccentric tone still provoked a silent, miffed scowl from Meadow. Her vexed glare thankfully lasting for only a second as a series of heavy knocks abruptly echoed from behind the front door. Styx calmly floated in with his flapping leather wings to very kindly see who was on the other side. "Worry not master, I shall answer the door" he uttered in his raspy impish voice.

Styx's slender fingers twisted like ivy around the decorative doorknob and he strenuously heaved open the front door, but was swiftly engulfed by a howling, icy gale. "Greetings and welcome to my masters homeeeeee!" cried Styx over the blustering blizzard which bombarded and blew him backwards, sending him careening across the floor of the foyer. In waddled Hector, covered head to toe in a thick layer of snow, "Delivery!" he announced before promptly rushing behind the front door and using all his might to close it shut against the icy tempest. After a slight struggle, the door slammed shut and Hector breathed a sigh of relief, taking a few precious moments to compose himself before removing his woolly scarf and protective goggles. "Greetings Swiftwing, once again you have endured the icy breath of the Frostveil Mountains, braved its chilly claws and sought refuge and comfort in my oasis of warmth, but to what end I say!?" declared Clyde. Hector rolled his feathery head and released an exasperated wheeze. "My name isn't Swiftwing Clyde! And you know I deliver letters so why not take a guess as to why I've travelled here!" Hector fired back.

After shaking the snow from his long feathery wings, Hector the harpy reached one of his sharp talons into his large delivery sack and rummaged around for Clyde's letter. "Such insolence! Maybe I should change my courier!" grumbled Clyde. After a little rummaging, Hector found the right letter in his bulky sack, whipped it out and shoved it into Clyde's face. "Yeah, good luck finding a courier willing to traverse this frozen wasteland! You've got another request for aid, just one this time" answered Hector.

Grouchily, Clyde snatched the letter and was abruptly consumed by frustration. "By the stormy breath of the legendary dragon Tyras! Another request for aid!? The last one was little more than a couple of weeks ago!" he exclaimed. As he stomped away towards the kitchen with the letter in hand, Clyde remained trapped in a realm of disbelief. "Honestly, ever since Meadow became my apprentice, I've never been so busy!" he proclaimed. A tiny chuckle fluttered from Meadow's mouth as she watched Clyde's cranky fluster unfold. "Never mind him, he's just been focusing on his own little project too much, would you like to stay for a cup of tea?" asked Meadow.

While a cup of delicious hot tea sounded as welcome as a moment of sunshine in this wintery wasteland, Hector had to reluctantly shake is head and refuse. "I have far too many deliveries ahead of me and I want to be home early tonight, got a feeling me and my wife are going to ruffle our feathers, if you know what I mean?" replied Hector with a wink. As soon as these words left Horace's beak, Meadow slammed her eyes shut and slapped her forehead with her palm. "No, I'm not entirely sure what you mean, but I'm pretty sure I don't want to know" she groaned. After tightening his woolly scarf again, Horace playfully slapped Meadow on the shoulder and laughed. "Well, I have to go, good luck with your alchemy Meadow, believe it or not, your being taught by the best" replied Horace. In a gesture of hospitality, Meadow prepared to open the front door for Horace. "Oh, trust me, there are days when it's hard to believe!" she joked before letting the bellowing blizzard back in. "Fly safe dear Swiftwing! Fly safe!" Clyde called when popped his head out of the kitchen to utter a fond farewell, only for Hector to jadedly roll his eyes.

Hector remained steadfast against the whistling icy wind and salvos of cold snow. Pulling his goggles back over his eyes, spreading his long elegant wings and taking flight into the frigid storm of white. He quickly vanished from all sight as the screaming tempest consumed him like a sandstorm sweeping over a lost traveler. Which prompted Meadow to summon all her strength to shove the door shut and silence the shrieking squall. Upon slamming the door shut, a smidgen of snow fell onto Meadow's head from the vibration, but she shook her fiery, carrot colored hair clean of snow and pursued Clyde into the kitchen.

Clyde had already poured himself a cup of fresh steamy tea and his eyes diligently perused the latest letter for aid, "So, what's the job this time?" asked Meadow as she strolled in. "Seems trouble is afoot in the city of Orstone, also known as Blooda Ruznik, which translates to Blood Rock in the ancient tongue of the orcs" answered Clyde after taking a refreshing sip of his tea. Surprise struck Meadow like a hidden arrow, "What could the orcs need aid with? Aren't they the greatest warriors in all Resplendia?" she asked.

After studying the letter of its contents, Clyde gently placed it upon the oak kitchen table and casually slumped into one of the surrounding chairs. "Potentially greatest yes, but only when it comes to smashing things and not all problems are solved with might" he answered. A fragrant aroma drifted from the pot of recently made tea and made the air taste as sweet as honey, "So, what's todays tea?" asked Meadow as she took a seat opposite Clyde. "Today it is a rather ravishing combination of moontear petals, sandstar root and frostwitch flower, creating a tea that is sweet, earthy and alluring" answered Clyde. Meadow gave Clyde a respectful nod as he kindly poured her a cup of the plum colored tea and passed it to her. "From what I've read in the letter, it seems the orcs have a ghost problem" uttered Clyde.

The warmth of the cup touched Meadow's fingers, yet her face remained befuddled as she gazed at Clyde, wondering if she had heard him correctly, "Did you just say ghosts?" she asked. Despite ghosts being utterly mysterious and a rare phenomenon, Clyde nodded and shrugged it off like it was a common occurrence. "Yes indeed, the letter says something has disturbed the sealed spirits resting in one of the orcs sacred crypts for fallen warriors" he replied. Baffled by Clyde's aura of calm, Meadow continued to speechlessly gawk at him until a burning tingle scorched her fingertips. In her moment of disbelief, Meadow hadn't even realized she was still touching the side of the hot cup of tea. "Ow! But honestly, ghosts? How exactly do we combat something that is already dead?" asked Meadow, quickly pulling her fingers back.

A crafty grin crept along Clyde's face as he reclined in his chair. "Do you still doubt the power of alchemy? Are you still blind to its boundless world? A world rife with a myriad of possibilities!?" he proclaimed. Meadow gave a few soft blows upon her hot tea before taking a hearty gulp and feeling its delightful fruity flavor sweep over her lips. "Of course not, alchemy is now a part of my heart that I never knew was missing, but surely ghosts cannot be harmed!" she answered. Instead of gulping the tea and drowning within its alluring taste, Clyde preferred to sip and savor it, especially when his mind was thinking hardest.

After several seconds of thoughtful silence, Clyde placed his teacup upon the table again with a slight slam and leaned forward. "Yes, in most cases you are right, and the letter states that some orc warriors have already been killed fighting these apparitions" he replied. "Cleary, these ghosts are capable of attacking others while being immune to harm themselves, it certainly makes for an irksome foe!" Clyde added with a dab of annoyance. Once she had quaffed the last of her refreshing tea, Meadow raised an eyebrow at Clyde, wondering if he was approaching a point. "So? I assume you haven't run out of tricks genius" she answered with a hint of sarcasm. "Ha, never!" Clyde declared with gusto, devouring his last droplets of tea, bolting out of his chair and confidently sauntering out of the kitchen. Meadow playfully chuckled to herself and shrugged, "Guess that's my cue to follow him" she uttered and pursued after Clyde.

Waiting patiently in the portal room was Clyde's loyal little imp Styx, "Are you travelling again master? Where are you visiting this time?" he asked in his same demonic voice. Clyde gazed at the large, elegantly framed map of Resplendia that hung upon the wall and dramatically pointed his finger up at it, "Orstone Styx! Deliver us close to Orstone!" he declared. Obediently, Styx saluted Clyde, "Aye, aye Captain Clyde!" he declared and raised his miniature magical trident. A churning aura of vivid energy began swirling around Styx's trident as he pointed it at the circular stone pedestal in the center of the room and channeled his demonic magic. At the same time, Clyde ardently marched back into his bubbling alchemy lab brimming with beautiful brews, mysterious mixtures and captivating concoctions in order to prepare his precious potions for the journey.

Picking his potions wisely was perhaps the part that enthralled Clyde the most. His delight bordering on reverence as he shrewdly and strategically selected which would be essential and slotted them into his harness. Meadow joined him a few moments later, the peculiar pungent odor of the alchemy lab wafting into her face the moment she entered. "What are we taking today Potion Lord?" she asked in a playful tone.

A stern expression abruptly surfaced upon Clyde's face as he watched Meadow vault over the shiny handrail coursing along the steps leading to the lab. Choosing instead to bypass it by leaping down, "Use the stairs! And who are you calling potion lord!?" remarked Clyde. Cluelessly, Meadow scratched the side of her face with her finger. "I'm sorry? Mixture Master? Brew Baron? Concoction King? Remind me which it is again" answered Meadow in a teasing tone. "I've told you a thousand times minion, my title is Alchemy Emperor! Remember it well, for one day my greatness and splendor shall be uttered upon the breaths of every citizen in Resplendia, if not the world!" Clyde haughtily declared.

As he slammed his hands upon his hips and unleased a maniacal bout of laughter, Meadow slapped her face with her palm and sighed. "Of course, forgive me oh great one!" she replied sarcastically. It took a few seconds, but Clyde managed to overcome his delusion of grandeur and temper his euphoria. "Forgive my delirious outburst, I fall prey to the vision of my vast renown, choose your own potions again my apprentice" he uttered. Granting Meadow, the choice to pick her own potions again proved Clyde had faith in her skill and guile, their last expedition no doubt aided in verifying that as well.

Meadow rested her finger upon her lips as she carefully considered which potions to take. "Life detection potions are pointless since ghosts are dead, and I doubt breath potions such as sleepy-gas and frost-breath won't have much effect either" she uttered. Clyde's eyebrows quickly shot up and he released a slight hum of admiration. "Very astute observations my disciple, it pleases me to see how much you have learned!" he proudly remarked. Clyde proceeded to pass a small glass vial of gooey, cobalt colored liquid to Meadow which she studied with a curious expression, but swiftly stashed it into her sturdy leather harness. "Don't drink that, it is not a potion meant for consumption, yet is vital when dealing with ghosts, spirits, specters and other manner of ethereal undead" uttered Clyde.

Before Meadow could ask why the vial of viscous liquid was essential, an abrupt boom shattered the tranquility and bellowed through the air. "Styx's portal is surely complete, don't take too long my apprentice!" declared Clyde as he finished sliding one last potion into the harness attached to his body and hastily dashed out of the room. Meadow rejected the desire to rush and wisely perused the potential potions she could pick. She weighed her options and selected a few more for the journey, then slotted them into the last empty spaces in her harness then departed the lab.

Soon she joined Clyde in the portal room but heard the familiar deep humming of the magical portal before she even approached the door. "I assume we are all set then?" asked Meadow as she stood beside Clyde and gazed upon the infinite swirling void of colorful vibrancy, constantly shifting between a plethora of pretty hues. "I am ready to plunge headfirst into the mysterious realm of boundless possibility if you are my most esteemed lackey!" declared Clyde with his usual dramatic flair. Styx fluttered over by using his little leathery wings and rested his trident over his shoulder as he proudly observed his whirling portal. "Travel safe and remember your dealing with the orcs, they can be quite brutish!" he hissed. "We shall be fine Styx; I've met enough orcs to know it is simply part of their charm!" answered Clyde and he confidently strolled into the depths of the magical abyss. Clyde then allowed the portal to devour him, offering no resistance and quickly vanishing from sight. "Guess it's time to lend another helping hand!" Meadow cheerfully uttered and playfully pranced into the portal's depths.

A fast, flashy fleeting moment later, her vision was awash in a sea of sublime shifting colors that whizzed by with such wonderous speed. Travelling through the portal was truly a moment she could never forget, like she was a shooting star speeding through the heavens. Of course, the transition ended as soon as it began, and Meadow soon found herself emerging into a sweltering hot plain of rocky canyons and jagged plateaus. "Welcome, to the Jagged Steppes! a region of harsh rock, rough stones and mighty beasts, the Jagged Steppes are the very outskirts of the endless desert beyond known as the Burning Plains!" answered Clyde.

The Jagged Steppes was a place that certainly suited the tough, stoic nature of the orcs. Nothing existed except stretches of dusty wilderness and rocky canyons as far as Meadow could see. Clyde raised his hand to his forehead to shield himself against the relentless glare of the burning sun and surveyed his surroundings. "Come my dear, we must traverse this rocky realm and locate Orstone, lest this heat scorch us into oblivion!" he declared. Alas, before they could take a single step further, a sinister hissing sound echoed behind them. "Uh Clyde, I think we have to deal with that first!" uttered Meadow with shaky breath as she turned around and looked up. It crawled above them upon the coarse ceiling of a giant chunk of rough canyon rock that jutted out and loomed above them. A monster unlike anything Meadow had seen before, "A salrodela!" shouted Clyde. The giant bulbous eyes of the salrodela fixed upon Clyde and Meadow, its long slimy tongue slithering around like a snake as it observed them, until without warning, the salrodela pounced.

It tried to land upon Meadow, but she managed to clumsily dive out of the way at the last second. "What in the celestial heavens is a salrodela!?" she cried after quickly picking herself up. "Giant thorny carnivorous desert lizard is the best description!" shouted Clyde as he grasped one of the potions from his harness. His description was accurate, the salrodela was larger than a luxury carriage, its body a vibrant emerald color speckled with a scarlet red pattern. Dozens of thorny tips mimicking the very pointy rocks it lived among also covered most of its back.

With a fierce whip of its thick scaly tail, the salrodela smacked Clyde right in the chest, knocking the potion he held out of his hand. "Curses!" Clyde shouted with agony as he felt the wind be knocked from his lungs. Meadow quickly captured the scaly creature's attention again by hurling a nearby rock at its head, "Over here you spiked-brained beast!" she yelled. Ominously, the salrodela shifted its gaze back to Meadow, its bulging spherical eyes creepily glaring at her. Then, just as Meadow raised her arm to lob another rock at it, the salrodela suddenly lashed its long, slender tongue towards her.

A grimace overcame Meadow as she felt its slimy tongue wrap around her arm and halt her throw, "Ewwww!" she cried in repulsion as she watched its saliva drip along her wrist. Despite her best squirming, Meadow was unable to free her arm from the salrodela's slithery tongue, that was until she received an unexpected serving of help. A fierce orc warrior who saw the scene unfold, fearlessly leapt from the edge of the jutting plateau that loomed above and came crashing down with his battle-axe. "Ugwahhh!" he shouted as he sliced the salurodela's tongue in half.

Pain and panic assailed the salrodela, evident by the way it quickly leapt back with a flustered hiss, "Never start what you cannot finish!" roared the orc as he gave chase. Without its tongue, the salrodela had to rely on brute strength and its tail, which it quickly lashed to try and knock the charging orc aside. Luckily, the burly orc was a little nimbler than he looked and managed to roll under the monster's mighty tail and remain unscathed. Dust scattered into the air from the frantic skirmish and the salrodela's attacks became increasingly berserk. Yet, the courageous orc warrior steeled his resolve and swung his huge battle-axe into one of the scaly limbs of the salrodela as it swung to strike him.

The thick gleaming blade of the battle-axe cut deep, and the thorny green lizard was once again wounded and recoiled in anguish. However, the orcs battle-axe was firmly lodged into the monster's limb. Thus, forcing him to release his grasp upon the hilt of his weapon and continue the fight unarmed, which the orc warrior did with little qualm. Fearlessly, the orc charged towards the salrodela, showing no care for his own safety, raising his mighty green fist and punching the thorny lizard in one of its large bulbous eyeballs. Another dose of pain engulfed the beast and this time it found the wisdom to retreat, which it did with all haste, swiftly scurrying away along the sides of the canyon walls. The orcs battle-axe that was deeply lodged into the salrodela's leg came loose as it scurried to safety, falling and clanging upon the ground, waiting to be reclaimed by its master again. Calmly, the hulking orc warrior cracked his knuckles and sneered, before wandering over to reach down and collect his battle-axe. "Greetings, I'm Bashe!" he declared as he turned to face Meadow and Clyde.

Bashe's greeting was met with speechless awe from Meadow and Clyde, until Bashe gradually wandered towards them and spoke again. "This is the part where you thank me for saving your puny hides!" he said in a rugged tone. Clyde managed to unshackle himself from the chains of amazement that detained his attention and approached with a hearty handshake at the ready. "Of course, forgive my manners my good green sir! My apprentice and I are profoundly grateful for your timely rescue, we shall sing songs about your glorious act of valor for all time!" declared Clyde. One of Bashe's eyebrows quickly arose as he watched Clyde, unable to tell if he was being sarcastic, "Not necessary!" growled Bashe.

He rejected Clyde's handshake by keeping his arms firmly folded and stood like an iron statue. His impenetrable glare remained unwavering like the watchful eyes of a hungry wolf, "What brings you weedy whelps to this harsh land?" he asked. Despite saving them from danger, Meadow didn't apprentice his tone, evident by the cross glare she gave. "We came to assist the people of Orstone, if that's okay with you!" she snapped. Urgently, Clyde uttered a nervous chuckle and bowed his head. "Ah, please forgive my disciple's manners, she is still young and unrefined, we are the alchemists Orstone requested for aid!" Clyde quickly uttered.

Strangely, an impressed smirk spread upon Bashe's lips as he observed Meadow, "Don't apologize, I like her fire!" he answered. "I was hunting the salrodela that attacked you, that's how I noticed your predicament, follow me, I shall escort you to Orstone!" growled Bashe, turning his back and treading away. Just as Clyde was about to follow, Meadow quickly scooped up a gleaming glass vial of potion that rested upon the dusty ground and halted Clyde. "Wait, don't forget this! It's the vial of potion you dropped during that skirmish" she uttered, offering the container of magical mixture towards him.

Happily, Clyde placed the vial of potion back into his harness from whence it had fallen, "Many thanks my lackey, I knew you would be helpful in some way" he answered. A miffed scowl brewed upon Meadow's face as she watched Clyde serenely march away. "Oh, so I'm only here to pick up your potions now? And could you stop with the lackey part?" she growled. Unsurprisingly, Clyde remained aloof, "I'm truly grateful my dear, that potion is a new one I've been working on, still untested, but will surely come in handy" he replied.

The journey to Orstone was far from pleasant for the sweltering sun sapped their strength, causing Clyde and Meadow to seek refuge beneath the shady shadows of rocky alcoves. Not to mention the rough, stone-strewn terrain which regularly tested their balance. Meadow had nearly gone head over heels more than a few times, "Ugh, this sun is relentless!" groaned Meadow as she wiped her forehead of sweat. It seemed Bashe had adapted to this unforgiving climate quite well, for he strode across the rough, sunbaked ground like he was traversing a path of gentle clouds. "I heard our chieftain hired the help of two alchemists, not sure how a pair of such delicate flowers could aid us though" he uttered in a mocking tone.

Once again, his words cut Meadow and summoned a bitter frown, but she was far too hot and weary to retaliate, instead it was Clyde who countered his response this time. "While we may seem like little more than frail glassware, I shall have you know that ridiculing our potential would be quite a grave blunder!" he answered. Suddenly, Clyde stood tall and proud with hands on hips and unleashed another one of his dramatic boasts. "We possess the limitless power of alchemy! The myriad of magical wonders it creates is ours to control! We laugh in the face of any adversity, for the magnificent miracles of alchemy allow us to…..." rambled Clyde. "Shut up, it's too hot!" Meadow quickly shouted, desperate to silence Clyde's ever waffling voice which drained her stamina even more than the rocky hill she was jadedly climbing.

A hearty surge of laughter erupted from Bashe as he lent Meadow a helping hand climbing the coarse hill. "I'm glad you shut him up, my axe was about to find another victim!" he jest. His moment of levity brought much needed succor to Meadow, along with a playful smile. "Very well, I shall enlighten you once we are in the shade" uttered Clyde as he wearily pursued Meadow up the seemingly endless hill. But, climbing such a jagged knoll proved tedious and grueling, especially with such unyielding heat looming above them. upon reaching the top however, they finally laid eyes on the city of Orstone.

Orstone, city of the orcs, this was the first time Meadow had laid eyes upon it. Then again, she never imagined herself travelling to the vast variety of regions scattered across Resplendia. "Welcome to Orstone, or Blooda Ruznik in our ancient orcish tongue, which means Blood Rock in yours!" declared Bashe as he marveled at the sight of his city from atop the rocky hill. Carefully, all of them descended the craggy slope, but Meadow's attention kept getting ensnared by the utterly spectacular vista spreading across the landscape. Gleaming sunlight drenched the city, a city that was surrounded by nothing, nothing but miles of exposed plains strewn with rugged rocks and jagged spires as far as the eye could see. Orstone was craftily built into the side of a giant mountain, no doubt as a defensive tactic. Yet, much of it extended beyond the mountain halls and the closer Meadow approached, the more daunting the city appeared.

Wooden watchtowers and a lofty wall of spike tipped oak surrounded the entrance to the city. Meanwhile, orc guards kept a vigilant watch upon their borders as they strolled along the walkways above. "Looks well-fortified" uttered Meadow as Bashe escorted them to the city's imposing wooden gates, halting only when two burly orc guards raised their shields and lowered their heads respectfully. "Berserker Bashe, welcome home! Shall I ask them to open the gate?" asked one of the orc guards in a humble tone. "Yes brother, I must see the chieftain, these two outsiders are with me also!" growled Bashe as he flung his thumb towards Meadow and Clyde behind him.

Obediently, one of the orc guards proceeded to powerfully slam his palm against the side of the fortified oak gate a few times. "Open the gate, berserker Bashe seeks entry!" bellowed the orc guard. Gradually, the formidable oak gates began to part and passage into the city of Orstone was provided, "Berserker?" inquired Meadow as she trotted to Bashe's side. "It's one of our titles, a title given only to the fiercest orc warriors, a title I had to work hard for!" growled Bashe as he briskly stomped ahead. Eagerly, Meadow skipped behind him, the many sights and sounds of Orstone consuming her curiosity.

Orcs both male and female worked tirelessly together beneath the scorching sun, diligently toiling away. Everyone one of them pouring all their focus into their chosen vocation, each one a cog in the mighty empire of the orcs. Currently, Bashe was leading Clyde and Meadow past a bustling bazaar. A bazaar abundant with stalls selling all manner of spices, herbs, meat and vegetables, "I see your people aren't lacking for food" noted Clyde. His observation was accurate, stalls supplying slabs of succulent meat were especially common. "Yeah, no one seems to be going hungry, doesn't seem like anyone is homeless and in rags either" added Meadow. A torrent of pride washed over Bashe as he marched through the crowds of his people with swagger in his steps. "Our people are taught to hunt and bring back what they kill, everyone pulls their weight, everyone is useful, everyone contributes to our city, those who don't are exiled for being a burden!" declared Bashe.

Such a disciplined lifestyle was nothing short of admirable, it was so surprising that it caused Meadow to shake her head with disbelief. "I was under the impression that most orcs were bloodthirsty savages, cruel barbaric brutes that know only war and fighting" uttered Meadow with a tone that sounded surprised. As they left the bazaar, they approached a strange stone pit hollowed deep into the earth. Deep from within the pit, Meadow and Clyde could hear thundering chants and bellows of excitement erupt, "Oh, those stories are still somewhat true!" announced Bashe. His arms firmly folded and he looked down into the gaping stone pit. Meadow and Clyde also peered down to observe what was causing such ecstatic ruckus.

Two hulking orc warriors stood facing each other with their eyes locked and were ferociously pummeling each other with their bare fists. Iron mesh surrounded the two fighters in their sandy pit making it look like a circular cage, it was from behind the safety of the iron net that crowds of cheering orcs looked on. "This is our arena, the place where we blow off steam and test our strength!" shouted Bashe as he watched one of the orc fighters slam his mighty green fist into the face of his opponent. This knocked the orc down while the orc who remained standing proudly pound his chest. Another rumbling wave of cheers bellowed from the excited crowd and the orc warrior bathed in their applause, raising his arms and giving a glorious roar.

Until his opponent gathered his bearings, shook off the mighty blow he had been delivered and assailed his fellow orc. Seizing him while his back was turned, and his attention captured by the worship of the people and the barbaric battle of fisticuffs resumed. "You measure each other's strength by knocking each other's lights out in a brutal cage battle within a stone pit with no means of escape?" asked Clyde in a ridiculing tone. Sternly, Bashe looked away from the arena pit and the two orc fighters currently smashing their knuckles into each other's faces. "If you have a problem with this, I'll have you know I used to be a slave in an arena once!" he growled. Bashe seemed imposing and gigantic as he stomped up to Clyde, appearing like a mountain in front of a frail weed. "Any true orc loves a good fight, our strength should be constantly tested, but at our arena death is not allowed and neither are weapons, we fight for honor and glory!" Bashe added while glaring at Clyde.

After taking a final glance upon the fatigued, blood-soaked fighters within the arena and listening to the thrilled chants of the crowds, Bashe led Clyde onwards. "Come, our chieftain is not much further!" he growled. A vast, sandy training yard devoid of shelter from the searing sun awaited Clyde and Meadow on their little journey through the city of Orstone. Orc children barley able to swing a blade tirelessly trained beneath the harsh heat. Striking wooden practice dummies with axes and maces while burly orc instructors barked into their ears. "Good, now give it fifty more!" roared one of the orc trainers as he watched one of the children slam his axe into the ribcage of the dummy.

However, another orc child nearby abruptly collapsed onto his knees, likely from exhaustion and dropped his weapon upon the sandy yard. "Are you defeated? Are you going to allow yourself to fall because of a little heat!?" bellowed the beefy orc instructor as he paced along the young fighters. A growl of rage erupted from the orc child, joined by a burning fire in his heart and he dragged his knees off the sand, raising his weapon and striking his wooden foe once more. "Our children grow up fast here, after they learn to walk and talk, they learn to fight, we teach them to find their strength, their resolve and how to use it to survive, the world is unforgiving and devours the weak!" barked Bashe as he looked on.

Next, they travelled into the rocky halls of the towering mountain itself. "This is the blacksmiths quarter, where we forge the strongest steel in all Resplendia!" boast Bashe as he led Clyde and Meadow through the sweltering halls. Swarms of flaming embers fluttered through the air like fireflies from the blazing stomachs of the iron forges dotted through the mountain halls. Torrents of melted steel tipped from their scorching iron maws, while orc blacksmiths echoed the stony halls with the persistent din of hammers smashing upon metal. Sweat dripped along Clyde's forehead despite the fact he was merely passing through. "Goodness, it feels like I've been thrown into the boiling waters of a witch's cauldron!" he remarked. This time Meadow was sympathetic to his plight and rubbed her face clean of sweat. "Your telling me! If nothing else, I can honestly say the orcs are disciplined and dedicated!" she groaned in a muggy tone. Through the haze of fiery ash, they travelled, shutting out the incessant racket of hammers clashing upon steel, until they finally left the steamy boundaries of the blacksmiths quarter.

Yet, the mountain halls travelled deep, it was more than a mere den for their blacksmiths, the mountain was the true city of Orstone. Hundreds of homes and thousands of spiral steps had been carved into the soaring stone mountain, turning the interior into a towering fortress of rock, "Incredible!" gasped Meadow as she gazed up. The central core of the mountain had been hollowed away; it was now a vast space stretching upwards with hundreds of homes carved into its sides.

The mountain itself was lit up in a dazzling sea of light as candles burned brightly by many of the windows. "Our chieftain awaits in her quarters, at the very top of the mountain" Bashe uttered as he pridefully strode towards a sturdy oak platform surrounded by thick iron chains. Dismay engulfed Meadow, for the idea of climbing every step sculpted into the mountain seemed like a herculean task, "We have to climb to the very top!?" she groaned. "Ordinarily yes, but luckily for you, we've built this lift inside the mountain for when moments of disaster are upon us" answered Bashe. He then stepped onto the oak platform in the center and nodded his head to a nearby orc.

Clyde and Meadow joined Bashe and trod by his side, before the nearby orc proceeded to pull a long iron lever and after a firm jolt, the lift began to move. The immensely long chains embedded into all four corners of the platform echoed the halls with their iron rattling as they gradually pulled the wooden lift upwards, towards the rocky peak of the mountain. Watching the hundreds of orc citizens and the luminous sea of candles in their windows pass her by while the lift smoothly carried Meadow further and further upwards was a truly splendid sight to behold.

A gasp of wonder fluttered from her lips as she slowly spun in a circle, gazing at the empire of glowing lights all around her. It felt heavenly, like she was being lifted into the stars. "So, when you say your chieftain is waiting in her quarters, you mean your chieftain is a woman?" asked Clyde as he stood by the edge of the lift and peered over the side. "Yes, our chieftain is a woman, but don't think for a second that makes her weak or unworthy, she earned the right to be our chieftain, she is wise, tactful, and strong enough to snap your neck in a heartbeat!" growled Bashe. "Ooh, I like her already!" Meadow joyfully declared, while a nervous gulp suddenly entered Clyde's throat and he responded to Bashe's words with a tense smile. "I shall keep that in mind" he uttered in a feeble tone that made him sound about as firm as a withering dandelion.

Just at that moment, the groaning chains gave a final jolting rattle when the wooden lift came to an abrupt stop. "Follow me, our chieftainess Umgra Brazoth awaits in her quarters just ahead!" barked Bashe as he heavily stomped onwards. Two more muscular orc guards stood facing the lift to greet Bashe, both orcs were clad in fearsome black armour and guarded a set of winding stone stairs with their huge battle-axes. One of the fearsome orc guards lowered his battle-axe and adopted a much more amicable and relaxed stance upon seeing Bashe approach. "Berserker Bashe, good to see you brother! It's been too long since we enjoyed an ale together!" he jovially boomed. Respectfully, Bashe shook the hand of the fellow orc and performed a gesture akin to a hug and a chest bump, "Berserker Tyrog, I would enjoy such a treat again my friend!" he answered. Meanwhile, the second orc guard remained stern and silent, like a stalwart rock amid fierce thundering wind, "Berserker Dragmaz, still learning how to talk!?" Bashe taunted.

His tone was ridiculing yet also seemed friendly, even welcomed by the second guard, who grinned, shook Bashe's hand and gave him a quick hug. "You know me, I prefer the silence, I have to do enough talking at home with my wife!" he bellowed in a mocking tone, followed quickly by an eruption of laughter among all three of them. Once the resonance of laughter gradually faded, berserker Dragmaz shifted his watchful eye to Meadow and Clyde, both of whom appeared like a pair of clueless fish out of water. "Who're the two snowflakes you've brought?" he asked.

Meadow overheard his remark and invaded the conversation with a determined stomp in her stride. "We're the alchemists from the Frostveil Mountains, the one's your chieftainess requested!" she growled. "We even have a letter to prove it, so how about letting us pass dung beetle?" Meadow added in a tone that flickered with flames of tenacity. Unfortunately, her demeanor only served to incite a dubious glare from berserker Dragmaz, while berserker Tyrog was powerless to repel his bubbling amusement, "Dung beetle, ha!" he chuckled.

Sternly, Dragmaz folded his arms and refused to yield to Meadow's fiery bluster and obstructed anyone from climbing the stone steps to the quarters of chieftainess. "Show me this letter, whelp!" barked Dragmaz with the wrath of a fearsome hydra in his voice. Before Clyde and Meadow had chance to produce the letter of aid as proof, another unknown voice chimed in from above the stairs, "It's okay my berserkers, allow them an audience!" it echoed. Obediently, berserker Dragmaz lowered his cagey stance and stepped to one side, uttering a low grumble and allowing Clyde and Meadow passage beyond. However, Bashe still insisted on escorting them and gave his berserker brothers a swift nod of respect as he passed by them.

Faint glimmers of fiery light were cast from the wax candles nestled inside the iron cages spread along the mountain walls and illuminated the spiraling stone steps. Clyde and Meadow shadowed Bashe along the winding stone steps that led upwards, to the very peak of the mountain. Until finally, they emerged inside a large open room, "Welcome, I am Umgra, chieftainess of Orstone!" boomed a voice. Sitting upon an astonishing stone throne carved into a huge hunk of solid rock was chieftainess Umgra, who vigilantly watched Clyde and Meadow as Bashe led them in. Umgra's living quarters were certainly opulent as far as orcish décor went, with Meadow immediately feeling the soft lushness of fur beneath her feet. Upon gazing down, she quickly noticed the large furry rug stretching across the room. It looked like the skinned hide of a taurian, one of Resplendia's most fearsome beasts. Immediately, it gave Meadow a moment of fascinated pause, wondering if chieftainess Umgra had slain the monster herself.

Hanging from the ceiling was an ornate chandelier filled with several burning candles. The chandelier itself was made not of iron, but of high-quality monster bones that had been pristinely polished. A roaring hearth stood beside Umgra's stone throne, its searing flames dancing wildly upon a pile of thick wooden logs, "Approach!" Umgra abruptly decreed. Humbly, Bashe marched into the light beneath the chandelier and pressed his fist into the rock floor as he bowed his head and knelt before the chieftainess. "Berserker Bashe reporting my lady, I have escorted the alchemists you requested!" he answered.

Umgra may have been a woman, but she possessed an aura of ferocity and fortitude that seemed profoundly imposing. Meadow could feel it in her piercing eyes and unyielding posture. Umgra was swathed in a variety of thick furs belonging to a mixture of different beasts, a necklace made of bones dangled from her neckline with a single large, jagged fang at the end and a large crown made of thick, black iron rested upon her head. "The mysterious man in the black mask only told me about one alchemist, not two!" growled Umgra while leaning forward to inspect Clyde and Meadow further.

Once again, mention about this black masked man of mystery had arisen and Meadow had grown insanely weary of it, causing her to briefly clench her teeth and scowl. Meanwhile, Clyde waltzed into the light and bowed, before performing his familiar song and dance of decorum. "Delightful to meet you Lady Umgra, this is my apprentice Meadow, I am Clyde Alrime, the skillful alchemist you sent for!" He boasted. Umgra remained skeptical and baffled as she watched Clyde swagger and bombastically flaunt his way forward. "I hereby vow to faithfully serve you and neither storm nor beast shall stop me from banishing whatever perilous plight plagues your people!" declared Clyde.

Umgra's hand coiled around a large iron goblet encrusted with blood red rubies. Slowly she took sip of whatever liquid it contained, "So you are happy to be our errand boy as long as the gold is good?" she asked. Her words rendered Clyde speechless and unsure how to answer, luckily Umgra spoke further for him. "I shall speak plainly; I despise the idea of seeking outsiders to solve our problems!" she growled. Umgra's firm grip upon the iron goblet tightened and she gently swirled it around, her mind reflectively churning like the liquid within. "A problem has befallen my people that mere strength cannot solve, a problem that requires a more magical solution, something my people are unfamiliar with" Umgra reluctantly added.

It must have been difficult for a race as proud and mighty as the orcs to request aid from others, especially humans. No doubt it would feel like quite the blow to their dignity, facts Clyde made sure to keep in mind. "Yes, your letter spoke of spirits haunting the halls of your sacred burial chamber, any additional information you can provide would be most helpful" Clyde humbly answered. Slowly, chieftainess Umgra climbed out of her throne and stomped towards Clyde, her true height revealing itself and showing that she towered over him, "Arise Bashe!" she commanded. Without questioning, Bashe obediently arose and even he whom was at least six feet tall, seemed like an ant before the colossal chieftainess. "My people tell me the ghosts that haunt the halls of our sacred crypt are invisible and immune to all physical attacks yet are still able to harm and kill" uttered Umgra. Firmly, Umgra folded her arms and watched the glowing flames frolic within the gaping maw of her fireplace. "Several of our warriors have perished, including two berserkers, so I am hesitant to send in more" she added.

Such sacrifice seemed needlessly excessive to Meadow considering it was just to make an ancient crypt of dust and bones safe again. "I know little of orc culture your highness, is this crypt really so important to risk the lives of your people? Surely another crypt can be built" uttered Meadow. Clyde and Bashe suddenly spun their heads towards Meadow so fast that it seemed like they risked decapitating themselves. "Sincerest apologies for my disciple's lack of respect and etiquette chieftainess Umgra!" Clyde swiftly uttered. Umgra revealed her orcish fangs as a toothy grin spread over her face. "Tis no disrespect, I prefer those that possess the courage to speak their mind!" she thundered in her deep voice.

A large golden ring of luxurious quality pierced Umgra's nose, something Meadow did not fully notice until Umgra casually flicked it as she spoke. "The crypt these ghosts haunt is our most sacred tomb, legendary orc warriors, chieftains and shamans are buried there, it is a place many in my city visit on a regular basis and an important piece of our history!" growled Umgra.

Although she attempted to bury any weakness beneath a shroud of conviction and authority, Meadow and Clyde could see the mask slipping with every concerned breath Umgra took. Umgra brushed aside the long, fur-skinned skirt she wore as she paced towards a gaping hole carved into the side of her quarters and pointed her finger. "Look, you can see the sacred tomb from here!" she declared while looking into the horizon. As Clyde and Meadow wandered to her side and gazed out of the gaping hole, they were powerless to oppose the utterly spectacular vista, "My goodness!" gasped Meadow. Stretches of sun-drenched canyons, lush green forests, snowy white mountains, boundless blue oceans and gold sandy deserts sprawled before their very eyes, "Yes, incredible!" whispered Clyde with awe.

Beams of warm sun carried upon breaths of breezy wind caressed Meadow's face, as she hypnotically gazed upon the majestic land from the peak of Orstone's mountain. Even Umgra whom had witnessed this resplendent vista many times over, allowed herself to marvel upon it once more. "Indeed, the beauty of this land is one of the main reasons we orcs desire peace now" she uttered. It became increasingly challenging to tear her eyes away from the view, thankfully Meadow managed it at last, "Your talking about the Green Banner War, right?" she asked. "Yes, the dreadful war that soaked this land with blood, when my people foolishly forged an alliance with the goblins and tried to usurp Resplendia for ourselves" replied Umgra.

Calmly, chieftainess Umgra sat upon her colossal stone throne again and casually crossed one leg over the other. "So, that's the sacred tomb? Doesn't look too far from the city gates" remarked Clyde, changing the topic. "It isn't, but be wary, its far enough that our guards cannot reach you in time should you be attacked by monsters!" Umgra explained in a stern tone. Suddenly, Bashe knelt before his chieftainess again and bowed his head, "Milady Umgra, I humbly request permission to join them!" he asked. In response to his request, Umgra gave a firm nod. "I was about to suggest that very idea Bashe, it would put my soul at ease, for no one other that orcs are allowed to enter our sacred burial chamber" she answered.

Umgra's fearless focus abruptly swung in Meadow and Clyde's direction. "No offensive, but I'd rather have one of my people there with you, to see that nothing is disturbed or stolen" Umgra bluntly explained. Being suspected as potential grave robbers was a thought that Meadow despised and took insult with, but she refrained from keeping out and kept her tongue locked behind her teeth. Unsurprisingly, Clyde succumbed to modesty and gave a bow of compliance. "No offensive at all chieftainess, I give you my word your sacred tomb shall remain untouched and my disciple and I shall banish these sinister spirits will all haste!" He proclaimed. It was difficult not to admire the passionate gusto in Clyde's voice, which impressed Umgra and rekindled the sleepy flames of motivation in Meadow. "My only request your highness is that you allow the use of some of your weapons for this task" Clyde humbly added. Such a request struck Meadow as odd, Clyde had never wielded nor requested a weapon since she had met him, potions and poisons were his weapons. Yet, Chieftainess Umgra still granted his request all the same, "Very well, I promise you shall be spoilt for choice!" she declared.

Briskly, Clyde and Meadow left Umgra's quarters with Bashe in tow and rode the large iron chained lift all the way to the base of the mountain again. "I don't understand Clyde, you've never used conventional melee weapons before, why start now?" asked Meadow as the rattling lift carried them down. A heavy thud followed shortly; the lift had reached the base of the mountain again, "We must wield weapons if we are to defeat these nefarious specters" Clyde answered. "Haven't you been listening fool? We already tried to attack them with our weapons, it was like hitting thin air!" growled Bashe.

After departing the wooden lift, Bashe promptly escorted them to the grand orc armory, "No matter how strong our steel, no physical harm came to these ghosts!" Bashe grumbled. As Clyde paced along the armory and perused the wooden racks lined with every weapon imaginable, he remained calm and impervious to Bashe's words, "Patience, I shall reveal all in time" he answered.

Meadow perused the magnificent armory and found herself honestly impressed by the quality and quantity of weapons presented. "Fine, but your plan better knock my socks off!" replied Bashe as he studied the weapons on show and decided to pick a giant bladed black battle-axe with a short shaft. No Doubt the shorter shaft upon the axe was meant for close encounters, ideal for swinging in an enclosed tomb, but the larger sharp blades upon the head compensated for the shorter reach. As for Clyde, he was currently inspecting the longsword section and settled upon a slender black sword he could comfortably swing with one hand. "Perfect!" he declared after giving the ebony blade several practice swings, swishing and swooshing it up and down, fantasizing himself as a gallant duelist no doubt. "Then all that is left your little helper, I'll show her the dagger section, orc weapons tend to be bulky in human hands, but I'm sure we have something she can use" uttered Bashe. However, Meadow had already found her ideal weapon. "No thanks, I'll use this!" she replied with a devilish grin as she re-appeared wielding a fearsome black mace covered in deadly steel spikes.

Without delay, Clyde, Bashe and Meadow left the city of Orstone and promptly began traversing the sun-soaked rocky wilderness of the Jagged Steppes. "I still can't believe you chose that as your weapon! Honestly, you scare me sometimes!" remarked Clyde. Meadow held the spiked mace in both hands, even though it was meant to wielded in one hand. "I don't want a feeble dagger; I want something that has punch!" she dominantly answered.

Although the journey to the sacred burial tomb was not far, the searing sun made it felt like an odyssey of a thousand miles. The heat felt inescapable and seemed to sap every ounce of energy from Meadow and Clyde, while the rough, rocky terrain caused them to infuriatingly stumble more often than they could tolerate. Only the occasional placid breeze provided any modicum of renewal, its fleeting current flowing through their hair and bestowing a brief sensation of serenity. It baffled Meadow how the orcs could endure such a punishing climate so effortlessly, treating it like a mundane chore. "Orcs must truly have warrior spirits to tolerate such a harsh land so regularly!" she gasped.

Bashe, appeared impervious to the merciless heat as he marched across the dusty wasteland seemingly unhindered. "This land is what aided in discovering our warrior spirits!" he declared with a proud snort. "Only those who are strong in spirt, body and mind can survive this unforgiving region, this land tempers our spirits, just as a blacksmiths forge tempers steel!" Bashe growled. Wearily, Clyde reached for a leather flask strapped to his hip, unbottled it and took an ample guzzle of the quenching cool water within. "And how long does it take before I find my warrior spirit? I'm hoping to find it before I pass out!" he panted in a ridiculing tone, making Bashe utter a grouchy grumble.

Crossing the several sandy miles from Orstone to the ancient orc burial tomb felt grueling, but finally they made it, although Bashe was the only one who made it seem simple. "Okay......here......at last!" Clyde gasped with fatigue and glee as he swiftly sought shade beneath one of the soaring stone pillars built outside the tomb entrance. Meadow also desired a vital moment of respite and used one of the pointy stone columns to conceal herself from the scorching fury of the sun. "And how I've missed the sweet shade!" she panted. Meanwhile, Bashe watched the pair of them clumsily slouch against the stone pillar. "Aw, you two butterflies need a nap? Don't rest too long or I'm gonna need to be buried in that tomb!" he mocked. Refusing to be subjected to such mockery, Meadow stood up, defiantly pointed her finger and was on the verge of uttering her own words of warfare. Until, she wearily flopped her head and quickly crumpled back onto her bottom, "Forget it......too hot!" she groaned.

After indulging in a brief rest and guzzling more of their cherished water, Clyde and Meadow rose to their feet, feeling revitalized. "Ah, my spirit is renewed! Let us push on with the journey my comrades!" he declared. His abrupt revolution in attitude made Meadow utter a giggle and she jovially joined Clyde's side as he began to ascend the dusty stone steps leading to the entrance. Clearly, the ravages of time had not left the bulky steps unscathed, for countless numbers of chips and cracks covered the otherwise exceptional stonework.

Upon reaching the top, Meadow rejoiced and marveled at the magnificent doors of the tomb entrance, "These doors are huge! You could fit a taurian through here!" she declared. Her comment was precisely timed, as the colossal stone doors of the ancient tomb were instantly demolished and reduced to rubble. A raging taurian suddenly smashed right through the doors and gave a ferocious bellow as the furry beast charged past. The collision caused Meadow and the others to yell cries of surprise and tumble backwards. "Be careful what you wish for!" shouted Clyde after toppling over the side of the stone steps, falling face first into the ground and spitting out a mouthful of sand.

Bashe went flying the furthest and glided several feet, before slamming against one of the stone pillars, "A taurian!? That wasn't in there before!" he gasped after losing his breath. In the same moment, Meadow painfully rolled across the stone entrance of the tomb, scraping her arm and knee. Soon she finally rolled and fell over the side like a ragdoll, "I heard taurians were docile!" she cried. She heard right, taurians were normally tranquil creatures, until they were provoked of course. They could be highly territorial too, but this was something else, something Bashe had not experienced.

Once the initial distress of almost being trampled to death by a taurian had worn off, Clyde, Meadow and Bashe quickly noticed something unusual. The taurian was being ridden by a nefarious little imp wielding a sharp little magical trident. Watching the wicked little imp gleefully stab his tiny trident into the air while manically laughing as he rode the rampaging taurian was jarring to see. "Ha, ha, ha! I knew I sensed something approaching! My master instructed me to cause chaos in this tomb and let none enter, so that is what I shall do!" it proclaimed. The imp then used its magic to command the taurian to take a great leap from the top of the stone steps.

A powerful tremor quaked the earth as the formidable taurian slammed all four feet into the ground upon landing, "The imp, it must be controlling the taurian with magic!" shouted Clyde. Meadow was nearest, so the beast turned its attention towards her, "Charge!" hissed the imp as it pointed its magical trident right at her. This was the first time Meadow had seen a taurian, she had only heard about them before, but they were far more menacing than she could have imagined. Taurians were hulking beasts, built like a moving fortress, as large as a griffon, their hides grey like stone, covered in ashen shaggy fur, possessing an array of terrifying tusks and thick horns upon its head.

Its terrible charge trembled the ground and left Meadow frozen with shock as it stormed towards her, "Don't freeze! Move!" bellowed Bashe. His deep, booming voice was still audible over the taurians charge and snapped Meadow's mind back into focus at the last vital moment. Resulting in Meadow clumsily diving to the side and narrowly eluding the beast's path of fury. It stampeded straight past her, scattering dust into the air and causing whirlwind of confusion and panic within Meadow. "My mace!" Meadow cried once she noticed her mace had slipped and flown out of her grasp. Once the brief wave of dust had settled, Meadow saw her gleaming spiked mace buried beneath the sand several feet away from her, but it was too perilous to chance grabbing it. The taurian had already begun rushing towards her again and was remarkably fast for a creature of its size.

Luckily, Bashe swooped in to lend her aid by running across one of the solid stone steps, leaping off the end and hurling himself at the barbaric beast. "Ugggaaaaah!" roared Bashe as he fearlessly swung his huge battle-axe in a dramatic act of valor, one that yielded reward. Bashe's hefty battle-axe struck one of the taurians tusks and cleaved it in half, causing the beast to lose balance and topple over. Sadly, the colossal creature was not stunned for long and managed to quickly roll onto its paws again.

Meanwhile, the malicious imp still clung onto its back, "Up you beast! Get up and crush them!" it hissed. A furious snort of rage erupted from the taurian's snout and it recklessly stomped towards Meadow and Bashe, more berserk and wrathful than before. However, during that moment the monster briefly collapsed, Meadow had seized the opportunity to collect her mace. Meadow had also just finished gulping a vial of enhanced strength potion from her harness, "Chew on this!" she yelled as she flung her mace at the beast. With her temporary enhanced strength, throwing the mace was akin to lobbing a twig now and with whizzing speed, the spiked, black steel mace whooshed through the air. Possessing the speed of a sharp arrow, the mace flew towards the taurian with the ferocity of a shooting star, pummeling the brutal behemoth right in the head. Its thick scaly hide protected it from death, but such a blow still drew blood and sent the taurian careening across the dusty wasteland in a tumble, which also resulted in the despicable imp being flung off.

Despite the wallops it had endured, the taurian's wrath refused to soothe and it began to angrily stamp its feet while unleashing a series of enraged roars. "I think it is time to test my new potion!" Clyde abruptly declared as he came running over and bizarrely removed his harness packed with colorful potions. Again, the taurian began to mercilessly charge, determined to trample anything foolish enough to obstruct its path. Yet, Clyde remained fearless as he tipped the vial of potion towards his lips.

Tremors from the taurians terrifying charge caused the ground beneath Clyde's feet to quiver, luckily the new potion took effect within a couple of seconds. "Ha, ha! It works like a charm!" shouted Clyde, while Meadow and Bashe were left in awe as they watched him quickly grow taller and taller, until his height rivalled that of a giant. Of all the magical effects alchemy could conjure, Meadow found this new potion to be the most ludicrously astonishing so far. "Unbelievable!" she gasped, with Clyde towering over her and the ancient tomb itself.

Although the beastly taurian sustained its thundering charge, it found itself quickly swatted aside like a fragile leaf as Clyde swung his mighty, gargantuan fist into its face. His colossal fist was now larger than the taurian itself and easily clobbered the puny beast, knocking it onto its back upon impact. Clyde proceeded to subdue the taurian while it was still dazed by reaching down and scooping the beast up in his palm. Like he was a god snatching up a troublesome rat and threw the taurian across the air like he was throwing a pebble. Never had Bashe witnessed anything like this before, he watched the taurian soar across the sky, roaring with confusion, until it smashed into the side of a nearby looming stone column. It wasn't getting up for a while after that, the beast was finally knocked out cold as its body slammed into the ground.

Despite Clyde's immense new height, his clothes thankfully grew along with his new size, as strange as that was. "Ha, ha, ha! Bow before me world! I am your new lord and master!" Clyde boomed, his voice echoing across the rocky valleys. Meadow flopped her face into her palm and groaned as she watched him childishly savor his moment of supremacy, "Ugh, great! Seems the potion also enlarged his ego!" she uttered. Urgently, Bashe began whizzing his head around, vigilantly surveying the area, "The imp! Where did it go!?" he angrily bellowed. "Over there! Its fleeing into the tomb!" declared Meadow, quickly catching a glimpse of the imp's slender spiky tail and purple leathery wings vanishing into the remains of the tomb entrance. Seeing the irksome little imp hastily flee enraged Bashe and he relentlessly chased it down, refusing to allow it a swift retreat, "After it!" he bellowed.

Without hesitation, Meadow quickly pursued Bashe up the cracked stone steps. However, she soon spun round when she realized Clyde wasn't following, "Come on Clyde, what are you waiting for!?" she shouted. Sheepishly, Clyde rubbed the back of his head and awkwardly chuckled, "Waiting for the potion to wear off, I'm a bit too big to fit in there! It'll wear off soon though" he answered. Meadow and Bashe traded glances and suddenly exhaled jaded sighs, "Great, guess we have no choice but to temper our eagerness for now" uttered Meadow. With options in short supply, Clyde stomped his colossal body over to the tomb entrance and rested his gigantic rear upon the stone steps nearby.

His titanic frame ended up eclipsing most of the building from sight, "That imp said his master instructed him to cause chaos in this tomb" Clyde uttered. "I'll bet my best underwear that the imp is the one responsible for these ghosts in the tomb" he added as they waited. Another theory promptly glimmered inside Meadow's mind, "That imp, do you think it could be working for him? For the black masked man we've been chasing?" she asked. Unknown to her, Clyde had already considered the same theory and the speculation gleamed in his eyes, "Possibly, which is why we must capture it alive" he answered. After another minute passed, the potion abruptly wore off and Clyde started to swiftly shrink and reverted to his original size at last. "Ah, there we go! Being a giant has its advantages, and disadvantages sadly" he remarked. Even with all the miraculous effects Meadow had seen alchemy create, it remained baffling to watch Clyde alter his size so drastically with such ease. "How did your garments not rip? You should be as bare as a newborn baby!" joked Meadow.

It took a moment for Clyde to readapt his perception upon the world around him again. "I had all my clothes magically enchanted a long time ago, they adapt to my size and form, comes in handy for certain experiments!" he answered. A glaze of shock abruptly flickered in Meadow's eyes and she gave a shudder, "Glad I didn't use your new potion then" she replied. Impatience overwhelmed Bashe, causing him to restlessly groan, "Can we go in now? Or shall we serve that imp tea and biscuits too!?" he growled. "The only thing we shall be serving that imp, is the bitter taste of justice!" announced Clyde after claiming his harness again and strapping it back on.

The mystery intensified, Meadow wondered whom the imp served, why it was sent with the purpose of being a pain in the rear and what was the goal in this game? Clyde approached the wrecked entrance of the sacred tomb from where the taurian smashed and peered into the profound darkness within, "Okay, in we go" he uttered. As soon as they stepped foot inside the sacred halls of the orc tomb, Bashe drew one of the wooden torches from his leather backpack. "Time for a bit of light" he uttered as he struck the oil-soaked cloth at the end with a flint and set it aflame. Warm light instantly engulfed the shadowy halls of the crypt, banishing the darkness and providing a means to navigate its depths.

Sadly, as soon as Bashe set the torch alight, dismay devoured his soul when the torches glow also revealed the fallen bodies of several orc warriors. "My brothers! May the gods grant them peace now" he whispered. Maggots had begun to feast upon the banquet of bodies and the stench of rotting flesh infused the stale crypt air, creating a pungent pong that rivalled the sewers of Deepshade. As gruesome as the sight of decaying, maggot infested bodies were, Clyde inspected them as closely as he could endure. "Ugh, looks like they have been here more than a few days! bodies are relativity intact, looks like the ghosts in this place used physical force to kill them" remarked Clyde. He kept his arm raised closely against his nose as he studied the corpses, his eyes watering slightly. "That's what the survivors said, these ghosts can hit us, but we can't hit them and they're invisible, so what's your plan genius?" grumbled Bashe. After learning what he could from the dead, Clyde turned away and drew the longsword he borrowed from the orc armory. "Ready your steel my companions and all shall be revealed!" he declared.

Next, Clyde removed one of the vials of potion from his harness and popped off the cork. It was the gooey cobalt colored potion, the one Clyde instructed was not meant for ingesting. So, instead of consuming it, Clyde proceeded to coat it over the blade of his sword. "This is no mere potion I am applying; it is an oil deadly to the undead, capable of banishing them from this world" he explained. After carefully glazing his sword in the magical oil, Clyde nodded towards the fiery torch Bashe held in his hand. "However, it also requires fire, hand me your torch if you would be so kind Bashe" asked Clyde.

Remaining silent and curious, Bashe warily passed his burning torch to Clyde, "Now behold!" announced Clyde as he hovered the flames of the torch beneath the blade. Within a couple of seconds, the blade of Clyde's sword burst into a delightful dance of sapphire flames. "It's also completely harmless to the living" remarked Clyde as he held his palm over the radiant fire.

Visually, it appeared like the elemental enchantments Meadow heard enchanters and battlemages use on their weapons. The fire coated the edges of the blade and its lustrous light captivated her, "Is there enough oil for all of us?" she asked. "Yes, I brought a second vial just in case" answered Clyde as he revealed a second vial of the valuable oil and handed it to Bashe. Bashe wasted little time in popping the cork from the neck of the vial and coating the shimmering blades of his mighty great axe with the magical oil. Meadow copied his actions with the flask of enchanted oil she carried, drizzling the oil upon the sharp spikes of her fearsome mace. "Alight, let's go ghost hunting!" Meadow courageously remarked upon using the burning torch to ignite the sticky oil covering her weapon, watching the head of her mace burst into a luminous plume of intense blue fire.

With enchanted weapons in hand, they ventured into the depths of the ancient orc burial tomb. Quietly creeping along its cobwebbed halls, treading past sturdy stone coffins which held the corpses of fallen orc heroes of days long past. Wails of whispering wind would occasionally sweep along the winding halls, chilling the nerves of Clyde and the others like the sound of a howling wolf before a full moon.

Sprinkles of thick dust would also plummet from the ceiling as they walked beneath it, while mysterious shadows would dance upon the walls from the radiant torchlight. "We still have no means of seeing these ghosts should we encounter them" whispered Bashe as he warily turned another curving corner with his burning axe at the ready. "True but lay your concerns to rest my imposing green guardian, I have a potion that will allow us to see them" answered Clyde. Cautiously Clyde then swayed the burning torch towards the continuing path of darkness, "But, we must wait to encounter them first as its effects are quite fleeting" he added.

A small set of musty stone steps came into view upon turning the next shadowy corner. "Steady your focus!" growled Bashe as he took lead, vigilantly inching his way down the steps into the next room. Clyde followed close behind with the amber light of the torch in one hand and the sapphire flames of his longsword in the other. Along the way, Clyde noticed how much nature had managed to invade the tomb, with many colorful varieties of fungi beginning to blossom in the gloomy corners and cracked stonework. Being an alchemist, ingredients such as these enthralled him like a lustful siren seduces a sailor at sea and Clyde was quite tempted to halt their advance so he could swipe them all up.

Yet, before he even had a chance to do so, the nearby tumbling of an archaic ceramic vase snatched his attention. The sound of it shattering upon impact with the ground resonated along the ancient crypt halls. "Did that vase just fall over on its own?" asked Meadow in a spooked tone, while Clyde and Bashe swapped nervous glances with each other. To make the atmosphere more unsettling, they began to hear deep ominous breathing echoing from in front of them, yet there was naught to see but an empty, dusty room of stone and pottery. "It might be time use that potion you were talking about!" rumbled Bashe before he was violently pummeled in the chest by some unknown force and flung across the room.

Seeing Bashe be abruptly launched through the air and slammed against the wall was all the proof Clyde needed to know that the spectral forces of the dead were upon them. "Meadow use the undead detection potion!" shouted Clyde as he began to wildly swing and swish his longsword, enchanted with the fury of sacred blue fire. He must have landed an accidental blow upon the invisible entity, for Clyde suddenly heard a piercing shriek of pain erupt from the air in front of him.

Meadow obeyed his orders without question and hastily ripped the cork from the vial of potion and gulped half of it down. She then passed the other half to Bashe who was still dazed and floored. Wearily, Bashe reached for the vial of potion, pulled it from Meadow's hand and imbibed what was left. "Huh, I was expecting it to taste like troll pee!" Bashe joked once he stumbled back onto his feet. "A little assistance when you are both ready!" shouted Clyde as he was suddenly walloped in the jaw and knocked face first into the ground. Before he could regain his rattled senses, Clyde was then promptly levitated into the air and tossed aside like a piece of moldy bread.

Pain and confusion engulfed Clyde as he clumsily rolled across the ground, scraping his elbows while also losing his grip upon the torch and his enchanted longsword. With Clyde briefly stunned, Meadow took it upon herself to retaliate, "I see it Clyde, I see it!" she shouted, charging towards the ethereal phantom with her burning spiked mace raised high. Meadow did not confess to knowing how the undead detection potion worked. It seemed similar to life detection potion, except in reverse, seemingly detecting the spiritual energy that lingered within the wandering souls of the dead instead. What truly mattered is it worked, and Meadow could perceive the once invisible specter now, yet she was more than a little surprised and frightened by what she saw.

The sinister spirit before her seemed to have a body that resembled a haze of grey ash, but also possessing a bright white outline of light. It was muscular and hulking, like the body of an orc, yet had no legs, instead it seemed to float a few feet about the ground like it was resting upon a grey cloud. However, its face invoked the most fear within Meadow, its eyes were nothing but wide abyssal black sockets, as was its mouth. Its ghostly visage indicated a profound sense of torment and melancholy, like the warrior ghosts had been disturbed from a peaceful slumber and were reliving days of battle again. Despite being confronted with such an adversary, Meadow bravely assaulted the apparition and with one tremendous swing of her magical fiery mace, she banished it from all existence.

A small but brief explosion of white light erupted from the blow, accompanied by a weeping wail of intense pain and for a moment there was silence. "Did you banish it!?" cried Clyde as he rose to his feet, shook the lingering daze from his senses and scooped up the burning torch and his magical longsword. Before any of them could revel in victory, the eerie echo of more ominous breathing crept into the room, except much louder than before. "Yes, I stuck it down, but err, it looks like there are about eight more of them now!" shouted Meadow.

Eight more, eight more of the spooky spirits began gradually phasing through the walls and into the room. Their ghostly gazes fixated upon Clyde and the others, the exorcism of the previous specter likely attracting their attention. "Alight then, lets send these accursed clouds of mist back to where they came from!" roared Bashe as he gallantly stormed towards the one closest and swung his axe. Bashe's blow was tremendous and would've easily spilt the head of anything living in two. Instead, the blazing blue flames around the edge of his axe blades passed straight through the face of the weeping ghost. An eruption of light burst upon impact, causing the specter to swiftly vanish with a screech and Bashe's axe to slam into the stone wall behind it.

Without the ability to see the deadly phantoms, Clyde was of little use in the spooky skirmish. Hence the reason why he quickly fumbled for his own vial of undead detection potion and hastily swigged it down. "Come on, time is of the essence!" Clyde muttered as he waited the couple of seconds it took for the potions effects to begin. Only to see the tortured, spectral face a of ghost right in front of him when the potion finally worked. Fear seized Clyde as the ghost bellowed a haunting scream in his face, before raising its ethereal arm and violently swiping Clyde across the cheek, making him painfully tumble backwards.

This time Clyde managed to keep a firm grasp upon his longsword. Despite the blow knocking him off his feet, he was able to avoid getting struck again from another ghost near him by swiftly rolling to the side. Two of the sinister phantoms advanced upon his position, trapping Clyde in the corner, thankfully one of them was reckless and rushed directly at him. Clyde took advantage of the moment and raised his enchanted longsword as the spirt stormed towards him, braced himself and stabbed the ghost through the chest. Another brief flare of radiant light exploded from the phantom as its body touched the magical blue flames swirling along the blade of Clyde's longsword. This caused the specter to wail and phase straight through Clyde before vanishing entirely.

With one more ghost effectively exorcized, Clyde confidently raised his blade and pointed it towards the second ghost nearby, a haughty smirk spreading across his lips. At that point anarchy consumed the room, Clyde, Meadow and Bashe became entangled in a ferocious and frantic battle with the group of ghosts, a climactic clash of the living versus the dead. Meadow managed to banish another anguished spirit with her magical fiery mace by using both hands and swinging it with all the strength she could muster.

Alas, misfortune struck Meadow when another eerie phantom assaulted her from behind, gripping her by the throat and slowly dragging her up towards the ceiling. To make matters worse, her enchanted spiked mace slipped from out of her fingers and clanged onto the floor, all Meadow could do was squirm as she felt the ghost choke the life from her body. Thankfully, Bashe noticed her predicament and was able to lend his aid by raising his colossal great axe over his head and using his tremendous orc strength to hurl it across the room. Meadow felt the air rush back to her lungs and fell to the floor as the ghost felt the full force of a giant battle axe infused with the magical energy of divine fire. Causing the malevolent spirit to burst into a cloud of light and a screech of sorrow.

However, Bashe was now defenseless, which another ghost hastily took advantage of. Viciously, it pummeled him across the face with its fist, causing him to smash through a cluster of ancient ceramic pottery in the corner. Unsurprisingly, the spiteful specter swiftly floated towards Bashe, eager to pound him to dust. But it didn't count on Clyde suddenly charging in and rescuing Bashe by leaping into the air and slashing his burning blue longsword down the ghost's body. A shrill screech resonated the room as Clyde's flaming sword struck the ghost, causing it burst into a dazzling explosion of light and vanish like the others before it. "Need a hand?" asked Clyde as he smugly extended his hand out to Bashe. Bashe, who was still lying among the shards of shattered pottery, gave an impressed sneer and smiled as he refused Clyde's assistance and pulled himself up, "No, but thanks" he replied.

Only three ghosts remained now with one trying to assail Meadow while she was still recovering her breath. Despite succumbing to an ephemeral moment of shock, Meadow managed to snatch up her fearsome mace and furiously swung it as the chilling phantom flew towards her. The steel spikes of the mace tipped in scorching sacred flames instantly banished the screeching specter from all existence, creating another abrupt flash of blinding white light. The last two remaining spirits tried to assault Bashe and Clyde, but with Clyde still being armed he was able to repel their ghostly onslaught, at least for several seconds. Battling the two vindictive spirits proved daunting and they soon overwhelmed Clyde by avoiding his frantic sword slashes and rushing him once they saw an opening.

Air was knocked from Clyde's chest when the ghosts slammed him against the wall, tightly pinning him. At the same time, Bashe hastily scurried towards his battle axe, eager to lay his fingers upon it. One of the ghosts trapping Clyde released its grasp and scornfully chased after Bashe, refusing to allow him to claim his weapon again. This moment aided Clyde, for with only one ghost now pinning him against the wall, Clyde was able to move his arm and thrust his burning blue blade, piecing the misty heart of the specter. Instantly, another flash of luminous light engulfed the room, along with a shrill wail as the phantom was exiled from this plane of existence.

As for the last ghost, its efforts to prevent Bashe from reaching his weapon and obtaining it were futile. Bashe wrapped his huge orc fingers around the hilt of his great axe, turned to face the weeping spirit and prepared to strike it down. Alas another problem quickly arose, "Where is it? I can't see it!" shouted Bashe as his eyes darted around the room. No doubt the potion which enabled them to see the spirts had worn off, fortunately their presence was not invisible to Clyde just yet as he took the potion later, "Behind you!" he shouted.

Placing faith in Clyde's directions, Bashe quickly spun around and vigorously swung his huge magical great axe, slicing the empty air with his blow. This caused a brief but beautiful surge of resplendent light to burst into existence. Clyde was spot on, for a tormented cry resonated from the invisible phantom, lasting only a couple of seconds and haunting the gloomy halls of the crypt with its eerie echo. Then, everything gradually became serene, the ghostly screams faded, the fury of battle subsided and soft murmurs of wind fluttering through the nooks and crannies of the tomb became the only sound anyone could hear. Yet, the twisted faces of the ghostly assailants, all aghast and anguished was still seared into Meadow's mind. Such imagery sent a chilling shudder crawling along her spine, "Can we find that meddling imp now?" she asked. "Yes, but we should be vigilant, I have little doubt it was the imp who invoked those ghosts, imps have all manner of devious magic up their sleeves!" answered Clyde.

In the past, Meadow had heard rumors and myths about the magical prowess of imps through simple folklore. But to summon ghosts? She didn't realize such power existed, "How is such magic possible?" she asked. "It is the forbidden magic of necromancy, this tomb is rife with the spiritual energy of the dead, imps excel in the art of curses, hexes, ailments and taboo sorcery" explained Clyde. Such matters did not concern Bashe right now, fury filled his heart and his only goal was to bring the blade of his axe down upon the imp's scrawny neck. "Come on, let us keep moving! I want to hang that imps head on my bedroom wall!" he growled.

Although Clyde could understand and sympathize the turmoil thrashing within Bashe, capturing the imp alive was still the top priority. "Cool your flames my friend, that imp serves a master and we have questions that need answering" replied Clyde as he scooped up the still burning torch and led the journey onwards. By this point, the enchanted magical flames dancing along the edge of their weapons had faded, Clyde just prayed no more phantoms would arise from their eternal slumber. Even without the threat of ghosts, the twisting stone corridors of the crypt were eerie, drenched in darkness and exuded a chilling aura that was difficult to rival, "How much further?" Meadow whispered impatiently.

Meadow trailed behind Clyde so close that she accidently stepped on his heel and almost tripped him up, "Relax, I think I see a room ahead!" Clyde answered in a fiery whisper. "I think we're approaching the Hall of Renown, where our most legendary orc heroes and leaders are buried! Memorialized forever with statues!" Bashe explained in an admiring tone. His guess was correct, dozens of majestically crafted stone statues lined both sides of the walls upon Clyde entering the room. Some of the statues showed fragments of time such as cracks and chips, but all the statues were of prominent orc figures from history and this was their final resting place.

A raspy voice suddenly broke the silence when it hissed from behind a stone pillar at the far end of the room. "Leave this place! You're not welcome here!" it snarled, revealing itself to be the despicable imp. "Yeah? Well right back at you!" yelled Bashe, whose blood instantly began to boil upon seeing the nefarious little creature, and he didn't hesitate to charge towards the imp with his great axe raised. "Bashe, no! Beware its magic!" cried Clyde as he watched Bashe the orc berserker rush towards the imp with the fury of a tornado.

A sinister chuckle seeped out of the imps forked tongue as it watched Bashe charge forth, "Ha, ha, so reckless!" mocked the imp. Boldly, it pointed its shimmering magical trident at Bashe and swiftly summoned a surge of fiendish magic, unleashing it in the form of a glowing green bolt that struck Bashe directly. Upon being struck by the sickly green bolt of magic, Bashe allowed his great axe to slip from his fingers and he toppled to the floor like a sack of potatoes, sliding face first into the ground, "Ugh! So hungry! So tired!" he groaned.

At the same time, Meadow and Clyde quickly sought cover behind two nearby stone pillars in the room, "What the heck happened to Bashe!?" declared Meadow. "He's been hit with a lethargy hex; all his energy has been sapped!" answered Clyde, who took a quick peek around the pillar, only to duck his head back in as the imp blasted another bolt of magic his way. "So weak, so tired! I need a nap!" groaned Bashe as he crawled along the ground and tried to reclaim his axe, failed and lazily sprawled face up onto his back. Clyde snatched a vial of potion from his harness and swiftly wrenched the cork out of its neck, "We need to get close!" he declared, swigging the black murky liquid within.

In the next breath, Clyde peeped his head from around the safety of the stone pillar and belched a hazy mist of ebony smoke from his mouth. He had cleverly used a smokescreen potion and gradually, he and Meadow were obscured from the imp's fiendish eyes thanks to the miasma of black fog swathing the room. Hastily, they plunged into the cloud of darkness to seek refuge, sadly, this also meant the imp was obscured from their sight. Thus, Meadow and Clyde had no option than to dash through the blanket of smoke, but it aided in helping them safely close the distance.

Anxiously, the imp surveyed the room, trying to catch a glimpse of Meadow and Clyde, "Arghhhh, no fair! Where did you go!? I can't see you!" it snarled. Suddenly, from out of the cloudy mist, Clyde burst forth, his body quickly coming into view, but he emerged closer to the imp than he intended, "Aha, I see you!" shouted the imp. Having to capture the imp alive proved infuriating since it limited the amount of options Clyde had at his disposal, "Curses!" hissed Clyde as he frantically reached for a potion in his harness. Alas, the imp was already alerted to his presence and Clyde was devoid of the time required to let another potion touch his lips. For the despicable imp raised its little trident and cast a mystical ball of emerald colored magic at him.

Upon being struck by the spell, Clyde's entire body was quickly imprisoned within a floating sphere of magical green energy from which he could not escape. "Enough of this, release me at once you vile little devil!" shouted Clyde as he watched the imp through his translucent hovering bubble of fiendish sorcery. "Ha! Caught you in my trap little fly! My master shall be so pleased!" mocked the imp as it smugly smirked, cavorted and stuck its tongue out at Clyde. "Don't forget about me!" Meadow shouted after dashing from out of the foggy confines of the smoke cloud, holding an empty glass vial in her hand. Whatever potion was in the vial, it seemed Meadow had already consumed it.

Just as the imp glared and raised its magical trident at her, Meadow abruptly unleashed a belch of purple sleepy-gas potion from her mouth. As the violet colored gas rapidly crawled over the imp and infused its senses, the imp began to woozily raise its trident, trying desperately to summon a last surge of debilitating sorcery. Yet, the imp's efforts were to no avail, the pungent sleeping gas exhaled from Meadow's mouth seduced the imp with its promise of sweet slumber.

Gradually, the imp's magical trident gently slipped away from its slender fingers and clanged against the hard-stone floor. "Master......my...master......will......get......you...." slurred the imp as it drifted into a jaded torpor and toppled over like a youthful princess after a tankard of rum. The hexes that the imp cast upon Bashe and Clyde also faded when the imp shut its spiteful little eyes and fell into a sleep rivalling that of the dead. As soon as Clyde was released from his floating spherical prison of magic, he swiftly jogged over and scooped up the imps enchanted trident, "Ha, ha! No more magic without this!" he declared. Meanwhile, Meadow haughtily towered above the snoozing imp and gazed upon it like it were a feeble like lamb, "What a nuisance! Sweet-dreams!" she growled.

Chalice of Renewal
Chapter 9
Mind games

To think that so much trouble had been caused by such a little creature, it was quite difficult to comprehend. Nevertheless, Clyde and Meadow could now proudly revel in another job well done. Except, Bashe didn't see it as a victory just yet, evident by the way he snatched up his great axe and began ominously stomping towards the imp once his strength had returned. "Stand aside, that imp has disturbed our most sacred burial tomb! Resurrected the ancient spirts of this place and used them to kill some of our best warriors! Its time it faced the judgment of my axe!" snarled Bashe. Bashe's fearsome demeanor struck terror even within Clyde and they were on the same side and it was fortunate the imp was asleep, otherwise it may have died from fright. "Despite your fury I shall stand my ground, for I cannot allow you to harm that imp, as wicked its actions have been!" declared Clyde as he obstructed Bashe's path of rage.

Thankfully, Clyde's words were enough to momentarily halt Bashe's stampede. "My disciple and I have been caught up in a perplexing plot, this imp may have some answers" Clyde explained. Calmly, Bashe lowered his hulking axe and took a deep breath, "Alight, say you take it prisoner, what's to stop it causing such disaster again?" he grumbled. Confidently, Clyde held up the imp's puny trident in his palm and laughed, "Because, without its little fork it has no conductor for its magic, it is as now as troublesome as a fly!" he proclaimed.

Although such a fact soothed Bashe's apprehension, he still desired more comfort and removed his thick leather belt. "Even so, use this to restrain the pest, I think that's fair since I'm not going to kill it!" he growled. It was a fair request and one Clyde was happy to oblige since he was on the verge of suggesting the very same thing. "Agreed, best not to leave anything to chance!" he replied as he took Bashe's belt. Since the imp was no larger than a new-born baby and Bashe's belt was meant to wrap around the waist of an adult orc warrior, Clyde easily tied the belt around the scoundrel. "Can we leave now? I mean no disrespect but, these gloomy crypts give me the creeps" Meadow nervously uttered.

Once the slumbering imp had been restrained, Clyde nodded his head. "Indeed, my petrified pupil! I see little reason to linger in these sacred halls of stone, I also wish to grant you a pat on the back, you proved your worth once again today!" Clyde replied. Clyde then proceeded to pat Meadow on the back, which created a rosy blush in her cheeks. "Glad to hear I'm not worthless then, and I'm not petrified of this tomb! I just find it a little too creepy for my taste!" Meadow declared assertively. Their chemistry evoked a carefree chuckle from Bashe, and he casually leaned his great axe over his shoulder. "Ha, I have to say you both fought well, better than I expected for such scrawny humans!" he declared. "Perhaps I shouldn't be so quick judge, I travelled with a human before and she showed me the strength and resolve your people possess" added Bashe.

Curiosity enveloped Meadow as she tilted her head and studied his words, "Oh really? And who was it? Knowing you, it was probably a great human warrior" she uttered. Meadow's remark abruptly dragged Bashe from out of his realm of reminiscence, "Never mind, I shouldn't dwell on the past!" he uttered. "On behalf of Orstone and chieftainess Umgra, you have earned our thanks and our respect! Report to the chieftainess back at the city to receive your reward!" declared Bashe.

Regretfully, Clyde shook his head and declined Bashe's invitation. "Sadly, I'm afraid we cannot, the sleepy-gas potion my apprentice used shall only last several hours at the most" he replied. Being unable to reward Clyde and Meadow and drink to their triumph displeased Bashe, causing him to despise the imp further. Yet, Bashe understood Clyde's decision, "I shall escort you back to the crypt entrance at least, I shall also tell chieftainess Umgra all you have done!" Bashe declared.

The journey back to the entrance of the sacred burial tomb felt just as gloomy as the journey in. The haunted whistle of desert wind still creeping along the cobweb covered halls of the crypt. Along the way, Clyde dragged the sleeping imp behind him like a common leather sack by using the long bulky belt Bashe had bestowed. "So, out of curiosity, how do you plan to pry answers from that creatures' lips?" asked Meadow.

It was a fair question, one to which Clyde hadn't a genuine answer. It was also very unlikely the imp would spill any secrets if Clyde simply served it tea and asked nicely, "Let me worry about that my dear!" he proclaimed. Even Meadow knew that meant Clyde hadn't formed a plan just yet, "Okay, so basically you have no idea, understood" Meadow answered in a ridiculing tone. Her sarcasm succeeded in causing a grumpy frown to swathe Clyde's face. "Restrain your ridicule my minion of mockery, lest you want to be the one dragging this infuriating imp next" he grumbled.

Sunset greeted them upon finally emerging from the murky tunnels of the burial crypt. The brisk breeze rejuvenating their weary souls, "At last, feels good to taste the fresh air again!" declared Meadow as she inhaled. Seeing the amber radiance of the blazing sun descend behind the mighty mountain city of Orstone made Bashe utter an elated sigh. "Thanks again, you may not possess the strength of an orc, but you both have the heart and courage of one and proven that strength alone cannot win every battle, a warrior is also measured by his cunning!" proclaimed Bashe. Like many clients before him, Bashe respectfully extended his hand for Clyde to embrace and shake. Clyde's hand was swallowed up and lost within Bashe's huge hulking palm when he happily went to shake it. It remained a majestic sight all the same, with the glowing sunset and towering city of Orstone on the horizon. "It was a more taxing ordeal than I could've imagined and fraught with surprises at every turn, yet my apprentice and I were only too happy to help good sir!" answered Clyde.

Soon, Bashe ended the handshake and slung his tremendous battle axe over his shoulder, "Well, I'm not a fan of long goodbyes" he uttered. "So, with that said, good luck to you both on your travels, its time for me to report back" added Bashe, turning his back and strolling towards the sunset. Meadow and Clyde watched him drift away for several seconds with smiles upon their cheeks, until Clyde raised the ring on his finger to his mouth and spoke into the chatterstone. "Styx? Styx? Are you there? Our business in Orstone is concluded, we're heading back to the same spot you created that portal!" declared Clyde.

Silence followed for several seconds, until Styx's raspy voice abruptly resonated back. "Yes master, sorry! I was cleaning up your alchemy lab, I keep finding goblin ears and minotaur horns in the strangest places!" he echoed. "Worry not though, I shall be ready to create a new portal as soon as you give the order!" Styx added with hearty devotion. Eager to escape this region of rough canyons, gritty sand and scorching sun, Meadow promptly began marching west, "Lets hurry then, it was this way wasn't it?" she asked. "Indeed it was my astute assistant, let us depart the Jagged Steppes and return to the frigid domain of the Frostveil Mountains from whence we came!" proclaimed Clyde.

Traversing the Jagged Steppes and navigating back towards their initial portal point was both daunting and tedious. Especially with the sweltering sun on their backs and the slumbering imp in tow. Fortunately, Clyde had a much better memory than Meadow gave him praise for and parts of the land began looking familiar again. "Have to say, I find it remarkable how well you know your way around" noted Meadow. "Tis only natural to be worldly and possess an impeccable memory when you've travelled as much as I have, not having to live among people aided me greatly though" replied Clyde.

Travelling across Resplendia to the furthest corners of the land sounded adventurous and exciting. But Meadow never considered the social aspect of it until now, "To be honest you don't often strike me as a people person" she uttered. Despite being skilled at maintaining healthy relations with his clients, Clyde succumbed to her shrewd remark. "I prefer to treat people as clients, it makes things easier and I prefer to keep things professional, too much can go wrong otherwise" he replied.

How Clyde phrased his words was mysterious and intriguing, there must have been a specific reason for his outlook. But Meadow took care not to pry too much, "And what about me? Have I earned your friendship and trust?" she asked. As soon Meadow asked this question, Clyde halted in his tracks and kept his back turned to her, "You've become tolerable at the very least" he answered. Naturally, a furious scowl that could have scared away a grumpy swamp troll appeared upon Meadow's face, "Tolerable? Really? Well thanks so much! Great to know I'm not a burden!" she grumbled. Her moment of frustration only served to make Clyde loudly chuckle as he disappeared into the mouth of a canyon ahead, dragging the snoring imp behind him. "Hey, don't just walk away! Wait for me!" cried Meadow as she gave chase.

Sprouting formations of jagged rock jutting up from beneath the earth appeared the deeper they travelled into the jaws of the looming gorge. Little lizard creatures scurried and hid beneath alcoves of rock as Meadow and Clyde walked by, while the wind occasionally echoed with the howls and growls of mysterious beasts in the distance. Dusk was upon them, causing vibrant streaks of gold and purple light to appear across the sky, giving the atmosphere an aura of eerie twilight. "I think we're close" uttered Clyde.

Soon, he came to an abrupt halt, which delighted Meadow, for her feet felt like they had traversed several miles of hot coal and even a minute of rest was welcome. Clyde promptly raised his hand and spoke into the ring embedded with the chatterstone, "Styx, we have arrived at the same spot and are ready to return" uttered Clyde. "I understand master, I shall create a new portal with all haste! Just please don't come home with muddy shoes again!" echoed Styx's voice a few seconds later.

All that was left was to wait a couple of minutes until the portal materialized, Meadow just hoped they were in the right spot. Night was on the cusp of appearing, so finding their way to the correct portal location in the dark was not something Meadow enjoyed the thought of doing. Especially not while the slumbering imp they captured continued to intrude their thoughts with its loud snoring. "Hope Styx makes a portal soon, if I have to listen to this imp snoring a second longer, I'm going to rip my own ears off!" grumbled Meadow. Fortunately for Meadow's ears, the air was torn asunder by a rumbling tremor which bounced and resonated all along the rocky walls of the canyon.

The magical portal appeared at last, only it was several dozen feet away rather than several inches. Meadow could easily perceive the glowing portal of mystical energy against the shadowy hue of dusk and she bestowed Clyde a brooding frown. "Okay, so, we weren't in the exact spot, but close enough!" Clyde declared. Eager to return to a relaxing bath, a soft bed and a steaming cup of tea, Meadow remained silent, mustered her motivation and began trudging towards the swirling portal. Fate proved nothing was quite so simple though, for the eerie sound of hissing began to creep across the air.

When Clyde and Meadow looked back to see what caused it, they were met with dozens of glowing eyes. "Salrodela! Lots of them! The vibrations from the portal must've caught their attention!" Clyde anxiously gasped. He and Meadow watched with dread as the pack of huge beasts slowly crawled along the walls of the canyon towards them. Judging by the way the bunch of lethal lizards slithered their slimy tongues and ominously advanced, it became clear that Meadow and Clyde were the evenings dinner.

Every so slowly, Clyde began to back away, keeping his gaze focused upon the approaching horde of hungry salrodela. "Great, we could really use Bashe to come leaping in with his axe again!" Meadow nervously whispered. "Our only option is to escape through the portal, so with that in mind, run!" Clyde shouted, turning tail and dashing as fast as he could towards the portal. Meadow didn't need to be told twice, she quickly joined Clyde in his frantic retreat and scurried behind him like a rat chasing a wheel of rolling cheese. Upon seeing them flee, the pack of hissing salrodela viciously chased after them, mercilessly pursuing their prey along the stretching gorge. It was thankful the captured imp was exceptionally light, meaning Clyde could easily sling it over his shoulder and carry it as he ran. "Styx, we are being chased by a pack salrodela! Get ready to close the portal as soon as we enter!" Clyde shouted into his chatterstone.

Sweat dripped along Meadow's forehead, her heart was beating so fast it felt like it would burst any moment. But she kept on running, gathering every fragment of strength she could to keep her legs moving. Despite their determination, the dreadful hissing and ominous snarls of the salrodela grew louder and closer. No doubt if it were not for the large gap of distance they started off with, Meadow and Clyde would have been caught already. Suddenly, Meadow noticed a few of the large spiky lizards rapidly crawling along the sides of the canyon walls, likely trying to use it to pounce upon them from the sides. Even through Meadow's legs burned like two pillars of fire and her lungs begged for air, the portal was finally within spitting distance. "Jump through!" cried Clyde as he dove headfirst straight into the mouth of the mystical portal floating in front of them.

Meadow could hear the deadly horde of horrid lizards hot on her heels and one of them stopped and lashed its long, slithery tongue towards her leg to ensnare her. It was too close, another second longer and Meadow would have been caught within the slimy grasp of the salrodela and been a tasty meal for the horde of monsters. Luckily, Meadow gave one last surge of effort and dove towards the vibrant portal just before the lizards long lashing tongue had chance to coil around her leg and yank her back.

A blinding myriad of captivating colors consumed Meadow as she was devoured by the portal and blasted from one region to another like a shooting star. She soon emerged a few seconds later and landed in a messy heap within the familiar portal room. "Now Styx, close it!" shouted Clyde, whom was already on the other side awaiting Meadow's return. "Right away master!" cried Styx who frantically raised his magical trident, pointed it at the portal, conjured his magical power and sealed it shut. Before the portal fully vanished, fierce snarls and hissing could be heard from the other side. Fortunately, nothing managed to get through, which caused Clyde and Meadow to gasp with relief, "Okay, I really need a cup of tea!" wheezed Clyde.

Swirling plumes of intoxicating tea infused Meadow's senses when she inhaled from the quaint cup she held, it was an aroma akin to sunflame flowers, elf blossom and chasmberry. Blissfully, Meadow meandered into the kitchen, her radiant fiery hair still wrapped in a thick towel from the bath she had recently taken, "Ahh! I finally feel alive again!" she declared. Clyde, who was already sitting at the kitchen table, glanced her way and narrowed his eyes upon seeing her, "And who said you could wear my bath robe!?" he demanded.

Innocently, Meadow admired the soft, thick robe of dyed cerulean blue wool and shrugged, "Well, it is a little big for me, but by the heavens is it comfy!" she jovially replied. Her quirky carefree attitude irked Clyde further, easily perceivable by the way he frowned at her. "Did it not occur to you to ask before wearing someone else's garments!?" he grumbled. However, Meadow easily parried his frustration with more insolence, "If you didn't want me to wear your robe, you should've stitched your name into it!" she answered. Ultimately, Clyde surrendered to fatigue and defeat, his only response being a jaded sigh, "Ugghhh!" he exhaled, taking a much-needed sip from his teacup.

Styx was also in the kitchen, lazily lying on his side upon the oak dinner table also drinking tea from a cute little teacup that appeared like it had been crafted just for him. "It's been three hours since you brought it back master!" he hissed. Styx was referring to the imp they had captured, Clyde tied it with rope to one of the wooden dining chairs and it remained soundly asleep. "I assume it's not said anything then?" asked Meadow. Clyde rested his chin upon his palm and watched the imp with the vigilance of a hawk, "Not yet, that sleepy-gas potion is taking a while to wear off" he grumbled impatiently. "Well you never know, maybe it'll talk in its sleep and let slip something juicy" Meadow replied, taking a seat at the dining table to join Clyde.

All three of them sat there, drinking tea and watched the imp sleep, "Master, I must say how unwise this idea is, my kind is exceptionally deceitful and scheming" remarked Styx. "Yes Styx, you've said that several times now" answered Clyde, brushing aside Styx's concerns and continuing to scrutinize the sleeping imp. Meadow made a distinct slurping sound as she sipped her tea and drummed her fingers upon the dining table. "Even when it does wake up, how will you pry any answers from it mouth? You're not going to torture it are you? Or do you have truth potion?" Meadow inquired.

As much as Meadow detested the devious imp, she did not wish to see any living creature suffer. "You may rest your concerns about torture, I have no intention of doing anything barbaric" Clyde answered. "And yes, I do indeed possess an elixir called truth potion, sadly it has no effect upon magical beings such as imps" he added with a disgruntled grumble. Just at that moment, the imp prisoner began to murmur, and his eyes slowly opened. Which in turn ensnared the attention of everyone in the room, "Wakey-wakey at last you little fiend!" declared Clyde.

As soon as the imp awoke from his drowsy dimension of dreams, it began frantically writhing and squirming. Only to be struck with dismay upon realizing it was firmly tied to a chair. "Let me go, let me go or my master will unleash his wrath upon you!" hissed the imp in a spiteful tone as he tried to wrestle out of the binding rope. The imp quickly froze in place and was rendered speechless however, when Clyde revealed a shimmering magical trident he had been secretly resting upon his lap underneath the table. "Your trident, the magical wand that allows all imps to cast their heinous hexes and cunning curses, I presume you want it back?" asked Clyde as he lay the trident upon the table.

A vindictive glare flashed within the imps beady red eyes and it menacingly clenched its ashen fangs together. "Give it back! Not yours! Give it back you thieves! It is precious!" snarled the imp. "Depending on what you say, you accursed little pest, I shall either return it to you or take it outside and hurl it over the nearest cliff!" barked Clyde. Everything fell silent after that, even the villainous imp dared not utter a single word or move a muscle, until its gaze wandered towards Styx. "You, you are an imp too! Help me brother! Why are you allied with these humans!?" it hissed. Luckily, the imp's pleas for aid fell upon deaf ears, "Silence yourself and speak only to my master if you wish to leave with your skin!" Styx hissed back.

Clyde swiftly regained control of the questioning by slamming his fist upon the oak table, "Tell me about your master, who is he!?" he demanded. It was rare to see Clyde reveal even a fragment of ferocity or intimidation, so it surprised Meadow when he showed it so authentically. Sadly, it was to no avail, for even though Clyde made the imp jolt, he received only one answer, "I don't know who he is!" cried the imp.

His reply infuriated Meadow, causing her to angrily bolt up and slam her palms upon the table. "Liar! Do not play dumb! You're telling us you don't know your own master!?" she yelled, lunging forward. Her sudden outburst caused the imp to recoil and it vented an alarmed yelp, but Clyde succeed in settling Meadow down, "I shall rephrase the question once more!" he barked. "Kindly reveal the identity of your master and you won't have to deal with my apprentice!" Clyde demanded, placing his hand upon Meadow's shoulder and gently easing her back into her chair. Alas, the imp remained motionless, silently gawking at them like every word they uttered was unintelligible, which caused another flurry of frustration to afflict Clyde.

Once the silence had overstayed its welcome, Clyde passed the imps magical trident to Meadow and sighed, "Very well, Meadow, be a dear and throw this over the cliff outside, will you?" he asked. "Okay, such a shame though, I was hoping to use it as a backscratcher" muttered Meadow as she took the shimmering trident from him and began strolling out of the room. That was the breaking point, the imp could contain his silence no longer. "No wait, truly I do not know! My master always wore a black metal mask! He kept his face hidden even from me!" cried the imp. Mentioning a black masked individual baited Clyde's attention again, it had to be the same one, "The mysterious man with the black mask, I knew it" he uttered. Meadow came strolling back into the room, lay the trident upon the oak dining table and pierced the imp with her glare. "The same masked man who's been the cause of the jobs we've been handling!" she growled.

Finally, Clyde was a step closer to unravelling the mystery of this black masked man, however, anger clouded his diplomacy skills. "Why is he doing such things? What is his purpose? Where is he located!? You shall answer me at once!" Clyde shouted, shoving his face closer towards the imp. Perhaps that was a mistake, Clyde felt a sliver of regret for allowing his calm to slip in front of his apprentice, especially since it yielded no answers, "I know nothing more! Nothing!" yelped the imp. They had hit another stone wall and frankly Clyde and Meadow had become increasingly jaded by the exchange. "Maybe he really doesn't know anything, perhaps he's just a puppet" whispered Meadow.

Reluctantly, Clyde agreed on this, shook his head and hopelessly shrugged. "I think you might be right, we learned next to nothing and I admit, I'm unsure as to what our next course of action should be" he muttered. Suddenly, Styx joined in with their discussion, "Master, If I may? I have an idea; I think I might know of a way to obtain the answers you seek without asking another question" he whispered. As the three of them discussed, schemed, plotted and planned, the imp looked on, tilting its ear towards their backs in hopes of overhearing their secret stratagem. To the imp's dismay, it could only hear faint muttering and inaudible murmurs, leaving whatever scheme they had planned up to the imagination. Clyde briefly shifted his gaze towards the curious imp for a moment, before swiftly swerving it away again. Then, he abruptly marched out of the room, "What are you planning? What is happening!?" cried the imp.

Its tone was perturbed, its mind trapped within a tumultuous tempest of turmoil as turbulent as the twisting snowstorm relentlessly pommeling outside. A sharp fragment of sympathy pierced Meadow in the heart, for she could detect the imp's unease, yet her and Styx remained bound to a veil of silence. Clyde returned several seconds later, revealing a glass vial containing a plum colored liquid, proceeded to yank the cork stopper from out of the neck and imbibe the purple fluid. Next, Clyde aimed himself towards the imp and spewed a hazy cloud of purple mist into its face, it was another batch of sleepy-gas potion he unleashed. Despite the imp's best efforts to resist, the violet vapor swirled over it and lulled the imp into a heavy slumber. "Okay Styx prepare the portal, I just hope your right" echoed Clyde's voice as everything turned black.

Deep within the lush sprawling forests of Resplendia, everything was ordinary, everything was tranquil. A small babbling river lay nearby, flowing gently like it hadn't a care in the world. A young fisherman watched a group of vibrant butterflies from the riverbank as he lay upon the soft grass. He gazed at the butterflies as they sailed serenely through the air with their graceful wings. Whoever the young fisherman was, this moment felt like he had found paradise, he didn't even mind if he never caught a single fish with his makeshift wooden rod and string. Basking in the radiant sunshine as it peeked through the towers of swaying trees and listening to the birds singing their songs was enough for him.

Until, a ferocious rumble rippled the peaceful air, shattering the calm atmosphere, creating a thundering roar and causing the young fisherman to jump out of his skin. Whatever caused the disruption came from nearby and as soon as the young fisherman raised his head over the hill to see what was responsible, a most astonishing sight greeted him. A luminous portal of swirling colors hovered in the air no more than twenty feet from him. "What in the healing waters of Soulspring is that!?" gasped the fisherman as he watched the floating vortex. From within the levitating whirlpool of wizardry walked a young redheaded girl, a slender older man with bushy black hair and a purple skinned imp which rested upon the man's shoulder. Upon seeing them emerge from the portal, the young fisherman simply decided to duck his head back behind the hill and pretend like it was all an illusion. "What kind of mushrooms did my mother put in that soup?" he quietly muttered.

Gradually, the humming portal of magical sorcery vanished, "I don't see anything, Styx are you sure we are in the right place?" asked Meadow. Styx hopped off Clyde's shoulder and scoffed, "Of course we are! I never make mistakes; this is the place! It has simply been hidden from view!" he declared. A loud boorish snore shattered the tranquility of the verdant forest around them and when Clyde turned his head to find the culprit, he realized it was the captured imp. It would be several hours more before the imp awoke, so Clyde had resorted to stuffing the imp into a linen sack and hauling it along like a piece of luggage. "Please lead on Styx, I wish to be rid of this headache I keep dragging along!" he uttered. Wearily rolling his eyes as he looked upon the imps sleepy drooling head poking out of the top of the sack.

Styx gave a loyal salute, flapped his little leathery wings and promptly glided away, flying deeper into the lush forest. "Hey, slow down! Wait for us!" called Meadow as she quickly chased Styx into the labyrinth of towering trees, dashing through the dense thickets, catching small glimpses of Styx ahead. Thankfully, Meadow didn't have to run very much, for she soon caught up to Styx and came to an abrupt stop several seconds later. "Whoa, that's quite a tree!" she gasped upon emerging within a sunny clearing.

Soon Clyde joined them, and he too had a moment of awe once his eyes beheld the sight of the colossal tree standing before him. "So, this is it? I confess this my first time visiting too!" he declared. The tree was rooted right in the middle of the forest glade and its branches seemed to pierce the very clouds. Most alluring of all was the absurd number of mushrooms scattered across its body. Nearly every single color of mushroom imaginable lay upon the tree. Hues and patterns that ranged from stripy gold to spotty caerulean, some of the mushrooms even glowed different colors like they were on fire from the inside. Adding to the wonderful whimsy, the leaves upon the tips of the tree's branches were a truly bizarre color, some being a shade of light lavender and some a deep amethyst.

It was like something out of a mythical storybook and though Meadow had seen many magical sights, she was beginning to grasp just how mystical the land of Resplendia was. "So, where's the door? How do we get in?" she uttered cluelessly. With a flamboyant spin of his trident, Styx pointed it at the tree and scoffed, "Opening the way is a trivial task, but only if you know the ancient magic of the imps!" he hissed. Styx then proceeded to murmur a series of mysterious chants in a language that was completely incoherent to Meadow and Clyde's ears.

Upon finishing the string of mysterious invocations, Styx's trident began to glow with an aura of radiant scarlet. A bellowing rumble quickly followed and caused the entire forest to tremble, "What's happening!?" cried Meadow. She soon received her answer, for the gargantuan tree in the center of the glade abruptly tore itself asunder, splitting down the middle and revealed a giant swirling portal. After that, everything slowly became calm once again, "There it is, the entrance to Duskglade! City of the imps!" declared Styx. Now, Meadow was certain nothing could surprise her at this point, for she gawked upon the titanic mushroom clad tree. It seemingly coming alive when it fractured its body apart and revealed the humongous glowing portal within its heart.

Even Clyde was reduced to a state of astonishment, "Come, we must enter quickly lest anyone sees!" Styx hissed. Clyde was so stunned he had to wrestle his way free from the grip of captivation that had befallen him, but he gave an affirming nod, "Right, let us focus upon the task at hand!" he declared. Seeing Meadow's mind still wandering in a world of wonder, Clyde repeatedly clicked his fingers in front of her face. "Come my apprentice, it is time for your attention to return from the celestial clouds!" he jest. "Yeah, yeah, I'm right behind you" answered Meadow in a dreamy tone, becoming dizzy as she stretched her neck up at the giant portal as they entered, and the tree devoured them whole.

Once they stepped foot beyond the borders of the colossal humming portal of magic, they heard the leaves of the tree rustle loudly, joined by the sound of snapping wood. As soon as they marched into the stomach of the tree, it twisted and contorted itself like a living wooden doll, until it magically fused itself back together exactly like it was before. As far as Meadow could tell, the portal functioned exactly like the one Styx would create, it was just much, much larger in size. After a couple of colorful seconds of whizzing later, they emerged upon the other side. "Where are we? This cannot be real!" gasped Meadow, for the first thing she noticed was eerie blue moonlight that veiled the sky, despite the fact it was a glorious golden day when she entered. "Duskglade exists within our very own plane of reality, a magical region untouched and unseen by most, it is where we are born, and where our tridents are forged!" hissed Styx.

Duskglade appeared as an enchanted forest at night, like something out of a fable and the ghostly blue moonlight enhanced the otherworldly atmosphere. Styx acted as their guide and led them further in, while Meadow and Clyde began noticing how fanciful this new realm was. "Look at all these mushrooms! Look at the size of them!" Clyde gasped. It was an alchemist's dream here, gigantic mushrooms taller than trees sprouted from beneath the ground. Some of them radiating a luminous glow and functioned as lanterns along the moonlit path. Marvel swept over Meadow as she traversed the main path and passed beneath two glowing mushrooms that loomed over her head.

Along the way to the settlement of Duskglade, a swarm of dazzling fireflies whizzed and whooshed through the shimmering air, creating a brilliant ballet of color. Their bodies seemed resplendent against the ethereal moonbeams and after Meadow watched them with fascination, she noticed the butterflies. There were oodles of them, all fluttering along the sky or resting upon the tops of giant mushrooms that grew like weeds amidst the sprawling twilight forest. No two butterflies appeared the same either, they all possessed their own unique patterns and colors, their wings literally glowing like fire, adding to the enchantment.

Never had Meadow envisioned a place so otherworldly, nor did she expect to ever reach out and touch one. Yet here she was, soaking in the eerie beauty of this spellbinding realm, treading upon its mysterious soil. It was only after Meadow and Clyde pursued Styx through the dense thickets of tangling trees and mountainous mushrooms that the secret imp city of Duskglade came into view. Duskglade was more of a small town than a true city, but the magical moonlight and fanciful atmosphere veiling the settlement imposed a bewitching beauty that was difficult to rival.

It also seemed a quaint, odd little settlement that revealed more of its charm the closer Meadow approached. "Stay close, my people relish playing tricks on visitors, for they rarely see any!" hissed Styx. First, they had to cross a timid stone bridge overlapping a steady stream, which possessed water that was strangely violet in color. Upon making the trivial crossing, the streets of Duskglade awaited, as did the mystified glances from the imp citizens as they gawked upon Meadow and Clyde with profound curiosity. At last Meadow knew how it felt to be like a luminous fish in a pond, "So to be clear, we're allowed to be here right?" she asked, nervously glancing left and right. "Yes, yes! Of course! All are welcome here; we just like to make sure everyone doesn't know here exists!" answered Styx in his raspy voice.

As Meadow and Clyde slowly meandered along the crooked cobbled streets of the town, they felt a strong surge of powerful magic sweep over them. "What's happening!?" cried Clyde as he and Meadow found themselves floating into the air. A winding coil of blue sorcery wrapped itself around their bodies, hindering their movements. "Styx, long time no see! Who have you brought to our city!? You know the rules!" barked a couple of armored imp guards as they fluttered over with their tridents raised. Clearly it was the imp guards who were hexing Meadow and Clyde with their magic, keeping them levitating in the air and rendering them helpless. "Please my brothers, let them go! This matter is vital; speak to the matriarch we must! We need her to rummage through the memories of another imp!" pleaded Styx. Whatever spell the imp guards were inflicting upon Meadow and Clyde, it felt like a giant magical snake had scooped them up.

Like a powerful python had wrapped itself around them and was gradually crushing them as slowly as possible. However, the two guards swapped piqued glances upon hearing what Styx had to say. Finally, after levitating and squeezing Meadow and Clyde for a few seconds longer, they kindly dispelled their magic. Gravity still functioned the same way in this realm, resulting in Meadow and Clyde abruptly dropping several feet to the ground in a crumpled heap. "Ouch! Quite the welcome!" grumbled Meadow. "It is fortunate Styx is one of the most trustworthy citizens in Duskglade, which counts for a lot in a settlement of imps!" hissed one of the guards as they stood aside and granted passage. After batting the dust off his coat, Clyde bowed his head, secretly in sarcasm, "Yes, how very lucky for us, we appreciate the kind gesture!" he answered.

After that little skirmish, Styx raised one of his slender arms and pointed his scrawny finger forward, "That gigantic mushroom ahead, that is the home of the matriarch!" he announced. The mushroom Styx was referring to was difficult to miss, for of all the mushrooms that existed in this realm, the matriarchs was by far the largest. "This matriarch lives inside a colossal mushroom?" asked Meadow as she strolled along the cobblestone path gazing up at the towering fungus. "Yes, at the very top, her magic is the most potent of all imps, she can perform the ritual to see into the memories of others!" declared Styx.

Clyde took a brief glance at the imp they had captured; it was still slumbering inside the sack slung over his shoulder. "Then let us hope she can pry some answers from this one's nefarious noggin" he replied. Meanwhile, Duskglade remained such an oddity to Meadow, for the shroud of luminous blue moonlight continued to persistently veil the town with no sign of time changing. Intricately decorated iron poles dotted the cobbled pathway and glass jars dangled from them. Each jar contained a cluster of glowing fireflies, clearly meant as ingenious sources of light. Even the huts and houses which the imps dwelled in were unique, for they were built not from wood or stone. Instead each house was sculpted and carved into the gigantic mushrooms that permeated the spooky forest.

The only part of the houses that consisted of wood were the doors and windows, but each mushroom house was uniquely distinct, having its own color and pattern. On the way to the mushroom tower belonging to the matriarch of the town, a pungent stench drifted across the air and captivated the attention of Clyde and Meadow. Whatever this mysterious new aroma was, it came from another mushroom hut nearby. "Oooooo, what is that smell?" remarked Meadow with bubbling interest. "Ah, that is the smell of duskbrew! The most popular beverage in Duskglade! Stands serving duskbrew are quite common here, would you like to try some?" asked Styx.

After being exposed to such an aromatic aroma, Meadow concluded it would be a crime not to indulge and nodded her head. She then gave a cry of glee and hastily marched towards the little mushroom hut. "So glad we could stay focused" sighed Clyde, shaking his head and chasing after Meadow and Styx. Both claimed their seats and rested their rumps upon the circular toadstools that surrounded the bar area. "Styx, how've you been!? It's been a lifetime since you returned to Duskglade! I bet you've missed a cup of duskbrew eh?" remarked the floating little imp who was serving. Styx gazed at the bubbling cauldron of purple liquid that hovered above a blazing firepit and smacked his lips. "Good to see you too Zeal! Indeed, I have missed the taste of duskbrew greatly!" answered Styx. Clyde wandered over, planted his rear upon one of the toadstool seats alongside Meadow at the mushroom hut and sighed again, "One drink okay?" he uttered.

Reluctantly, Meadow saluted him and rolled her eyes, "Fine, one mug of your finest duskbrew for each of us please!" she heartily declared to the imp serving. "Coming right up, and since your new to Duskglade there is no charge! First time visitors drink for free!" announced Zeal. Who promptly took their order, dunked a large wooden ladle into the batch of bubbling brew and poured it out. Three bulky wooden tankards were pushed towards them, each filled to the brim with the purple liquid known as duskbrew, with plumes of steamy warm mist rising from them.

Meadow felt a hefty weight when she raised her mug, which admittedly caught her off guard, "Ah, smells delicious!" she remarked before taking a humble sip. Although it was hot, that one sip possessed a fantastical flavor the likes of which Meadow had never imbibed before. So much so that she pursed her lips together and blew upon it, hoping to cool it and take her next sip sooner. At the same time, Styx took a braver swig from his mug and gasped with delight after swallowing. "Ahh, it has been so long since I savored the taste of a mug of duskbrew! To an imp it is the greatest delicacy!" he exclaimed.

To Meadow it tasted thick but smooth, possessing a mixture of flavors that reminded her of fresh plomberry pie. But also, sweet cherrybutter herbs and the spicy kick of nightfire nuts all rolled into one. "By the golden flames of the legendary Embermire! This beverage is sweeter than a sirens kiss during a shower of shooting stars while a celestial full moon hangs in the air!" proclaimed Clyde. Meadow raised an eyebrow as she watched Clyde drink from his mug, then chuckled and pointed her finger at him. "Yes, what he just said!" she added after swigging another mouthful now that it had cooled. A strange sensation swept over Meadow and she started to feel slightly light-headed, but in a surprisingly pleasant way. "Hey, do you guys feel that? I feel funny! Also is it just me or is everything starting to glow brighter?" pondered Meadow as she gazed upon a group of vibrant butterflies floating above her head.

Clyde began to feel a similar experience and gawked at the jars of beautiful buzzing fireflies dotted around the moonlit town. "Yes, everything is becoming so radiant! And I feel so light, almost like I could float away!" he uttered in a dreamy tone. "That is the duskbrew you are experiencing, it grants imbibers a harmless state of pure serenity and euphoria!" explained Zeal, who was diligently cleaning mugs behind the counter.

A river of relaxed bliss cascaded over Meadow and she felt a wave of warm tingles swell inside her heart with every sip of duskbrew she took. "Ah, makes sense! Such a wonderful beverage and such a wonderful town!" she jovially remarked. Clyde then raised his wooden mug to propose a toast, "I shall drink to that, and to fond memories with my favorite imp and my cherished disciple Meadow!" he announced with jolly gusto. Meadow and Styx reveled in his toast and clanked their oak tankards together with his. Culminating with all three mugs pressing together to from the perfect symbol of their unity and friendship, "Here, here!" proclaimed Meadow.

It was a delightful sentimental moment, brimming with joy. For Clyde, Meadow and Styx chatted, laughed and drank together on their little toadstools by the quaint mushroom hut, basking in the ethereal moonlight. "Incredible, it feels like I'm floating, like I'm just a feather sailing upon a soft breeze!" gasped Meadow as she innocently swayed from side to side.

Clyde took another gulp of the delightful duskbrew and whimsically watched the majestic, azure moon in the starry sky. "Amazing, I feel as though I could take a wonderous waltz through the heavens and dance beside the gods!" he remarked. Styx felt a profound sense of elation too and playfully twizzled his tail, "I feel blissful and warm, like a hundred glowing sunsets are shinning upon me!" he hissed. Each of them was aware of what was happening, each of them cherished the unique sensation the mug of duskbrew bestowed upon them, it truly seemed like a drink of kings.

Sadly, soon after consuming the last drops of the magical purple liquid, their moments of euphoria ended, but the positive energy lingered within them. "Well, that was amongst the best drink I've ever had, but I fear we must procced with our original goal now" remarked Clyde, tipping the wooden tankard into the air and slurping down the last few droplets. "Agreed, but it was worth visiting Duskglade for that drink alone!" declared Meadow as she spun around and hopped off the small blue toadstool acting as a seat for her rump.

Slouched against the side of the mushroom hut was the captured imp. Still confined within its linen sack and slumbering away, "Let's us venture on then!" Clyde heartily announced. "Thank you for such a wonderful drink, we shall have to come again!" Meadow happily exclaimed, offering a bow of appreciation. Zeal the imp bowed his horned head back to her and flashed his sharp fangs when he smiled. "My pleasure, thank you for stopping by and please, make sure Styx doesn't get into any trouble!" he answered. "Me? Never! I never get in trouble, at least not anymore!" joked Styx as he flapped his wings and fluttered away, chuckling and waving goodbye to his fellow imp friend Zeal. All of them departed the glowing embrace of the steamy mushroom hut and strolled along the crooked cobbled stone path leading towards the colossal fungus tower in the distance.

Upon approaching the towering mushroom, Meadow spotted two imp guards clad in admittedly cute armour. Little spikes protruded from their shoulder plates and they wore steel horned helmets that appeared slightly too large. Both imps defended the entrance with minimal effort as one was lazily slouched against the side of the mushroom, resting his trident upon his shoulder. Meanwhile, the second imp guard rested his bottom upon a small flat rock and spent his time mindlessly tossing smaller rocks into the distance. "They look bored" Meadow noted as she approached. "Duskglade is not exactly a main attraction for visitors, they guard simply out of duty" answered Styx. He then proceeded to wave his trident when the guards spotting him advancing. "Styx? It's been a while since we've seen you around here, Still serving a human I see!" remarked one of the guards who swiftly shifted into a more attentive stance.

Clyde was unsure how to interpret such a comment and almost gave into to his desire to accuse the imp guard of implying slavery. Yet, he bit his tongue and allowed Styx to speak on his behalf. "It has been a while my brothers and yes I still serve a human, but Clyde is good to me! I serve him out of my own volition!" Styx firmly answered. One of the imp guards gave a pleased nod and took a stab at the reason for Styx's visit, though it was surely easy to guess. "Glad to hear it, but if you're here to see the matriarch you know the procedure, perform the sigil" he replied. Styx gave a weary sigh and reluctantly channeled the power of his mysterious imp magic into his trident, "Can't believe I still have to do this!" he remarked.

Curiosity consumed Clyde and Meadow as they silently watched and witnessed Styx's enchanted trident radiate a magical red aura. Just as Clyde pondered what kind of sorcery Styx could be conjuring, the symbol of a single eye appeared and hovered above the tip of his trident. The eye was swathed in magical purple energy and levitated over the end of Styx's trident for a couple of seconds before promptly vanishing. "Thank you, Styx, you know the rules, that sigil can only be created by those not banished from Duskglade" remarked one of the guards. In a friendly gesture, the guard swished his palm towards the innards of the lofty mushroom tower and ushered them in. "In you go, the matriarch awaits you all!" hissed the imp guard.

Within the hollowed center of the massive mushroom stood a lone imp upon an ornate circular platform of stone, decorated with a small set of stone steps leading up to it. Styx guided them towards the stone structure, "Going up! We have been granted an audience!" he announced, as he floated up the stone steps and approached the circular platform. Everything else inside the shell of the mushroom was odd and unique, like the jars of glowing fireflies hung upon the walls. Or the contorted vases containing strange flowers Meadow had never seen before and the plush furniture that had a peculiar, warped shape to it.

Duskglade was a realm only the imps could treat as ordinary, as with every new glance Meadow and Clyde took, there was always something bizarre to behold. Styx impatiently tapped his toes and disrupted their daydreaming with a deliberate cough, "Okay Styx we're coming, keep your horns on!" barked Meadow. "Yes Styx, tis not every day we visit an alternate realm, walk within the halls of a giant mushroom tower and to see the queen of the imps" added Clyde after seeing Styx's impatience.

Upon climbing the set of small steps and planting her feet on the ornate stone platform, Meadow was on the verge of asking what happened next. Until the imp stationed upon the sturdy stone pedestal channeled a surge of magical energy into his trident and began slowly levitating the entire platform into the air, carrying them to the top of the tower. While Meadow rode the stone platform as it magically levitated towards the peak of the mushroom tower, she gawked back and forth at the imps diligently performing their duties. The tower possessed several floors and most imps were busy using the power of their magic to levitate brushes, mops and buckets of water to clean the hallways and rooms. Although some also couldn't resist playing tricks on each other, like when Meadow spotted an imp levitate and tip a bucket of water over the heads of two other imps nearby. Upon being drenched by the water, the two furious imps began chasing the chuckling prankster, using their magic to levitate their mops and attempt to slap the culprit in the face.

Suppressing a giggle at the sight of the nefarious imps as they goofed off and pranked each other proved impossible for Meadow, so she allowed her laughter to be set free. "Try to control yourself Miss Meadow, I beg you both to be respectful around the matriarch, I may be banished if you don't!" Styx hastily hissed. An abrupt bump shook the magically levitating platform when it reached the peak of the mushroom tower, causing Styx, Meadow and Clyde to disembark, with the still slumbering imp they captured in tow. Not long after leaving the stone lift however, they all heard an exotic, strangely alluring voice. "Ah, some new guests enter my domain! Welcome to Duskglade, I hope your visit here has been pleasant!" uttered the slithery voice from across the room.

Styx instantly ceased flapping his little leathery wings and swiftly knelt before the voice, "Matriarch Melevola! It is I Styx, your most loyal of servants!" he gasped. At last, Clyde and Meadow were confronted by Matriarch Melevola, queen of the imps, who was currently sitting upon her lofty throne. A throne constructed of pure silver, adorned with glimmering jewels and sparkling gems. Overlooking Melevola's unique appearance quickly became impossible. For unlike the rest of her imp citizens, the queen of the imps was distinctly taller, her tail and horns were much longer, and she possessed spiralling, ruby red hair as long as her body. "Arise from your knee Styx, I have missed you, but you are my faithful servant no more! Your duty to me has been paid!" declared Melevola.

Her words caused Clyde's eyebrows to shoot up, while Meadow failed to repel an astonished gasp. "Wait, you were once the personal servant to the queen of the imps!? Why are you serving a troll brain like Clyde!?" she cried. A stern scowl smeared Clyde's face, "I shall commit that comment to memory the next time I am brewing you a cup of tea my apprentice!" grumbled Clyde. An amused chuckle erupted from Matriarch Melevola upon watching their dispute and nearly caused her shimmering, jewel encrusted crown to topple from her head. "I bid you all welcome to this realm I created, I hope you've been treating Styx well" uttered Melevola after regaining control of her laughter.

As usual, Clyde marched forth, took center stage and performed another grand display of etiquette. "Greetings mighty Matriarch Melevola, May I first comment on how majestic your realm looks? I've seldom seen anything so beautiful, except maybe for you!" he announced. Naturally, this caused Styx and Meadow to slap their faces in embarrassment, while Melevola's cheeks blushed a rosy red. Clyde's performance was far from over yet though, "My name is Clyde, a humble alchemist from the frozen reaches of the Frostveil Mountains milady!" he confessed. "You shall be delighted to hear that Styx has been instrumental to our endeavors and proven himself a worthy friend!" Clyde added.

Upon giving a dignified bow, Clyde prepared to reveal his intentions for seeking out the hidden sanctuary of Duskglade and prayed his request would be granted. "I bow here before you great and beautiful Matriarch to respectfully ask for your assistance in a matter most perplexing!" he uttered. His passionate little speech seemed to capture the matriarch's slender pointy ears, causing her to lean forward on her plush red cushion. "Very well human, you've interested me and got my attention, but for your sake I hope I don't lose it and get bored now!" she answered with a sinister chuckle. Clyde quickly dragged the snoring imp he had captured along the floor while it slumbered in the old sack. Then he dumped it before the feet of Matriarch Melevola like he was dropping off a delivery of spuds. "During the course of our travels we captured this imp, it was causing trouble, more trouble than usual for an imp! I believe it possesses knowledge that could prove vital to us!" declared Clyde.

Melevola bestowed the sleeping imp a fleeting glance from her majestic, lofty throne before raising her shimmering scarlet eyes to Clyde again, "Interesting, and what help do you think I can be?" she asked. Any other time Clyde embraced and even enjoyed the waltz of words, but this time he preferred to simply strike at the heart of the matter. "My friend Styx here tells me you possess the art of plunging into one's memories!" he answered. "I only ask you wield that magic for us and use your gift to peer into this perplexing imp's past, I seek answers, nothing more!" Clyde continued.

Upon hearing his request, Matriarch Melevola silently pierced Clyde with her shrewd glare, drumming her uniquely long fingernails upon the arms of her throne. "Rummaging into the realms of someone's memories is a personal and intrusive art, it's an ancient form of sorcery I alone know, the question is why? Why should I do this for you?" she inquired. Her signs of reluctance began to wane Meadow's spirit and made her squirm with impatience. "Because it's the right thing to do, this imp serves a killer! And we need answers!" she fired.

Naturally, Meadow's little outburst quickly enflamed Melevola's ire, but Clyde was swift to mend the damage and raised his hand to Meadow in order to stop her from speaking further. "Mighty Matriarch, this imp is in service to one whom has taken the lives of innocent people! We must discern the identity of this imps master!" Clyde announced. Although the horrid snoring echoing from the maw of the slumbering imp spoiled Clyde's gusto, Melevola could see the fire flicker in his eyes and feel the steel in his words. A smile akin to one of both admiration and cunning crossed her lips. She proceeded to flap her wings and float down from her throne, "I admit, I have so missed having visitors to my realm, I shall grant your request" answered Melevola.

Her response delighted Clyde, Meadow and Styx, but each of them deemed it wiser to hide their joy rather than allow it to spill out. "Just know I'm only fulfilling your request because Styx is your friend and you've treated him well, it's the least I can do after all the years of loyal service he has given me!" added Melevola. Before performing the ritual however, Melevola bestowed a glare that was both icy and cunning at Meadow. "Do not cause such an outburst in my chamber again though girl, remember the power you stand before, for if it weren't for Styx, I would've turned you inside out!" she snarled. Gently, Matriarch Melevola rested her slender hands upon the temples of the sleeping imp, shut her eyes and focused while Meadow uttered a nervous gulp. "I shall begin searching its most recent memories, please talk only if necessary, for I must concentrate" Melevola whispered.

Soon after placing her fingertips upon the imp's temples, a radiant veil of vibrant magical energy shrouded the sleeping imp. it originated from Melevola's fingertips, which were glowing a burning, bright orange. "I remember this imp, his name is Faux, he was banished from Duskglade a long time ago for killing another imp, the most serious crime among our people" uttered Melevola. As the magic gradually engulfed the captured imp, more of his memories revealed themselves to Melevola. "Faux lived a hard life outside of Duskglade, he was shunned and mistrusted everywhere he went" she whispered. "Here, I shall allow you to see what I see" uttered Melevola, opening her eyes and showering the room with a dazzling blast of golden light.

Thankfully, the blinding light lasted only a couple of seconds and once it had faded, Clyde and Meadow winced as they looked upon the hazy memories of the imp. Faux, the captured imp, they watched a memory of him, locked up in a small cage like an animal among piles of other cages filled with various animals and creatures along a bustling market street. It looked like it may have been the city of Greydawn, but Clyde couldn't be sure. However, there was a man, a scruffy, tubby man stood in front of the cages yelling incoherently. He appeared to be an animal merchant of some kind and Faux the imp kept desperately reaching for his trident which was stuffed into the pocket of the tubby merchant's coat. As Clyde and Meadow watched the memory unfold in their minds, they could easily see how miserable Faux was being locked up in his cage, he clearly longed for freedom. Suddenly, a mysterious man strolled along the busy market street, a mysterious man whose face was hidden by a black mask, "It's him, it has to be!" gasped Clyde. The mysterious man with the black mask bent forward and studied Faux in his cage, it was a shame his face remained unidentifiable.

The hazy memory concluded with the shadowy figure pointing his finger towards the caged imp. He traded a bulging pouch of gold coins for the imp and shook hands with the chubby merchant. Such a memory gave enough information on how the imp Clyde captured came to serve the black masked man, but sadly little else. "There must be more, there must be something more substantial!" grumbled Clyde. "Patience, I am searching the maze of memories as we speak but it is proving difficult and draining, imps have greater resistance to sorcery such as this!" echoed Matriarch Melevola's voice.

Another memory abruptly appeared within the minds of Clyde and Meadow, like watching a theatre performance inside their own heads and this memory felt relatively recent. As the next memory they viewed unraveled like an intricate web, Clyde and Meadow discovered they were inside a gloomy little room decorated with a wall of brightly lit candles and a roaring fireplace. Yet, the rest of the room looked ruined and abandoned, the stonework was crumbling, ivy seeped through the cracks and rumbling thunder and pattering rain echoed beyond.

Standing in front of the crackling fireplace was the shadowy figure, his back turned as he watched the flickering fireplace embers fly into the air. "You understand what I want you to do Faux? Head to Orstone, city of the orcs, cause as much trouble as you can, I will inform the orcs about Clyde and how he can help them" uttered the masked man. Faux the imp gleefully accepted his master's orders and nodded intently. "Yes master, as you wish! My life and freedom are yours to command! I shall do an admirable job!" exclaimed Faux. Upon hearing this snippet of information, a slither of fury began to brew within Clyde and Meadow, for it confirmed what they already suspected. This mystery man had been the orchestrator behind most of the ordeals they had solved. "Once you have performed this task for me, your service is concluded, you shall be free to live life however you wish my friend" uttered the masked man.

Watching the murky memories of the imp unfold vexed Clyde to no end, for still no tangible answers revealed themselves. Until the memories showed the masked man turning around and speaking again. "Soon I shall depart for the floating city of Cloudvale, for another clue to the location of the chalice rests there, hopefully it shall be the last clue I require" uttered the masked stranger. Just as the masked man finished speaking, a radiant wave of light enveloped Clyde and Meadow. Banishing the hazy maelstrom of memories and tossing them into back into the realm of reality again. Matriarch Melevola gasped as she pulled her fingertips away from the temples of the slumbering imp and toppled onto her knees. "Ah, forgive me, but I fear that was all I could muster!" she declared.

Styx flapped his wings and flew over to her side, aiding her back onto her feet. "Peering into the past is a sorcery that takes its toll upon the caster, more so when performed upon an imp!" uttered Melevola in a breathless pant. Clyde folded his arms and pondered upon what he had just witnessed and heard. "Do not apologize Matriarch Melevola, if it wasn't for your aid we would still be stumbling in the dark" he answered. A mixture of thoughts and feelings weighed heavily upon Clyde, but he hid them well. Meadow on the other hand felt her own thoughts and feelings deluge her, to the point where it felt as though she would drown.

One part of the memories that intrigued her and Clyde most was the mention of a chalice. "The masked stranger talked about finding the last clue to the chalice, your searching for a chalice too, the Chalice of Renewal, could it be the same one?" Meadow asked. It had to be the same chalice, Clyde knew it couldn't be a coincidence, someone else was looking for the Chalice of Renewal. "The memories revealed that the stranger is heading for Cloudvale soon and it was a recent memory, this might be our chance to catch him!" he declared. Why this masked stranger was looking for the Chalice of Renewal or how he knew Clyde was looking for it too was mere speculation and Clyde didn't wish to waste any time wondering.

Matriarch Melevola climbed back onto her shimmering silver throne and rested her weary body upon the plush red cushion adorning it, "Well, I have done all I can, I just hope it was enough" she uttered. Her act of support warranted a reward of some kind, at least that's how Clyde felt, yet he had nothing to offer in return except his humble gratitude. "It was more than enough your highness, I'm just sorry to say that my heartfelt appreciation is all I can do to repay you!" Clyde replied.

A tired smile crawled over Melevola's lips and she tilted her head while twirling her flowing, ruby colored hair. "Remember, do not mistake my gesture, I have enjoyed your company, but I aided you out of gratitude to Styx" she answered. Rather ominously, Melevola started drumming the sharp pointy nails upon each of her fingertips together, "To be honest, I find most humans a bore, interested only in war and politics" she uttered. "Often, I end up punishing most visitors with my magic, but you two have proven an interesting diversion to my curiosity, so I shall allow you to leave unharmed" Melevola added.

A nervous prickle tingled Meadow's spine accompanied by a bead of wary sweat, for it was then she remembered they were speaking with the queen of imps. Somehow, Clyde shrugged off Melevola's words and remained unfazed. "I'm pleased to hear our company was sufficient matriarch, I only wish we could linger longer, but time is not our ally" he responded. Melevola understood Clyde's desire for haste with a slight nod of her horns, "Styx will show you the way to the portal pedestal here in the tower, use it to depart quickly" she replied. "You may also leave Faux, the imp you have captured here, I look forward to punishing him myself when he wakes!" Melevola added. Gratefully, Clyde and Meadow offered a bow to Matriarch Melevola, appreciating her hospitality and aid and promptly shadowed Styx out of the ornate audience chamber.

Once they were all out of earshot, Meadow voiced her thoughts. "So, now we travel to Cloudvale, that's the city of the harpies isn't it? I've heard it rests among the very clouds, how in Resplendia do we reach it?" she asked. As Styx led them along the mushroom corridors of the tower, Clyde vaguely brushed aside Meadow's questions, his mood becoming one of intense focus. "Let me worry about that, right now I'm more concerned with finding the Chalice of Renewal before this masked stranger" he answered. It sounded like a treasure hunt, a race to see who could find this mythical chalice first. Meadow remained clueless as to why Clyde desired it so badly, but then an interesting thought occurred to her. "Wait, what if that's the reason this mysterious masked stranger has been making us chase our tails? To distract you from finding the chalice before him?" she asked.

It surprised Clyde that he didn't come to such a conclusion first, his apprentice was a step ahead of him in terms of reasoning and logic this time and it was quite a plausible theory. No, in fact it was more than plausible, it was quite likely. "Hmmm" Clyde muttered while stroking his chin, trying to keep his mind from wandering. Across the giant hollow hall, opposite Matriarch Melevola's audience chamber was a sturdy oak door built into the wall of the giant mushroom. "In we go, it is a gesture of great respect for first time visitors to use portal room here in the matriarchs tower!" hissed Styx.

Two more imps clad in spiky little armour guarded the door, however, one of them unhooked a shiny key dangling from his waist belt and inserted it into the door's keyhole. "Hold on, if there's a portal pedestal here, why didn't you just portal us here to begin with and save us lots of time?" grumbled Meadow. The imp guard who unlocked the oaken door, suddenly stood to one side, held it open and ushered them in. "Because using the matriarch's portal pedestal without her written or verbal permission is a crime in Duskglade, one punishable by execution!" Styx answered crankily. Meadow followed Styx into the room and nodded her head amicably, "Okay, sure, that's a valid reason" she replied.

Inside the center of the portal room stood a grand golden pedestal, circular in shape. Embellished with lustrous jewels, ornate swirling patterns and engraved with magical runes all around the sides. Four golden pillars were erected on the pedestals outer rim and they too were adorned with a variety of jewels and gemstones. Ultimately, it made the portal pedestal back home look like a glorified skimming stone. "Wow, that looks valuable! I don't suppose you can portal it back with us, can you Styx?" asked Meadow as she gazed upon the golden pedestal, admiring every inch of its beauty.

With a jaded roll of his beady red eyes and a flick of his spiky tail, Styx ignored Meadow, raised his trident and began channeling his impish sorcery. "I shall begin creating a portal at once master!" he hissed. Currently, Clyde kept his arms folded and drummed his fingers against his arm. "First we must return home, for I must acquire the necessary funds to buy passage into Cloudvale" he answered. "As you wish master, home we shall return!" Styx declared, entering a deep state of mind, conjuring the magic necessary for the portal spell and unleashing it towards the gleaming pedestal.

As usual, it took a couple of minutes before Styx's portal spell was fully cast. But the abrupt tremor shattering the air, the thunderous roar and the brief eruption of vibrant light signaled its completion. The portal came into existence, its colorful swirling vortex seemingly beckoning them to enter, "Okay, we know the routine my friends, into the void we go!" announced Clyde. At last it was time to leave the mystical realm of Duskglade, the hidden city of the imps. Clyde was the first to be devoured by the magical portal and Styx pursued close behind. Meadow entered last, pausing and enjoying an intimate moment of reflection upon the memories she had made with Clyde thus far, then allowed the portal to consume her.

Chalice of Renewal
Chapter 10
Sky's the limit

Everything Meadow had experienced during the months she'd spent with Clyde, the ordeals they had overcome, the places they had visited and sights they had seen. Meadow couldn't resist dwelling upon it all. If Meadow told people, she travelled through a gigantic portal hidden within an ancient tree which could only be revealed by having an imp cast a secret spell upon it. All so she could enter Duskglade, the magical moonlit realm of the imps so she could visit their queen who lived inside a giant mushroom tower so she could use her sorcery to show her the memories of another imp. If Meadow told someone she had done all that, people would surely wonder if she were drunk or mad.

For now, Meadow's resolve remained unyielding like rock against crashing waves, she sought answers as much as Clyde and was eager to travel to Cloudvale and find them. Also, the idea of visiting the floating city of the harpies made her heart tremble with excitement. Various images of the city pranced around in her head, making it even more difficult to remain settled.

Trails of warm steam coming from the mug of tea in front of Meadow's face swirled upwards and caressed her cheeks. The mug felt warm and welcoming against her palms like the flickering flames of a cozy hearth and she quenched her craving to savor fragrant tea with a timid sip. The plans to travel to Cloudvale were delayed momentarily, for Styx needed to rest in between creating portals since it drained his magical prowess significantly.

Even if Clyde and Meadow were to travel to Cloudvale on foot for five days straight, they still wouldn't make it before Styx could portal them there. "The tea tastes delicious as always, let me guess, you used grimweed herbs, shadow-weave petals and a handful of crushed sea-thorn spines" uttered Meadow after another sip. Clyde, who was sitting opposite Meadow, leaned backwards in his chair, muttered an impressed murmur and took a swig from his mug. "Hmm, correct on all guesses my apprentice! You've certainly been paying attention to all I've been teaching you" he replied. In a gesture of respect, Meadow raised her tankard of tea into the air and winked. "Well, you might be a passionate, crazy oddball at times, but I have to admit, you know how to teach alchemy!" answered Meadow.

Both savored the moment of tranquility infusing the air, relishing sips of hot steamy tea. Listening to the oddly serene howling blizzard relentlessly pummeling the walls of the house outside. "Tell me, what do you know about Cloudvale?" asked Meadow, tightly pressing both her palms against the side of her warm mug. "Tis one of the grandest cities in all Resplendia, it hovers hundreds of feet in the air, is the city of harpies and they have a strict hierarchy of class when it comes to their citizens" answered Clyde. A curious tilt appeared in Meadow's head, indicating confusion, "A hierarchy of class? In what way? You mean in wealth?" she asked. Clyde promptly waved away her comment and elaborated further. "No, no, it's more to related to the color of their feathers, golden feathered harpies are upper-class, white feathered harpies are middle-class and brown feathered ones are lower-class" he explained.

Such a questionable hierarchy formed a flurry of mixed emotions in Meadow but being Clyde's apprentice had somewhat taught her to quell such tempestuous storms. "Sounds a little unfair, deciding one's social status and worth based on the color of their feathers?" she remarked. Although Clyde obeyed his code of not meddling in the laws and customs of other races, he believed Meadow's ire to be justified. "Indeed, tis why many harpies leave Cloudvale and attempt to find fame, success and fortune upon the surface, Resplendia is becoming far more lenient towards other races" remarked Clyde.

Upon taking a subtle whiff of his tea, Clyde cherished the enthralling aroma drifting from it and indulged his lips. "That's not to say those of lower or middle class can't find success and fortune in Cloudvale, tis merely harder, but most are thankful not to be born with black feathers" he uttered. Meadow's curiosity was promptly captured again, and she pressed Clyde further, "Why? What happens to those with black feathers?" she inquired. "Sadly, harpy children whose feathers are black upon birth are immediately banished from the city, for they are seen as omens of calamity and death and left to fend for themselves upon the surface" answered Clyde.

A whirling veil of fury brewed inside Meadow, thankfully she kept it mostly subtle and contained. "Really? They banish them even as babies!? They just toss them away!? What about their parents?" she barked. Clyde merely gave a powerless shrug, "Parents of black feathered harpies are given two choices, abandon their child or be banished along with them" he answered. A blustery huff leapt from Meadow and she had to take a swig of tea to calm herself down. "Well, Cloudvale sounds lovely, can't wait to see it!" she ranted sarcastically.

Poignantly, Clyde chuckled at her satirical remark, smirking at the shadow of irony that had been cast. "Actually, you would adore Cloudvale, the city itself is magnificent, a sky paradise, an oasis among the clouds!" he remarked. Such a description didn't change the flustering feeling of disapproval in Meadow, evident by the way she swirled the tea in her mug. "An oasis you have to pay to enter, speaking of which, I assume you've got the coin?" she replied. A small leather pouch of jingling gold coins was abruptly flopped onto the kitchen table by Clyde. "Indeed, tis not cheap to enter Cloudvale either, one-hundred gold is the entry fee, one more way the haughty harpies keep the riffraff out, we leave as soon as Styx is rested and ready" answered Clyde.

Just as Clyde uttered his sentence, Styx came fluttering into the room with his little flapping wings. "I ready now master; my magical essence has recovered! I make another portal!" he hissed. Clearly Clyde had been eager to depart, for he arose from the kitchen table with half of his tea still left in the mug. "Excellent, then we shall voyage to Cloudvale with all haste! But first, to the lab my lackey! We must prepare our potions for every plight!" he declared. A keen aura brimmed Clyde's steps as he marched out of the kitchen at a speed just shy of a jog. "Keep your hair on, I'm coming!" replied Meadow, quaffing the rest of her tea.

The familiar odor of bubbling brews and simmering mixtures invaded Meadow's nostrils the moment she entered the alchemy lab. The sight of scattered scrolls, piles of colorful powders, plumes of vibrant smoke and jars of strange herbal ingredients captivated her as much as it did the first time. Without delay, Meadow snatched her harness off the wall, slammed it upon one of the labs workbenches and began slotting potions into the pouches. Like a buzzing bee, Clyde dashed back and forth, grabbing various potions from the shelves. "Don't ask me what you might need my apprentice, you know how it goes now, trust your own instincts!" he declared.

For starters, Meadow decided to take two vials of steel-skin, one sleepy-gas, two fire-breath, one vial of ethereal, one vial of invisibility and two vials of smokescreen. As Clyde reached for a glass vial containing an amber colored liquid and removed it from the wooden rack, he watched and admired Meadow as she prepared. "Don't forget a vial of enhanced-strength my apprentice, and here try this one, it may come in handy in the sky city of Cloudvale!" replied Clyde. Gently, he tossed Meadow a flask of potion the likes of which she had not seen yet. "I haven't seen this mixture before but judging by the color and texture it looks like it contains powdered griffon talons and wisewind herbs" she replied. Again, Meadow impressed Clyde with how much she had learned, "Correct my dear! At least on the first two ingredients and it will surely come in handy!" he proclaimed. While curiously gazing upon the new vial of orange liquid, Meadow's tongue was on the verge of asking what it did. Until a roaring rumble resonated the air and ruptured her focus, "Sounds like the portal is ready!" announced Clyde.

Travelling by portal had become routine and verged upon being mundane at this point. Meadow had lost count of how many times her emerald green eyes had gazed upon one of these magical floating doorways. Yet, here she was again, gazing into the vibrant void of another. Ready to be whisked away and emerge at a different region of the land in the blink of an eye, "Alight, let's find some answers!" she declared. "Hopefully" added Clyde as he finished tying the small leather pouch to his waist which contained the gold needed to enter Cloudvale.

With their preparations finished, Meadow and Clyde boldly strode into the pulsating portal of cascading colors and vanished within its luminous maw. A whirlwind of wonder waited on the other side, for these fleeting seconds of flying through the portal were Meadow's favorite. The sensation of gliding through a magical dimension of constantly altering colors, dazzling dots and smears of starry light was majestic beyond any words could describe. Alas, it soon ended again, and the portal concluded with a radiant deluge of blissful light and she was cast into the realm of Resplendia once more.

This time, Meadow and Clyde emerged in a sunny glade surrounded by towering pine trees and one very confused rabbit as it watched the portal appear and spit them out. "Are we here? Is this Cloudvale? Doesn't seem like we're in the sky right now" remarked Meadow as she surveyed her surroundings and fixed her fiery hair. "Nay, Styx's portal traversed us to a place close to the entrance of Cloudvale, for tis probably best if we appear to travel like ordinary folk" answered Clyde. To obtain a better grasp of their current location, Clyde and Meadow spared little time admiring the bouquets of lush lilies and charming critters.

Instead, they promptly navigated their way through the dense thicket of trees and departed the sylvan glade, discovering a vast grassy plain awaiting them on the other side. Weathered windmills and quaint cottages dotted the stretching landscape, accompanied by the feel of a refreshing airy breeze, "Ah, there! Upon the peak of that cliff!" announced Clyde. Meadow swiveled her gaze across the windswept plain, rested it upon whatever Clyde was referring to and saw three individuals standing near the tip of the cliff edge.

A cobblestoned pathway led along the ground, stretching and winding like a stone snake, eventually ending at the peak of the cliff edge, "That's the way to Cloudvale?" asked Meadow. "Indeed, for at the tip of that cliff is the griffon station and if you look up right, you can even see Cloudvale, at least the bottom of it" answered Clyde, pointing a finger skywards. Meadow stretched her neck back and turned her head towards the sky, gasping with disbelief, "Yes I see it!" she exclaimed. It was only the rocky underside of the city, but there it was, Cloudvale, city of the harpies. Gently floating hundreds of feet above Meadow's head like a giant chunk of the earth had been ripped out and left to dangle on a giant invisible string.

Eager to witness this floating wonder for herself, Meadow jovially cavorted along the cobblestoned road leading up the grassy hill towards the three golden figures in the distance. Her cheerful frolicking brought a smile and a soft chuckle to Clyde as he leisurely followed behind, taking a moment to cherish the sunny hike. Upon reaching the peak of the cliff, several large, bushy nests made of straw covered by a tall wooden shelter came into view. The three golden figures Meadow had seen from a distance were harpies, clad in gleaming golden armour and equipped with equally lustrous spears and shields.

All three of the harpy warriors possessed white feathers and wings although their beaks, talons and feet were of a sandier color. "Halt, what is your purpose here!?" squawked one of the harpies. "No need for concern bird brain, my apprentice and I are simply travelling alchemists, we humbly request passage to the grand city of Cloudvale and wish to peruse its many exotic ingredients!" proclaimed Clyde. Resting within one of the large shaggy nests upon the tip of the cliff was perhaps the grandest sight of all. It was a fully-grown adult griffon, the first of its kind Meadow had ever seen.

Meadow marveled at the majestic beast, admiring its gallant eagle head and wings and its elegant lion body. Meanwhile, the harpy guard obstructing Clyde's path perused him from head to toe with suspicion, "Humans, I don't trust your kind!" growled the guard. "Hey, is that any way to treat visitors? No wonder tourism to Cloudvale is so low!" squawked a tender female voice, revealed to belong to a young, chirpy harpy girl. "Nice to meet ya, my name is Saphris!" declared the chipper young harpy girl, who possessed celestial white wings and feathers akin to the color of snow. Clyde gripped the claw of the harpies outstretched arm and exchanged a handshake. "Tis a pleasure my feathery friend, my name is Clyde, and this is Meadow! Are you the one whom can grant us passage to your sky sanctuary?" asked Clyde.

Proudly, Saphris placed her talons upon her hips and nodded, "Yep, I am one of the official griffon-masters for the station here and you're in luck! One of our griffons has just finished resting and is good to go! You just need to pay" she answered. Her request was soon granted, for Clyde coiled his arm around his waist and removed the jingling pouch of gold coins which dangled from it. After handing the leather coin pouch over, Saphris carefully inspected it and produced a satisfied smile, "Alrighty, that's enough gold!" she cheerfully remarked. "Follow me and hop onto the griffon when you're ready, have either of you ridden a griffon before?" Saphris asked while finishing her duty of brushing the griffon's body with a small brush. Excitedly, Meadow shook her head but was left unsurprised when Clyde nodded his. "Okay, well all ya need to know is to be gentle if you want to stroke its fur, don't pull on the griffon's tail and jump around while riding it" explained Saphris.

Saphris's lecture lasted a little longer than Meadow expected but she listened intently. "Also, do not ride upon it while drunk, because yes, we've had fools do that before" uttered Saphris as she finished cleaning the griffon's nest in the large wooden stable. As important as her explanation was, the prospect of taking to the skies upon the back of a griffon caused Meadow to miss the latter half of the explanation. "Also stroke only the fur if you wish to stroke the griffon at all, do not put your fingers near its beak and hold onto me or your partner at all times!" concluded Saphris.

A lethargic yawn is how the griffon chose to greet Meadow and Clyde when they ambled towards its giant nest. Awe and fright slithered within Meadow's heart when the beast raised its giant eagle head and lay its piercing stare upon her, simultaneously padding at the nest with the lion claws adjoining its paws. "Don't be scared, griffons can be fierce, but they're also smart and noble creatures, let me hop on first!" declared Saphris. Fearlessly, Saphris coiled her talons around the saddle adorning the griffons back and mounted the beast without any kind of resistance or defiance, save for a brief squawk from the creature's beak.

Gradually, the griffon arose from its lying position, pulled its body back and stretched its front paws out, a characteristic from the lion half of its anatomy. "Easy girl, easy" whispered Saphris as she gently stroked the griffon's opulent fur and watched the beast extend its majestic golden wings out to the side. "Okay, both of you climb on one at a time and keep hold, unless you wanna be mushy red stains adorning the side of a mountain somewhere!" declared Saphris. The playful tone behind her message made the image even more unnerving. Yet Meadow approached the side of the griffon, mounted its back and wrapped her arms around Saphris's waist with an impressive amount of courage.

Surprisingly, Clyde advanced towards the creature like a timid baby rabbit taking the first steps out of its burrow, climbing somewhat clumsily onto the griffons back. "Forgive my hesitancy, I confess, I've never been an avid fan of heights nor flying" uttered Clyde as he tightly coiled his arms around Meadow's waist. Without a whiff of warning, the griffon proceeded to dash across the plain and charge straight towards the edge of the nearby cliff. "Here comes the fun part!" yelled Saphris as the beast valiantly pounced off the side. Meadow and Clyde felt their stomachs shoot straight into their throats as they plunged like comets towards the jagged rocks jutting out from the ocean below. "Gods save me!" cried Clyde as he felt the furious rush of air sweep over his face and heard the shrieking gale of wind bellow past his ears. "Wooooooo!" screamed Meadow as she embraced the plummet, relishing the thrill of the fall and the whistling wind as it whooshed through her fiery hair.

Just when it seemed like they were on the verge of being smashed against the jagged rocks, the gallant griffon used its magnificent wings, took flight and soared. It soared into the vast blue sky, towards the beaming ball of sunlight floating high amongst the fluffy white clouds, elegantly, like a ship drifting across a calm ocean. Words alone failed to express the beauty Meadow beheld when the griffon ascended above the cluster of ashen clouds and the grandiose vista of Resplendia was laid bare.

Snowy mountaintops, sandy dunes, sprawling forests, ancient ruins, stone towers, mysterious castles, picturesque towns and bustling cities, it was all on full display from the sky. Seeing the vast, magical land of Resplendia from such a viewpoint gave Meadow an essential moment of pause and reflection. Thus, she inhaled deeply, felt a refreshing euphoria wash over her and smiled when she allowed her breath to escape. Clyde on the other hand, he made the blunder of taking a glance down and seeing naught but hundreds of feet between him and the hard ground. Dread sunk in and he tightly shut his eyes and began whispering sobs of sweet words to comfort himself. His arms suddenly felt like Meadow had a pair of cobras coiling around her waist and were trying to squeeze the life from her body. "Loosen up, will you? Scaredy cat!" Meadow teased as she listened to his whimpering.

Although his face turned as pale as the clouds they soared among and it looked like he was on the verge of spewing up his morning tea, Clyde managed compose himself. "Overlook my moment of debility if you would be so kind, though I am a dashing, talented, alchemical genius, even I have my defects!" he proclaimed. "Ruby on the other hand, she would've cherished this view" uttered Clyde, his voice gently trailing off. However, it didn't trail off enough for Meadow to be unable to overhear him, "Who's Ruby?" she asked, her head turning, eyes glimmering with curiosity. A flicker of fright flashed upon Clyde's face and he quickly disregarded the question with a fragile smile, "Never mind" he uttered softly. "There she is, jewel of the sky! Cloudvale! Home of the harpies!" Saphris abruptly called as the furry griffon flew through one last blanket of clouds.

Once the city of Cloudvale came into view, Meadow's breath was immediately stolen by its astonishing, verdant beauty. Cloudvale appeared as a lush green island abundant with tropical fruit trees and dotted with scenic ruins of sandy stone. The main city rested quaintly upon the very edge of the floating island, overlooking the world below. In the center of the hovering isle stood a colossal marble tower gleaming with lines of curving gold travelling all the way to the peak A giant violet jewel gently levitated inside the top of the tower and radiated beams of alluring magical light. "See that jewel atop the tower? That's what keeps Cloudvale from becoming a plummeting meteor!" declared Saphris, pointing one of her talons towards it.

Ahead of them was a crowded sky dock, packed with merchants, diplomats and visitors. Some of whom were just arriving in the city upon the backs of griffons, while others were beginning to depart, likely on business. Saphris gently guided her noble winged beast towards the sky dock and its large furry paws touched down on one of the many hay nests that dotted the edges. Lazily, the griffon sprawled out its belly upon the nest and lay all four of its paws out flat, "This is where we get off, hope you enjoyed the flight!" Saphris jovially remarked.

As Meadow dismounted the griffon, she took an amused glance at Clyde, whose legs seemed as stable as a pile of old leaves, then chuckled and turned back to Saphris. "Well, I cannot speak for Clyde, but I enjoyed the trip immensely! Seeing the land from the clouds above was certainly an experience I shan't forget!" declared Meadow. While bent over and groaning wearily, Clyde uttered what words he could. "By the way, we seek a stranger in a black iron mask who has visited this city, any information will aid us greatly!" Clyde grumbled as he wrestled with vertigo.

Saphris scratched her pointy hooked beak with one of her talons for a moment, until a candle suddenly came alight in her head. "Now you mention it, I did see a stranger that fits that description! He arrived here a couple of days ago, but it was one of the other griffon-masters that flew him to the city" Saphris replied. Hopefully, it was the culprit Clyde and Meadow were chasing, the visit to Duskglade and the rummage through the imps' memories proved worthy. "Do you know where he went or if he is still here!?" Meadow swiftly inquired, her hands clamping firmly around Saphris's arms.

It was easy to hear the urgency in Meadow's voice and see the intensity yearning in her eyes, which caused Saphris to chuckle nervously. "Ahh…erm, no sorry, but speak to the dock-keeper, it's his duty to record everyone who enters and leaves" answered Saphris, nodding her head towards the individual she spoke of. A large, white-feathered male harpy sat at a small wooden desk and tended to a queue of people that had formed before him. "Very well, we shall make that our next move, many thanks to you griffon-master Saphris!" announced Clyde. Meadow gently released her intense grasp upon Saphris and offered a humble bow. "Sorry, I got a little carried away there! Thank you for the ride and may you always be well" she uttered.

Meadow barely had chance to finish her sentence before she felt Clyde abruptly latch onto her arm and hastily drag her away. "Yes, yes! Thank you immensely, now let's go!" he declared. Awkward smiles were traded between Meadow and Saphris as they parted company with an equally awkward wave goodbye. "Ugh, okay you can let go of me now!" grumbled Meadow once they were amidst the hustling crowds.

Instead of obeying protocol and merging with the queue of various visitors, Clyde carved a path straight through the horde and approached the white-feathered harpy directly. "You there, I am led to believe you are the dock-keeper! We are on the trail of a masked stranger clad in black, relinquish all the information you have on this individual at once!" Clyde demanded. However, the rather bulbous bodied dock-keeper feigned ignorance, not even bothering to lift his feathery head and meet Clyde's gaze. Instead, the white winged harpy adjusted the golden monocle around his eye, dipped his quill into the pot of black ink on his wooden table and jotted names into the thick book of parchment paper before him.

Frustrated by the harpy's aloof nature, Clyde thought it a good idea to press him further. "Did you not hear me dung beak!? My apprentice and I are pursuing the trail of a dangerous criminal and we seek information!" he barked. A jaded huff crept from the dock-keepers beak, causing him to abruptly cease his scrawling and tilt his head towards Clyde, "Join the queue like everyone else" he muttered. Naturally, this vexed Clyde, but just as he was on the verge of protesting more, the infuriating dock-keeper repeated his words. "Join the queue, unless you want the guards to throw you back to the surface" he uttered in a droning tone.

Clyde silently gazed at the glassy eyed harpy with a sullen scowl, until he uttered a cranky growl and stomped to the back of the queue. Before accompanying him, Meadow frowned upon the tedious dock-keeper and defiantly stuck her tongue out at him, causing the docile harpy to raise a curious eyebrow. "Such insolence, that I have submit to the monotonous wheel of social etiquette at such a crucial moment! The iron is still hot; hence we must strike! But nay! That puppet of authority demands we yield to the system!" barked Clyde.His uproar caused onlookers to turn their heads, while Meadow concealed hers with her hand to shield her from public embarrassment. "Normally I don't beg, but I'm begging you Clyde, please shut up!" she mumbled.

Waiting in a queue proved tedious, but at least it allowed Meadow to soak in the atmosphere of the sky dock and the surrounding city of Cloudvale. Griffons were a common sight here; they flew in quite regularly and all landed upon the large fluffy nests dotted around the dock which acted as stations. All the sky dock workers were harpies and all of them had dark brown colored feathers and wings, which meant they were considered lower-class in the hierarchy of Cloudvale. It seemed Cloudvale received a regular mixture of different races though. Meadow noticed fenix traders, orc blacksmiths, elven alchemists, skarl mercenaries and even a couple of satyr travelers.

Despite being a city based on a hierarchy of class, Cloudvale was quite multicultural and accepting of visitors of many different races. Watching the sky dock bustle with travelers, traders and seeing the mighty griffon beasts swoop in and take off was a pleasant distraction, as was the view of endless blue sky and horizon of fluffy white clouds. Alas, it lasted only so long before the tedium of waiting in a queue took root and impatience began to emerge. "Ugh, this is getting unbearable! How much longer will this take!?" grumbled Meadow. Soon, another visitor ahead of them had been handled and the line diminished a little more, "Now do you see why my ranting was justified?" asked Clyde as he shuffled forwards.

After what felt like eons, the line gradually shrunk more and more, until at last, to Clyde and Meadow's joy, they were up next. "Names, professions and reasons for visiting Cloudvale" uttered the joyless harpy dock-keeper from earlier as he watched them eagerly waddle forwards. Waiting so long in a dull line had clearly caused Clyde an insufferable amount of attrition, as he slammed both palms upon the dock-keepers desk the moment he approached. "Finally, praise the gods! My name is Clyde, this is Meadow, we are alchemists from the Frostveil Mountains, we seek an iron masked criminal that has recently visited this city!" he declared. Ever so slowly, the harpy dock-keeper adjusted his golden monocle, dabbed his quill into his ink pot and scrawled notes into the thick logbook in front of him. "Okay, Clyde and Meadow and I assume that's Clyde with a C?" he asked. Mustering all the patience he could summon, Clyde nodded his head and smiled at the harpy with gritted teeth and clenched fists, "Yes, Clyde with a C!" he growled.

Sounds of more scrawling upon the harpy's logbook followed and Clyde looked like a bubbling volcano about to erupt as he watched the dock-keeper nonchalantly perform his duties. "Okay, I hope you enjoy your visit to our city, please don't try to feed the griffons and remember that troublemakers will be thrown to their death" droned the dock-keeper. In retaliation, Clyde chimed in once more, "Hold a moment, bird-brain! We have waited in your line, now I demand you tell me what you know of the masked stranger we seek!" he barked. With a jaded sigh, the harpy dock-keeper flicked his talons through the pages of the logbook and rolled his eyes, "Fine, if it shall move you on quicker" he groaned.

Upon flipping through several pages of the logbook, the harpy dock-keeper finally settled his gaze and examined the list of previous visitors. "Ah yes, here we are, difficult to forget such a unique character, naturally I couldn't see his face, but he said his name was John Smith, probably a lie but also quite possible" uttered the dock-keeper. Refusing to be content with such meagre information, Clyde fiercely pressed the harpy further, "What else? What did he say he was here for!?" he demanded. His uncouth demeanor ruffled the harpies' feathers, but the discombobulated dock-keeper assisted all the same. "Settle down, settle down, the stranger identified himself as a scholar here to study the ancient ruins on the edge of our island, if you're looking for him, he's likely still there" answered the dock-keeper. A gleeful gale swept over Clyde as soon as this delightful news reached his ears. "Truly? Then we must head to these ruins at once! Thank you for your assistance commoner, it seems waiting in your tedious line bore fruit!" he exclaimed.

Before the harpy dock-keeper could utter a single word further, Clyde feverishly dashed past him. "What he said!" declared Meadow as she gave a cheerful wave and chased after Clyde. Both burst into the main city of Cloudvale and despite not wanting to squander a single grain of their time, Clyde and Meadow were swiftly enslaved by the city's opulence. Vibrant banners of ruby red and sapphire stripes adorned the lavish corners of the golden stone streets and bards at every turn filled the air with harmonious music. Performers such as jugglers and acrobats also scattered the streets, putting on a fine display of skill in exchange for the applause and coin of spectators nearby.

Merchants were as plentiful here as sand in a desert and lined the saffron colored stone paths in droves. Peddling wares from common fruits and vegetables, to exotic animals and magical trinkets. Beyond the entertainment and shopping, there were also several regal looking taverns dotting the bustling streets, all of them embellished in an assortment of gorgeous flower gardens and magnificent marble fountains of sparkling water. The crowning adornment of the spectacular stone plaza was a towering silver statue of a harpy knight. Wielding a spear with a blade made of emerald and riding a silver griffon whose eyes were made of amethysts. Naturally, Clyde and Meadow were rendered awestruck by the city, "Looks pretty nice here" muttered Meadow in a state of astonished sarcasm. "Come, we must find a guide who will show us the way to these ancient ruins" remarked Clyde. Freeing himself from the shackles of amazement that bound him and pushing past the jolly crowds.

Merriment and joy adorned the air it seemed, and the hordes of onlookers proved a tough, unyielding obstacle to overcome. Most were relishing the balmy sunlight, melodious music coming from the bard's flutes and harps and the sight of elegant dancers as they twirled upon the golden stone streets. "Here Meadow, let us enter this fine establishment in search of a guide!" declared Clyde as he approached the entrance of a rather classy looking tavern called the Golden Wing Inn.

Several strangers drank from polished silver tankards and were sitting outside the inn upon smooth marble benches that surrounded a stunning, circular stone fountain. Shimmering golden borders circled the fountains edge and a small statue of a golden harpy maiden pouring a jug embellished the top of the fountain. Sparkling crystal-clear water flowed directly from the jug and it was majestic to behold. As were the alluring marble planters flourishing with juicy plomberry bushes, proving this tavern was far different from the rough, grimy rat dens Meadow saw in Deepshade. It was topped off by a most tranquil ambience infusing the air here in Cloudvale, it was serene and welcoming, like a floating haven of sunshine and bliss.

A tide of delight submerged Meadow and Clyde as they entered the Golden Wing Inn, for they were quickly enraptured by how plush and placid everything appeared. From the gentle sound of the large oak fan spinning around in the ceiling, to the luxurious cushions of red silk that decorated the elegantly crafted oak chairs and tables. Thankfully, it was far busier outside the tavern than in, hence Clyde was able to reach the bar at the far end with relative ease. A young, captivating harpy female with copper colored feathers and wings served behind the bar as Clyde approached. "Hello good sir, welcome to the Golden Wing Inn! What can I get you?" she asked. "Greetings, fair pourer of drinks! My apprentice and I are in search of a guide, for we wish to visit the ancient ruins beyond the city, mayhap you know of someone?" answered Clyde.

After wiping a bead of sweat from her brow, the brown-feathered harpy girl gave a clueless shrug. "Sorry, wish I could help but I'm just a lower-class harpy here, maybe ask around" she replied wearily. With that, the young harpy barmaid scooped up a couple of nearby empty tankards that had been neglected upon the bar and scurried away with them, "So what now?" asked Meadow. After taking a pensive glance around the room of the tavern, Clyde hastily nabbed an empty silver tankard and spoon from the table in front of him and began repeatedly clanging them together.

Gradually, the droning chatter in the tavern fell silent and all eyes were upon Clyde. "Attention patrons, it is urgent I find a guide who can take me and my apprentice to the ancient ruins outside of the city" he announced. "Naturally, I shall pay a handsome sum of gold, so please step forward if you wish to accept my offer!" Clyde concluded, turning his back to the bar and waiting. However, the monotonous babble of the room soon picked up again and the patrons all returned their attention back to their drinks. "Maybe we should try to find these ruins ourselves" uttered Meadow. No sooner after she spoke these words, a large silver tankard abruptly slammed onto the bar beside her, "So, you two need a guide eh?" asked a voice.

Turning their heads to see from whom the voice came; Clyde and Meadow were greeted by the cheerful face of Saphris again. "Hey, Saphris! Good seeing you again!" declared Meadow. Saphris casually rested her elbow upon the bar and ran her talons along her silky flowing hair. "Saw you both waiting at the check-in line, I get to skip right by it since I'm a citizen of Cloudvale" she answered haughtily. Meanwhile, Meadow was quick to notice the quiver of silver arrows and the ornate silver bow strung over Saphris's shoulder. "Nice bow, when you're not flying griffons, are you a hunter or a guide?" she asked. Saphris glossed over Meadow's question and changed the topic. "I was having a drink in the corner when I heard Clyde's announcement, if you want to find those ancient ruins then I'm just the harpy for the job" she replied. To seal the deal, Saphris held out her talons for Clyde to shake, which he did so gladly. "Very well Saphris, our options are in short supply, therefore we gladly enlist your aid! But we must leave at once!" he proclaimed. After leaving several gold coins upon the bar as a generous tip, Saphris casually wandered away, "In a rush eh? Let us get moving then!" she uttered.

Beyond the sparkling fountains and golden stone walls of the city, the rest of the floating island of Cloudvale was covered in a thick layer of untamed jungle and buzzing insects. Squawks, hisses, howls and growls from all manner of exotic birds and beasties resonated throughout the tangles of giant vines and tropical trees. Culminating in an environment that was as chaotic as it was vibrant.

Several hours had already passed since Clyde, Meadow and Saphris began their little expedition into the wilderness in search of the ancient ruins. "Okay, lets rest here!" declared Saphris, deciding it was about time to take a break after brushing through a dense thicket of shrubbery and emerging upon a secluded clearing. However, Clyde, playing the part of stubborn persistent fool right now, refused to yield to fatigue. "Nay I say! We must venture onwards and endure, for time is of the essence and I shan't let lethargy consume it!" he decreed.

Despite his objections, Saphris declined to budge another step and instead rested her rump upon a fallen log nearby. "Have it your way, don't blame me though if you become a snack for a hungry capamandra, they tend to prey on the weak and vulnerable" she uttered. Wearily, Meadow slumped onto the ground like a puppet that just had its strings cut, sprawled out like a starfish and basked beneath the cool shade coming from a giant tree leaf overhead. "Listen to her Clyde, I want to catch this culprit as much as you do but let us recover our breath first! Also, I'm not sure all this sweating and humidity is good for my beautiful porcelain skin!" moaned Meadow. Reluctantly, Clyde surrendered to their demands and gave a cranky grumble as he slouched onto a nearby rock. "What's so important anyway? The ruins aren't going anywhere" inquired Saphris.

Unsure how to explain in a brief short sentence, Clyde sighed as he gathered his words. "We learned from the memories of an imp that a devious criminal, whom has been sending us on wild goose chase, may be at the ancient ruins in Cloudvale, we're here to apprehend him" explained Clyde. Surprisingly, Saphris's reaction was rather mundane, prompting a slight nod and little more than an intrigued murmur. "Sounds like you've had a tale or two to share" Saphris replied.

A small, scarlet backed frog with luminous blue legs suddenly hopped out of the bushes. The frog then gave a quick leap and landed upon Meadow's face as she lay sprawled upon the ground, causing her to bolt up and emit an alarmed gasp. "What about you? Why were you so quick to assist us in our journey to the ruins? You haven't even haggled over payment yet" Clyde uttered. Innocently, Meadow poked and played with the frog in the background while Saphris and Clyde spoke. "Life is not all about gold, sometimes a good adventure is payment enough" Saphris answered as she leant her arms back, rested upon the log and gazed at the sky.

Clyde tilted his head and curiously observed her while stroking his chin. "Feigning innocent naivety shall yield no fruit girl, I'm onto your gambit, clearly you wish to wait until the time is right and demand I cough up more gold later!" he proclaimed. An empty echo of chirping birds accompanied the ensuing silence, while Meadow kept trying to chase the frog as it hopped away, "Don't worry, he's an oddball" she uttered. "Well, I like to think we're all a little odd in our little way, maybe it's a gift!" chuckled Saphris as she regarded Clyde with both curiosity and amusement. To her delight, Meadow finally managed to scoop the frog up in her palms and held it towards the sun with triumphant joy. "You like adventures then? I confess I do too! I bet you've got a tale or two to tell" remarked Meadow as she stroked the frogs head and released it back into the wild.

A bittersweet smile spread upon Saphris's beak, a smile that radiated warmth, but possessed the frailty of a sunflower. "I have one, but it's a long tale, a tale that taught me the value of friendship and forgiveness, but a tale that did not end happily" she whispered. Before Clyde and Meadow could inquire further, Saphris abruptly sprung from the log and adjusted the bow slung over her shoulder. "Well, I think that is enough rest for now, we should aim to reach the ruins before nightfall!" she heartily declared, before marching off into the depths of the jungle.

Her tenacity took Clyde and Meadow by surprise and they had to briskly jog in order to catch up with her. "Hey that was sudden! Come back, I wanna hear the tale!" Meadow cried as she gave chase. Dismay quickly walloped Meadow however, when she took a wrong turn through the sprawling thicket of emerald green leaves and exotic shrubbery, only to plunge headlong into a pit of sinking mud. A repulsive splodge sound followed and before Meadow had a chance to react, the viscous mud had already devoured her legs and stuck to her waist like a bunch of begging children. "Great, I don't believe this! Clyde! Clyde help! I'm stuck!" cried Meadow. Frantically, she fought against the mud pits sticky grasp, made all the worse by the fact that both her hands were already dunked in.

All ten digits attached to Meadow's hands were unfortunately ensnared by the gooey pool of muck, thus her struggle was in vain, until Clyde came rushing into view. "Meadow, Goodness! let this be a lesson to not simply charge into the unknown!" yelled Clyde as he knelt and reached out to grab her. "Yes, yes! Lesson learned now get me out of here! This is not my idea of a mud bath!" Meadow hysterically cried, still trying to wrestle to freedom. Alas, even though Clyde could reach her, no amount of pulling or tugging on her arm would liberate Meadow from her murky predicament. "It's no use, you're really stuck! I haven't the strength!" shouted Clyde. "Strength potion use strength potion!" yelled Meadow, watching in fright as the mud now swallowed her elbows.

In theory, strength potion should have been the answer, until Clyde thought about the potential risk. "I can't, I could end up ripping you in half like a smoked sausage!" he declared as he watched Meadow continue to sink. Luckily, another idea came to him and Clyde acted fasted as he reached for a potion slotted inside his harness and frantically popped the top off. "Here, swallow this!" shouted Clyde as he held out the vial of potion above Meadow's face and tipped the liquid into her mouth. Whatever potion Clyde had just given Meadow had to act fast, for the gobbling mud had reached her shoulders and nothing was happening. And nothing continued to happen, at least for a second or two, until finally Meadow felt the potions effect kick in. The parts of her body that were still visible suddenly became ghostly and see through, "Ethereal potion, clever!" declared Meadow. The viscous clutch that the filthy mud pool had upon Meadow slipped away, Meadow had become physically intangible and was able to stroll out of the mud pit like it wasn't even there.

An exhausted sigh of relief blew from Clyde's lips as he watched Meadow gaze upon her spectral form, "Thanks Clyde, you really saved my skin!" uttered Meadow. A moment later, Saphris suddenly burst through the bushes of the jungle and reappeared again. "I heard all the shouting, what happen...oh my gosh! A ghost!" she screamed. Meadow exploded into laughter upon seeing her rection and played the part of being a real phantom for a moment, "Wooo-ooh! I died and came back to haunt you!" she mocked.

Her juvenile moment and lack of care in the face of near death made Clyde grimace and wearily shake his head. "She took a potion that made her untouchable, looking like a ghost is a side effect, more importantly, where were you? Why dash ahead like that?" asked Clyde. Guiltily, Saphris rubbed the back of her neck, "Sorry, I forgot to warn you about the mud pools in this jungle, but I found the ancient ruins, we were really close when we stopped!" she answered. Spreading the long, angelic white wings adjoining her back, Saphris began ascending into the air as they began flapping up and down. "Just look to the sky and follow me, I will show you the way!" she announced. "Must be nice to be a harpy sometimes" muttered Meadow as she pursued Saphris, her ghostly body phasing straight through the thick foliage of the jungle. Beyond the gaps of flourishing vegetation, Clyde and Meadow began to see glimpses of weathered stone and their pace suddenly quickened. They shadowed Saphris, who continued to fly overhead and upon traversing past one last cluster of obscuring bushes and snarling vines, the ancient ruins revealed themselves.

A crumbling archway made of ancient grey stone acted as the entrance to ruins. Ornate patterns of swirling gold were embedded into the architecture of the stonework, indicating a lost but once prosperous society. Ivy and moss also crawled and draped across the ruins, testaments to the age of these dormant remains of a civilization now vanished to the winds of time. After passing beneath the crumbling archway of solid stone and dull gold, Saphris flew down and landed in front of the cracked steps that led up and into the proper ruins. "So here we are, the ancient ruins, my people still have no idea who lived here, some scholars believe it was a race of magical beings who wished to try and enter the heavens!" remarked Saphris.

Meadow gazed upon the crumbling walls and shattered stone towers with fascination. "Interesting, maybe that explains why the island of Cloudvale floats high above Resplendia" she answered. Meadow's astute observation reaped an amicable nod from Saphris. "Could be, it wasn't my people that created the mysterious tower that keeps Cloudvale floating, it was apparently here to begin with" she replied.

As captivating as the theories were, Clyde had not the time nor focus to indulge in them, as much as he wished to. "Alright let's go, and the keep chatter to a hushed minimum, hopefully our criminal will be here and I would prefer to ambush him" he uttered. Catching this culprit was top priority, but whoever this masked stranger was, his reasoning for visiting these dusty, decrepit ruins inflicted a shudder of excitement upon Clyde. After all, Clyde knew the criminal had come here to find another clue to the location of the chalice, hopefully the Chalice of Renewal which Clyde was seeking. But the further along the stone steps Clyde climbed, the more he understood what the ruins were. It seemed like a sort of temple, as defaced statues and shrines of familiar idols and gods dotted the many alcoves and walls. Judging by the layout of the dusty ruins, Clyde also got the sense that it was a place of great wisdom. "These ruins may have been an academy as well as a temple" he whispered.

By this point, the ethereal potion Meadow had taken had long worn off, thus she had to physically brush aside the layer of cobwebs that greeted them around the next corner. After swatting aside the cluster of sticky cobwebs that blocked their path, they stumbled upon a towering bronze statue as soon as they reached the final step of the winding stairs. The statue was of a woman holding a mighty golden great-sword in one hand and holding a shiny orb of gold in the other. The orb was made to look like the bronze woman was holding the sun in her hand and she also possessed hair made entirely of solid gold that appeared on fire. "That's got to be a statue of Inferna, the goddess of sacred fire!" Meadow declared, admiring the exquisite craftsmanship of the statue.

A necklace of small bronze stars was engraved around the statues neck, along with an ancient star symbol carved into Inferna's forehead. "The goddess of sacred fire isn't that the same kind of power wielded by Emperor Helios?" asked Clyde. "That madman? The one who proclaimed himself emperor and currently rules the slave city of Helios? Yeah, I've stories of his power" answered Saphris. A nervous shudder crept along Clyde's spine, prompting him to remember the real reason they were here, "Come on, we're not here to discuss theories and admire statues" he uttered.

Further exploration of the ruins revealed a vast great hall of stone with beams of golden sunlight cascading into the room from cracks and holes in the ancient ceiling. The floor was emblazoned with a huge, golden emblem of a mighty griffon, but many clumps of grass, weeds and ivy crawled up through the numerous crevices scattered across the ground. Six thick pillars of towering marble also adorned the room, three on each side. All of them stretched up and touched the ornate ceiling above, creating a profound atmosphere of significance in the room. Yet, as the initial wonder and awe gradually dwindled away and Clyde's eyes surveyed the rest of the room, it was then Clyde spotted him.

A strange masked figure in black, his back turned, his focus upon a wall of mysterious carvings, silently scribbling into a roll of parchment with his ink and quill. It was the one they were searching for, Clyde knew it, he could feel it. This mysterious stranger was the one who had been manipulating them from the shadows all along. A quiver of discomfort rattled Clyde's heart, but he remained watchful and silent, as did Meadow. Although she also narrowed her eyes and scowled upon the back of the hooded stranger with fierce contempt. After taking a deep breath, Clyde marched forth, rested his foot upon the first step of the grandiose stairway and glared at the hooded stranger at the very top. "At last we meet! You are the criminal whose messes we have been cleaning up! Reveal your face and your intentions villain! For your elaborate game is at an end!" proclaimed Clyde. However, the masked stranger pretended like Clyde wasn't even there, choosing instead to ignore his words and diligently scribble down the strange and ancient looking language carved upon the wall.

Until at last, after a short uncomfortable silence, the masked stranger ceased the sound of his scribbling, slowly turned around and began to speak. "Well done Clyde, I can't imagine how difficult it must've been to track me down, but then again, you always were very resourceful!" answered the masked stranger. Finally, they had cornered and confronted the mysterious stranger, who decided now was the perfect moment to remove his mask and unveil his identity at last. "We meet again, face to face! I hope you haven't forgotten me Clyde! But how could you with a face like mine!?" growled the stranger.

Meadow quickly raised a hand to her mouth to stifle a gasp of horrified shock, for the skin upon the stranger's face was swathed in ghastly scars and burns. Meanwhile, Clyde was rendered utterly speechless, becoming frozen like a lump of ice, his eyes wide like he had seen the secrets of the cosmos, "Lorenzo! It can't be!" he managed to sputter out. A repulsive smirk spread across the stranger's lips, made even more grotesque because of the horrific damage sustained to his face. "After all these years you still remember your old master! That truly warms my heart Clyde, even though you took everything from me!" snarled Lorenzo.

Again, Clyde could not find the words to respond, he became like a stunned galamare in front of a raging chimera, Meadow on the other hand, she had a plethora of questions. "Clyde, you know this stranger? Who is he? You told me you never had a master! Why didn't you mention him?" she asked with increasing intensity. Her relentless questioning and yearning for answers were to no avail, Clyde lingered in a state of gob smacked bewilderment. "Judging by that potion harness your wearing and your age, I'm guessing you girl must be his apprentice" replied Lorenzo.

Slowly, Lorenzo took a few steps down the stone stairs and drew closer to Meadow, his sinister, eerie glare radiating an aura of pure, unquenchable hatred. "Can't say I'm surprised Clyde never mentioned me, he should've just taken the memory erasing potion and made life easier on himself" Lorenzo added. The mere presence of Lorenzo seemed to infuse Clyde with an overwhelming aura of unease and discomfort. "I killed you, you're supposed to be dead!" he muttered with gasped breath. Meanwhile, Saphris, who was still tagging along with them, took a humble bow and began to slowly back out of the picture. "Okay, I think I've stumbled onto something personal here, I'm just going to take a walk" she uttered.

No one paid her any attention; an ominous black cloud had fallen upon the room and the tension was so dense it felt like a swamp. Parting his long black coat, Lorenzo revealed an inner side pocket, drew an empty glass vial from within and held it up for all to see. "Indeed, I should be dead! And I would've been, if not for that very last potion I asked you to make Clyde, for this vial is from that same potion all those years ago!" declared Lorenzo with a hysteric laugh. Meadow hadn't a clue what he was talking about, but it seemed like Clyde did judging by the spreading shock in his eyes. "The levitation potion! No…I had forgotten!" he gasped.

Lorenzo seemed to cherish Clyde's surprise and dismay, to the point where it seemed like he was feeding off Clyde's despair and using it as a source of nourishment. "Yes Clyde, you tried to kill me, but you also ended up being the one who saved me!" he laughed. As soon as he heard this astonishing revelation, Clyde seemed to fall cold and lifeless like a lump of clay, his eyes becoming empty like a fresh corpse. Which meant the duty of divulging Lorenzo's scheme fell upon Meadow, "So it was you who created all those problems! And it was you who steered us towards them!?" she shouted.

Arrogantly, Lorenzo smirked, calmly shrugged and took a conceited bow. "You're the one that paid the satyr! You're the one who poisoned the fairy and sent her mad! You're the one that unleashed the capamandra on Crestwood and the giant spiders in the sewers of Deepshade!" roared Meadow. Lorenzo didn't even try to deny any of her accusations, instead he seemed to reveal in them. "Guilty as charged on all accounts, and I was the one who ordered my little imp helper to cause trouble in Orstone" he answered. A gust of fury whipped over Meadow as she glared upon Lorenzo's hideous scarred face, his repulsive grin appearing like something out of a nightmare. "Good innocent people have died because of you! Why have you done this!?" she cried.

Slowly, Lorenzo's sinister smile faded, and he callously pointed his finger at Clyde. "To slow down Clyde, I know he searches for the Chalice of Renewal, just like I am, and I shall do anything to stop him from obtaining it!" he growled. A frustrated scowl accompanied Lorenzo's words, "But, I did not expect Clyde to solve the problems I created so swiftly! I clearly underestimated him" he grumbled. Despite this, Lorenzo's annoyance quickly shifted to back confidence. "Not that it matters now, I have studied the ancient carvings in these forgotten ruins and I've finally unraveled the resting place of the chalice! I know where it is!" he proclaimed. His announcement promptly dragged Clyde's attention back into the realm of reality and Clyde, almost on the verge of begging, stepped forward and asked to know. "Where Lorenzo!? Where is the chalice? Please, tell me!" he pleaded.

Alas, Lorenzo refused to surrender any details and snapped his fingers, commanding a ferocious, snarling griffon to suddenly swoop down upon them. The icy hand of fear quickly grasped Meadow and Clyde as they confronted the formidable snarling beast. Its fangs gleamed like deadly mirrors, its body poised to pounce at any moment, "Do you like my little pet?" asked Lorenzo. Strangely, the griffon's eyes glowed a vicious eerie red color, but Clyde knew why. "He's done something bad to the griffon! Just like the fairy in Soulspring!" he gasped. Simmering hatred twisted Lorenzo's already maimed face, "Tell your apprentice it was you that gave me this face Clyde! Tell her you took Ruby from me!" he shouted.

A whirlwind of emotions whipped and thrashed within the pit of Clyde's soul right now, while Lorenzo reached into his coat and drew a vial of potion from his harness. "Goodbye Clyde, enjoy being mauled to pieces!" he growled, before uncorking the vial of potion, gulping it down and becoming a transparent ghost a couple of seconds later. Clearly, he had consumed ethereal potion and Lorenzo used his new phantom form to arrogantly vanish through the wall behind him, leaving no trace of his existence.

Now Clyde and Meadow were left to face the ferocity of Lorenzo's berserk griffon alone, "Clyyyde…!" Meadow nervously uttered as she began to slowly back away. "Yes, I think now would be an opportune time to run!" he shouted, suddenly spinning around on the steps, almost toppling over his panic and slamming chin first onto the hard-stone ground. Meadow followed him and allowed the fright in her heart to enhance the speed of her steps. Alas, the griffon spread its grand golden wings, soared into the air and mercilessly flew after them. It proceeded to stomp all four of its powerful lion paws onto the stone floor, obstructed the exit to the ancient ruins and unleashed a piercing screech from its sharp eagle-like beak. "It's no good, it's not going to let us escape!" cried Meadow.

Fortune shone its warm rays upon them though, as a silver arrow suddenly whooshed overhead and struck the griffon square in the chest. A tinge of agony abruptly enraged the griffon and it furiously recoiled. "Hey, hope you didn't forget about me!" announced Saphris, who reappeared, quickly drew another arrow and readied her bow. Rage consumed the once majestic griffon and it unleashed its wrath by recklessly pouncing straight ahead, trying to trample over Meadow and Clyde like they were a pair of delicate daisies. Clumsily, Clyde threw himself to the right and evaded the beast. Meadow desperately dodged to the left, also managing to elude the griffon's deadly talons, while Saphris bravely stood her ground and fired her next arrow.

Sadly, it was a fruitless hit, as the arrow whizzed towards the griffon's head only to strike its hard-bony beak and be knocked aside like an annoying fly. Scarce time remained for Saphris to draw and fire another arrow as the griffon charged her with the wrath of a dragon and leapt towards her with the ferocity of a hungry wolf. Wisely, Saphris spread her white harpy wings and flapped as hard and fast as she could, rapidly soaring into the air, flying over the griffon just in time to escape its violent assault.

Dust scattered into the air from the griffon's onslaught and it slammed into the set of grand marble stairs, erupting a piercing screech upon impact. "You might want to run away now!" cried Saphris, who flew overhead. "And leave you? Not our style!" called Clyde as he reached for a vial of potion in his trusty harness, proceeded to uncork it and swallow all of the beneficial liquid within. Again, the enraged griffon charged and this time its target was Clyde, however, Clyde had taken a vial of sleepy-gas potion. He then spewed a swirling, plum colored cloud from his mouth as the griffon approached, clearly his intention was to end the battle quickly and without harm. Sadly, this was not the case as the sleepy-gas cloud hadn't the time to build up, resulting in the griffon swiftly dashing through most of it. Almost none of the gas was inhaled by the griffon, its speed and ferocity overwhelmed Clyde and it bashed him aside with its head, slamming him on his back. Pain and panic engulfed Clyde in equal measure and he froze with fear once he was confronted by the sight of the growling griffon stood over him, ready to sink its beak into his throat.

Thankfully, Meadow was the beautiful princess who came to his rescue. Grabbing the griffon by the tail and with all her strength, pulled it off Clyde, tossing the beast behind her like a common stone. An alarmed squawk burst from the griffon's lungs as Meadow threw the beast aside, lobbing and slamming it into one of the mighty marble pillars nearby. Hastily, Clyde scrambled up from the ground, his jaw agape as he gazed upon Meadow. "Took a strength potion!" she declared, playfully dangling an empty potion vial between her fingers. Yet, the griffon remained enraged and its fearsome red glare indicated it was far from surrendering. "You may be strong my disciple, but be careful, you can still bleed!" cried Clyde.

Just as the griffon recovered itself, luck graced them again in the form of a whistling arrow overhead, an arrow that plunged into one of the griffon's furry lion paws. Saphris had joined the battle once more and swooped overhead with her trusty silver bow, causing a furious holler to erupt from the beast. Eager to tear Saphris to shreds, the griffon took flight, expanded its wings and relentlessly chased her through the air.

This caused Clyde to notice somewhat of a weakness, "In its poisoned berserk state, it is easily provoked!" he cried. "Meadow, use that new potion and aid Saphris in distracting it!" ordered Clyde in a hurried breath. The potion Clyde referred to, was the one which possessed the astonishing amber hue. "Okay, here goes!" answered Meadow as she pulled it from her harness, uncorked the vial and gulped it down. Like most other potions, it took little more than a second for it to work, and as soon as it did, Meadow could feel the difference. "I feel something on my back! what is that?" she asked as she turned her head. Beauty dazzled Meadow's eyes as she suddenly beheld a pair of large magical wings upon her back, glowing with a radiant golden energy.

Saphris struggled to fend off the snarling griffon much longer as the beast hunted her without rest. Desperately, she kept trying to dive and swoop in and out of the towering pillars of the hallway. It was becoming fruitless, the griffon was far faster and far more ferocious that she thought, its speed and tenacity ensuring that she couldn't even find time to fire off another arrow. Then, just as Saphris was looking back into the jaws of certain death, Meadow came flying in at great speed with her magical golden wings. She also ensnared the beast's attention with a powerful punch to its beak.

The strength potion still coursed her veins, that combined with the flight potion made Meadow appear like a fabled heroine, the kind bards would sing mystical ballads about. Meadow knew it too and she savored the moment, looking down upon the fallen griffon with her arms folded and a cocky grin smearing her face. Angrily, the formidable griffon fixated its wrath upon Meadow now and ruthlessly flew after her. Its ire and savagery continuing to bubble like a volcano on the verge of eruption. It was all part of the plan though and Meadow had snatched the creature's attention. Now Meadow played the part of bait as she flew around the room with her majestic new wings but didn't exactly like the idea of playing chase with a berserk griffon.

Still, she played her part well and lead the beast on a frantic pursuit along the hallways and balconies of the ancient grand hall. She could hear the infuriated griffon behind her getting closer, hear its cacophony of screeches, growls and squawks as it recklessly lashed its talons at her. The strength potion had worn off at this point, Meadow could feel it, but the plan was complete. After another sharp turn she saw Clyde at the ready and dove straight at him with the griffon in tow.

Clyde too had taken a vial of strength potion and was ready and waiting with a large chunk of ancient marble pillar, which Meadow was easily able to fly right under. The griffon was not so lucky however, and despite seeing the marble pillar ahead, its sheer size and speed rendered it powerless to take any evasive maneuvers. It was literally a smashing sight as the griffon collided with the chunk of marble that Clyde held with his newfound strength and the wild beast slammed into the ground, skidding across the floor from the momentum.

Dust and rubble scattered everywhere from the impact and the noise of the smashing marble echoed the chamber. Yet as bruised and bloody as the griffon was, it still attempted to get up and fight. "It's not done, finish it my apprentice!" Clyde yelled to Meadow who hovered above the creature with her pair of flapping magic wings. "Already on it!" Meadow shouted back, swiftly reaching for a vial of stone-form potion and quaffed the liquid down her throat as quick as she could.

Wearily, the griffon staggered up, blood dripping from the cuts adorning its body and it mustered its strength for another pounce. That was until Meadow came crashing down upon it rump first, her body weighing far more than normal now that she had temporarily changed her flesh to stone. Enhancing her body weight so immensely was a clever tactic as it felt like several suits of steel armour had just slammed upon the griffon, making it collapse to the floor and uttered a defeated growl. Although it was severely injured, the griffon was rendered unconscious and alive, which was fortunate since it was only acting violent as a result of whatever vile concoction Lorenzo had fed it.

To avoid causing the griffon any further harm or suffering, Meadow quickly rolled her incredibly heavy body off its back, creating a rumbling thud when her feet touched the ground. Every footstep Meadow took when she stomped her way to Clyde's side was heavy and thundering, like the steps of a giant, "Will it be alright?" she asked. Meadow made it clear she was speaking to Saphris by the way she made eye-contact and gazed back upon the poor injured beast. "Yes, griffons are tough creatures and I've seen them in worse shape, I'll make sure my people nurse it back to health" replied Saphris.

After patting the dust from her outfit, Saphris shouldered her bow again and prepared to take off, "I have to say, you two sure know how to show a girl a good time!" she declared. "Whatever your caught up in, I wish you luck! It's been quite the experience!" Saphris cheerfully added, before spreading her wings and soaring into the sky. Clyde and Meadow silently watched her fly into the burning sunset for a moment and although everything was calm again, a tornado of turmoil brewed within their hearts. Fatigued and confused, Clyde abruptly plummeted to one knee. He didn't wish to show any weakness, but couldn't contain it any longer, "Lorenzo, so he's alive! I saved him!" he gasped.

Frustration gnawed at Meadow like a beggar chewing upon a fresh leg of cooked deer. "Are you going to come clean and tell me what the heck is going on!? I think I have the right to know!" she demanded. It seemed to take every ounce of strength Clyde could muster to raise his head and rise from his knee again. Shock had shattered his mind, rendering him little more than a frail old man in a cage fight against a group of orcs. "Later, first I must study these symbols on the wall, Lorenzo showed great interest in them, they likely hold the final clue to the resting place of the Chalice of Renewal" Clyde answered in a shaken tone.

Whatever past Clyde shared with Lorenzo; Meadow could clearly see it rattled him to his core. Especially the realization that his old master was still very much alive, "Fine, but I'm not dropping this!" she grumbled. With unwavering focus, Clyde observed the strange symbols upon the wall, examining each one with profound attention, until he quickly realized something remarkably familiar about them. "These symbols, I've seen them before! They're from an ancient, long dead language, the kind I've been studying in my lab back home!" he exclaimed.

Meadow took a glance upon the bizarre symbols, but she could only express baffled confusion, "They look difficult to decipher, you know what it all means?" she asked. "Not at all, I've seen bits of bizarre language like this scattered all over Resplendia in its various nooks and crannies and I've yet to learn what race it originated from" Clyde confessed while rubbing his chin. Whilst Clyde diligently studied the archaic symbols and pondered their meaning, a familiar face swooped in again. "It's ancient harpish, the language of my people, before we learned the language of humans!" declared Saphris.

Her voice surprised Meadow and made her head spin, truthfully she didn't expect to see her again so soon, "Saphris? What brings you back?" she asked. As Saphris strolled closer, her eyes were drawn to the weathered wall and its ancient symbols. "I found a group of harpy guards on patrol nearby, I told them about the wounded griffon" she answered. "Can you read these symbols? Can you translate them? If so, then please, I beg of you! Their significance is immeasurable!" implored Clyde, cutting straight to the chase. Playfully, Saphris winked and gave a simple nod, "Well, since you said please!" she answered and began studying the symbols upon the wall meticulously. "It's a riddle, it says, to find the chalice and hold it in your hand, venture to a tower concealed by sand, search for it when the sun is nearly dead, for only then will the shimmer fade and its stone walls be fully made" uttered Saphris.

Cryptic was the best way Meadow could think to describe such a riddle and she made no secret of how it sounded like nonsense. "Sounds like a perplexing jumble of jargon, did you read it right?" she asked. Saphris brandished a frown as looked at Meadow, "Yes I read it right, learning the ancient tongue of my people was one of my ordeals to end my exile from Cloudvale" she answered. "But in truth, this is also the deepest I've ventured into these ruins, my duties usually keep me too busy, so I don't know what it means" added Saphris as she pondered the wall of words. Meanwhile, Clyde reflected upon the riddle and recited every word until it felt like it was the key to unlocking a part of his mind, like he had found a lost puzzle piece. Suddenly, he whizzed around to face Meadow, his eyes practically gleaming with insight. "I think I know the answer, we must return to the lab at once my apprentice!" he gasped.

There was no halting him, Clyde briskly marched off before Meadow could utter a single word further. But Meadow believed Saphris was due some appreciation though, "I'm sorry, we're both very thankful for all you've done!" she uttered. Humbly, Meadow bowed to show her gratitude further, "Today has been quite a shock for both of us I'm afraid" she added. Thankfully, Saphris seemed to show no signs of being insulted, instead she gave a cheerful giggle and smiled. "It's okay, go after your master, finish your journey, I'm just glad I could help!" she remarked. With that, Meadow saw that Clyde was getting a little too far ahead and promptly gave chase after him, she was supportive of his goal to find the chalice, but she was determined to get some answers too.

Chalice of Renewal
Chapter 11
Heart of stone

From the moment Clyde and Meadow re-emerged through the doorway of the mystical portal, Styx knew their experience had not been entirely pleasant. It was clear as a crystal lake by the brooding black clouds looming over their heads. They trudged from the depths of the magical portal with about as much effort as a pair of grumpy old dragons and with a veil of sullen silence soaking their thoughts. "Is everything well master?" hissed Styx. Clyde couldn't even begin to muster the energy to answer him, instead he wandered straight past like a fresh risen zombie, leaving Meadow to supply an answer. Clyde seemed troubled and shocked, whereas Meadow was clearly more frustrated and vexed. Evident by the way she stomped past Styx without even making eye-contact, "Don't ask!" she grumbled.

Clyde wasted no time in lumbering straight to his alchemy lab and diving face first into the bundle of parchment paper strewn across his desk, but Meadow had other plans in mind. A scowl smeared her face as she chased after Clyde, entered the alchemy lab and saw him sitting at his desk. His mind becoming consumed by work as always, pretending like there wasn't going to be a conversation. "Hey, I think it's time you tell me what's going on!" barked Meadow as she hurried down the steps and approached him, only to be met with silent ignorance.

Either Clyde wasn't listening, or he decided to ignore her entirely. Whichever it was, it was a stupid decision to infuriate Meadow further, "Hey!" she yelled, slamming both hands upon his desk. "What? What do you want? You want answers!?" Clyde cried back, becoming flustered at Meadow's tenacity. "I want the truth!" Meadow fired back, her frustration steadily increasing at the lack of honesty. "You can't handle the truth!" yelled Clyde, his shock finally erupting into a climatic outburst infused with fury. Yet, an intense sorrow also seemed to weigh heavily upon him judging by the way he slumped into his chair, hid his face with his palm and wearily sighed.

In fact, Meadow started to feel a hint of shame or guilt resonating from him, which cooled her tenacious, fiery spirit. "What happened? I deserve to know; I think I've earned the right!" she adamantly pressed. She made a fair point, Clyde couldn't argue with her and he couldn't fault Meadow for being angry, all she wanted was honesty from her master. Especially after the personal things she had shared with him in the early days. "Very well, you are right, I hoped this would not be a story I would have to recite, but I shall tell you the truth, I shall tell you the history between me and Lorenzo" replied Clyde.

Clyde cast his mind back over ten years ago, searching for the earliest memory he could. Searching for those golden days of sunlight beaming through the laboratory windows and the smell of fresh alchemy ingredients. Those days when he was an eager young apprentice, spending hours in the lab memorizing every potion recipe in every alchemy book until he felt like his mind was about to explode from knowledge. The air was fresh, everything was tranquil, cauldrons and beakers would gently bubble away, and everyday Clyde would hear an angel sing.

This day was the same as the many other cherished ones before it, Clyde was diligently concocting a new potion his master Lorenzo had tasked him with making. When suddenly, he would hear that familiar angelic singing coming from outside. Every time Clyde heard that singing, he would cease his work and walk over to the window to watch her. Ruby, beautiful majestic Ruby, her beauty and enchanting voice were the only things that could pry Clyde away from his passion for alchemy. Ruby would always grace the hidden sanctuary Lorenzo had created with the gift of her singing; her musical chords sailing into the air like graceful petals upon a warm breeze.

Truly, Clyde wondered if Ruby's voice was magical, for she always seemed to cast a spell upon him. Clyde would watch from the window as she strolled along the garden, singing away and he would never be able to return to work until she stopped. Or until he heard the laboratory door unexpectedly creak open, which it did right now, "Clyde, how is that potion coming!? Have you finished it yet!?" called Lorenzo. Being the diligent, passionate student that he was, Clyde averted his eyes from the window and the world outside, choosing instead to hastily return to his work. "Yes, master Lorenzo, it is almost complete! I am certain you'll be delighted with my work!" Clyde awkwardly responded, zipping back to the mixing station in a desperate attempt to look busy.

Lorenzo inhaled the sweet aroma of powders, herbs, liquids and tonics upon entering and waltzed his way towards Clyde, "Ah, nothing beats the smell of a lab!" he declared. Clyde briefly reminisced about the first time he met master Lorenzo and the day he was shown around his lab. It was Lorenzo who ignited his passion for alchemy and constantly reminded him of how captivating the art was. Clyde shared his master's sentiment and reveled in the atmosphere of the lab. "I agree master, few things get my heart and soul tingling as much as the scent of a well-stocked alchemy laboratory!" he proclaimed.

Happily, Lorenzo stroked the wispy golden hairs upon his goatee and rested his hand upon Clyde's shoulder. "I'm glad to hear that my boy, the world of alchemy is wondrous and vast, its mysteries profound!" he replied. Carefully, Clyde poured a glass beaker of gooey, shimmering silver liquid into a glass retort which hung over a small lit candle. The liquid was then distilled and poured into a small glass vial held tight by the arm of an iron ring stand. Once the glass vial was filled, Clyde removed it from the clamp and presented it to his master. "Here you are Master Lorenzo, one potion of levitation!" he pompously proclaimed.

To add an extra slice of dramatic flair to his presentation, Clyde confidently blew out the burning candle nearby and awaited his master's approval, a prideful smile smeared across his lips. Meticulously, Lorenzo's jade colored eyes examined the glass vial for any discernible imperfection in the mixture. "Name me the three primary ingredients for the concoction and the volume" he ordered. "Three pinches of crushed pixie wings, one spoonful of oil extracted from mistgale flowers and four dashes of ashfall herbs!" Clyde answered without a second of hesitation or doubt.

Impressed by his astute response, Lorenzo gave an approving nod. He then placed the vial of potion into one of the leather pouches adorning the exquisitely designed harness strapped to his body. "Excellent Clyde, for it is not just about knowing which ingredients to add, but also how much" Lorenzo uttered. "This is a basic yet vital rule of alchemy, follow it well or all you'll end up with is a vile taste on your tongue or incredible ill" he lectured. Every word Lorenzo spouted, Clyde took heed with profound interest, his attention sharp like a newly forged dagger. "Yes, master Lorenzo, I promise to keep such a vital rule in mind!" he proclaimed. This made Lorenzo release an amused chuckle and he playfully slapped Clyde upon the arm. "Don't fret my boy, you're the first apprentice I ever had and your far better than I could've hoped" he replied. "Alchemy is in your blood Clyde, your heart is a cauldron of potential, but I think that's enough studying for today, let's go eat with Styx and my wife Ruby!" added Lorenzo.

Hearing such positivity directly from his master's mouth caused Clyde to swell with pride. He longed to be a wizard of alchemy himself, maybe even one who could surpass Lorenzo someday. Meanwhile, a quiet rumble in the pit of Clyde's stomach made him agree with his master's idea to take a break and eat. "A most excellent suggestion master, I admit I've not stopped to quell my hunger yet!" he replied. The two talented alchemists promptly departed the lab, guided by the groans of their famished stomachs. Leaving behind the curious scent of mysterious powders and brewing herbs, in exchange for the aroma of roasting fish.

Outside the lab Ruby awaited, the bottom of her rosy red dress damp and dirty with water and mud, indicating that she had been fishing again. She had created a small campfire near the edge of the cliff where the cottage and the alchemy lab rested upon, their private little sanctuary overlooking the whole horizon. "I think I'm getting better at fishing!" Ruby cheerfully uttered as she turned the beautifully cooked fish upon the spit over the flickering campfire and drizzled oil upon them with a large ladle. What was it about Ruby? Clyde struggled to narrow it down to just one aspect, she infatuated him, every word, every smile, every breath more magnificent than the last.

Her glowing golden skin, her flowing scarlet hair blowing in the breeze, her azure eyes shimmering like jewels or her delicate voice sounding as serene as a sun-soaked stream. It was all these aspects to Ruby and more which caused euphoria to inflate Clyde's soul until it began to ache. Feelings he had never felt for anyone before bubbled to the surface, perplexing feelings he could not understand or explain. Then of course, a tinge of jealously would follow as Clyde watched his master Lorenzo approach his wife Ruby and the two would exchange love filled kisses. Clyde would quickly avert his eyes he would glance anywhere else, anywhere except at the sight of the two of them together. He hated himself when he felt like that, but it pleased Clyde to see his master knowing how lucky he was.

Dinner was served, the fish that Ruby caught were served upon wooden plates and one was passed to Clyde, "Clyde? Are you okay? It's time to eat" Ruby uttered softly. Her angelic voice snagged Clyde's averted gaze back and he savored the chance to trade eye-contact with Ruby. "Oh, yes! Thank you, Ruby!" he clumsily uttered while taking hold of the plate. Slowly, Clyde sunk his teeth into the crispy skin of the cooked fish, taking a sizeable bite and relished its delicious juicy meat, "Mmmm, positively scrumptious!" he remarked.

Soon, Styx flapped his little purple wings, fluttered over to the campfire and joined them, carrying three tankards of fresh brewed tea. "The tea you asked for miss Ruby!" he hissed. Gratefully, Ruby took hold of one of the tankards and deeply inhaled the steamy aroma rising from it, "Ah, smells delicious, thank you Styx!" she answered. "Will there be anything else miss?" Styx asked after passing the other two tankards of tea to Clyde and Lorenzo. "No, that will be all Styx, you can go enjoy some rest now" Ruby answered, rewarding Styx with a caressing stroke upon his pointy purple ears and spiky horns. Styx cherished the moment of affection, then bowed his head and flew back towards the cottage. "Styx is such a loyal servant, you are truly kind my love, few people would even talk to an imp" uttered Lorenzo. Ruby picked up a nearby wooden stick and gently prodded the crackling campfire with it, "Styx isn't my servant" she replied. "I'm glad I took him in, he was abandoned, hungry and scared when I found him lost in the woods all those years ago, now we're like the best of friends" Ruby added.

Over the horizon beyond the cliff edge, the entire landscape appeared ablaze from the stretching rays of burning sunset. Everyone was engulfed in a glorious glow of golden light, "Well, I propose a toast!" announced Lorenzo. He arose from the little wooden stool he sat upon and raised his tankard of tea above the crackling campfire, "To friends, good memories and everlasting happiness!" he declared. "I shall drink to that, and to the majesty of alchemy!" Clyde added as he too raised his rear from his wooden stool and tapped his tankard against Lorenzo's. "Here, here!" announced Ruby in a jolly tone, also raising her tankard of steaming tea and clattering it against the two other tankards hovering above the roaring spit. It was a moment of purity, harmony and perfection, a moment they all cherished, right up until the sunlight faded and it was time to turn in for the night.

Morning arrived as inevitably as an orc accepting a fistfight, but this time Clyde had been kicked out of bed early by his master. Currently, Clyde was wandering in the nearby sunlit woods, for Lorenzo had bestowed him a special task to perform. The woods were tranquil, sunny and flourishing with echoes of life another reminder of why Clyde adored this place so much, truly it was a sanctuary of secrets and serenity.

In fact, it was so peaceful and picturesque that Clyde's mind would often wander, causing him to daydream and make it a struggle to focus upon his duty at hand. Lorenzo had tasked him with gathering a couple clusters of dragontail mushrooms for another batch of fire-resistance potion, a potion Clyde was still learning how to concoct. Finding the mushroom shouldn't prove challenging though, as Clyde knew this particular mushroom was in season. The real test was not getting his attention ensnared by the beauty of the forest. So far Clyde's hunt had been a leisurely scenic stroll, hands in his pockets and the sun on his face. Until something besides the elegance of the woods captured his focus.

A beautiful fair maiden with ravishing scarlet hair and honey colored skin innocently waltzed among the trees sniffing a purple shadow-weave flower, humming a gentle tune. It was Ruby, Clyde recognized her right away, but she hadn't noticed him yet. So, Clyde decided to sneak like a timid mouse and hide amongst the columns of thick forest trees and observe her from a distance. Why Clyde decided to do this was uncertain even to him, he couldn't explain it, what was he watching her for? What was he hoping to see? It was a mystery he couldn't discern; all he knew was he enjoyed watching her. Seeing her prance and skip through the forest like a wild, graceful galamare was pure poetry.

Against his better judgement, Clyde secretly followed Ruby deeper into the forest, following the melodic sound of her humming. Until she finally ceased her waltzing and stopped at a gentle, winding river, the same river she liked to try her hand at fishing. Except this time, Ruby decided to remove her shoes, dip her feet into the cool water and enjoy the refreshing feeling that followed. Clyde watched her from behind and was tempted to inch closer, he wanted to get as close as possible without her knowing.

Hence, he took a few careful steps forward, his heart beating with excitement and fear, but froze like a statue when his foot snapped a fallen branch. Even with the noise of the stream, the crack of the branch was painfully loud, making Ruby quickly spin her head and glance behind. Fright leapt into Clyde's chest upon being discovered, causing him to plummet onto his knees and search the ground frantically. "Clyde?" called Ruby as she curiously watched him. "Oh, forgive me Ruby, I didn't mean to startle you, just searching the forest for mushrooms! Thought I saw one!" he answered in a panicked tone. His panicked demeanor caused Ruby to smother an amused giggle with her palm, "It's okay, come sit with me, the water feels cool and refreshing!" she answered.

Sheepishly, Clyde accepted her invitation, ceased his pretend searching and approached the riverbed. His cheeks appearing like a pair of rosy red apples from the embarrassment, "Oh...th...thank you!" he stammered. Clumsily, Clyde plonked himself alongside Ruby, untied his laces, removed his boots and dipped his feet into the babbling river. "Ah, yes! Very refreshing, perfect for a sunny day!" he uttered nervously. Ruby was suddenly forced to hold one palm over her aching rib as a tinge of laughter struck her, "I'm glad you like it here" she chuckled.

Ruby could see how nervous Clyde felt around her, Ruby knew why, but she didn't mind, she found it quite cute. "Does my charm and beauty make you nervous?" she asked, innocently playing with her hair. Clyde peeked upon Ruby's deep red hair and cherished the glance, since he couldn't find the courage to look into her shimmering eyes while she was this close. "No, not at all, why would I be nervous? I am a man of science, I am immune to any kind of temptation except for alchemy!" declared Clyde. This made Ruby howl with laughter and she powerlessly flopped backwards onto the lush riverbank, "Ha, my husband Lorenzo used to say the same thing!" she announced.

Her inescapable fit of squirming laughter infected Clyde and he couldn't resist yielding to the intoxicating merriment bubbling up inside him, until his amusement eventually escaped too. Both resonated the forest with their laughter, but they finally managed to reel it back in. "Ahh, Lorenzo really likes you Clyde, you've shown such promise, I hope you'll stay with us" Ruby softly uttered. Thoughtfully, Clyde turned his focus downwards towards the sparkling river. "Working with master Lorenzo has been truly enlightening, I plan to stay by his side, but my greatest fear is making him disappointed" he poignantly answered.

In that same moment, Clyde felt the delicate, smooth touch of Ruby's fingers upon his chin as she gently pulled his face towards hers. It felt like a dream when Clyde deeply gazed into her eyes which shimmered like a pair of jewels upon a sandy beach. "I know my husband Lorenzo, so believe me when I say he is really proud of you, you sought him out, you showed how passionate you were about alchemy, you could never disappoint him" she whispered.

Clyde prayed that were true, just as he prayed this moment would never end, what was it about Ruby? She was neither witch nor sorceress yet possessed a magic that always made Clyde feel so weak and yet so powerful. Clyde remained paralyzed with infatuation; his soul captured by Ruby's tender touch. Until she pulled her hand away from his face and slowly stood up, "Come on, let's go!" she cheerfully declared. However, Clyde gazed up at her like he was worshiping the statue of a divine goddess and tilted his head curiously. "Lorenzo has you hunting for ingredients, right? Well let's get finding them!" Ruby gleefully added. She then offered her supple hand to Clyde and playfully heaved him to his feet, before the two of them happily strolled deeper into the forest.

While absorbing the radiant sunlight that shone through the gaps of lush green forest trees, Ruby enhanced the stroll with a spot of her soothing singing. "How the forest blooms, how it blooms, we're off to find some mushrooms!" she sang. Clyde chuckled at her gaiety and watched her elegance with unrivalled captivation. "I've always thought your voice is beautiful, as beautiful as the forest we walk among" he remarked. Ruby flashed a smile as bright as the sunlight, before gradually vanishing amongst the labyrinth of trees and verdant shrubbery.

Clyde gave chase and searched for her whereabouts, becoming increasingly perplexed when her mellow singing fell silent. "Ruby? Ruby! Where did you go?" he uttered in a puzzled tone as he surveyed the surroundings. "That's odd, she was just here" whispered Clyde, baffled at the fact that she had eluded his sight so effectively, while the chilling thought that a horrible fate had befallen her crept into his mind. "Boo!" Ruby suddenly shouted as she leapt from behind a nearby tree, flanking Clyde and pouncing her palms upon his shoulders. Clyde practically leapt out of his skin in fright, while Ruby held her ribs in splitting laughter, "Oh, you're so easy to sneak up on!" she chuckled.

A weary groan left Clyde's lips as he collected his breath again, "Thanks, I'm sure Lorenzo wouldn't like to hear you killed his favorite apprentice by sheer fright!" he gasped. It took some effort, but Ruby managed to quell her laughter and held out a bright orange mushroom she had picked while hiding, "Is this your mushroom?" she playfully asked. A quick examination revealed that it was indeed the dragontail mushroom Clyde had been tasked with finding, "Indeed, you certainly have a keen eye!" Clyde answered.

Ruby handed Clyde the vibrant mushroom and gave a modest shrug, "What can I say? I'm a girl of many talents" she remarked. Before their interaction could go any further, a familiar raspy voice intruded upon them. "Ah, miss Ruby and young Clyde, I've been searching for you, master Lorenzo has prepared some fresh tea!" announced Styx. Secretly, Clyde cursed his intrusion and hated himself for hating it too. "Thank you, Styx, we'll be right along!" Ruby jubilantly replied. She bestowed a glimpsing smile to Clyde, then promptly pursued Styx with a hop and a skip in her steps.

Clyde remained motionless and silent as he watched her disappear into the forest. "Everything is perfect here, everything is wonderful, I cannot complain, so why do I yearn for more? What is this feeling in my chest? Why do I adore you Ruby? Why do I feel confused?" whispered Clyde. Solemnly, Clyde placed the burning orange mushroom into the gathering satchel strung over his shoulder and slowly followed Ruby's footsteps, releasing a muddled sigh as he walked. Ruby was several years older than Clyde, but also several years younger than his master Lorenzo, yet despite being significantly older than Clyde, Ruby retained such carefree youthful purity. On the other hand, Ruby also possessed a sense of mature classiness and seasoned elegance that she could brandish on a whim. perhaps that's why Clyde adored her so much, the fact that she seemed flawless. Her beauty, her charm, her kindness and grace, there were too many reasons why she was so enchanting. It frightened Clyde, especially when he tried so hard to resist putting her on a pedestal.

Yet, upon a pedestal she was, at least in Clyde's heart, her voice and presence brought such calm to his mind and tranquility to his soul. Doubt lingered no longer within Clyde; he loved Ruby and would give anything to have her. She devoured his thoughts on the sunny stroll back to the cottage and Clyde was greeted by the scenic image of master Lorenzo standing upon the wooden porch. One arm wrapped around the shoulders of Ruby, his other hand raising a tankard of hot tea to his lips.

Both watched the horizon glow from the wooden steps of the nestled cottage. A warm, brisk breeze blew past the lush green trees nearby, making them gently rustle and sway. Then came the mellow kiss upon Ruby's forehead, it was perfect, they were perfect. As much as Clyde cherished the life he now had, the beautiful sight of Ruby and Lorenzo together made his heart ache and Clyde would always picture himself there, instead of his master.

Scents of pungent powders greeted Lorenzo as he opened the rustic oak doors leading to his alchemy lab, followed closely by the sound of bubbling concoctions of magical liquid. It was a new day and Clyde was hard at work, diligently adding a dash of lime green powder to a new alchemy mixture that Lorenzo had entrusted him with creating. "Morning Clyde my boy! How goes the mixture?" asked Lorenzo. "Tis proceeding nicely master!" Clyde heartily proclaimed, stretching his arm and reaching for a glass bottle of sunflower seed oil upon the wooden shelf above him. Various alchemical tools lay strewn about the wooden workstation, a sight Lorenzo adored seeing, for it indicated an assiduous alchemist.

He watched Clyde uncork the bottle of sunflower seed oil and meticulously pour it into a small wooden cup. Stopping when the liquid reached the halfway level, indicated by a mark carved into the side of the cup. The precision of alchemy, the possibilities, it infatuated them both, as did the many essential tools of the art. "The fire-breath potion, did you finely chop, grind and boil the dragontail mushroom?" Lorenzo asked, picking up a set of iron tongs in front of him and examining how clean they were. "Indeed, I did master, I also remembered to place it in first to help the mixture thicken!" declared Clyde, gently tipping the wooden cup and pouring the sunflower seed oil into the flask of mixture. A calm ambience then fell upon the room as Lorenzo paced around. One question lingered upon Clyde's mind though, one he couldn't shake, "Master? I was wondering, what is the most powerful potion of all?" he asked. Lorenzo chuckled at his question as he looked out the window, "That my boy would be mana-breath potion" he answered. "A potion of great destructive power, one that is also incredibly difficult to make as the ingredients are immensely rare!" Lorenzo added.

Master Lorenzo then wandered over and peered into the flask of honey colored liquid and decided to test Clyde, "Now, name me the three primary ingredients of this new concoction" he asked. "Easy, one dragontail mushroom, a handful of chopped nightfire nuts and one grinded up magma beetle!" announced Clyde. Lorenzo quickly spun his head towards Clyde and gasped, "A magma beetle? No! It's supposed to be a lava worm!" he cried. Those were the last words Lorenzo uttered before the bubbling mixture of liquid in front of him suddenly fizzed up and spewed like a volcano, burning his face.

A scream of agony leapt from Lorenzo's lungs as the boiling alchemy mixture scorched his skin, melting it like dragon breath upon ice. Panic engulfed Lorenzo, causing him to stagger backwards and fling his arm wildly. Creating a clatter of noise as he smacked aside the various alchemy equipment upon the workbench and shattered a couple of glass flasks. Clyde was seized with terror and numb with shock, but with great effort managed to recapture his senses and rushed to his masters aid with a nearby jug of common spring water, "Master! Hold still!" he cried.

As Clyde poured the jug, Lorenzo felt the cool, refreshing water splash upon his face, dousing the raging hot alchemy mixture. That one alchemical mistake forever altered Lorenzo and the future he and Ruby shared together, and it would haunt Clyde with eternal guilt. It was a harsh reminder of how cruel the art of alchemy could be if the mixture were incorrect or if the alchemist became too overconfident. It was a mistake Clyde couldn't believe he made, the magma beetle in the mixture was the cause, it proved too potent and created a volatile reaction. A mistake that shattered the peaceful harmony they all shared forever, it was Clyde's greatest calamity and the point of creation for all the pain that Lorenzo left in his wake.

Rain plummeted from the dreary black sky, it seemed only fitting and Clyde took it as an omen after what happened. He silently listened to the endless patter of raindrops hitting the cottage roof, sitting there upon the sheltered porch, sitting and gazing at the bleak, grey horizon normally aglow with light. Behind him, he heard the front door of the cottage open and saw Ruby emerge when he turned around, an expression of anguish and sorrow adorning her face. "How is he?" asked Clyde in a tone ripe with remorse and uncertainty, but for the moment Ruby couldn't even form words. She took a seat alongside Clyde on the wooden steps of the cottage porch and had to muster every ounce of strength she possessed to reply. "He's…he's…he's sleeping…." she whispered, unsure of what else to say.

A sullen blanket of dreary darkness draped Clyde, "I don't even know how to begin, except by saying sorry, I was foolish, it's all my fault" he whispered. Ruby wiped away a cluster of tears welling up within her eyes and took a much-needed breath. "His…his face, its…it's never going to heal is it?" she asked. Dismay drenched the moment between them, and Clyde reluctantly shook his head, "I'm afraid even alchemy cannot fix it" he whispered. Further tears began gushing within Ruby's eyes causing her to stand up and walk out into the rain to hide them. "Sorry, I need to be alone" she uttered softly, with thunder rumbling above.

Over the next few days, Clyde remained deeply distracted about what to do next. So far Ruby had not banished him from this idyllic haven of alchemy and study, nor had Ruby openly blamed Clyde for what happened. However, master Lorenzo hadn't departed his room since the accident, causing Ruby to bring all his meals to him, on the rare occasions he ate anymore. For the moment, Clyde was without a master, forcing him to instruct himself, a task that seemed to sour some of the wonder of alchemy. In fact, Clyde feared he may have lost his passion for alchemy altogether. Preparing the ingredients, chopping them, grinding them, boiling them, distilling them. It all felt mundane and monotonous, like he had fallen into an unending pit of desolation.

Clyde's gaze wandered, drifting into nothingness as he watched the glass flask of murky violet liquid bubble away above the burning candle in front of him. He kept expecting to hear the alchemy lab door creak open and see Lorenzo stride in. He kept visualizing Master Lorenzo approaching him, full of vigor and merriment, eager to discuss notes and reveal new mysteries of alchemy. Sadly, another week passed without a single word or appearance from Lorenzo and Clyde knew he had to move on, it wasn't the same anymore, he had destroyed everything pure about this place.

It was upon the eighth day, while Clyde was mindlessly toiling away in the lab, that was the day he finally snapped and decided to abandon alchemy once and for all. Clyde decided to concoct a batch of shrinking potion but was having difficulty ensuring the potion shrunk everything attached to the imbiber too, namely clothes. It was a much more advanced potion, rife with complexity and Clyde had begun to regret attempting it as it began to enflame his patience. Then, while stirring the mixture with a long wooden spoon over burning candlelight, he failed to maintain attention for a moment and spilled some of the concoction upon his hand. "Agh!" Clyde shouted as the liquid scalded his skin and forced him to release his grip upon the wooden spoon and retreat his hand back. Frustration and fury quickly enveloped Clyde, his love for alchemy shifting to pure hatred and he couldn't quell his rage. "Curse you!" he yelled and swatted aside the glass flask, smashing it and the mixture across the workstation. Shards of broken glass scattered everywhere, while the bubbling hot concoction splashed across the wood and onto the floor causing quite the mess.

Seeing the chaotic mess he created caused further anger to boil within Clyde. He was mad at the mess, mad at alchemy, but most of all, he was mad at himself and it took every ounce of willpower he had to reel his anger back in. A much-needed break was desired, and Clyde marched away from the workbench in a fluster. He cleared his thoughts by leaning upon the window ledge, watching the endless torrent of pattering raindrops and exhaled a frustrated deep breath. Beyond the veil of hammering rain, Clyde also spotted Ruby, armed with a sturdy wooden umbrella and wandering into the forest with Styx at her side.

Curiosity and a yearning to escape the alchemy lab prompted Clyde to hastily snag his nearby coat, dash into the downpour and pursue Ruby. Unknown to Clyde at the time, Lorenzo happened to be at the window in his cottage and spotted Clyde head into the woods after Ruby. Clyde ventured a guess as to where Ruby may have wandered, and after several minutes of stomping through the rain-soaked forest, he found her. She was sitting quietly upon a mossy rock along the bank of the babbling stream.

She had decided to don her elegant creamy dress, but it was the victim of many splotches of mud and moss, not that Ruby seemed to care. She seemed more intent on gazing at the cascading current at her feet. Warily, Clyde crept closer like a hungry cat stalking a precious bird, ensuring not to snap any branches underfoot this time. "What should I do Styx? Lorenzo seems so closed off to me, we barely talk anymore, his heart is full of hate now and I feel my love for him slipping further and further away everyday" uttered Ruby.

Although her voice was barely audible above the gushing stream and pounding rain, Clyde had crept close enough to hear her and hid his presence behind a nearby tree. "You should always follow your heart, so what is it telling you to do?" hissed Styx as he twirled his impish tail around one finger and floated by Ruby's side. "It's telling me I have to move on, I need to escape this place, I don't want to be here anymore, I wish to start fresh" Ruby earnestly uttered. Upon hearing her words, Clyde quickly emerged from his hiding spot and revealed himself, mostly out of a jolt of fear that he may never see Ruby again, "As do I!" he declared.

His sudden appearance caught Ruby by surprise and as she watched Clyde nearly stumble over, a flicker of dread seized her. "Clyde! You were following me again? Did you hear everything I said!?" she demanded. Guiltily, Clyde nodded but spoke quickly before Ruby had a chance to counter-react. "Yes, I heard, but I'm glad I followed, I wish to move on from this place too" he answered. As the icy rain bombarded them, Ruby maintained an unwavering, silent gaze upon Clyde, one that felt as though it was piercing his very soul, "Styx, could you give us some privacy?" Ruby politely asked.

Obediently, Styx offered a humble bow, granted her request and fluttered back towards the direction of the cottage. "It's probably for the best that you leave, you've already caused enough damage" uttered Ruby with a tone devoid of any feeling or emotion. Despite her words cutting Clyde's heart like a cold spike of ice, Clyde endured the harshness of them. "I'm sorry, your right to blame me, I have caused enough damage, I shall leave soon" he answered. A frustrated huff blurted from Ruby's cherry lips, "I don't blame you; I know it was an accident, it's just......" she replied, her voice trailing into oblivion. Clyde watched Ruby lean forward, her face powerlessly falling into her hands and sobs of sorrow followed soon after. "Just what?" asked Clyde as he swiftly moved to her aid and knelt in front of her.

After emitting a series of tearful cries, Ruby managed to compose herself enough to form words again. "Lorenzo, he wanted to kiss me, and I couldn't help but turn away from him" she sobbed. Clearly, she was fraught with woe and Clyde refused to leave her in such a distraught state. "Oh, I see, but that's nothing you should feel ashamed or guilty about" he replied, gently stroking her arms. After giving a sad sniffle, Ruby watched the rushing raindrops and allowed them to splash her face and drown her grief. "We've been married for years; I can't remember the last time I refused to kiss him" she uttered.

Then Clyde posed the one question that hounded his mind the most. "Do you still love him?" asked Clyde as he took a hold of her soft slender hand and caressed it gently, hoping that Ruby would see him as someone to which she could confide in. "I still want to love him, but his face, I shouldn't love a man just from the way he looks, I know that seems awful and selfish, but I also cannot deny how I feel now" she answered.

Her beautiful teary eyes wandered into the depths of the forest, making her appear like a lost soul after a surviving a shipwreck at sea. Clyde felt a stirring within his heart, a yearning that could not feed, "I also cannot deny how I feel Ruby" he answered and suddenly lunged forward and pressed his lips against hers. It was a kiss both sweet and passionate, a kiss soaked in both fear and excitement, a kiss that made Clyde tremble to the very depths of his soul. Yet, Ruby did not recoil, she expressed surprise and wide eyes and when their lips finally parted, a sparkle of desire gleamed within her.

A sudden surge of emotions blew within Ruby's heart, sweeping her off as easily as her umbrella when a swift breeze came along and snatched it from her fingers. Despite this, Ruby didn't even look back to see where her umbrella had been carried off to. Instead she and Clyde continued to peer deep into each other's eyes with gasped silence, before passionately kissing again in the rain. Sadly, this created an unquenchable anger and hissing hatred within Lorenzo, who was secretly watching them from a behind a nearby tree. Any fragments of good left in his heart were shattered further and hatred devoured his soul. Eclipsing it like a giant black shadow, but Lorenzo did not intrude upon them, instead he carried his wrath with him when he stomped away.

Clyde and Ruby continued to exchange one sweet embracing kiss after the other. Each one making Clyde's heart beat faster than the last, until eventually they parted lips and released breathless gasps. The river beside them seemed to rush faster and the rain above seemed to pommel harder, drenching them both head to toe. "How I've yearned to kiss those lips!" Clyde whispered intensely. Gently he pressed both his palms against her wet rosy cheeks and leaned his forehead against hers. "How I've thought about this moment, how I've dreamt of it!" he gasped.

For the moment, Ruby was still speechless and caught up in a whirlwind of emotional turmoil that whipped and thrashed her around, until she felt like she was about to burst. No words came to the surface when she parted her lips and tried to speak, hence why Clyde proceeded to voice his thoughts and feelings. "Come with me Ruby, let us leave this place together, it seems cruel I know but what else can we do? Let us start fresh!" Clyde declared, tenderly holding her silky hands. Alas, a spear of dismay pierced Clyde when Ruby retreated her hands from out of his and turned away from him to face the rumbling river once more. "Maybe, but I just don't know" she uttered softly.

To rescue the tender moment, Clyde placed his arm around her shoulder and supported the overwhelming burden of weight upon her mind. "However, there is one thing I know I must do" whispered Ruby. A long strand of soaked crimson hair flopped in front of her face and Ruby adamantly flicked it back. "I must leave this place and Lorenzo; I no longer feel happy" she added. Ruby's resolve burned brightly again, like a recently lit forge in a blacksmiths workshop and she arose from the large hunk of stone in the ground. "I must be honest with him, I shall tell him tomorrow, I shall leave tomorrow, I must do it or face being trapped here in misery forever" she remarked. She spoke not a word further to Clyde, instead, Ruby silently walked back along the forest path to the cottage. Walking through the rain, leaving Clyde alone on the rock alongside the river.

Tomorrow arrived, but it brought another dose of pummeling rain, except this time it was joined by bellowing thunder. The day seemed ominous and uncertain; Clyde could feel it in the air. Today was also the day Clyde decided he would renounce the art of alchemy for good. But decided to pay one last visit to the alchemy lab and look upon the various tools, powders and containers, just for sentimental sake. Strangely, when Clyde pushed open the creaky door of the lab, the smell of magical smoke and burning liquid assailed his nose, "That's odd, someone's been working here" he uttered. That much was clear, even before Clyde walked further into the lab, approached the messy workbench and spotted the cluster of filthy flasks and stained mortar and pestle. "Lorenzo, were you working here?" whispered Clyde as he gazed upon the array of alchemy equipment.

Most of the tools were stained a variety of deep murky colors, but what snagged Clyde's attention most was the number of tools. Almost every piece of alchemy equipment had been brought out and Clyde had never seen so many utilized before. "This looks complex, what were you working on Lorenzo?" he uttered. Meanwhile, Ruby had spent the morning packing a small leather travelling sack and plucking up the courage to face Lorenzo. Timidly, Styx creaked opened the bedroom door and poked his head in. Ruby found his intrusion most welcome and flopped herself upon the soft cushy bed behind her. "Styx, I'm glad you came, I can't find Lorenzo, I think he's decided to get some fresh air finally!" she declared in a huff. Styx remained meek and shriveled as he entered the bedroom, "Master Lorenzo is outside, he just came back from a walk and wishes to speak with you Miss Ruby" he answered.

Upon relaying the message, Ruby sat up and surrendered to a curious head tilt. "Oh, okay, I shall go to him at once then, I need to speak to him anyway" she answered. A strange tremble traversed Ruby's bones and followed her steps for reasons she couldn't understand, still, she departed the cottage and strolled out front where Lorenzo awaited her. Lorenzo stood upon the edge of the cliff, his back turned as he surveyed the stretching horizon of forest and mountains, clad in his favorite shadowy black robe. "Lorenzo!?" Ruby called over the ceaseless patter of rain. Ominously, Lorenzo turned around and faced her with a gaze that was both piercing and sinister, "You wanted to speak to me?" asked Ruby. Although Ruby tried her best to maintain eye contact, her resolve faltered at the sight of Lorenzo's horrifying, scarred visage and shattered her gaze. "Yes, my dear, for I have a confession to make" he answered.

His tone was barren and flat like a dead savannah, his smile warped and disfigured from the harm inflicted upon his face, creating a smirk meant to haunt the dreams of children. "I've not been the best husband to you, I've let you down my love, I'm sorry for being difficult to deal with and I know I need to do better" Lorenzo uttered softly. Despite his gruesome outward appearance, his words sounded sincere and apologetic, impaling Ruby's heart upon a sharp stab of regret. "It's okay, I understand, its natural what you're going through" Ruby replied as guilt continued to tug upon the strings of her heart, making her writhe in shame inside.

Slowly, Lorenzo revealed a small glass vial of liquid from his pocket. "I made something special for you, a new potion, one which will to bring happiness and clarity to those that drink it" Lorenzo uttered. Happiness and clarity were certainly on Ruby's list of desires and she studied the glass vial of murky potion which Lorenzo held out in his palm with intrigue. "Thank you, that is very thoughtful of you my love" she answered. However, Ruby moved closer to Lorenzo and placed her palm over his, forcing it shut and gently pushing Lorenzo's hand back against his chest. "But I think you are more deserving of such a potion than I am" she answered with a delicate tone. Ruby's reaction was not what Lorenzo intended or expected, evident by the way a sour, spiteful glare suddenly flared up within his hideous face. "Shut up and drink it you lying harlot!" he snarled. A shriek of fright burst from Ruby as Lorenzo flew into a rage and lunged for her. Wrapping his fingers around her throat and slamming her into the wet, muddy ground.

Using his teeth, Lorenzo ripped the cork off the vial of potion he held and forced it into Ruby's mouth as she struggled and squirmed to wrestle free from his grasp. "I saw you with Clyde, this was all part of your plan! You two planned all this! I know it!" yelled Lorenzo as he watched Ruby panic and gasp for breath. Both of Ruby's arms leapt up flailed around wildly like a pair of octopus tentacles from beneath the ocean and they scratched and scraped against Lorenzo's face and skin. Alas, a few minor lacerations weren't going to stop Lorenzo's fury and Ruby felt the liquid within the potion slither down her throat.

At the same time, Clyde witnessed what was happening from the window of the alchemy lab, not to mention he could hear Lorenzo's shouting and Ruby's choking screams for help. "Lorenzo, stop!" shouted Clyde as he came barging out of the alchemy lab in a confused fluster, slamming the door and charging into the icy rain. Thankfully, Clyde's intrusion caused Lorenzo to finally release his hateful grip upon Ruby's throat. "Ha, your too late Clyde!" bellowed Lorenzo as he held up the now empty vial of potion and playfully swayed it back and forth between his fingers.

In a scared dazed panic, Ruby scurried away from Lorenzo on her hands and knees, gasping for breath, "Clyde! Clyde!" she screamed hysterically. Clyde rushed to Ruby's side, enveloped his arms around her body and lifted her back onto her feet, "Ruby, It's okay! I'm here!" he declared. A sinister laugh roared from Lorenzo's maw, causing Clyde to glare at him furiously, "Clyde, he forced me to drink something!" panted Ruby. "What did you do to her!?" Clyde shouted, before noticing that Ruby began feeling increasingly heavier in his arms. "Clyde, I feel strange! I feel so heavy and cold!" Ruby panted and Clyde looked upon her rosy red cheeks, only to see the beautiful glow in her face fade to a hard grey.

A frightened gasp leapt from Ruby's throat as she looked upon her hands and watched them turn a dull ashen color, becoming completely solid. "No...no, no, no, no!" Clyde uttered in a panic as he witnessed her slowly turn to cold stone. "Clyde!" Ruby gasped and that was the last word she ever spoke again. For Clyde watched with horror and despair as she turned into a lifeless, unmoving statue. "Ruby...no...this isn't real, this isn't happening!" sobbed Clyde as he collapsed to his knees in front of Ruby's new stony form.

He was rendered speechless and empty, like some beautiful piece of him had been shattered. "It's your fault Clyde, it's all your fault! You Destroyed my face! You stole my love! This was all part of your scheme! You planned that accident in the lab, I know it!" snarled Lorenzo. Relentlessly, rain pummeled Clyde whilst he knelt there in front of Ruby. "Your wrong Lorenzo! And your insane! How could you do that!?" Clyde bellowed back. Solemnly, Clyde caressed the side of Ruby's stony face, feeling her rough, hard edges scrape against the skin of his palm and gazed into her pebble eyes.

His tears dripped onto her rocky body but were washed away by the pounding rain. "It should've been me; it should've been me! I was the one you should've punished, Ruby had nothing to do with this!" he yelled. Hateful glares were traded between Clyde and his once master Lorenzo, hate so profuse it seemed thick enough to wade through. "When I saw you both kiss I could see how much you loved her and how much I had lost her!" growled Lorenzo. "Well now if I can't have her, no man can!" Lorenzo shouted at the top of his lungs with insane glee, causing a flood of agony and hatred to bombard Clyde. "Curse you, curse you to the deepest pit of torment!" Clyde roared as he charged for Lorenzo, determined to knock that repulsive, demented smirk off his face.

Fearlessly, Clyde stormed towards Lorenzo with fury rivalling that of an enraged minotaur. This took Lorenzo by surprise and by the time he had reacted, Clyde had already shoved him off the side of the cliff edge. Except, as Lorenzo stumbled backwards and spewed a shocked howl, he luckily managed to grip the edge of the cliff with one hand. But now Lorenzo dangled precariously above the frightful drop by only a handful of dirt and the mercy of Clyde who stood above, watching him try to twist and squirm his way back to safety. Clyde watched him like one of the gods of the heavens judging a mere mortal trying to claw his way out of eternal dark pit of Diablos, watching with a cold, merciless heart. "So, this is how it ends eh Clyde? Just know that you have forever ruined the peace and prosperity of this place! Remember that it was all your fault!" snarled Lorenzo. Silently, Clyde stomped away, turning his back upon his hideous master, stopping only when he heard Lorenzo's echoing scream as he plummeted to his death once his grip failed.

To Clyde's knowledge, Lorenzo was dead and by all rights should've been. But that must've been the moment when Lorenzo remembered the potion of levitation in his jacket pocket. The same potion Clyde had brewed for him over a week ago. It was common for Lorenzo to forget about what he had in his pockets, of course Clyde had forgotten all about it too, but it was undoubtedly that potion that saved Lorenzo's life that day. Believing Lorenzo had fallen to his death, Clyde shambled towards Ruby's stony form like a mindless zombie and jadedly collapsed in front of it. The final words of his former master still haunting him, even to this day.

Chalice of Renewal
Chapter 12
A sandtastic discovery

A metallic clicking sound echoed from within the keyhole when Clyde inserted his slender silver key into the sturdy oak door. It was the door leading to the mysterious room, the one Meadow had been curious about ever since she first arrived. Now Meadow wasn't sure she wanted to see what awaited on the other side after Clyde had finished spinning his tale, for a fog of turmoil lingered in the pit of her stomach. "I promised I would be honest with you my loyal disciple, your devotion has earned you the truth, I only hope you do not condemn me for keeping it from you" uttered Clyde as he unlocked the door. Clearly the door had been firmly sealed, evident by the stiff jerking movements from its hinges, likely to stop even the smallest of critters entering.

Styx had also come to join in and witness the unveiling of the door, almost like it was a sentimental event or festival. "It's been a while master, but it never gets easier" hissed Styx. Clyde bowed his head and gestured Meadow inside with his hand, ushering her in as the first visitor, "Go ahead" uttered Clyde. Warily, Meadow poked her head into the room, which would've been pitch black if not for the natural light coming in through the alchemy lab windows. The first thing Meadow noticed was a plush, comfy red chair made of exquisite velvet cushion and a nearby table stand holding a half-burnt wax candle, placed firmly in an ornate, golden candleholder.

The rest of the room was unremarkable and was devoid of anything worth mentioning, until Meadow's eyes finally fell upon the spooky stone face of a young woman in the center. As soon as the statue's stony visage greeted Meadow, she covered her mouth with one hand to smother a frightful gasp, "So it's true!" she cried. The statue was no doubt of Ruby, still frozen in time with a body of stone, "I kept this room a secret just for me, to preserve her from the elements outside until I find a cure" Clyde solemnly whispered. Mournfully, Clyde approached Ruby's statue and caressed the side of her cheek with his hand, "Look at her, she hasn't aged a day, while I'm now a few years older than her at this point" he whispered.

Seeing Ruby in her empty, stony form caused a haunting shiver to trickle over Meadow's shoulders, for it meant Clyde's tale held heart-breaking truth. "In my rage, I didn't think to ask Lorenzo what ingredients he used in the vile potion that made Ruby this way, I thought I killed him, but Lorenzo has returned to plague me again" Clyde said softly. Meadow pondered the statue sensing the deep bittersweet tragedy flowing from it, for even with her body made of stone, she could see Ruby possessed immeasurable beauty and elegance. Then, Meadow studied the chair nearby, "I'm guessing you like to visit her from time to time? I also take it you haven't discovered the cure yet?" she asked.

Sadly, Clyde shook his head and uttered a jaded sigh, "Alas no, there were at least eight different ingredients in the potion Lorenzo used and that's hundreds of thousands of combinations" answered Clyde. It was blatantly clear that Clyde's heart felt as heavy as an anvil and as hopeless as a wilting rose, "Still, I've been trying to figure out the recipe for years and I've been getting very close" he said. "The problem is even if I did figure out a cure, I would have to get Ruby to swallow whatever concoction I create, a difficult task for one made of stone" Clyde added with a dab of frustration. A different side of Clyde was on full display now, a side seeped in unbearable guilt, tragedy and melancholy. "You will find a cure master and I swore to stay by your side to see that day come!" replied Styx.

The sorrow swamping Clyde's soul was so powerful that Meadow felt like it would swallow and drown her too. "Ruby, her smile, her laugh, I remember how she used to frolic, she was so full of life, but look at her now" whispered Clyde. Disdain emerged in Meadow and she made it clear by her tone, "You really did scar Lorenzo's face and steal Ruby from him? That's true then?" she pressed. Her attitude and words were victorious in bothering Clyde and riling him up, but he managed to keep it mostly suppressed. "I'm not expecting anyone to think I'm perfect! I have my share of guilt, but Ruby was still an innocent victim in all this!" he fired back.

Gradually, Clyde quelled his frustration and soothed the thrashing flurry of emotions within with a calming breath. "Contrary to what you might think, as much as I admired Ruby, what happened to Lorenzo was a genuine accident" Clyde uttered. In the background, the blustering snowstorm continued to howl, its fury seeming to mirror the same kind of emotions Clyde and Meadow were going through right now. "Anyway, this is why I have sought the Chalice of Renewal, for tipping its magical water upon Ruby's skin should restore her flesh and I'm so close now, I just need to revise the clue we found in Cloudvale" he added. Everything finally made sense to Meadow, like an elaborate jigsaw puzzle, the picture becoming clear once the last piece had been placed. "That's why Lorenzo is after it as well, he knew you'd try to find it, he doesn't want you or anyone else to have Ruby again, hence all them requests for aid, to slow us down" explained Meadow.

Clyde took another sentimental glance at Ruby and rummaged his mind over the many memories and the moments he spent with her. But he knew it was time to say goodbye again, so he slowly shut the door to her room, locking away her stony body in the darkness once more. An irked grimace then smeared Clyde's face, "If I know Lorenzo, he'll use the chalice to first restore his face, then destroy it, for he knows Ruby would never forgive him" he replied. It felt as through the entire weight of the world rested upon Clyde's shoulders as he slumped against the door and rested his body upon it. "I must find the chalice first; I have to review all the notes I've accumulated" he said with a heavy sigh.

Clearly, the riddle they had discovered in Cloudvale had detained Clyde's attention, for he began pacing up and down the alchemy lab, reciting the riddle incessantly. "To find the chalice and hold it in your hand, venture to a tower concealed by sand, search for it when the sun is nearly dead, for only then will the shimmer fade and its stone walls be fully made" uttered Clyde. Gradually, Clyde's pace quickened, became increasingly flustered and he looked like a caged, hungry cerberii awaiting its next meal.

The only time Clyde ceased his relentless pacing was to scratch his head in perplexity. "It must mean the Burning Plains southeast of Resplendia, but that's not enough to go on" he mumbled. "The Burning Plains is the largest expanse of land in Resplendia, much of it unexplored, that's thousands of miles! There has to be another way of narrowing the search!" Clyde exclaimed. With no answers coming to fruition, Clyde hastily jogged to his desk and began digging through the mountain of scrolls and notes upon it. "What am I even supposed to be searching for? There must be another clue, the clues I've found so far must be linked! There has to be a connection!" he remarked.

Seeing his tenacity and passion for answers becoming aroused also inspired Meadow and she failed to repel a respectful smile, "He's determined!" she remarked. Meadow's gaze then shifted towards the extensive collection of jarred alchemy ingredients, neatly aligned tools and pristine workstations, "Perhaps I should be too" she pondered. The gentle touch of a small, slender hand suddenly rested upon Meadow's shoulder and when she turned around, she was greeted by Styx, "Perhaps we both should" he hissed. A curious shimmer draped Meadow and she waited for Styx to speak further as it seemed he too had something in mind. "While you've both been on your little adventures, I've been crafting something special for master Clyde, it's almost finished but I could use a hand" he uttered.

So, it began, the quest to unravel the mystery of the Chalice of Renewal and where it rested. But it would not be a quick process, that much became clear by the way Clyde succumbed to regular outbursts of confusion. Thus, while Clyde poured his eyes over ancient pages and rattled his brain with riddles, Meadow and Styx devoted themselves to their own projects in the meantime. Styx kept busy by crafting something that would surely prove essential against Lorenzo. Meanwhile, Meadow dedicated every waking moment of time to studying Clyde's alchemy notes and sharpening her alchemy skills. Honing her craft by spending hours upon hours in the alchemy lab in hopes that she may one day call herself a master like Clyde. To that end, Meadow spent the next several days pouring over every text relating to alchemy that Clyde possessed, arming herself with nothing more than a cup of tea and her full attention.

When she wasn't studying, sleeping or eating, Meadow spent every fragment of her free time gazing at bubbling alchemy beakers. She spent oodles of time distilling different liquids, weighing various ingredients on scales and grinding them into powder with her mortar and pestle. Hours were spent inside Clyde's indoor garden too, with Meadow practically picking it clean of all the colorful insects and vibrant flowers. Again, and again and again, Meadow studied, mixed, grinded and distilled, like she was possessed by some fanatical force compelling her to keep improving.

In all her time in the lab with Clyde, Meadow had never chased the art of alchemy so determinedly. Even when her motivation started to wane, she found a way to inspire it again and keep going. During all this time, Meadow, Clyde and Styx barely even spoke a word to each other, instead they remained focused and absorbed in their own little worlds. Over a week passed and finally, weariness began to erode their foundation of resolve. But only when every single glass vial on the shelves had been used, did Meadow swim to the surface and catch her breath.

A fifty at least, Meadow had crafted at least fifty potions, she ceased counting half-way through the week. "I did it, I actually did it!" she gasped as she gazed upon the colorful collection she had concocted. She sat there, slumping jadedly into a wooden chair, captivated by the astounding assortment of vibrant potions on display, still in disbelief that she had created them all. Many, many mistakes were made along the way, but she never allowed it to hinder her confidence. She marched forth with greater wisdom with each new mistake and in doing so, she had excelled herself to a new level as an alchemist.

Soon, Clyde wearily wandered into the lab and stumbled as he sloppily descended the stairs, having to seize his grasp upon the handrail at one point. "I've done it! I'm certain I've deciphered the location of the chalice!" he remarked. A swift bolt of awe struck him however, once he saw the multitude of mesmerizing mixtures neatly assembled along the entire workstation. "Incredible, you've been a busy little bee my dear! You crafted every one of these yourself!?" he gasped. Still drained from the whole ordeal, Meadow answered his question with a tired smile and a proud wink. "To have come so far in the fascinating field of alchemy like you have is heart-warming to say the least, mayhap I shall even cease calling you my lackey!" declared Clyde.

Gently, Meadow brushed aside a lock of ruffled hair that had swept in front of her face. "And that's not all, Styx has been working on something special too" she replied, her eyes gesturing behind Clyde. As Clyde curiously turned around, Styx waited behind him, hovering above the ground by flapping his little leathery wings, "For you master Clyde!" he hissed. In his tiny arms, Styx held out a leather harness, "We only had time to make the one but try it on, it should fit nicely!" explained Meadow.

Happily, Clyde received the leather harness and eagerly tried it on. The leather seemed of much higher quality than his old one and was a glossy, black color with ornate golden buckles, "You made this for me?" he uttered. A ray of delight shone upon Clyde once he realized how tight fitting, yet comfortable the harness was to move in. "Incredible, there's literally no wobble! My potions will stay tightly strapped!" he remarked. Without a doubt, the most pleasing revelation about this new harness came next. "You'll also be happy to know that this new harness can hold even more potions than your last one could!" declared Meadow.

Such a kind act of friendship rendered Clyde flabbergasted, he was at a loss for words, but the expression on his face was more than reward enough. "Thank you both so much! Truly, I am blessed to have such devoted helpers, you have aided me greatly and I am fortunate to have your support, you are more than assistants, you are both my best friends!" he remarked. His tender little speech brought solace and pride to Meadow and Styx. Their bond together had been forged stronger than steel after the adventures and experiences they had witnessed and now the most personal one was soon to come. "We have to assume Lorenzo has also deciphered the location to the Chalice of Renewal, he always was extremely crafty, but I too have now unraveled its location!" Clyde proclaimed.

With a tilt of his head, Clyde gestured for Styx and Meadow to shadow him into the portal room. Wherein he quickly mounted the set of wheeled ladders and studied the grand map of Resplendia upon the wall. Reaching his arm upwards, one of his fingers slammed onto a small section in the bottom-right of the exquisite giant map. "Scorchwind, home of the fenix, that is our first stop!" he announced. Casually, Meadow crossed her arms and slouched as she contemplated the elaborate map, "Scorchwind? You're sure?" she asked. "That last clue we found in Cloudvale was too vague on its own, but I dug up other old clues I've found over the years, I discovered they're all linked!" Clyde professed.

Leaping from the set of wheeled ladders like a little boy escaping a tree, Clyde scurried towards his desk and nosedived into the papers scattered upon it. "Look here, this is a clue I found a few years ago, I had to have it translated from ancient elven!" he declared. "Having it translated took a hefty amount of time and gold in itself let me tell you!" Clyde added as he shoved a weary looking scroll into Meadow's face.

Meticulously, Meadow perused the ancient, almost faded writing upon it, but quickly gave up trying to read it, "So, what does it say?" she asked. "Venture to the place where swords rust and bones decay, stay the course, follow the ruins and find the tower you may" Clyde answered cryptically. Such a vague, puzzling riddle prevailed in confounding Meadow, but the last part about the tower snagged her interest. "You think it's talking about the same tower?" she asked. Adamantly, Clyde nodded before rummaging through his cluttered desk and laying hands upon yet another dusty scroll and revealing it for all to see. "This one I found about a year ago and like the one before it, I had to spend precious time and money to find someone to translate it, this one was written in the tongue of the ancient orcs" Clyde explained.

Intrigued by whatever words were written upon this next scroll, Meadow and Styx gathered around Clyde's desk, "So what's this say?" asked Meadow as she peered upon it. "Those who would seek the chalice must seek the shimmering palace, endure the burning fire and find the crescent spire, only then will you have what you desire" uttered Clyde as he read the translated scroll aloud. On their own the clues didn't seem to mean much, but together they formed a picture, a story, even Meadow could see that now. "Interesting, instead of one big riddle, the riddle was split into three pieces? Clever" she uttered. Clyde echoed her sentiment with an admiring hum. "Indeed, and all clues point to the Burning Plains, the large sea of sand southeast of Scorchwind, I believe the clues relate to an ancient legend, the legend of Shimmermyst Tower!" he concluded.

Shimmermyst Tower, a fable Meadow had heard upon the tongues of travelling wanderers, adventurers and merchants passing through her village. Though none had ever confessed to ever laying their own eyes upon the structure. It became something of a whimsical fairy tale to tell around warm campfires on cold nights, the tale of a mystical tower that appears out of thin air, its walls shimmering like crystal. Many believed it to be nothing more than the trick of the mind, for the tower is said to vanish as swiftly as it appears, stealing away anyone who happens to inside. While the idea of a magical, shimmering, disappearing tower likely seemed absurd to most common minds. Meadow believed herself to not be among them anymore, not based on everything she had seen so far.

Still, the thought that she and Clyde were on the trail searching for the legendary Shimmermyst Tower both fascinated and astounded her. "The Chalice of Renewal must be inside it somewhere, so I guess it's time to chase a mythical tower then!" Meadow declared with a playful shrug. Clyde couldn't agree more, and a renewed flame of determination burned brightly within him again, "You heard her Styx, you know what to do!" he declared. Styx punched the air with his little demonic trident in hand obeyed Clyde with invigorated loyalty. "You can count on me Master Clyde, if there's a chance to cure Miss Ruby I shall do whatever it takes!" he answered. Scorchwind was their next destination and as Styx scurried away to begin creating the portal, Clyde and Meadow headed into the alchemy lab to stock up and prepare.

The temptation to haul every potion across the land was irresistible. Yet Clyde and Meadow defied such seduction, for they knew packing the right potions was far more vital than the amount. "We must prepare for anything should we encounter Lorenzo; he was the one who came up with the potion harness design, meaning he carries his own arsenal of concoctions" uttered Clyde. As he studied the plethora of potions across the workstation of his bubbling, scented alchemy lab, the vast option of which potions to take weighed heavily upon Clyde's mind.

This was not like all the other ordeals they had faced; Lorenzo was merciless and able to craft every potion Clyde could and more, making him a very unpredictable foe. "Lorenzo's skill as an alchemist surpasses even my own, he used to boast how he could create potions the likes of which should not even be possible" uttered Clyde. As Clyde's finger glided above the vials of magical tonics upon the work bench, it came to an abrupt halt and loomed over a bottle of fire-resistance potion. "The scorching heat of the Burning Plains is often the reason no one returns alive from that sizzling wasteland; thus, we need fire-resistance potions if we are to increase the probability of our success!" Clyde proclaimed.

Adamantly, Clyde slotted two vials of fire-resistance potion into two of the pouches upon his extravagant new harness. "Beyond that, we must try to foresee every outcome and have defenses ready for anything my dear!" announced Clyde. Meadow couldn't agree more, for she already knew the potential of potions in the hands of a master alchemist, and soon they would be facing possibly the greatest alchemist in all Resplendia. Leaving nothing to chance, Meadow grabbed a mixed bag of all the most essential potions that could easily turn the tide of battle against an opponent. Clyde did the same thing, taking full advantage of his new pouches and the extra space they bestowed.

An abrupt, booming tremor tore the air asunder, rupturing the moment, shattering it like a rusty blade being struck against rock. To Meadow it was a signal and meant only one thing, "Guess it's time to go" she remarked, as she finished grabbing a couple more precious potions. Hastily, Clyde conjured his wisdom, picked a few more essential vials of magical mixture and prayed his choices were shrewd. Clyde also did not wish to prolong the next encounter with his former master any longer, as unpleasant as seeing Lorenzo was for him. "Yes, time to go, time to face him again, time to face the horror I created and somehow atone for my mistake, for I cannot be haunted by it any longer" Clyde uttered.

Following the sound of deep humming led Clyde and Meadow into the portal room, where another floating doorway of magical sorcery awaited them. Levitating up and down upon the circular, marble pedestal with carved glowing runes. "Whatever happens Meadow, just know that you have been a fantastic apprentice and it has been an honor to work alongside you!" announced Clyde, tenderly resting his hand upon her shoulder. His heartfelt remark caused a confusing concoction of serenity and concern to begin brewing within Meadow as sure as a bubbling flask of potion. "The honor has been mine Clyde, you've shown me the wonders of alchemy and fascinated me with its magic, for that I am truly grateful!" she answered heartily. Both traded a blissful smile with each other, then turned their eyes towards the humming maw of the magic portal and at the same time, stepped inside, "Good luck master!" cried Styx. As the portal devoured Clyde whole, he turned back, gave a playful salute and a confident wink to Styx, then disappeared into the mystical void.

Into the fabulous realm of cascading colors they bravely plunged. Soaring through a tunnel of radiant ruby, captivating cobalt, luminous lavender, elegant emerald, glorious gold and opulent orange. like being swept away upon a rainbow river, lasting no more than a few seconds. But how Meadow cherished the feeling of flying through it, completely weightless. Until very soon, upon reaching the end of the shimmering portal, a splendid burst of dazzling white light engulfed Clyde and Meadow. Bathing them within its luminous embrace, until they finally emerged on the other side.

Fragments of light still dazed Meadow and Clyde's vision as they departed the jaws of the magical portal, instantly feeling the soft, porous ground beneath their feet. A vast sweltering dune of golden windy sand greeted them upon arrival, coupled with the sound of the soft, desolate breeze gliding through their hair. Scorchwind was visible in the distance, half-buried by the burning desert, but still large enough to be called a city. "So, that's the exotic city of Scorchwind, looks interesting!" Meadow remarked. Shielding her eyes against the sun to better gaze upon the city's spiky ornate spire towers and lavishly patterned stone walls.

Already Meadow was beginning to suffer the heat, it was like nothing she had experienced before, even the rocky landscape of the Jagged Steppes wasn't this hot. "Ugh, this heat is intense, we need to find shade!" she moaned. At the same time, something on the horizon suddenly snatched Clyde's focus. "I think shade has found us!" he answered as he narrowed his vision and peered closer. At first, he thought it might be some sort of illusion, a trick of the heat, but it looked like a tamed snazzle, "What the heck is that!?" Meadow shouted. Her reaction made Clyde burst into laughter, "Remain calm and lay down your fear my dear, it's called a snazzle!" he chuckled. Snazzle were a type of giant desert snake, but with long fish-like fins upon the side of their head and body, "The people of Scorchwind use them to traverse the desert quickly" added Clyde.

As the snazzle slithered across the desert dunes towards them, Meadow remained trapped in a tempest of awe and a fear of being gobbled up. Strangely, from upon the back of the slithering snazzle, Clyde heard one of the riders calling his name. "Clyde? Clyde! I thought that was you!" called one of riders while waving happily. Clyde stretched his sight to better glimpse who was uttering his name, studying the giant saddle attached to the back of the snazzle. Examining the bunch of riders who were seated beneath the colourful umbrella attached to the seat. The ethnicity of all the riders were the foxlike fenix, but one such furry face stood out in particular, "Nera!" cried Clyde as the snazzle approached.

Gleefully, Nera hopped off the saddled seat attached to the back of the giant snazzle while it was still slithering across the dusty desert dunes and brandished a toothy fanged grin. "It's been a while since Soulspring, what brings you here?" Nera asked, adjusting the ruffled silk hood shielding her face from the harsh desert sun. "As preposterous as it may be to hear, we seek the fabled Shimmermyst Tower, For I am certain the equally fabled Chalice of Renewal rests within!" Clyde declared. Not content to leave such a statement there, Clyde took a voyage upon his own ship of monologue. "Such an undertaking may seem foolish, fantastical and fraught with peril, but confidence drenches me! For I have unraveled the cunning clues behind its location at last!" he proclaimed.

His torrent of flamboyant passion produced an irresistible chuckle to leak from Nera's furry mouth, "Same old Clyde, you haven't changed a bit!" she remarked. "Indeed not, though I'll thank you to leave out the old part my fuzzy friend" replied Clyde as the hulking yet docile snake-like snazzle came crawling up beside him. Along with a group of four, well-armed fenix guards who dismounted the snazzle saddle and studied Clyde and Meadow suspiciously. Two had their furry paws resting tightly upon the hilt of their swords while the other two had an arrow readied in their bows. "Easy, easy! These are my friends; we can trust them I promise!" declared Nera, gesturing for the fenix warriors with her to lay down their arms. Clyde came prepared for a level of hostility from the fenix, they were shrewd diplomats and traders but also a tightly knit community that seldom trusted other races entering their borders.

Hence the reason why a profound sense of relief engulfed him once he saw Nera was here. Fenix were far more likely to tolerate and trust outsiders if one of their own vouched for them. Gradually, the group of fenix warriors relaxed their shoulders, the suspicious scowls faded from their bright beady eyes and their paws slowly released upon their weapons. "Very well, but your responsible for them" sternly uttered one of the fenix escorts. Nera didn't seem too bothered by his tone and gleefully spun round to face Clyde again, jumped into his arms and treated him to a tight hug. "I saw your portal from the city walls and there's only one person I know who travels like that, so I told these fleabags to come and give you a lift" she explained, nodding towards the other fenix. "And Meadow, nice to see you again! Hope Clyde isn't being too strict of a teacher! How've you been?" asked Nera with evident joy. Meadow gave Clyde a playful shove and smirked, "I'm doing alight but honestly, I think I'm starting to surpass the master now!" she joked.

Clyde's head performed such an abrupt spin towards Meadow that it looked like it could've flown off. "Tame that wild ego of yours my naïve lackey, lest it rush away as sure as a fair maiden on a surprise date with a goblin!" he growled. Watching their brief quarrel proved entertaining for Nera, who oozed another cheery chuckle, "Come on, lets ride the snazzle back to city, we can talk more on the way" she uttered. Sailing across the blazing sunny sands of the Burning Plains upon the back of a giant snake-like creature with fins was certainly a pleasant experience for Meadow to say the least. The large, patterned umbrella attached to the seating provided ample shelter from the sweltering sun. Not to mention the majestic golden dunes were an exceptionally beautiful sight to behold despite being so desolate.

A carefree breeze blew upon Meadow's cheeks as she rested her arms upon the wooden paneling of the carriage and leaned her head over the side. There was something undoubtedly enchanting about watching the sea of glowing sand gently glide by. "So, why are you here Nera? You were in Soulspring last time we saw you" inquired Meadow. "I came home to pick up some supplies and visit my people while everything was settling down in Soulspring" Nera answered, resting her head upon the plush seating with her arms outstretched.

Clyde sat opposite Nera and mindlessly watched a colourful beetle scurry between his feet upon the wooden floor of the carriage, "How fares Soulspring now?" he asked. "Far better, now that the fairy has restored the healing waters that flow through the city, repairs have also begun now that the people had regained their sanity" answered Nera. A sudden gust of sand swept into the carriage upon the back of the colossal snazzle and blew into Nera's face, causing her black wet nose to itch. "I've forgotten how different this place is to Soulspring" she uttered after banishing the itchiness from her nose with a wipe of her paw. Hypnotically, Clyde continued to watch the beetle scurry around until a pair of elegant, translucent wings popped out from the beetle's shiny blue back. "An indisputable statement, I confess I have ventured little in this part of the land, yet I'm aware of how hostile it is, even for seasoned adventurers" answered Clyde.

Without warning, the beetle used its wings to take to the air and flew away upon the desert breeze, "But a land filled with beauty also" uttered Clyde. The hulking moss-green sand serpent known as a snazzle continued to carry them towards the half-sunken desert city of Scorchwind. Along the way, Clyde explained the situation in greater detail and revealed the clues he had gathered thus far. "So, you two need a guide eh? Well I used to play in the Sandscar ruins further west of the Burning Plains when I was a child so I might just be able to help you" explained Nera. Clyde's ears quickly pricked up and he yearned to hear more, "Truly? You know of these old ruins? What can you tell me about them?" he asked. At first Nera responded with a casual shrug, "An old battlefield covered in even older ruins, you said the first clue says to find the place where swords rust and bones decay and find the tower you may" she answered.

Thoughtfully, Nera rubbed her furry orange chin with her paw. "The Sandscar Ruins are the only place that comes to mind, it's the site of a bloody battle waged many years ago, a battle lost to history" she added. A lonely whistle from the desert gales pursued her words and left a lingering aura of silent reflection inside the carriage, until the slithering snazzle slowed its speed to a complete stop. "And here we are, the jewel of the sands, the city of Scorchwind!" declared Nera as she vaulted over the side of the carriage and hopped down.

Scorchwind, the next majestic sight for Meadow to witness on her travels and what a sight it was. "So unique and exotic, the architecture is like nothing I've seen!" Meadow remarked as she gazed upon its splendor. Each stone the city was built of was adorned with an intricate pattern consisting of various colors and flamboyant swirls, with spiralling towers that pierced the sky. Circular looming barbicans ending with long spiky spires and onion shaped watchtowers dotted the elegantly crafted stone city walls also. Nera gently patted the side of the humongous snazzle that had carried them to the city gates and playfully reached up and stoked one of the fins upon the side of its head. "We'll need supplies first, like plenty of water, the Sandscar ruins are a decent distance!" remarked Nera as she pulled down the silky hood covering her head and approached the city gates. Like every other city Meadow had seen before this one, it had stalwart guards protecting its gates or diligently patrolling along its high stone walls.

The furry foxlike fenix seemed to don a mixture of light leather armour swathed in long flowing capes and silk or cloth hoods, likely to aid against the relentless heat of the desert. Most of their equipment appeared worn and well-used, their capes and hoods torn and frayed in various places and their armour seemingly cobbled together crudely yet still effective. Their weapons appeared as light as their clothing, most were armed with curved scimitar swords. Though the hilts were wrapped in cloth or leather, likely to stop them getting hot from the searing sun. Although their armour and weapons were not the same mighty weapons of war crafted by the master blacksmiths of Orstone. Meadow had heard how the Fenix relied on their cunning wits and superb agility to vanquish their foes instead.

Although the imposing iron gates were well guarded, they were at least open for now. Meadow guessed it was because of the surprising number of traders flowing out of them, "Fenix like to travel eh?" asked Meadow. "Scorchwind gets a fair number of visitors but not as many as we'd like, we often have to bring our goods to others to make coin" answered Nera as she spiritedly marched through the gates. Strangely, most of the traders were traveling on foot, with either a bulky backpack or a simple galamare to haul their goods, "Must be difficult traveling this desert" Clyde remarked.

Once they were inside the walls of the city, Nera couldn't resist browsing all the unique market stalls. Her gaze wandered between the assortment of glittering jewelry and her nose inhaled the aroma of exotic spices. "We fenix are well adapted to this kind of heat, our fur protects us, besides most traders travel to Orstone first and use it as a resting point since it's not too far" she explained. Orstone was only around thirty miles or so from Scorchwind now that Clyde thought about it, which clarified why a moderate number of orcs were also perusing the bustling bazaar. A mere stone throw away from the main city gates stood a pair of elegantly designed marble water fountains with fancy golden stars carved into their surface. Several fenix, a few orcs and a harpy sat around the pair of beautiful fountains. All of them chatted beside the sparkling blue water that gushed out, cherishing the bracing cool droplets that splashed against their skin. One of the fenix whom looked like a common citizen of the city learned forward, cupped his hands and took a refreshing sip from the fountain beside him. Clearly the water flowing from the fountains were for public consumption and graciously placed for any thirsty visitors just entering in city in desperate need of hydration.

Beyond the busy bazaar and the rows of sandy streets lay a grand marble palace that loomed over everything else in the city like a magnificent beacon of prosperity. Majestic towers sprouted like weeds all over the beautiful palace, all of which had been built with ornate spiralling and twisting spires while vibrant stained glass covered every window. "That's the palace of the grand tsar, the ruler of Scorchwind, only those of noble stature or with matters of great importance are granted an audience" uttered Nera upon seeing Meadow's astonished gawking face.

Market stalls lined the sandy streets of Scorchwind, some peddling rolls of glamourous silks that shone beautifully when they caught the reflective of light of the radiant sun. Other market stalls sold various colourful herbs, spices and flowers. All possessed such exotic odors and Meadow couldn't resist being enslaved by their intoxicating allure and leant closer to bombard her senses with their fascinating scents. Beyond that, there were an abundance of stalls flaunting a fabulously flashy array of gleaming gold jewelry, encrusted with sparkling jewels and gemstones of every conceivable color.

Truly, the city of Scorchwind was the real jewel of the desert, its markets prosperous and bustling, its architecture ornate and lavish. The very water sparkled like it were made of countless shiny gems and the many towering palm trees created lush spots of heavenly shade. Despite all this, much of the city was still buried beneath the sand, a fact Meadow and Clyde noticed the further they followed Nera inside. "This city is truly a wonder, but how much of it still lies buried?" Inquired Meadow. Scrupulously, Nera inspected the quality of goods lining the market stalls, taking care not to be lured in by some of the craftier merchants. "We're not sure, it might be over half the city is still buried, but we have diggers uncovering more and more of it every day!" Nera replied.

Nera wrapped her furry paws around a pair of apples being sold on a nearby fruit and vegetable stall and squeezed them hard to test their firmness. "It's one of the city's most ambitious projects right now and there's plenty of diggers hoping to uncover lost treasure and strike it rich!" she added. Once Nera had confirmed that the pair of apples, she picked up were juicy and ripe, she tossed them into a small leather sack tied to her waistbelt and handed over a handful of gold gleaming coins to the black furred fenix merchant. "Truth is, Scorchwind is ancient, legends say our ancestors were assaulted by a furious sandstorm caused by a huge monster which left most of the city buried" Nera added.

A local butcher was their next port of call, with Nera becoming engaged in a shrewd battle of tongues with the merchant. "I like you Nera, I really do, but I have to make a profit, I'll sell you that fine slice of salrodela meat for forty gold, okay?" uttered the merchant. Nera examined the juicy slab of salted salrodela meat and was subtly impressed by its freshness, but still attempted to bargain for a better price. "It looks fresh but if you lower it twenty gold, I will have plenty left to spend more" she answered.

The fenix butcher had pale, white fur almost like the color of smoke and more than a few scars along his face and body, indicating he might've been a hunter. "Curse you Nera, fine twenty gold! But only if you spend thirty more on my wares!" bartered the ash furred fenix butcher. "Deal!" Nera joyfully replied, gave a nod and proceeded to select a large, tender cut of salted fogfur meat, causing a vexed scowl to spread on the butcher's face. "Nera, that's fresh fogfur meat! Do you know how difficult it is to obtain and import!? I can't hunt that myself, I have to pay traders fees to acquire it!" he proclaimed. However, Nera produced a rather hefty pouch of gold coins and jingled it up and down in front of the merchant. "Eighty gold for both!" she offered, a bargain to which the butcher finally surrendered to.

Seeing their exchange impressed Clyde, yet also made him feel like he was imposing too much upon Nera as it was her own coin she was spending. "Nera, I thank you for purchasing such supplies for us, but are you sure it's no trouble?" he asked. Nera had the two chunky slabs of juicy salted meat wrapped and tied in sheets of parchment paper and slid them into the large linen sack slung over her shoulder. "After Soulspring this is the least I can do Clyde, I owe you greatly and I'm happy to assist" she answered.

After Nera had bartered and bought more vital supplies from a few other merchants scattered around the city, she decided it was best to depart soon. "Sunset is the best time to travel to the Sandscar ruins" she remarked. "We should arrive at the ruins by nightfall, which is when the Burning Plains are at their coolest, it will take half a day to reach the ruins by snazzle anyway" she explained. Seeing Nera in her home city made Clyde realize how much she was known, and how well she knew how to deal with the wily merchants that littered the streets. Truthfully, Clyde felt blessed that Nera was in the city at the time of their arrival, even more fortunate that she found him right away.

Finding a guide in this maze of streets and taking care not to be robbed of every coin by a sly merchant could've taken days. "I confess, I am surprised how much of an art haggling is and how labyrinthine these streets are, yet you seem to be a master at handling both, I take it you've missed your home?" asked Clyde. A delicate smile spread around Nera's furry snout and she gave a playful shrug as she strolled along the streets, "Maybe a little" she replied. "I admit, I've missed the feel of the soft warm sand beneath my paws, the exotic fruits and spices, the artful game of haggling with the merchants and seeing old friends of course" Nera added. Although Meadow was curious to ask why Nera didn't stay, Nera answered for her before she could ask. "But I have also grown attached to Soulspring and its people, I've made new friends there and I owe them a lot, besides, I enjoy the lush forests and cool air from time to time!" she remarked.

Outside Scorchwind's bulky, sandy oak gates, decorated with sturdy golden bolts and gold steel edges, the huge, scaly snake-like snazzle awaited. Ready to slither Clyde and Meadow across the shifting dunes of the desert and on to their destination. Nera approached the dauting beast and rested her palm upon the side of its shimmering jade body and tied the sacks of supplies she carried to the giant saddle upon its back. "I've convinced the stablemasters here to let me rent this snazzle for half-price, we're allowed to rent it up to the Sandscar Ruins but no further, otherwise it shall cost me an arm and a leg" uttered Nera.

Such a gesture provided a bountiful yield of delight to Meadow, for the journey would undoubtedly be much longer without the aid of a snazzle. Having to traverse the desolate dunes of the Burning Plains was also a thought she did not cherish. "Your generosity transcends the very heavens and stars my friend, alas it shames me to say that overwhelming gratitude is all I can do to show my thanks" Clyde remarked in a meek voice. Nera then proceeded to curl her furry paw into a fist and playfully punched Clyde in the arm. "Will you stop? Or have you forgotten how much you've done for me?" she answered.

Both shared a tender smile, with Clyde gently rubbing his arm, "Okay, fair point my dear, let us dismiss all debt and declare it even!" he cheerfully replied. Without delay and with the warm sunset now on their backs, it was time to depart the opulent city of Scorchwind and traverse the now crimson colored hills of the Burning plains. Once aboard the snazzle's back, Nera gripped the long leather reins attached to the creature's face, gave a firm yank and made a sound akin to imp quickly chuckling twice in a row. Upon hearing the sound, the mighty snazzle began to slither across the coarse desert sand, gradually picking up speed as it glided away from the magnificent walls of Scorchwind.

Going straight ahead was all that needed to be done for now, hence why Nera released her grip upon the leather reins. She knew full well that a tamed snazzle will simply keep slithering in one direction until commanded otherwise. "Now all we have to do is sit and wait, the Sandscar Ruins are easy to find but exhausting to reach, unless you're travelling upon the back of a snazzle" explained Nera. Despite danger likely looming on the horizon of their journey, Meadow took a long, captivated gaze at the ever-sinking sunset beyond. She admired the ruby colored luminosity radiating from it and basked in the tingly, warm desert breeze as the snazzle continued to sail along.

She felt a tranquil peace befall her and reveled in the feeling of the pleasant sandy wind as it flowed through the long locks of her fiery hair, "It feels serene" she remarked. Nera overheard her and decided to partake in gazing upon the glowing scenery as well. "I know, I remember I used to sneak off to watch the sunset with a boy I admired when I was younger" she answered. "We'd sit upon the tallest dune and watch for hours, sometimes in complete silence while holding hands, I've missed it greatly" Nera whispered.

As Meadow imagined the scene in her mind, she thought to ask one question. "Let me guess, did the boy you were with say that you were the still the most beautiful view of all?" she asked. Nera chuckled at her comment and responded with an amused nod, "He did actually, and I remember telling him that he wasn't looking for long enough then" she answered. Both girls covered their mouths to try and stop their laughter from spilling out. "Boys, they can be so predictable!" chuckled Meadow, rubbing away a small tear of laughter from the corner of her eye. Meanwhile, Clyde watched them from the seat on the opposite end of the carriage with profound perplexity. "Confound it, such mysterious creatures! The mystery of women will continue to elude me" he uttered after fruitlessly rubbing his chin.

Sunset gradually turned into dusk and the burning red dunes slowly became a shade of shadowy purple. But, the sight of ancient, crumbling ruins, half-buried beneath the sand popped into view. Meadow had dozed off from the trip and Clyde was halfway into a deep slumber when Nera's loud voice shattered their sleepiness. "We're here, The Sandscar ruins!" she barked. Meadow awoke with a jolt, her eyes quickly flicking open and she emitted a drowsy yawn, "Ugh! I must've nodded off from the desert sun!" she remarked.

At the same time, the snazzle came to an abrupt halt when Nera firmly yanked backwards on the leather reins. "Sadly, this is as far as I can go! I have no idea what lies beyond the ruins" she uttered. Ghostly whistles of midnight wind blew through the nooks and crannies of the ancient, towers and weathered walls of the battle-scarred ruins. "Are you sure? I thank you greatly for being our guide Nera, but will you be safe travelling back to Scorchwind at night?" asked Clyde.

Nera wrapped her furry arms around Clyde and hugged him tightly. "I'll be fine, travelling back to Scorchwind at night is easy by snazzle, but I'm afraid I wouldn't be much of a guide any further than here" she answered. Clyde returned her caring hug with one of his own and playfully ruffled the top of her furry mane with his hand. "In that case, I bid you farewell my fluffy friend, may the heavens watch over you!" he declared. Except, Nera couldn't depart before selecting Meadow as her next hug victim. "Stay safe Meadow, I know you'll be a legendary alchemist someday, just promise to look after Clyde and see he doesn't get into too much trouble" she uttered.

Nera's tender gesture of emotion touched Meadow's heart and made her realize how much she cherished the friendship they formed. "Ha, if anything I'm usually the one dragging that oddball into trouble, but I promise!" she answered. Once she had hopped back onto the carriage attached to the snazzle, Nera gave a final fond farewell wave goodbye. Then she pulled the reins to reposition the beast and commanded it to slither away, back towards the sandy city of Scorchwind. Swiftly, Nera vanished into the shadowy void of the desert horizon, becoming consumed by the veil of night. "These ruins shall provide suitable shelter until morning" said Clyde as he watched her. A sudden gust of chilly wind infiltrated Meadow's clothing and caressed her arms, causing goose bumps to spread across her skin and a shiver to her spine. "Lead the way, anything to escape the nippy bite of this wind, can't believe it becomes this cold at night!" Meadow moaned, hopping up and down to shake the chill from her bones.

A tall, ruined tower of stone was the spot Clyde had selected to make camp. Half of it was buried beneath the sea of sand, while the other half rested at an angle that was far from straight. To their good fortune, enough wood still lay around inside the battle-scarred fortifications. Clyde was able to get a small campfire going and currently roasted one of the thick slabs of meat that Nera bought from the market in Scorchwind.

Luminous firelight shone upon the crumbling stonework of the tower as Meadow and Clyde sat upon the soft sand and huddled around the little campfire watching its golden flames flicker and dance. "What will you do if you end up meeting Lorenzo again? You think it will end in bloodshed?" asked Meadow as she inched her hands closer towards the warmth of the fire. In truth Clyde hadn't thought about it or maybe he was trying not to. Regardless, his thoughtful silence and reluctance to answer Meadow's question said more than the words of a hundred books. Instead, Clyde decided to poke and prod the campfire with a short wooden stick and carefully watched the hunk of beast meat to change into a juicy brown. "When I was just a child growing up in my village, before Elijah razed it to the ground, I remember a moment when I was quite mean and made him cry" uttered Meadow.

Desperate to occupy his mind with anything other than Lorenzo, Clyde ceased poking the campfire and keep his focus frozen upon Meadow. "Although our woodland village was quaint and isolated, we had a baker who made the most delicious sticky buns" added Meadow. A distant howl of a desert beast and the sudden snap of burning campfire wood intruded upon the tale for a moment. But Meadow allowed the atmosphere to settle before speaking again. "Giant doughy sticky buns, glazed with the sweetest honey, layered with the freshest cream and dotted with flaked chocolate and juicy plomberries, ugh! They were amazing!" Meadow declared, practically drooling.

A raised eyebrow from Clyde indicated that he was curious to know where she was heading with this story. "As utterly delicious as these sticky buns sound, are you making a point or merely seeking to torture me with the imagery?" asked Clyde. Although his tone ruffled Meadow's temper slightly, she overlooked his snarky comment and promptly hurried towards the meat of the story. "One day I used some of the gold I had been saving up that week and went to buy one as they were my most favorite treat" she continued. While telling her tale, Meadow causally scrawled crude drawings into the sand using her finger while appearing lost in thought. "As I went to the village bakery to buy one, I realized Elijah had bought the last one, there were no more left, and it really irked me" Meadow uttered.

Her story started to intrigue Clyde, so much so that he had to keep remembering to push around the sizzling slab of juicy meat over the campfire. "I saw Elijah walk off with the sticky bun, likely to go and meet his sister, so I followed him, waited until he was alone, then confronted him and demanded he hand the treat over" explained Meadow. A sudden trail of black smoke from the meat made Clyde quickly jerk it away from the fire, "And did he?" he asked. Dismay descended upon Meadow as she shook her head. "He offered to share it with me, but I refused, I wanted all of the sticky bun, I had been saving up and craved it, so I swiped it from his hands and forcefully shoved him to the floor" she replied. Memories of her home village that Meadow once assumed buried began to bubble to the surface of her mind again. "Elijah was always known as quite a cry-baby and he was no different when I shoved him, but what stuck with me most was I never apologized" Meadow uttered.

Upon reciting the childhood tale, a glassy gleam sparkled in her eyes, "I felt so bad afterwards, I obtained my sticky bun, but was it really worth the pain I inflicted?" asked Meadow. "Sometimes I wonder, if I hadn't been so mean to Elijah that day, would he still have destroyed the village? Would things have turned out differently?" she added. Clyde pondered her tale, then let his head powerlessly droop once he was aware of the meaning Meadow was trying to make. "I too wonder where the hand of destiny would've dropped Lorenzo had I not been so quick to succumb to my own selfish desire" he mumbled.

It brought no delight to see Clyde lost in a pitiful fog of doubt, devoid of light, but she graced his ears with one last uttering of wisdom. "However, despite what I did to Elijah, it was still his choice to destroy my village and kill all my family and friends, I don't blame myself and you shouldn't either Clyde" uttered Meadow. A small shimmer of solace shined brightly upon Clyde's face, creasing his frown into a fragile smile at the sound of Meadow's wise words. Sadly, they weren't enough to quell the harrowing hurricane currently whirling around inside the tormented prison of lament that was Clyde's soul. "Thank you Meadow, your loyalty and support as both an apprentice and a friend has proven to be instrumental and I treasure it greatly, but for now, we should eat and rest, we shall need plenty of stamina for tomorrow" he uttered.

Sleeping in a forgotten sand swept tower amidst an ancient battlefield littered with the rusty blades and decaying bones of fallen warriors was not Meadow's ideal camping spot. Yet options were in short supply and the crumbling tower provided shelter from the chilly night air at least. The sand beneath them also proved comfortable enough to curl up and sleep on, and the warm campfire burned for most of the night. It was not a comfortable night's rest by any means, but it was just for one night since the morning desert sun soon came and woke Meadow by blasting her in face with its hot rays.

The scorching light beamed though the various cracks and holes scattered across the tilted tower and Meadow begun the morning by shielding her eyes against the dazzling light. "Ugh, Clyde? Is it time to continue our journey?" she groaned, surveying their small campsite in the tower, still half-blind. Clyde sat across from her, leaning against the stone tower, using its wall as support while he slept, but awoke upon hearing her voice. "Ugh, yeah, I think time dictates we resume!" he declared while stretching his arms up high.

Now that the sun had risen again, the desert looked and felt a whole lot different. The purplish dunes of night had been replaced by endless stretches of burning gold and the cool breeze replaced with sweltering heat. After stretching the last lingering feeling of sleep from their bodies, Clyde concluded it was time to resume to hunt for the fabled Shimmermyst tower. "Before we take another step across this desolate wasteland of boundless sand, I declare that we imbibe the fire resistance potions I formulated my ever-loyal lackey!" Clyde insisted. Already the searing heat was sapping the energy from Meadow's body, hence the reason she swiped one of the vials from Clyde's outstretched hand with all haste. "I had to make the mixture far weaker to make it last longer, it will stave off the heat for several hours, perhaps I should name it heat resistance potion!" Clyde joked with a hearty laugh.

After twisting the cork from the neck of the glass potion vial, Meadow heard that familiar, satisfying pop sound, "Don't take up comedy!" she replied. Meadow then quaffed the entire mixture of bright, butter colored liquid and tossed the empty vial over her shoulder. "Now where do we go from here?" she asked, her voice trailing off with a deep sigh of comfort as she felt the relentless heat fade. Clyde gulped his vial of precious potion, released a refreshed gasp and wiped his chin clean with his sleeve. "The second part of the clue states that we are to find a crescent spire" he answered. A blank, baffled gaze persisted within Meadow's eyes as she regarded his words. "Your expression says it all but fear not! For the first clue says to follow the ruins and stay the course!" added Clyde.

With no better theories or ideas rising to the surface, Meadow yielded to his and shrugged, "Okay then, let's keep following the ruins" she uttered. It sounded simple enough, but the ruins of this ancient battlefield seemed to stretch for miles into the distance, for it was built like an ancient frontline wall. So began the long march across the sandy dunes of the Burning Plains, Clyde and Meadow followed the trails of crumbling towers, decaying bones, rusty swords and shattered shields. They were travelling along a path of war and death, a place ripe with nothing but empty howls of wind and the ominous cawing of vultures. A path few had travelled and even fewer returned from.

Even with the heat being suppressed from the potions they had taken they still had to rest every so often, for traversing the deep sands and steep hills proved laborious. Quenching the arid desert in their mouths with fresh water was of course a regular labor, but Meadow began to show glimmers of concern the further their waterskins emptied. Onwards and onwards, they marched, step after step, travelling east into the ever-expanding region of the Burning Plains, the largest unmapped region of Resplendia.

Occasional sandstorms would whip up and bluster them from head to toe. Bombarding them with a maelstrom of sand and wind, further hindering their progress and trying to misdirect them. One furious sandstorm lasted for nearly an hour and made any kind of travel almost impossible. Yet Clyde and Meadow refused to halt, they covered their faces with cloth hoods and stubbornly marched on, following the seemingly endless wall of crumbling ruins and broken towers. It had to be midday now, as the beaming sun of dandelion yellow had shifted into a deep, blazing red. Making the desert sands look like they were made of cinnamon and by this point the heat resistance potions had worn off.

Sweat trickled along the side of Meadow's face as she jadedly trudged behind Clyde, until at last they reached the final fortification at the end of the sprawling, ancient battlefield. Several hours had passed by this point, several hours of ceaseless wandering, a testament to how expansive the battlefield was. Yet there was no sign of anything significant, nothing except boundless stretches of sand as far as the eye could see. "There are no more ruins to follow, so where now?" groaned Meadow, before collapsing from the heat and falling face first into the sand.

Upon seeing Meadow topple like a pile of wobbly stones, Clyde tried to rush to her side. Unfortunately, with his stamina drained he could only wearily stagger to her instead, "Come on Meadow, don't give up now!" he groaned. Unable to find the fortitude to remain standing, Clyde soon joined Meadow and dropped to his hands and knees, "It's probably...only...a little bit......farther now!" he panted. Without rest and shade from the burning crimson sun, Clyde succumbed to fatigue and flopped onto his face, practically burying his head in the sand. Like an exhausted starfish, Clyde spread his body out and refused to move, "Okay, maybe just a short rest! Maybe it's a good idea!" he mumbled. He and Meadow lay on the sand next to each other for what seemed like ages, both searching for the strength to arise again and muster on. But it became clear why very few had ever travelled this far before, it was just fortunate that the sun had begun to descend again. Which also meant the heat was gradually diminishing, "What do we do now? There's nothing here" groaned Meadow.

Her remark was valid, for when she finally summoned the strength to pull herself up and view the horizon, she saw nothing but vast stretches of empty dunes. Despair seeped into Meadow's soul as she emptily watched the windy desert plains stretching far into the distance. But suddenly, something caught her eye, something she was drawn towards. Intrigued by the sight of this new entity, Meadow squinted her view and studied it carefully, "Wait, what is that? Is that the spire? Or is it merely a mirage?" she uttered. With seemingly tremendous effort, Clyde raised his face from the dirt, shook his head and spat a mouthful of sand from his lips. "What? What's going on? Are we dead yet!?" he sputtered.

Something stood in the near distance of the desert, something Meadow hadn't noticed until now, mainly because it blended in quite well with the sandy background. However, the longer Meadow gazed at the object, the more she could discern what it was. Then, when a gleam of sunlight sparkled from upon its surface, she knew it was no mirage. It was a small twinkle, just a brief flash, but Meadow caught sight of it, and it caused her to leap to her feet. "It's made of gold, a spire made of gold!" she declared excitedly. Without another moment's delay, Meadow began dashing towards the looming gold spire in the distance, her spirt becoming revitalized with hope. "Meadow wait for me!" cried Clyde as he dragged himself off the sand and gave chase, stumbling and almost falling right back down as he tried to find his footing again. Amazingly, the golden spire was much closer than Meadow realized, it was just so well hidden among the golden dunes of the desert. In fact, if they hadn't stopped to rest, there was a good chance they would've travelled by it entirely.

Upon reaching the solid, looming pillar of gold protruding from the sand, Meadow slapped her palms upon it and leaned against it in a huff. "This must be it, look! There's a crescent shape at the top!" she wheezed. Breathlessly, Clyde turned his gaze upwards and examined the top of the golden spire. A fatigued grin of joy crawled along his jaw when he noticed the crescent moon shape elaborately crafted into the peak. A stunning blue jewel of impressive size also rested in the center of the crescent moon, held by a thin golden pedestal. "Yes, this must be it! We have reached the second part of the clue!" announced Clyde.

Using the slender golden spire as shade, Clyde fell and slumped his back against it and took a vital gulp of precious water from his flask. As the cool shade shielded Clyde from the persisting, burning wrath of the sun, he rested his head back and cherished this moment of respite. Locating the next clue on their arduous journey was as welcome as the finest elven wine at a banquet. Yet alone it did not solve the dire circumstance Meadow and Clyde still found themselves in. "Well, instead of dying from hunger or thirst, we can wait for a nice desert beast to come and give us a quick death" joked Meadow upon joining Clyde's side.

They found shade but were still in the middle of nowhere, lost in a windy wasteland with nothing but sand to see every time they turned their heads. And no company except the sound of barren gusts and haunting howls in the distance. "Do not yield to fear yet, the third and final clue hints that we must wait until the sun is nearly dead and I remain certain that moment is when the sun has almost set" groaned Clyde. His usual bravado had diminished, no doubt depleted by the roasting heat and tiresome journey. Hence silence between the two of them followed as they patiently waited. However, Meadow soon began to ponder what they were waiting for, what did she think was going to happen now? She would've complained but lacked the energy to do so, thus, they waited, and waited, and waited some more. Both remained silent and slumped against the side of the golden spire, relishing the increasingly cool breeze as the sun faded. Until finally, just as Clyde was on the verge of questioning what he was doing here. The final moment of sunset arrived.

When it did, his eyes suddenly beheld what was possibly the most magnificent sight he had seen so far. For as the sun gradually dipped beneath the horizon behind them, its warm rays beamed directly through the giant, sparkling blue jewel embedded in the peak of the golden crescent spire. The suns radiant rays became an alluring shade of ghostly azure, and shone directly across the desert, "Meadow, Look!" gasped Clyde. "What?" uttered Meadow as she turned her slumped head around and found her jaw dropping with as she gazed upon the splendid sight now revealed to them.

A gigantic mystical tower made of strange, gleaming crystal had suddenly appeared before them. A tower whose heavenly walls sparkled like mirrors and shimmered before the luminous blue light, "Shimmermyst tower!" gasped Meadow. Every single one of Clyde's nerves began to twitch and tingle with excitement, "It was here all along, it was merely invisible until the light revealed it!" he spluttered. Naturally, Meadow and Clyde swiftly jumped to their feet and promptly hurried to the tower with all haste, "Quickly my apprentice!" Clyde remarked. "The light of the fading sun reveals the tower, if we delay too long, I'm sure the tower shall vanish from all sight again!" he declared, frantically dashing towards the main doors of the beautiful bastion. Such a mythical, marvelous discovery, Meadow was admittedly speechless as she ran towards the sparkling, glittering fortress of mystery.

She felt like an insignificant dung beetle when her gaze kept turning upwards to look upon the looming palace of shining crystal. Every square foot of the tower seemed to sparkle like it was built from the essence of stars and plummeted straight from the heavens long ago. Even more mysteriously, many parts of the tower seemed to vanish when it wasn't exposed to the constant shifting light of the sunset, like it was made of ethereal swirling smoke. Yet, here it was, the magical Shimmermyst tower of legend, a discovery for the ages.

When Meadow and Clyde finally, breathlessly approached its large, pearly crystal doors, they couldn't help tremble with delight. "Well, here it is my apprentice, the end of our long journey, we've found the fabled Shimmermyst tower! Inside its walls we will find the Chalice of Renewal at last!" announced Clyde. Meadow shared his sentiment and displayed a fulfilled smile, "I have to admit, its been quite the experience with you Clyde!" she answered. On that Clyde could agree, but every step they had taken together was finally worth it. "I want to thank you Meadow, you've helped me find the chance to redeem myself and correct a mistake I was partly to blame for" he uttered.

Once they had savored the moment, Meadow and Clyde realigned their focus onto the lustrous white doors of the crystal tower and eagerly strode towards it. "Ah, it seems I arrived just in time!" growled a sudden sinister voice from behind, causing Clyde and Meadow to quickly spin around. Spears of dismay pierced their hearts, for upon turning around to confront the culprit of the voice, they were met with the horrifying sight of Lorenzo's scarred face. A twisted, repulsive smirk spread over his maimed lips as he pulled down the shadowy black hood covering his head. His arrival was both unwelcome and unnerving, filling Clyde and Meadow with dread and paralyzing them to the spot. "Yes, I'm afraid I have that effect on people!" Lorenzo menacingly joked.

Chalice of Renewal
Chapter 13
War of the potions

Time was running out, it wouldn't be long before the beaming sunlight vanished, along with Shimmermyst tower, rendering it invisible once again. Yet, despite knowing this, Clyde remained in a frozen state of uneasy tension, "Lorenzo, please! I'm sorry, I succumbed to a weak moment of foolishness!" spluttered Clyde. His attempts to negotiate proved fruitless, for it only made Lorenzo clench his fists and scowl further. "Which part Clyde? Burning my face? Or stealing my wife!?" he growled. Lorenzo's fury and hate were palpable, but he suddenly averted his gaze towards the peak of Shimmermyst tower and keenly admired it, "Beautiful isn't it?" he asked. "I've been following your trail, in truth I worried I wouldn't be able to catch up, but here I am! The chalice is mine!" Lorenzo proclaimed.

An ominous gust of desert wind blew over the scene and the sight of Lorenzo's maimed smirking face chilled Clyde and Meadow to the bone. "Lorenzo, I implore you! Claim the chalice, but do not destroy it! Heal your face then let me use it to undo the curse upon Ruby, she is innocent!" Clyde pleaded. Sadly, the furious fiery gleam of odium that flashed within Lorenzo's eyes proved he was not open to debate. "Why? Just so she can hate me forever or fall into another man's arms!? Maybe yours!?" he bellowed.

Lorenzo was far from peaceful, a raging meteor storm of malice bombarded his thoughts, "I shall heal my face with the chalice and then destroy it!" he yelled. "Once the chalice is destroyed, I swear Clyde I shall maim you with the same torment I've had to endure all these years!" Lorenzo roared. Never had Clyde witnessed such overwhelming spite and rage, it was on a level so intense that he felt a sudden spike of trembling fear slither through his entire body. "No matter what, I won't let you have what you want!" Lorenzo shouted in a ferocious snarl.

Meadow had seen it before though, she had seen hatred of this caliber, she saw it with Elijah. "Forget it Clyde, he's not going to listen! He needs some sense knocking into him!" she cried. Although Meadow's comment stoked the burning flames of hatred within Lorenzo's heart, he regarded her with sympathy. "And you, Clyde's new puppet! Betray him before he betrays you, for it seems to be what he does best!" he hissed. This caused Meadow to narrow her eyes and vigilantly glare upon Lorenzo with anger and disgust. "Anyway, I tire of talking, your both in my way!" Lorenzo suddenly boomed.

Swiftly, he reached into the depths of his coat, revealed a vial of potion, firmly yanked the top off and proceeded to quaff it down his throat, "What did he just take!?" cried Meadow. "I...I'm not sure, it could be storm-breath potion!" Clyde hastily gasped as Lorenzo suddenly belched and unleased a blustering cyclone of wind from his mouth. Shock followed as Clyde and Meadow were quickly scooped up by the whistling maelstrom of white wind and flung aside like a pair of forgotten toys. The screeching whirlwind erupting from Lorenzo's mouth only lasted several seconds, but confusion lingered as Meadow and Clyde were slammed into the sand.

Lorenzo took this opportunity to dash past them and head to the front doors of the tower unobstructed, "Storm-breath potion? How is that even possible!?" cried Meadow in a daze. "Because alchemy that's how! Even I don't know how to make that potion!" growled Clyde. Lorenzo wasted no time in hurrying towards the entrance of the giant shimmering tower and pressed his arms against its colossal crystal doors. He gave the doors a mighty shove, only to not even slightly budge them. "Hmmm, a test, it seems one has to possess great strength to even step into the towers halls" Lorenzo muttered, reaching for another vial of potion concealed within his cloaked harness.

Meanwhile, Meadow and Clyde were left eating the sand, but after shaking it from their hair and spitting it from their mouths, they staggered back onto their feet. "We must make haste; I can see the tower beginning to disappear!" Clyde declared, gazing upwards and pointing his finger. The truth was clear to see, for the lower the sun plummeted beneath the horizon, the more Shimmermyst tower became invisible again. Meadow spotted Lorenzo again in the distance, but he appeared spectral, like a ghost, "Then let's get in there!" she growled with fiery resolve. Tremendous strength proved unnecessary for Lorenzo; a quick gulp of ethereal potion solved the test involving the terribly heavy doors. Lorenzo had become like a phantom, his entire body a translucent ghostly blue, meaning he was able to stride straight through the gleaming doors like they weren't even there.

By the time Clyde and Meadow had begun approaching the doors, Lorenzo was nowhere to be seen. "He must've gone through, but those doors look heavy, quick Meadow! Ethereal potion!" declared Clyde. Obeying his command, Meadow swiped a vial of ethereal potion from her harness, firmly yanked the cork from its glass neck and quaffed the liquid down her throat as she ran. Clyde quickly mimicked her and upon guzzling his own vial of mysterious ethereal potion, he and Meadow appeared as a pair of spooky spirits sprinting across the sand. Only the last fragments of fleeting sunset remained, the burning rays beaming through the lustrous blue jewel had almost entirely faded. Thus, only the main entrance of Shimmermyst Tower was visible now. Clyde had no idea what awaited inside, but he refused to allow Lorenzo to claim the Chalice of Renewal after he spent so long searching for it, so he and Meadow recklessly charged right in.

Through the pair of twinkling, white crystal doors they dashed, both easily materializing upon the other side thanks to the ethereal potion, just in time to be confronted by Lorenzo again. Amazement awaited inside the crystal tower, for greater beauty was found within, "Incredible!" gasped Meadow as she took a couple of steps forward and gazed all around. "Yes, truly, it is a legend more fantastic than I could've imagined" uttered Lorenzo, who remained fixated upon a hunk of sparkling, levitating crystal as it floated through the air.

He appeared fascinated with the chunk of silvery-blue crystal as it floated by him, his eyes peering deeply into its depths. But it was only one of many more in the room, as Clyde and Meadow quickly noticed the entire tower was made of majestic crystal. Inside the towers walls hundreds more chunks of crystal dotted the air, all of them different shapes and sizes. Some crystals were no bigger than beach pebbles, while others were larger than watermelons, but whatever magic existed in this tower made them calmly float around like gentle clouds. "This tower has already proven itself fascinating, I've already discovered the magic behind these crystals, if one peers into them, they act as mirrors into the past!" Lorenzo proclaimed. If that were true, it explained why Lorenzo was peering so deeply into the chunk of crystal floating closest to him. "Why not peer into one yourself Clyde? Take a gaze into the past! Or are you too ashamed!?" Lorenzo growled.

A small piece of magical crystal floated right by Clyde just as Lorenzo spoke these words, alas Clyde was far too afraid to stare into it. "I have not sought out this tower to reflect upon the past Lorenzo, I am truly sorry for what I did, but all I can do is try and mend the present!" Clyde fired back. No sooner after Clyde had finished speaking, the ethereal potion him, Meadow and Lorenzo had all taken suddenly wore off, their corporeal flesh swiftly returning to their bodies. "That crystal I just gazed into showed me visions of my past, the moments were random, but it showed her, it showed Ruby! It showed us together and how happy we were!" Lorenzo angrily hissed.

Tense silence engulfed the large, circular room made of a twinkling mixture of turquoise blue, emerald green and plum purple crystal. Until Lorenzo's unhinged, mutilated face contorted into a repulsive smirk again. "The chalice will be mine and when it is, I will be able to cast aside this new face you gave me Clyde!" Lorenzo announced as he raised his shadowy black mask and attached it to his face. Caution flooded Meadow and Clyde as they warily watched Lorenzo, waiting to see what his next move would be. Which took the form of him quickly nabbing another potion from his harness again.

Regrettably, Lorenzo was too far away from Meadow and Clyde to wrestle the potion from his grasp. Hence, Lorenzo succeeded in hastily unbottling the neck of the vial and consumed the glittering, glowing blue liquid within. Clyde was unsure which potion Lorenzo had just devoured, for it appeared to be one he didn't fully recognize again. However, Clyde quickly became aware of its effects, for Lorenzo suddenly spewed a screeching bolt of blue lightning from his mouth and blasted Clyde straight in the chest. As soon as the screaming bolt of lightning touched Clyde, it shattered the mystical ambience in circular crystal hall with a thundering boom.

Clyde was flung backwards from the ear-splitting bolt of crackling lightning and painfully slammed against the main door behind. "Behold Clyde, I call it bolt-breath potion!" Lorenzo cackled, then made a dash for the twisting, crystal staircase built into the side of the tower. "Clyde!" Meadow cried as she watched him collapse onto the floor and utter a groan of agony. Hot white smoke rose from his clothes, thankfully, Meadow could see Clyde was still breathing. Although it was painful, the bolt of lightning didn't seem as powerful as a real one, however, it remained powerful enough to daze him.

Above her, Meadow could hear Lorenzo's echoing laugh and she couldn't simply stand by and allow Lorenzo to claim the chalice so easily, hence she foolishly pursued him alone. The spiral, crystal staircase built into the side of the magical tower seemed to stretch all the way to the top, making it quite the climb. But Meadow remained determined to catch up to Lorenzo and stop him at any cost. However, several steps along the staircase later, large pillars of crystal began sliding in and out of the very walls of the tower, at quite a modest speed, "What the heck!?" Meadow cried.

It was as though the entire tower had suddenly come alive and as the thick columns of crystal shifted in and out of the walls, Meadow had to dodge in and out of them. It was either that or risk being pushed right off the side of the spiralling staircase and down to the bottom again. Thankfully, this somewhat evened the field, as it also slowed Lorenzo down, his path becoming blocked when a pillar of crystal abruptly flew out of the wall in front of him before he could cross. "Fascinating, this entire tower must be magically enchanted somehow!" Lorenzo remarked while waiting for the column of crystal to slide back into the wall.

Another column of crystal began pushing its way out of the wall in front of Meadow's path as she ran, but she managed to notice it in time and took a great leapt forward. Although she took a slight tumble from flinging her body, Meadow recovered with a smooth roll and dodged the pushing crystal pillar before it had chance to obstruct her path. Lorenzo watched her catching up from above and as more pillars of crystal began pushing and pulling out of the walls, he decided the spiral staircase wasn't the best place to deal with her. Thus, Lorenzo took flight and hurried ever higher along the twisting staircase with Meadow hot on his trail, "What's the matter? Scared!?" she yelled up at him.

Interestingly, upon climbing the winding path of spiralling, sparkling steps, a large circular platform made entirely of crystal hovered in the air in the middle of the tower shaft. The spiralling steps built into the side of the tower also ended abruptly, nothing but a deadly fall remained, "It seems I must jump!" Lorenzo remarked. Another set of curving crystal stairs also lay upon the other side of the tower, indicating the floating platform in the center was the only way to reach them. After taking a quick downward glance at the plummeting drop below, Lorenzo took a deep breath and performed a running jump towards the levitating platform. Successfully leaping over the empty gap and landing safely upon the crystal surface.

Impact from the landing briefly hindered Lorenzo and just as he was on the verge of finding his footing again and taking another running leap to the stairs on the other side, Meadow caught up. Her resolve was fierce and her spirit fearless, for she charged towards the floating platform and threw herself at it with reckless abandon. Shock seized Lorenzo as he turned around to face Meadow, only to see her fly and crash right into him, causing them both to tumble and roll across the platform. Vigorously, they both wrestled and rolled, reaching the edge of the circular platform and risking their lives to a plummeting drop all the way back to the entrance. That was until crystal bars magically formed all around the edges of the crystal platform and stretched upwards, each joining into a center point, making the platform appear like a levitating birdcage. Lorenzo painfully slammed against the crystal bars of the cage but managed to throw Meadow off him and the two of them were now trapped in the cage together.

Lorenzo traded glares with Meadow as they slowly climbed to their feet, "Clyde's apprentice! Meadow, right? You must be very brave or foolish to chase me alone girl!" Lorenzo taunted. "I'm just sick and tired of chasing your trail! You'll pay for all the trouble you've caused!" Meadow fired back and reached for one of the potions strapped to her harness. Lorenzo swiftly discerned that it was a vial of fire-breath potion Meadow had plucked from her harness, thus he quickly reached for one of his own mixtures in retaliation.

With all haste, Meadow ripped the cork head from the neck of the vial and guzzled down the potion, meanwhile Lorenzo proceeded to do the same with his. "Burn!" Meadow shouted as she unleashed a blazing belch of searing hot flames from her mouth, engulfing Lorenzo within the dancing stream of scorching flames. Despite erupting such a fiery onslaught, once the blistering flames had faded, Lorenzo emerged utterly unharmed. "Ha, fire resistance potion!" announced Lorenzo as he looked upon Meadow's dismayed face. Attempting to seize the upper hand, Lorenzo swiftly countered Meadow's attack with one of his own and nabbed a bottle of what appeared like frost-breath potion from his cloaked harness.

This was the moment when Meadow was incredibly grateful to Clyde for helping her identify various types of potions merely by looking at their color, consistency and vibrancy. All that crafting Meadow did while Clyde was busy also aided her in identifying potions and she knew exactly which potion to retrieve from her trusty harness. Once again, her and Lorenzo ended up pulling out of their vials and consuming their potions at roughly the same time. "Freeze!" yelled Lorenzo as he exhaled a chilly mist of freezing frost from his mouth, enveloping Meadow within its white, icy grasp.

Thankfully, Lorenzo's frosty breath was rendered futile as Meadow endured the frigid mist like it was a pleasant summer breeze. "Ice resistance potion!" she declared with a smug grin. Gradually, the bitter glacial mist spewing from Lorenzo's mouth vanished and Meadow remained completely unfazed and unfrozen. "Impressive, Clyde taught you well girl!" Lorenzo growled. "You've managed to alter your potions so their effects trigger almost instantly which is vital, for the time it takes a potions effects to trigger can mean the difference between life and death" he uttered.

With a scowl, Meadow snatched hold of another potion from her harness, "Let's just skip the lessons, I already have a master!" she snapped. This time, Meadow unbottled a vial of sticky-breath potion, a new one she learned to concoct and was eager to test it out and put the vial to her lips. Although Lorenzo tried to react by reaching for a potion of his own, he reacted slightly too late and Meadow fired a slimy blob of viscous green goo from her gob. Disgust smeared Lorenzo's face followed by a spear of pain as the sticky green blob stuck to his chest and slammed him against the side of the crystal bars of the cage. "Ugh, Effective but the taste really needs improving!" Meadow announced then teased Lorenzo with a playful wave, for the glob of goo had rendered him firmly stuck.

With Lorenzo tightly trapped against the bars of the crystal cage by the large ball of sticky green goo, Meadow was free to slurp another flask of potion and escape. Although her stock of ethereal potion had depleted, Meadow decided to consume another unique potion she had recently learned to craft. One that possessed a thin, watery consistency with an ashen grey hue to it. Upon consuming this new potion, which tasted like a mouthful of hazy smoke, Meadow's entire body disappeared and turned into a swirling cloud of grey mist.

In her new mist form, Meadow was able to easily travel through the bars of the cage like a plume of smoke, unlike ethereal potion, mist-form potion allowed her to float as well. Thus, Meadow floated towards the other side of the tower chamber and onto the next set of long spiralling steps, sadly the mist-form potion lasted far less longer than ethereal potion. Hence it only took a several seconds before Meadow's misty form faded and her earthly, physical body popped back into existence.

Still, she escaped the cage and didn't delay in hurrying along the next set of glittering crystal stairs, following them ever upwards, hoping the top of the tower was near. Meadow had achieved the lead in the race to the peak of the tower and infuriated Lorenzo immensely, but he refused to surrender, he wriggled and trashed against the viscous blob of slime binding him. After much forceful struggling, Lorenzo managed to wrestle an arm free, "Fine, two can play that game!" he growled as he grasped a flask of potion from his harness. Using his teeth, Lorenzo then yanked the cork from the neck of the bottle and chugged down the magical mixture within, his body also becoming a swirling plume of pallid mist. This allowed Lorenzo to easily escape Meadow's goo trap and the floating crystal cage and continue the pursuit after her.

Meadow had made quite a significant stride of progress up the tower; in fact, she was worryingly far higher than Lorenzo desired. So as soon as his new misty form escaped the cage trap and his worldly body returned, he instantly acted. A stern frown smeared his face as his glaring gaze turned upwards and watched meadow climb the spiral staircase above him, "You won't escape me girl!" he shouted. From within his cloaked harness, Lorenzo revealed another vial of mysterious tonic, this one glowing with a deep amber. With no time to waste, he gulped the entire concoction down his throat and a pair of radiant golden wings sprouted upon Lorenzo's back. Lorenzo smiled sinisterly as he quickly took flight and eagerly flew after Meadow.

All the way back down at the front doors of Shimmermyst tower, Clyde began to stir again, and he slowly roused from his unconscious state. "That was quite the shocking experience!" he joked while shaking the numbness and pain from his body. His attention became abruptly ensnared by one of the towers numerous floating crystals as it drifted right by his face. The small chunk of reflective crystal showed him flashes of the past as he gazed upon it. It showed memories of him, Ruby and Lorenzo when they were together, living peacefully and happily.

Images of the babbling river appeared upon the sparkling crystal, the same river Clyde and Ruby would sit beside in the sun and laugh together. More painful memories began to appear the longer Clyde investigated the floating piece of magical crystal, memories of the accident in the lab, when Lorenzo's face was forever destroyed. Clyde watched the memoires play out upon the crystal like he was watching a tragic stage play and witnessed the horror upon Lorenzo's face as the alchemy mixture scarred his skin.

Then of course came the memory which led to Clyde seeking out the tower in the first place, the day Ruby turned to stone. The day had been captured in perfect detail, the roaring rain, the yells of hatred, anger and the sight of fear and sadness upon Ruby as she turned into a statue of cold rock. Watching the memory play out made it feel like it happened yesterday, and Clyde hadn't the strength to watch anymore, but he refused to wallow in pity and regret. The echoes of Meadow and Lorenzo coming from high above him reinforced Clyde's resolve and his focus sharpened again as he glared upwards, his hand reaching for a potion in his harness.

Using the power of his new golden wings, Lorenzo soon caught up to Meadow and flew straight at her as she ascended the crystal staircase, "Going somewhere!?" he roared. Meadow froze in her tracks as Lorenzo flew in front of her, and a bolt of fear quickly struck when Lorenzo whooshed forwards. He gripped Meadow by the throat and slammed her against the wall, "This game ends!" he growled. Panic devoured Meadow as she writhed and squirmed against his tight grip and she tried to wrestle his arm off, to no avail.

A devious glint flashed in Lorenzo's cold, hateful eyes as he slowly choked the life out of Meadow and listened to her gasp for breath. "Remember, don't blame me, blame Clyde!" he scornfully hissed. Luckily, just as he spoke these words, an unknown figure suddenly slammed into him from behind and swiftly ripped Lorenzo's grasp away from Meadow's throat. "I believe your fight is with me!" announced Clyde after flying into Lorenzo and throwing him across to the other side of the tower, smashing him into the side. Agony struck Lorenzo with surprise following close behind, for once he looked up, he saw the sight of Clyde floating in mid-air with his own pair of golden flapping wings upon his back.

A frustrated snarl erupted from Lorenzo's throat and he furiously flew at Clyde with relentless hate and they both became twisted up in a vicious airborne brawl. The black iron mask Lorenzo wore provided him adequate protection; so, Clyde reached his hand to grab it as they tussled. After a little effort Clyde managed to rip it off his face, revealing the scarred skin beneath. Punches of hatred were traded between the two of them as they flew around the tower, both trying to overwhelm the other and gain the upper hand. They flew higher and higher, ascending ever closer to the top of the tower while also clashing and walloping each other, until their magical wings suddenly wore off and disappeared.

Gravity quickly took hold and they began plummeting down the central shaft of the looming crystal tower with alarming speed. However, they still possessed tricks up their sleeves and drew fresh potions from their harnesses but grabbing their potions while plunging to certain death proved tricky. Yet after a couple of moments of frantically struggling, Clyde and Lorenzo revealed their potions and made sure to hold them close to their lips.

Haste was essential, for gravity would surely spill the magical mixtures in the vials if they were too slow. After swiftly guzzling the potions down their throats, Clyde and Lorenzo soon realized they had picked the same potion. Great minds seemed to think alike, for they both consumed vials of levitation potion, effectively ceasing the speed of their plummeting to an abrupt floating halt. Although some distance to the top of the tower had been stolen from them, they saved themselves from becoming a pair of messy red stains upon the beautiful crystal floor. Swiftly, Lorenzo regained his bearings, his merciless glare suddenly resting back on Clyde who weightlessly floated a few feet away in front of him.

Both master alchemists traded stern scowls as they gently levitated several hundred feet in mid-air, ignoring the dauting drop below them. "Everything is your fault Clyde! You are the villain here!" Lorenzo yelled. Without warning, Lorenzo quickly delivered a cruel forceful kick to Clyde's chest, causing him to fly backwards and have the wind knocked out of his breath. In his weightless form, Clyde flew backwards with ease and banged against the nearby wall. Meanwhile, Lorenzo used his fleeting moment of levitation to slowly glide towards the spiraling staircase again.

During all this, Meadow had been reclaiming her breath after being subjected to Lorenzo's sinister grasp upon her throat and she soon realized that he and Clyde had gained quite a bit of height above her. It was vital she caught up quick, hence Meadow wasted no time in recovering her focus and reached for a vial of enhanced speed potion, "Okay, now I'm mad!" she growled. Suddenly, a sharp screeching sound from behind her caused Meadow to spin around and a flood of fright swamped over her when she looked back.

Clusters of sharp crystal spikes began shooting upwards out of the steps and travelled along the spiral stairs, "Ugh, who created this tower!?" Meadow cried. Quickly, she plucked the vial of enhanced speed potion from her harness and proceeded to consume it, for the spikes approached her with alarming ferocity. "Spikes! Clyde! The stairs are being covered in spikes!" Meadow yelled up as she used her newfound speed to swiftly scale the sparkling steps of the spiralling tower as the savage clusters of spikes relentless chased her. "Fantastic, that's all we need right now!" groaned Clyde upon hearing Meadow's voice echo below him. So, he hastily shook off Lorenzo's kick and resumed the pursuit as the levitation potion wore off and he slammed safely upon the steps again.

It was fortunate Clyde was much higher up the tower than Meadow, for it gave him significant headway in front of the deadly spikes. This was especially lucky since enhanced speed was one of the potions Clyde hadn't brought along with him. Desperately, Meadow and Clyde dashed, onwards and onwards towards the top of the diabolical tower, determined to outrun the chasing huddles of menacing spikes before they caught up. With her temporary burst of enhanced speed, Meadow soon began catching up to Clyde, but it was only a matter of time until it wore off and the shimmering spikes showed no sign of stopping. Clyde took a brief but foolish glance behind him and his legs briskly carried him away on their own once he saw Meadow and the sparkling rows of crystal spikes approach. Fear thundered in their hearts and empowered their feet as they both hurried up the tower. Hope finally appeared in the form of another large circular platform detached from the steps, floating in the center shaft. Meadow joined Clyde's side with her great speed and the two of them reached the gap, "Quick! Jump!" shouted Clyde.

With a hearty lunge they leapt from the stairs, flew across the air and safely landed upon the circular levitating platform and the onslaught of sharp spikes thankfully ceased chasing them. Messily, they tumbled across the circular platform but were otherwise unharmed, "It seems this tower can create a variety of crystal-based traps!" gasped Clyde as he struggled to catch his breath. A rest at this point would've been welcome, but they both knew there was not a moment to lose. "Come, let us carry on the chase my apprentice!" declared Clyde before some invisible force punched him in the face.

Upon being stuck by the blow, Clyde veered backwards with both pain and confusion, "What in the heavens!?" he shouted. Another punch followed and struck his jaw, causing him to stumble again. "What's happening!?" Meadow cried as she watched Clyde be assailed again and again by an unseen force and become helplessly knocked to the floor. It suddenly dawned upon Clyde what was happening when he felt a hidden presence wrestle against him, "Lorenzo, Its Lorenzo! He's taken an invisibility potion!" he shouted. "Correct Clyde, I thought I'd give you a nice surprise! Too bad you saw through it so quickly" hissed the invisible voice of Lorenzo as he pummeled Clyde with ruthless satisfaction.

Another painful blow to the face from Lorenzo's fist brought Clyde ever closer to the perilous edge of the floating platform, "Meadow, run on ahead! He's my problem!" he shouted. Despite being hesitant to abandon him, Meadow obeyed Clyde's request and fled the floating platform, leaping off the opposite end and onto the next set of spiralling crystal stairs in the wall. Securing the chalice at the top of the tower and ensuring it didn't fall into Lorenzo's grasp took priority, thus Meadow banished her concern and didn't look back.

Meanwhile, the vicious tangle between Clyde and Lorenzo persisted. But after escaping the perilous edge of the platform, Clyde rapidly fumbled for a flask of life-detection potion from his harness. An invisible punch to the face knocked Clyde down again and he tumbled across the levitating platform, sprawling into a messy heap. Thankfully, Clyde kept a tight grip upon his potion and swiftly consumed it and it only took a second for the life-detection potion to trigger. When it did, Lorenzo was no longer invisible to Clyde's sight, for he could see Lorenzo's aura of life energy glowing like a swarm of fireflies.

Lorenzo charged right at Clyde, desperate to shove him off the platform and send him plummeting to his death. However, Clyde quickly braced himself and endured the shove, resulting in the two of them locking in a forceful stalemate. "A most underhanded trick Lorenzo, but your presence is no longer hidden from me!" announced Clyde. Unfortunately, Lorenzo succeeded in pushing Clyde ever closer towards the edge of the hovering platform and closer towards his plunging demise. Until the crystal tower decided to spring another new trap and made a series of tall, crystal walls erupt from around the platform, forming a perfect square.

Clyde and Lorenzo quickly found themselves trapped in the square, the only way out being straight up. Problem was, the walls were over ten feet tall and things soon shifted from bad to worse, as two sides of the walls began moving towards each other. "The walls are closing in!" cried Lorenzo, who remained entangled in a scuffle with Clyde. Clyde took advantage of his surprise by headbutting him in the face as his invisibility abruptly wore off. This caused Lorenzo to grimace and recoil backwards in pain, breaking off the knotted brawl between them.

Unsurprisingly, Lorenzo stubbornly recovered his stance and furiously lunged at Clyde again and another twisting wrestle ensued between the pair. During the struggle, the tall crystal walls of the square surrounding them continued to move ever closer and would undoubtedly crush them into plomberry juice unless they acted fast. Mustering all his strength, Lorenzo managed to fling Clyde aside, slamming him onto the ground and banging him against one of the shifting walls behind. Little space remained, for the deadly crushing trap had almost closed, but Lorenzo quickly drew a vial of enhanced jumping potion from his harness and frantically devoured it. Once consumed, Lorenzo sneered, tossed the empty vial down at Clyde and took a mighty leap, whooshing straight upwards.

He managed to escape the fatal trap with ease, leaving Clyde to be crushed into dust and with only a couple of meters of space remaining. Clyde knew he had to act swiftly, so upon dragging himself off the ground, he hastily quaffed a vial of enhanced jump potion as well. Sadly, his stock of ethereal potion had been depleted, otherwise he could've simply walked right out of the crushing block trap. This was the next best potion he had and upon sipping the magical concoction, Clyde took a tremendous jump upwards and whizzed into the air, escaping the perilous trap by only a cat's whisker. Below him, he saw the crystal walls soon close in and meld together, forming a perfectly shaped cube of shimmering crystal.

A brief shudder of fright entered Clyde when he imagined how messily it would've ended for him had he not escaped in time. Meanwhile, Meadow continued to climb the seemingly endless spiral of crystal stairs, until Lorenzo flew right up alongside her. "Hello again!" he growled upon slamming both his feet down in front of her. Being confronted by the repulsive, hateful visage of Lorenzo made Meadow freeze in her tracks and stumble, "Curses!" she spluttered. Her reaction forced a dastardly smirk to contort Lorenzo's scarred lips, but Meadow fearlessly pounced at him once she had recomposed herself and the two tussled upon the stairs. At the same time, Clyde's enhanced jump wore off and his boots touched upon the staircase, "Hang on Meadow!" he cried, bravely dashing over to aid Meadow once he saw her predicament.

Although Meadow proved herself a handful for being so young, Lorenzo was victorious in throwing her off him and shoved her down the stairs. Meadow sustained a fair share of bumps and bruises as she painfully toppled down the hard crystal steps, fortunately Clyde caught her in his arms. "Easy fair maiden, I hope you are uninjured!" Clyde uttered once he had safely nestled Meadow and ceased her tumbling. "Fear not, my pride took the greatest blow!" Meadow remarked as she shook the dazing stars from her vision and found her footing again, albeit with a bit of dizzy staggering. Adamantly, Lorenzo kept his high ground upon the stairs and scowled at them with unyielding anger, "Sweet dreams!" he barked.

Clyde and Meadow glared back and charged at him head on but froze when Lorenzo unleashed a belch of hazy, purple sleepy-gas mist from his mouth. No doubt Lorenzo must've taken a vial of sleepy-gas potion while Clyde was saving Meadow from falling down the stairs. Thankfully, the creeping mist was slow, but if they inhaled it and fell asleep, it would all be over, and Lorenzo would surely win. Desperately, Clyde reached for a vial of fire-breath potion as the thick, purple fog descended the stairs towards them, attempting to lull them into a deep slumber.

The murky mist swirled over them like a noxious cloud, but Clyde was able gulp down his fire-breath potion and belch the debilitating miasma away in a scorching torrent of inferno. Clyde's fiery breath of bright burning flames succeeded in blazing away the cloud of sleepy mist and he cleared the path. Except, Lorenzo had used the opportunity to flee further up the tower. A tense panic lingered inside Meadow and her heart thundered like the stomps of an angry cyclops, "That was too close! If we breathed in that mist and fell asleep!" she gasped. "Reflect upon that later, I think we're finally near the top!" interrupted Clyde as he promptly persisted the pursuit and tenaciously chased Lorenzo's trail, wiping away the beads of nervous sweat trickling down his forehead.

To Meadow's disbelief and delight, Clyde's observation was correct, for after dashing along another several dozen steps of glittering stairs, the peak of the tower rested above them. The final spiral of stairs led upwards, into what appeared like a gigantic loft made of solid crystal flooring. Seeing Lorenzo flee into it only added to the joy, for it meant they had caught up and were right on his tail. "We're right behind him, quickly Meadow! we've finally reached the top!" Clyde gasped with excitement, his resolve burning brighter and bolstering his spirit to endure the climb.

If they hurried, they could possibly take down Lorenzo before he even had a chance to rest his despicable fingers upon the chalice. Such a thought empowered their determination and hope filled their hearts for it seemed like a chance to thwart Lorenzo's plan still beamed upon the horizon. That was until they reached the very last step, it was right upon the very last step that things suddenly took a dire turn. The tower suddenly decided to play one last trick on them and altered the entire spiral staircase into a giant crystal slide.

Clyde and Meadow's feet were instantly scooped out from under them as the slippery surface toppled them onto their rumps and sent them sliding back down. "No, no!" shouted Clyde as he watched in despair as the entrance to the tower loft slipped away from him. If they were departing the tower, it would've been a fun convenience, sadly it felt like a shattering bolt of cruelty. "This cannot be happening!" cried Meadow as the twirling crystal slide slid her deeper and deeper towards the bottom. "Meadow, do you have any vials of flight potion!?" Clyde shouted as he slid closely behind her with gradually increasing speed. "Yeah, right here! Just one though!" Meadow yelled back and frantically searched her harness for it.

She found the specified potion a few seconds later and quickly held it out for Clyde to grasp. Desperately, Clyde stretched his arm to grab the vial of precious potion from Meadow's hand, his fingers gently caressing the side of the glass. It was just out of reach, "Just a bit closer!" he growled. It was a tense predicament, for they lost valuable distance every second they spent riding the accursed crystal slide, but after one last stretch, Clyde's hand seized the vial. "Okay, hang onto me!" he shouted as he grabbed Meadow's arm, tore the cork out of the vial with his teeth and hastily swigged it down without delay.

Another pair of radiant, golden glowing wings quickly appeared upon Clyde's back and he swiftly took to the air. Meadow scrambled onto his back and the pair of them flew all the way back to the top with great speed. Clyde fiercely flapped his new wings and soared to towards the tip of the tower with tremendous intensity. His mind racing with panic as he contemplated the unpleasant image of Lorenzo reaching the chalice first. Thankfully, although they had lost a fair amount of distance, Clyde was able to fly back to it quick. He soared past the final spiral of stairs again and suddenly burst into the loft, "Lorenzo!" he shouted. Sadly, Clyde and Meadow were confronted by the undesirable sight of Lorenzo standing before a grand, ornate fountain of water. They were too late; Lorenzo was dousing his repulsive face with the water using an unspeakably beautiful chalice. Wonder washed over Clyde as he gazed upon the chalice within Lorenzo's hands when he held it up.

It matched every description Clyde had ever heard or read about; a chalice made of lustrous sparkling crystal that never lost its gleam. A chalice so clear and magnificent that peering upon it seemed to make time freeze in worship of its beauty, "The Chalice of Renewal!" Clyde gasped. Furthermore, after Lorenzo had swiped the chalice from its pedestal atop the ornate fountain, dunked it into the water and finished pouring the water onto his face. He slowly turned around to show his skin miraculously healed. "Behold Clyde, the chalice of legend is mine and it has finally undone the damage you inflicted upon me!" Lorenzo proclaimed.

Smugly, Lorenzo peered upon his beautiful reflection within the sparkling surface of water in the fountain nearby. "Very well, now please Lorenzo, hand it over! Let me pour its magical waters upon Ruby and return her to normal!" Clyde pleaded, still floating in the air with his golden wings. Lorenzo graced the smoothness of his skin with his hand and erupted in hysterical laughter, "No, I am a man of my word! I shall never let you have her again!" he cackled. "Now it is your turn to suffer as I have Clyde, you don't deserve a happy ending!" Lorenzo yelled and raised the chalice high, preparing to smash it upon the ground.

Clyde had to be reckless, there was no other way, he suspected all along that Lorenzo would resort to such action. Thus, he used the last few seconds of his golden wings to fly at Lorenzo full force. It was a hasty and risky move, but Clyde knew options were in short supply, meanwhile Meadow released her grip from Clyde's back and clumsily tumbled across the floor. Before Lorenzo had his chance to smash the chalice into dozens of tiny shards upon the ground, Clyde managed to reach him just in time. Alas, his potion of flight abruptly expired, causing his wings to vanish and the resulting momentum caused Clyde to wildly smash headfirst into Lorenzo.

As for the chalice, Clyde ensured it was his primary focus of concern and shifted his body upon impact, seizing control of the chalice and nestling it close to his chest as he rolled. Miraculously, the chalice had emerged unscathed and Clyde took a moment to offer a silent prayer to the heavens for such a lucky blessing. "Finally, the Chalice of Renewal!" Clyde gasped as he gazed upon its magnificence. The object he had spent so long seeking was in his very fingertips yet curiously seemed as light as air. Holding it in his hands and seeing the dance of shimmering light it performed as he rotated it brought Clyde satisfaction that could scarcely be described in words. "Meadow, here! Look after it!" declared Clyde as he held the mythical gleaming chalice of magical crystal out to her, Meadow naturally hurried over and dutifully obeyed his order. Yet, an expression of flustered fright rapidly veiled her face as she took the chalice from Clyde's hand, "Behind you!" she gasped while hastily hopping several steps backwards.

Clyde spun around and was confronted by the sight of Lorenzo charging at him like an enraged taurian but was too close to evade his assault. Resulting in Lorenzo painfully pinning Clyde against the sparkling water fountain in the middle of the room. Despite Lorenzo's face now being fully healed of all deformity and appearing as soft as a siren's embrace, his visage still scowled with unquenchable hatred. "I said no happy endings for you!" he snarled; his hands wrapping tightly around Clyde's throat. Both alchemists fought and wrestled, but Clyde mustered all his might and managed to force one of Lorenzo's hands away from his neck.

Alas, this also resulted in Lorenzo loosening his grasp and delivering a swift left hook to Clyde's lip, causing him to briefly stagger from the blow. Lorenzo's rage and savagery intensified, and he persisted in pummeling Clyde in the face, devoid of all remorse. "You stole her from me! You ruined everything!" bellowed Lorenzo as he relentlessly punched away. Meadow felt powerless as she watched, deciding it better to keep her distance now that the chalice was safely in hand, "Clyde, Come on! Fight him!" she cried. Her cry of support reached Clyde and he grew weary of being a victim of Lorenzo's hate.

Thus, Clyde managed to gather his bearings, waited for Lorenzo to take another swing and dodged his head to the side. Rather than Lorenzo's fist walloping Clyde's face, his knuckles collided with the sturdy crystal of the fountain instead and immediately made Lorenzo retreat in agony. A yelp of pain leapt from Lorenzo and he tried soothing the impact upon his hand by shaking it, while Clyde sprang at the chance to retaliate and delivered a fearsome punch of his own to Lorenzo's nose.

Clyde did not stop there however, he bestowed Lorenzo the same lack of mercy that he had shown him. Serving him a series of several more clouts to the face, until he finally knocked Lorenzo off his feet. Satisfied at the pummeling he gave, Clyde ceased his assault and exhaled all the frustration from his lungs, "Enough Lorenzo, end this war here!" he demanded. "Oh, don't worry Clyde, I intend to!" Lorenzo hissed after spitting a dollop of blood from his mouth, cowering away from Clyde and secretly reaching for another vial of potion.

Peacefully, Clyde took a few steps forward and leaned towards Lorenzo, who remained floored, "Please my old master! End this before it goes any further!" he implored. Cruel trickery lay in wait for Clyde, for Lorenzo had plucked a vial of enhanced strength potion from his harness, had already uncorked the stopper and consumed the liquid within. "I shall end this by ending you!" Lorenzo roared, proceeding to spin around and violently lash out at Clyde, giving him a mighty backhand blow. Under the effects of enhanced strength, the strike was powerful enough to fling Clyde several feet into the air, throw him backwards and pound him against the wall all the way opposite the room.

Frantically, Meadow came rushing to his aid once he collapsed to the floor utterly dazed from the devious attack, "Clyde!" she cried hysterically. "Death is your punishment, nothing less shall please me! Now behold Clyde, behold the most destructive potion of all!" Lorenzo shouted. It took a couple of seconds for Clyde to recover from his staggered state, but Lorenzo's words sped up the process. "The most destructive? It couldn't be!" he muttered while wearily rising to his feet.

Dread engulfed Clyde as he watched Lorenzo consume a vial of potion he had never witnessed before, a potion that pulsated and glowed with a brilliant, violent red hue. "Meadow hurry, take cover!" Clyde yelled, with an intensity Meadow had scarcely seen. She could discern the urgency in his voice and quickly sought shelter behind the sturdy, crystal fountain in the center. There was no time to prevent Lorenzo from imbibing the potion, the distance between them was too great for that and they had a mere second to hunker behind cover before the greatest power of alchemy was unleashed.

Back when Clyde was still Lorenzo's apprentice, he had once or twice heard his master briefly mention the most powerful potion of all. Lorenzo named it mana-breath, a potion that required nothing short of a unicorn's horn as one of its primary ingredients, a potion of immense rarity and tremendous power. It seemed too mythical to be true, and yet here Lorenzo was, proving it existed, unleashing the power of mana-breath potion from his mouth. Which took the form of a deadly, screeching beam of pure, scarlet-red sorcery. The shrieking beam of destructive magic proved unstable and caused a tremendous booming explosion of red fire upon impact. It effortlessly blasted the crystal fountain into shards, along with a large line of wall behind it.

It was a potion of sheer, chaotic energy, one that was powerful enough to shatter the sturdiest of steel armor and blow the mightiest of dragons out of the sky. Fortunately, the screaming beam of mana-breath potion lasted only a few seconds, but the destruction it caused within that time was devastating. For in its wake it left a titanic, scorching scar of blistering red ruin upon the crystal wall. Clyde and Meadow were covered in sharp cuts from the shattering of crystal and flung aside from the deafening shockwave the explosion created. Parts of their clothes turned a charred black from the sudden burst of flames and their ears rang incessantly. If wasn't for the fountain taking the brunt of the beam, they would've been surely obliterated into ash.

The entire room kept spinning and a vial of frost-breath potion that Clyde's fingers had been holding onto, slipped out of his hand and rolled across the room. When the dust finally settled and everything became quiet again, Lorenzo released a sigh of fatigue and rubbed his temples, banishing the blood rush that had entered his head. Although Clyde and Meadow had sustained wounds, the sight of them still alive succeeded in making Lorenzo's anger flare. "I admit, I didn't want to use a potion such as that, considering how difficult it is to make!" he announced. "But then again, I never expected you to survive it either!" Lorenzo added, his focus becoming drawn to the vial of frost-breath potion near his feet which Clyde had dropped.

Holding his aching bruised ribs, Clyde painfully staggered to his feet and slouched upon the wall nearby, "Meadow, the chalice! Where's the chalice!?" he groaned. Hearing Clyde's voice roused Meadow's attention back into reality, but her head ached like she caught the full force of a banshee's wail. "Oh no, Clyde! Look there! It must've flown out of my hands!" Meadow cried as her eyes perused the room and spotted the base of the chalice. Sadly, the rest had shattered into hundreds of gleaming fragments.

Seeing the Chalice of Renewal, the object which Clyde had toiled so hard for be rendered a sea of shimmering shards wrought more devastation than he could've imagined. Like a nefarious demon had swooped down and impaled his soul. "No, no, no, no, no, no" Clyde softly muttered as he collapsed onto his knees and hung his head, his fist repeatedly banging against the floor. Witnessing his defeat and melancholy brought oodles of delight to Lorenzo, "Now Clyde, now your spirit is broken! Now do you see how it feels to lose everything you care about!?" he cackled.

Lorenzo's insane laughter echoed within the room incessantly, his mind becoming drunk on a deranged euphoria, "By the way, I think you dropped this!" he announced. Lorenzo enjoyed twisting the dagger further by scooping up the fallen vial of frost-breath potion belonging to Clyde and uncorking the cork stopper. "How ironic that fate allows me to kill you with one of your own potions, don't worry though, once I've turned you to ice, I'll shatter you into pieces like that chalice!" Lorenzo jeered. Surprisingly, Clyde offered no resistance, he instead chose to remain on his knees and accept his fate. "Go ahead Lorenzo, my entire quest shattered as soon the chalice was destroyed, my purpose is pointless now" he wearily uttered. "Clyde, You can't!" Meadow suddenly cried, her ears adamantly refusing to believe what they just heard him say.

Torment clearly wracked Clyde's mind, the torment of losing the chance and to be reunited with Ruby, the torment of losing any future with her in his life. "It's okay Meadow, if this is the only way to quell the hatred within Lorenzo then so be it, I was the creator of his hatred after all" Clyde uttered. All fear vanished within Clyde's gaze when it returned to meet Lorenzo and he bravely pierced into his stare with unflinching focus. "Well, finish me Lorenzo! I assume it's what you want!" he demanded. Silently, Lorenzo studied Clyde, his desire to accept whatever fate was bestowed was surprising to say the least. "You assume right Clyde!" Lorenzo replied with a sinister smirk and he eagerly gulped the vial of frost-potion Clyde had dropped and prepared to unleash icy fury upon him. However, as soon as Lorenzo finished drinking the vial of potion, Clyde slowly arose with a victorious smile smeared upon his face, "It's over Lorenzo, you lose!" he declared.

Lorenzo blew as hard as he could, but try as he might, he exhaled nothing but harmless air from his lungs. "I don't understand, what did you do? What did you do!?" Lorenzo snarled as he fearfully tossed aside the empty vial of potion. A satisfied scowl of triumph lingered upon Clyde's face as he watched the potions effects take place upon Lorenzo. "I dropped and rolled that vial near you on purpose, I had to make it look like a convincing accident of course!" Clyde announced. That's when Lorenzo realized, he couldn't move, and terror struck him when he looked down and noticed his legs turning into solid grey stone.

Deeming him to be no threat, Clyde approached Lorenzo and watched the life gradually fade from him as his body turned to stone, "No! How!?" Lorenzo gasped. "I finally recently figured it out, I figured out what potion you used on Ruby to turn her into stone, which is why I know there's no cure for her, no cure except the Chalice of Renewal" uttered Clyde. Speechlessly, Meadow watched the scene unfold, her astonishment rivalling Lorenzo's, for she knew nothing of this.

Clyde hadn't mentioned a word of it to her, yet the sight of it happening caused her to rejoice inside. "But it was a vial of frost-breath!" Lorenzo gasped as the effects of the potion continued to render his flesh hard as stone, reaching past his waist by this point. "Oh yes, I merely altered it's coloring, otherwise I assure you it's still exactly what you used, I learned from the best after all!" Clyde answered in a haughty tone. Lorenzo was soon rendered unable to move an inch, for the potion had reached his neck and had almost turned him entirely into stone. "Clyde, Curse you! Curse you into eternity! Curse you!" he yelled.

Soon Lorenzo was able to yell no longer, his hisses of hatred became muffled upon turning into a solid statue of motionless stone. "Goodbye forever Lorenzo" whispered Clyde as he watched right until the very end. It was over, Lorenzo was no more and had destroyed the Chalice of Renewal. The one known cure to the same vile poison he himself had created, an ironic but seemingly poetic end. Seeing all that hatred, torment and rage being sealed away in a body of stone finally brought Clyde a measure of peace, yet the ordeal had left him jaded to say the least. "It is done, but have I atoned for my mistakes now? Do I deserve to celebrate? Or is victory supposed to taste so bittersweet?" Clyde uttered while pondering the events of what just happened.

A much welcome gesture of support came from Meadow, who wandered over and rested her hand gently upon his shoulder, "Come on Clyde, let's just leave this place" she answered. After taking one last gaze upon Lorenzo, his stony face frozen in an expression of twisted hatred, Clyde took a deep breath and nodded to Meadow. Both turned away from Lorenzo's statue, never to look back upon it again, although Clyde did take one more glance at the shattered remains of the chalice on the floor nearby. "The Chalice of Renewal, to think I actually held it in my hands for a short time, I briefly possessed the object of my deepest desires, alas, it seems it was not meant to be" Clyde uttered with a sad chuckle.

Playfully, Meadow punched Clyde in the arm, an act that hurt far more that it should have with how much his body ached. "I'm sure you're not going to give up though, you're a genius, you'll find another way!" she declared. Clyde rubbed the tender soreness on his arm and grimaced, but also smiled at Meadow's cheery energy. "Who knows? Perhaps I will my apprentice, perhaps I will" he answered softly.

Epilogue

For once, the Frostveil Mountains were devoid of a blustering blizzard of snow and ice pounding against the windows, this time the weather was tranquil. Clyde packed yet another pair of undies into his leather travelling backpack, despite cramming in a few pairs already, "Hmmmm, better safe than sorry" he muttered aloud. His leather backpack bulged with supplies, but Clyde knew he would likely be out on the road for quite some time. "Okay, I think that's everything!" he uttered after draping a cozy leather travelling cloak onto his shoulders. At the same time, a delicious aroma drifted through the air and he was powerless to resist its allure as it infiltrated his senses. "Mmmm, something smells good!" he declared, as he followed fragrant trail and it led him to the kitchen.

Inside, he discovered Meadow pouring a fresh cup of herbal tea, "Smells wonderful, what tea are we having today?" asked Clyde. A delighted smile spread upon Meadow's lips as soon as Clyde entered the kitchen. "Ah, good morning master! Today's tea is a blend of frostwitch flowers, elderking root and cherrybutter herbs!" she answered. Although a spot of tea was tempting, Clyde rejected the offer when Meadow was upon the verge of pouring him a cup. "As much as I relish a good cup of tea, the horizon calls, and I must begin my journey!" he announced. Meadow promptly poured out a cup of delicious steaming tea for herself instead and sighed. "Very well, but must you leave so early master?" she asked. Adamantly, Clyde nodded, "Tis prudent to travel while the weather is calm, and cease calling me master! You know we are like equals now my dear!" he answered.

As the swirling plumes of tasty tea floated into Meadow's face, she released a harmless chuckle, "I know, I just like teasing you!" she jovially replied. Suddenly, Styx flapped his way into the room and latched onto Clyde, hugging his arm tightly. "Master, please be safe, I can always create a portal for you!" he cried. His abrupt raid of affection warmed Clyde's heart and made him recoil happily. "Thank you, Styx, but that shan't be necessary, after all, I do not know where my path lies, I'm following the wind now!" he announced.

After subjecting Clyde to a long tight hug, Styx flapped his wings and flew upon his shoulder, while Meadow sipped her tea and looked on. "Have you packed everything? You won't be cold?" she asked. Confidently, Clyde shook his head and headed for the front door of the house. "After all the travelling we did in the scorching desert, I'm going to enjoy a bit of snow!" he answered. Wrapping his fingers around the front doorknob, Clyde gave it a hearty pull and exposed the white, snowy horizon waiting on the other side, "Here we go!" he announced.

Frosty air pinched Clyde's cheeks and when he took several weighty steps out onto the snow, he listened to it crunch beneath his boots. "You really think you'll find a cure for her?" Meadow suddenly asked. A newfound feeling of hope tingled within Clyde's heart as he gazed upon the boundless stretching scenery before him. "The chalice was destroyed, but I believe there's still a cure out there for Ruby" he answered. "My travels may take me far, but there's got to be a way, its waiting for me somewhere out there, I shall simply travel till I find it" he added. A new journey of discovery awaited, and Meadow admitted to being intrigued by the wonders he would see, "Let me join you Clyde, I can help!" she implored.

Her ardent desire to partake in this new odyssey brought Clyde much delight, however, he clashed against it. "Meadow, there was never a doubt in my mind that you could help, but this has to be my journey now" he answered. Before taking the first step upon his new voyage, Clyde plunged his hand into his pocket, drew a final gift for Meadow and held it out to her, "Oh, before I forget, this is yours!" he declared. Meadow was rendered speechless as she looked upon the gift, for it was none other than a glass vial containing the memory erasing potion, "For me?" she finally spluttered. Slowly, Clyde placed the vial of potion into Meadow's open palm and firmly nodded. "Indeed, I think you've finally worked off the payment for it and it's why you sought me out is it not?" he asked with a humble laugh.

Ironically, it had been so long since Meadow had reflected upon her original intention to find Clyde that it made her chuckle when she was reminded about it in tangible form. "Well, you weren't joking when you said this potion costs a fortune!" Meadow remarked. Sheepishly, Meadow stroked a long lock of her fiery hair aside and laughed as she reminisced about the first days between her and Clyde. Resting his hand gently upon Styx's horned head, Clyde gave him a final, playful ruffle. "Take care Styx and look after the place while I'm gone, your service to me is over my friend!" he uttered.

Despite feeling sad about his masters leaving, Styx dutifully obeyed his final command. "Thank you, Master Clyde, I swear to faithfully tend to this place! Good luck on your journey, I pray you find a cure for Miss Ruby!" he rasped. An icy gust abruptly sliced through the moment and caused Clyde to shudder, "Well, I shouldn't put this off any longer" he remarked. "Meadow, thank you! You have been the greatest friend I could ask for and what you do now is up to you!" Clyde declared, taking a final dramatic bow.

After a final tight hug between the two of them, Meadow offered a humble bow of her own. "Thank you too Clyde, for everything you taught me and everything you've shown me! You are a true master!" she replied. With that, Clyde turned and began traversing the thick snow, venturing into the horizon, refusing stop and look back. Meadow watched him from the doorway for a while, until she unbottled the vial of memory erasing potion in her hand and gazed upon it. A cheerful smile spread over her lips as she tilted the vial, spilling its contents all over the snow until it was empty. "Come on Styx, we have potions to make!" she declared, finally turning away and shutting the door of the house.

Printed in Great Britain
by Amazon